ics

CHRISTINA ELLEN STEAD was born in 1902 in Sydney's south. After graduating from high school in 1919, she attended Sydney Teachers' College on a scholarship. She subsequently held a series of teaching and secretarial positions before leaving for London in 1928.

There she met and fell in love with Wilhelm Blech (later William Blake), a married American broker at the financial organisation where she was working. They moved to the Paris branch of the same firm in 1929, eventually marrying in 1952 after many years travelling and writing in Europe and the United States.

Stead's debut novel, *Seven Poor Men of Sydney*, and a short-story collection, *The Salzburg Tales*, were published in 1934 to positive reviews in England and America. They were followed by novels drawing on Stead's time in Paris, *The Beauties and Furies* and *House of All Nations*, and in the 1940s a succession of major works, among them *A Little Tea, a Little Chat* and *Letty Fox: Her Luck*.

By the early 1950s Stead's sales, and her finances, had deteriorated. 'Her refusal to write for popular taste, her mobility and her left-wing politics,' Margaret Harris writes, 'all impeded her efforts to be published in the postwar environment.'

The republication in the mid-1960s of the autobiographical novels *The Man Who Loved Children* and *For Love Alone* renewed interest in Stead's writing; the former has in recent years been called a masterpiece by Jonathan Franzen, among others. Over the next ten years Stead published four new works of fiction, including *The Puzzleheaded Girl* and *The Little Hotel*.

Stead returned to Australia for a university fellowship in 1969, following William Blake's death. In 1974 she resettled permanently in Sydney and was the first recipient of the Patrick White Award.

Christina Stead died in 1983. She is widely considered to be one of the most significant authors of the twentieth century.

FIONA WRIGHT is a writer, editor and critic from Sydney. Her book of essays, *Small Acts of Disappearance*, won the 2016 Kibble Award, and her poetry collection, *Knuckled*, won the Dame Mary Gilmore Award.

ALSO BY CHRISTINA STEAD

The Salzburg Tales
Seven Poor Men of Sydney
The Beauties and Furies
House of All Nations
The Man Who Loved Children
For Love Alone
Letty Fox: Her Luck
A Little Tea, a Little Chat
The People with the Dogs
Cotters' England (US title: *Dark Places of the Heart*)
The Little Hotel
Miss Herbert (The Suburban Wife)
Ocean of Story: The Uncollected Stories of Christina Stead
   (ed. R. G. Geering)
I'm Dying Laughing: The Humourist

The Puzzleheaded Girl
Christina Stead

Text Publishing Melbourne Australia

textclassics.com.au
textpublishing.com.au

The Text Publishing Company
Swann House
22 William Street
Melbourne Victoria 3000
Australia

First published by Holt, Rinehart and Winston, New York, 1967
This edition published by The Text Publishing Company 2016

Cover design by WH Chong
Page design by Text
Typeset by Midland Typesetters

Printed in Australia by Griffin Press, an Accredited ISO AS/NZS 14001:2004
Environmental Management System printer

Primary Print ISBN: 9781925355710
Ebook ISBN: 9781925410143
Creator: Stead, Christina, 1902–1983, author.
Title: The puzzleheaded girl / by Christina Stead ; introduced by Fiona Wright.
Series: Text classics.
Dewey Number: A823.2

CONTENTS

Pieces of the Puzzle
by Fiona Wright

THE FOUR NOVELLAS that make up *The Puzzleheaded Girl*, first published in 1967, are all portraits of women— although they're referred to, by the characters that surround them, as girls. The distinction is important, and it's made most explicitly by two of Stead's male characters, Martin and George, both American expats living in Paris. They're talking about Linda, the beautiful, kleptomaniac daughter of one of Martin's friends, whom George desperately wants to marry, in what would be his fourth such partnership. Martin begins:

> 'A woman can't be, until a girl dies. I don't mean it indecently. I mean the sprites girls are, so different from us, all their fancies, their illusions, their flower world, the dreams they live in.'
>
> 'Women!' said George stormily. 'No, there is not a dead girl in them. They are just clay. When

a girl dies there is nothing. Just an army of aunts
and mothers, midwives and charwomen…I see girls
without sentiment, but I see how beautiful they are.
I cannot marry a woman who is a dead girl. I must
marry a living beautiful wonderful girl.'

Yet the drama in this story—the last in the collection, 'Girl
from the Beach'—occurs precisely because Linda refuses the
definition that these men seek to impose on her, refuses their
expectations, too. She is flighty and impulsive, embarking
on spontaneous trips to Spain, to Strasburg, to the French
countryside, with other young expats she meets in cafes
and bars; she shares a hotel room with a young gay man,
pretending they are an engaged couple, to save her money
and his reputation simultaneously.

At one point in the novella, Barby, one of George's
ex-wives, asks Linda if she intends to follow through with her
engagement, and she answers, 'I don't know…I think everybody wants to get rid of the problem. I'm a problem.' But
Barby, older, brasher and clearer-eyed than Linda, responds
by pointing out that George is the problem, that 'he's got
a complex' and hates American girls, but doesn't know it.
'He keeps marrying them to make them into his own little
girl,' she states.

Linda is a problem because she won't settle down,
because she doesn't know exactly what she wants, but won't
accept anything that she doesn't. She has her secrets, and her
own pain, but she is also having a riotous time, indifferent
to—although not unconscious of—the demands and desires
that men like George project onto her.

And project Stead's men do, across each of these novellas.

In 'The Dianas', Lydia, another American living and working in Paris, spends her time meeting and dining with men, all of whom feel some claim on her and try to pin her down. 'The Puzzleheaded Girl' is named for the descriptor Debrett, a city businessman, uses for the enigmatic Honor Lawrence, an oddly beautiful and socially inept young woman who drifts in and out of his life across many years. And in 'The Rightangled Creek', Sam Parsons, a male writer, goes on retreat in a country farmhouse, and dreams up a ghost based on a local story about the young woman who once inhabited the house. In each of these stories, Stead is making a forceful and sometimes brutal point, about the claims and the kinds of knowledge, patronising and paternalist, that these men assume they have over women—and girls.

I've been this girl, I can't help but think. This kind of girl somehow misapprehended by the world, or at least by the people around me, who've seen something in me or about me that I wasn't sure was really there. And because we are all constituted in part by the selves we see reflected back at us in our interactions, or because I think I somehow trusted other peoples' apprehensions more than my own, I couldn't help but play along. It's taken me years to recognise the damage this misrecognition can do, even longer to try to undo it. So it's remarkable to me that Stead is so uncompromising, so clear-eyed in examining this strange projection.

It's remarkable today, but all the more startling when you consider that the first novella in this book was originally published in 1965. In 1965, Robert Menzies was still prime minister of Australia. Bookshops were still being raided and publishers prosecuted for obscenity. The first Australian troops were sent to Vietnam. In the United States, Betty Friedan's *The Feminine Mystique* had been published only two years before, and it was still illegal for married couples to use contraception.

At this time, Christina Stead had been living away from Australia for thirty-seven years, and was residing on the suburban outskirts of London. Her novel *The Man Who Loved Children*, originally published in 1940, was reissued in the United States, and finally started finding its audience and acclaim. The world was changing, and so was Stead's position within it; so too, more slowly, were the lives of many women and girls. Against this backdrop, Stead's portraits are subversive and defiantly political. They are drawn from many angles at once, much like Cubist paintings, and are never stable, never definitive, but riddled with uncertainties, half-truths and secrets that conventional knowledge cannot capture or contain.

Honor Lawrence, the titular 'puzzleheaded girl', first appears at the offices of the newly formed Farmers' Utilities Corporation in New York City, carrying a book on French symbolism and claiming to be eighteen. The first description of her is entirely from the perspective of Guy Debrett, one of the partners in this firm, who is immediately intrigued by her: 'He saw a diffident girl in a plain tan blouse, a tight, navy-blue skirt, very short at the time when skirts were not short, round knees, worn walking shoes; she wore no overcoat.' In this passage, Debrett literally looks Honor up and down, and we see only what he sees.

Honor joins Debrett's office as a filing clerk, and is disliked by her women colleagues, but is strangely fascinating to the men. She is 'polite yet odd', an unsettling and intense presence, always reading her art books as she works. After some months, she is offered a promotion, but stormily declines, stating 'I have to earn my living in an office, but I won't mix in business…it is the enemy of art.' When pressed, she explains, 'I want to live with artists and live like them. I don't want to be like those earthy girls there…I prefer to die of hunger. Or go away.'

There are echoes here of Stead's other heroines—the principled, ambitious and hungry Teresa from *For Love Alone*, the rebellious and creative Louisa from *The Man Who Loved Children*. Honor's striving and desire lead her, later, to abandon the firm without warning, to almost travel to Europe as the companion of an older lesbian, to marry bigamously and float around the world, always unanchored, always unsatisfied and always barely avoiding destitution.

But the more that Honor passes in and out of Debrett's life, the greater his romanticisation of her becomes. She is an innocent and 'a rare human being', and then 'a repressed girl who is hunted by lechers, criminals and hags', 'a weak shade of lunatic', and finally one who 'partakes of a sacred character, those the gods love, or hate'. Other characters, caught in her thrall, begin to describe her as a person 'with great gifts who want[s] to create, but [is] not self-centred enough', 'a spirit in a dress of rags', and even 'the ragged, wayward heart of a woman that doesn't want to be caught and hasn't been caught'. To the men who perceive her, Honor is all of these things—but what she is to herself neither they nor we are ever allowed to know. All we see are pieces of the puzzle, never the image that Honor might carry in her own head.

And this is Honor's tragedy, just as it is the tragedy of Linda, traipsing around Europe with George hopelessly in tow, and the tragedy of Lydia, trying to make a life for herself and by herself, as her suitors scramble madly and often cruelly to pin her down. 'You're surely not going to refuse?' one of these men asks when he tries to take her to bed. Linda answers, 'We're travelling together, my dear Russell, but we're not intimate. We're comrades, remember; we scarcely know each other'—which doesn't prevent him from trying again, and again.

All four of the women at the heart of these novellas are, in their own way, trampled or tormented by the expectations or projections that are pressed upon them, but they are also defiant. They are distinctly modern women, waiting for the world to catch up. And this is precisely why *The Puzzle-headed Girl* is such a fascinating book—it is so thoroughly of its changing and confusing time. Stead is masterly in capturing the contradictions and complications of this era, and the effects, both devastating and decidedly mundane, that they had—and perhaps still have—on the lives of women and girls.

The Puzzleheaded Girl

To my friends
JESSIE AND ETTORE RELLA

Debrett liked his job in the old-style German Bank in Broad Street, but he soon saw that the partners' sons were coming into the firm and he could not rise far; so he joined three friends of his, Arthur Good, Tom Zero and Saul Scott, who had just formed the Farmers' Utilities Corporation. They were all in their early twenties.

It was a new office building, scarcely completed, built like a factory; everything was in contrast with the German Bank's offices smelling of old wood, the ink and grease of ledgers, hair oil and dust, crumbling bindings. Here the elevator opened into carpeted offices. There was a waiting room with soft leather seats, photographs of farms, farmers and machinery, a doorman, a pretty girl receptionist, an outer office with busy clerks. The uniformed doorman, Fisher, was a retired policeman, who looked like a fine old small-town banker; and could be useful as a bouncer. The head clerk was Saul Scott's secretary, Vera Day, who was studying law; and the head typist was Maria Magna, business-like, impatient.

One November Saturday afternoon, working overtime, they sent out for lunch; the paper cups were still on the desks when doorman Fisher told Debrett that a girl was waiting for an interview. They still needed a filing clerk. One of the typists, a boyish girl named Charlotte and called Sharlie, went out to look her over. A young seventeen, perhaps, dressed like a poor schoolgirl, she sat reading a small book, her light brown hair over her plain grave face. She looked up, a sweet and wistful expression appeared. Sharlie withdrew, and reported: "She's just a high-school kid reading art to impress the customers, an innocent—doesn't know she's alive yet."

Augustus Debrett, a stubby dark man with large hazel eyes, a round head, with pale face turned blue with the winter light, sat between two large windows, behind a big polished desk on which was nothing but a blotter and an inkstand.

She stood for a moment in the doorway looking at the room; the light fell on her. He saw a diffident girl in a plain tan blouse, a tight navy-blue skirt, very short at a time when skirts were not short, round knees, worn walking shoes; she wore no overcoat. "Miss Lawrence, come in."

She had a chin dimple and a dimple in her left cheek, a flittering smile; and when the smile went, her face returned to its gravity, its almost sadness. She had a full, youthful figure. She said she was eighteen. She sat down, keeping her knees together and holding her skirt on her knees with her brown purse. The little book she placed on the desk in front of her. It was a book in English on French symbolism. He looked at her face a moment before he began to question her. "Surely Honor Lawrence is a New England name? It sounds like Beacon Hill," and he laughed kindly in case it was not Beacon Hill. No answer. She said she had experience and wanted a good wage, and then she named a low wage and said she had no references: "Only my schoolteacher." "Where was your last job?" After a pause, she said, "I could start now if you liked." Debrett engaged her. "Come on Monday. If you've been out of a job for some time, you may be short of money. Do you need money now? I can give you an advance." "Oh, no, I have money." She got up and went to the door. There she turned and said quietly, "Thank you." As she was going out, Tom Zero, the young lawyer, one of the partners, entered. He was short, slender, debonair and so swarthy that he was looked at curiously in restaurants in the South, handsome and dark-eyed from two olive-skinned parents

4

from southern Europe, fastidious but with a faint sweet personal odour, like grass and olives; ambitious, bright and selfish.

"I've engaged Miss Lawrence as filing clerk: she's coming on Monday," said Debrett. Zero looked sharply. "Have you looked at her references? Can she type?" "Yes," said Debrett. The girl looked straight into Zero's eyes and moved away. Later, Debrett thought about her, her poverty and her book.

He had a socialist meeting that night and got home late. No food was laid out for him. His wife, who was up early and in the middle of the night with her newborn son, was asleep now. He got himself some bread and cheese and a cup of coffee and began to walk about the living room making calculations, repeating his speech at the meeting, the objections and the answers. He baffled professional hecklers by treating them as sincerely puzzled people; and he answered them in good faith. They would sit down, turn away, sincerely puzzled. He wanted to tell his wife what had happened; and he even thought of mentioning the girl to her. Miss Lawrence's address was on the fourth floor of a house in a tenement district far uptown. "A poor, prudish New England family—well educated, spoke a choice English—New Englanders are poor too—" Such a girl might preserve a girl's primness for years, might be really innocent. "What does a man really know about girls? A man feels he has to be a wise guy and he can misjudge."

Strangest of all were her grey eyes. They looked casually away into the distance, taking her far away, or they looked with hypnotic pinpoint intentness into his eyes, as if someone else were there, not this timid girl; someone indifferent, wise, uncaught.

It was his habit to walk up and down, up and down and go to bed long after midnight. His wife Beatrice was up several times before that with the sickly child. He admired her uncomplaining devotion, he admired her and her mind; but he was irritated by the disorder. He had no sympathy with the child. But his wife had said, "What did we get married for?" This was reasonable, customary. Yet he thought, "If you loved me, you would not need anything else." "My life is empty," she would say; "marriage sucks life out of a woman." She was not happy with the child, but she was busy, her life was not empty; and it seemed to him as if his life were empty. He felt he was not loved and never had been. "She has been very patient with me, since she does not love me," he said to himself.

Miss Lawrence always carried books on art and painters, ostentatiously perhaps, to mark that she was interested in better things than the office; but she read the books; and almost every day, Debrett encouraged her. She would listen in silence, as if not quite in agreement; but when he made social comments or deductions, she would lower her eyes or look out of the window. She was polite and yet odd. She lingered too long when bringing papers to executives; at a glance or word, she went out delicately, gravely or even with a slight smile; sly perhaps? She made few mistakes, typed well; if corrected, she pouted. A spoiled and favoured child? A coquette? She rarely spoke to the other girls; liked no one but the senior, Vera Day, who was kind to her. For weeks she wore the same navy-blue skirt; but presently she had a white shirt-blouse as well as the tan, and a beret and a short grey tweed cape; a singular outfit, though she looked neat.

Arthur Good, who originated the Farmers' Utilities Corporation, was dark, pale-skinned, middle-sized, slender, a joyous unprincipled schemer who turned out legal and illegal manoeuvres day and night. He saw loopholes everywhere. Arthur was of Italian origin, he had married an Italian girl, had, at twenty-five, already deserted her and was living with a serious French-Canadian girl he would never be able to marry. He was amused at Honor's delicate dawdling and once or twice ran his hand lightly down her hip and touched her stockinged knee. She drew back, ran out of his office. "Like a young cat, lascivious and scared," he said, "not for Artie." As for Tom Zero, he at once realized that she was attracted to him and he was abrupt with her, bored and hostile. He had a fair wife and two small fair children. She was out of place in the commonplace activity of his office.

"I know where you live," said Gus Debrett mildly; "I know that street. I was up there only the other day. I had to go to a meeting near there. I looked in at your place but did not see your name on the letter boxes. Are you a sub-tenant? A lodger?" She answered indirectly as usual. She lived alone with her father. And then, in an undertone, a spurt of talk. She wanted to live nearer to Greenwich Village. She wanted to find a room in that district, but everything was dear; she hadn't the money and she hadn't friends. She didn't know where to look. Where could she look? She knew no one but her brother, Walter Lawrence, the painter, who shared, with an actor, an old studio at the corner of University Place. They would not take her in.

Debrett listened eagerly now. Her brother was a painter who had just made his name by winning a prize and a fellowship, his was one of the new names in the city. "That is why you are interested in painting! It's your brother's influence? But perhaps you yourself paint?"

No; and she didn't agree with her brother's views. "He gives himself airs, people are running after him; but he hasn't a theory."

"Are your parents very proud?"

Her mother was dead.

"It must be rather difficult for you," said Debrett in a low voice. "I suppose you have to look after the house and your father when you go home from work." She did not reply, sitting up straight, gazing out the window and untranslatable feeling flickering in her face.

"Well, if things are difficult at any time, tell me; I'll do what I can."

She said nothing.

"I wish you knew my wife; she is very understanding, a great friend to women and she would know how to help you. But she's at her mother's at present, as you know," he continued to smile, "since you write my letters to her." The girl listened indifferently; Debrett, supple and enthusiastic, began to talk about his wife's nature, her intelligence and goodness. "She is very loyal and thoughtful; she understands people better than I do...In the meantime, perhaps her friend, Myra Zero, could have a talk with you. We all want to help you." He talked on and on, quixotically, looking at her with his beautiful dark eyes sometimes gay, sometimes mournful.

7

He paused. After a moment, she said, "My brother talks too much: he has an opinion on everything." "Well, you had better go now, if you want to."

Their business was growing. They added carbide to their commodities and were selling it in quantities in coal-mining districts. They had to buy more office machines, including a Moon book-keeping machine. An instructor was sent along with it. Debrett thought this a good chance for Miss Lawrence to earn more money. She had been with them all the winter; cold spring had come, and she had added very little to her office clothing; the cape but no coat, the same shoes, often sodden, and her hair worn simply as a little girl. Debrett called in Maria Magna, who set the girl to the machine. She learned quickly and got it right in an hour or so. Tom Zero, coming into the office, glanced over her shoulder and said to Maria Magna, "I see the new girl is getting to work on the book-keeping." "Yes, I think she'll do it," said Maria Magna, a little warmth in her voice for the first time. But when the instructor had gone, Miss Lawrence rose from the machine and, going over to Miss Magna, said she could learn the machine, but she would not, she would have nothing to do with accounts, money machines and sales. "I came here to make a living, but I won't mix in business."

Miss Magna bustled in to Mr. Debrett with this story. "Tell her to come in." She appeared at once.

"I understand that you're good on the new machine but you don't want to work it?"

"No. I won't do it."

"Why?"

"I have to earn my living in an office, but I won't mix in business. I hate and despise business and anything to do with making money."

"Do you think it's wrong?"

"It is the enemy of art."

"And you feel yourself an artist?"

"No. But I want to live with artists and live like them. I don't want to be like those earthy girls out there, like Maria Magna and Vera Day. I prefer to die of hunger. Or go away."

"But you have no money."

"No. But it doesn't matter. I can get along without money. In the Village, artists get along without money. They all help each other. It's a different kind of living. This is a terrible world here, everyone working for money, no one working for anything good."

"My God, I think so myself. Things ought to be different; and one day they will be." But, as always, when a word was said that was, however remotely, challenging on social matters, she shut her mind. "You don't think so?" She raised her brown head in its childish hair and he saw the maiden breasts move as she drew in a breath. "You don't think so?"

"I don't think so," she said primly.

"Well, you must feel you're an artist; that you have some other plan for living," he pressed her.

"I don't know; I don't know what these things are," she said vaguely. Tears came into her eyes. "I don't know why I am here."

"You're a good girl," he said getting up and about to go to her, but glancing at the half-glazed partitions which divided the offices. "Well, go out now and do your work. You do your work well."

"Yes, but I hate it," she said, frowning. She had dried her tears. "It's unworthy. It's not worthy of man."

"Man?"

"Mankind, people. Artists don't think like this; artists don't fight for money."

"That's the old Bostonian highmindedness," he said respectfully. "You don't meet it often in Manhattan."

With a flick of her short skirt she was out of his office. He saw her a few minutes later sitting in the middle of the clerks' room, a high window lighting her hair, as she bent over the telephone book. This surprised him, for she did not like the telephone and made a fuss about taking her turn at the switchboard; although, as at the Moon machine, she was competent. What was she looking at? He also liked to read the telephone book, pictures, data and conclusions forming in his memory as he read. He was stirred by her curious protests which he felt had a meaning; and he was puzzled. Later on, Tom Zero came to him and remarked, "What about this

9

new girl? Let's get rid of her. She's not obliging, she makes too much fuss."

"She's a sort of miracle in our age and town," said Debrett. "She's terribly poor and needs money, but she won't learn the machine because it's too close to gross money-making. She can do figures but she despises them. Her brother's Walter Lawrence, the painter, supposed to be one of our best painters, and she hero-worships him. We have to be human. Can you imagine a girl who needs fares and clothes, and probably even bread, giving up a raise on principle?"

"Well, if you're interested in her, all right, but I hope you're right."

"I'm a happily married man and I'm only interested in my fellow human being, when I see an ingenuous or a pure soul struggling with the world, man or woman; but it strikes me that women struggle oftener. Men don't fight moral battles."

"Moral battles arise when two sets of ethics clash, they're not in themselves admirable," said Tom Zero. "She'll adjust herself, I suppose. Let her do her work and keep her morals for home. Some buyers are in town today from Market Wheeling, Ohio, the brothers we wrote to. They want to go out tonight, want someone to show them around, the theatre, a nightclub, you know? Will you do it?"

"No, I won't," said Debrett. "You know what they want. They want an obscene show; that's what these hicks want in New York."

"Well, someone has to do it," said Zero "I can't. Myra has people to dinner. Scott has an opinion to write and he wouldn't anyway; Good has his father-in-law visiting, trying to patch up his marriage; and the others are tied up, too."

"Well, I'm tied up. Beatrice expects me to be home if she phones. She's not happy. The baby gets her up at six or four; her mother nags her. I'm her only friend. I have to go to my meetings; but she wouldn't understand that sort of night out and I wouldn't understand it myself. Let them hire a guide."

"No, it's a courtesy we owe them. I'd like you to do it. You're a sociable man."

"If that's the price of my staying here, I'll hand in my resignation. I won't do it."

"Don't get heated. Who will, though?"

"Try the sales staff, try the carbide men. Why not Big Bill? He's amusing and foulmouthed, known in every whorehouse from coast to coast. They'll like him." said Debrett, already laughing.

"Yes, you're right. If he's in the house."

He went out but turned as he grasped the door handle and shot a sharp glance at the mild man sitting at the desk. Debrett nodded gaily.

When he reached home, Zero said to his wife, "Pity we didn't invite Gus to dinner. He's lonely. Beatie's out of town."

"Oh, she's only gone off to her mother at Morristown." After a moment, she said, "Any particular reason?"

"How does Gus manage?"

"Oh, he scrambles for himself, I guess. He's never home when she is at home. Why, what about Gus?"

"Well, let's ask Debrett some night soon."

"Wait till Beatie comes home."

"All right."

"You have to pick your company for Gus Debrett. He doesn't care what he says. It's all right with us."

"He's diplomatic in business. He's a good wangler."

"But all his outside friends are mavericks."

"Is that what Beatie says?" asked Tom with a smile.

"Oh, Beatie's very loyal."

He smiled. "I see. Just the same, is that adult? To be always at her mother's?"

"Well, it saves Gus money, Beatie says. And I suppose Beatie's family help them out."

Zero laughed. "I'm sure they don't. More likely, Debrett has to lend them a hundred dollars to eat occasionally."

She said irritably, "Everyone knows how the Honitons spend."

"Yes," said Zero laughing. He added "I believe if they both died in an accident tonight, God forbid, the Debretts would have

11

to pay for the funeral expenses and be torn to pieces by screaming creditors as well."

"Still, it's her mother and she wants to be near her," said Myra. "What's your drift? You know how devoted Gus is."

"Too devoted."

"Explain that, Tom."

The guests began to arrive.

The next day Miss Magna reported that one of the visitors from Market Wheeling had been idling in the office, jaunty with the girls, when he passed his hand over Miss Lawrence's shoulder. She sprang at him and hit him with what she had in her hand— a file. "Send her in to me," said Tom Zero, holding Miss Magna with his eye. The girl came in softly. "I hear you hit one of my clients," he said insultingly. She scowled. He looked at her curiously. "Come here." She approached. He looked up at her, observing her charm. "Why?"

"No one can touch me," she said. They were close. His face flashed. He said gently, "Well, go and behave yourself," and touched her hand with his fingers. She took his oval fine hand and looked into his face. "I'll have a letter for you later on," he said. She went. Later he gave the letter to another girl. She seemed to take no notice.

The Zeros had an apartment on the sixth floor of a new brick building in the East Eighties. Over the sidewalk was a blue awning with the number on it in white. There was a square-tiled entrance hall with palms, behind which two staircases rose; an elevator, a doorman in blue uniform. The doorman sat at a small table near the entrance, his back to the radiator. He was supposed to examine callers and announce them through a house-phone, but he let those pass he summed up as respectable; and so he let pass a ladylike girl who said she was expected at Mrs. Zero's.

Myra Zero opened the door. The girl, in a new raincoat and hat, stood there without saying a word, looking at her. "Who do you want?" "I'm Miss Honor Lawrence." "Yes." "Are you Mrs. Zero?" "Yes." The girl stepped eagerly forward and Myra, in surprise, stepped back; the girl was inside. She herself shut the door and began taking off her gloves. "How do you do? You know of me, don't you?" she said politely. "I don't know you." "I work for your husband, Mr. Tom Zero." "Is something wrong?" "Wrong?" "Come in," said Myra with reserve, looking the girl up and down: brown velvet skirt, brown kid shoes and handbag, brown felt hat, no cosmetics, self-possessed. She looked around and said casually, "I didn't think it would be like this." "No? Won't you sit down?" She sat and looked around her critically. "I thought I ought to talk to you." "Why?" Myra said with a slight start. "I have such a long walk to work—my father won't give me the fare. You see, I have to give him everything. Someone gave me a skirt. He doesn't think I ought to have money for myself. He says, What is it for? And I won't explain. I'm too proud. It's a long walk. Then I have to go back and cook at night. If I go out the door afterwards, he's angry, very angry. And men do speak to me. I don't like that. If I could find a room, nearer the office, I'd make some friends. I thought you could advise me. My sister's married and doesn't come near us. She sent me this skirt. My mother died years ago. My brother—" She was looking at the paintings on the walls, and stopped, eyeing one of them.

"I'm sorry your mother is dead."

"Oh, she died years ago. She wasn't sick. She was miserable. We used to go and sit with the neighbours. Mother would never ask for anything, and neither did I. She wouldn't allow me to. When my father came home, he unlocked the door and we could go in. Or we sat on the stairs. But the neighbours asked us in and made us eat something. Father was afraid we would eat before he came home. My father locked all the windows and nailed them down. It was hot in summer and I liked sitting on the stairs. I have to scrub the floor and wash the things with water and no soap—" She told this in an interested tone. She then said trustfully, "I never told anyone all this before. I suppose it's a bit unusual. But I never knew there were happy families. I thought that was all a lie. I didn't know there were rich people either." She once more looked around the room. "Well, you see, he takes my money, to pay for the food and rent he gave me as a child. The others have left home, so I will never be through paying. I must leave. But I don't know where to go. I thought you might know. Perhaps somewhere here," she continued, looking out the window towards the other houses. "All the houses in the city! When I'm walking I look at them all and think, There are plenty of rooms in there, or at least someone who could give me a bed. My father takes all my money. He puts it away somewhere and he doesn't want to buy food. I don't want to think about it. I never think about it. But I want to leave."

"You're in trouble," said Mrs. Zero. "I'll make some coffee while I'm thinking about your problem." She went out and presently came back. "Do they know at the office that you're here? Does my husband know?" Miss Lawrence was looking at the paintings. She turned her head slowly, "I asked for the afternoon off." "To visit me, you mean?" "Yes." "Did my husband tell you to come here?" "No. But I heard you were a good woman." "Who told you that?" "They were saying in the office that Mr. Zero is a good man." "And that means I'm good." "Yes. He's a very good man."

Afterwards the wife said, "You want to pay rent, do you?"

"I can't pay much rent. Aren't there people who would give me a bed, just a bed? I could clean the house for them. I do it at home. Sometimes I have to do it over again in the middle of the night."

"Why?"

"He makes me get up. He says it isn't clean enough. So I could easily do two hours a day."

"That wouldn't be necessary, I think."

As Miss Lawrence was going, she hesitated, holding her purse tight and standing upright, looking expectantly at Mrs. Zero. "Is there anything you want?" The girl shook her head. "Are you going back to the office now?" "Yes." "Have you any money?" She did not answer. "You can't walk down to the office. It would take too long. I'll give you your fare." The girl smiled, held out her hand saying, "Thank you for the coffee. You've been very kind," and went towards the stairs. "Wait for the elevator." She did so. When the car reached their floor, Miss Lawrence said, "Could I see you again?" "Yes, if you like. Come to dinner some night." "Thank you very much. You are really very kind." Holding her empty purse tightly, she passed out of sight. Myra thought about the episode for some time, and when her husband came home she kept the surprise for a while. She was flattered.

"Miss Lawrence came to see me."

"Who is that?"

"From your office."

He thought for a moment and asked, "What for?"

"I am not sure. She said she had the afternoon off to see me. Isn't that odd?"

"Maria Magna wants her to go. Perhaps she gave her time off to look for a job."

"Well, she needs a room and she thought I might know of one."

"Why you?"

"I don't know." They came to no conclusion. "I asked her to dinner."

"Why?"

"She asked to see me again, and so I asked her. Don't ask me why."

"I don't want this," he said casually.

"No date was mentioned. She may not think of it for months," said Myra.

The next evening, about half past six, Miss Lawrence came to the door, looking exactly as before, said good evening and remarked, "I know I'm not late, because Mr. Zero was still in the office when I left."

Myra Zero was in a hurry. "What have you come for?"

"You asked me to dinner yesterday."

"I'm getting the children to bed. Come in. Go and sit where you were yesterday and I'll be in when I can."

When she came back, the girl was sitting in the same chair as before, with her legs stretched out and her eyes closed. As soon as Myra entered, she began to talk trustfully, "I saw my brother and told him you were helping me."

Myra watched her husband when he entered. He was a discreet man. He said, "Oh, it was for tonight, then?" and offered her a drink. "Oh, thank you. I don't drink," she said timidly. She refused

15

a cigarette in the same way, and when he said, "You don't play cards either?" she replied, "I don't know what they are. Do you mean—" she hesitated.

"So your family is religious. But you go dancing?" "Oh, no," she exclaimed with horror. "Do you think dancing is wrong?" asked Myra. "It's such a stupid waste of time." "Then what do you think people should do?" Myra asked, for she and Tom loved dancing and had once won a prize. "I don't know what others should do," said the girl. They had a light meal and the girl soon left, saying she had to be in by nine. "Are you walking home?" "Yes." "Why? Is it for health reasons?" said Zero sarcastically. But Myra went to the door and gave her a dollar. "You can pay me back when you've found a room and have the money. It's our secret." The girl was astounded. "Secret?" She examined the dollar bill. "I mustn't spend it?" She looked at Myra while she explained, a new and astonished understanding on her face. "Or you can have it, keep it." "Oh, no, I'll pay it back."

"I hope this is not going to become a habit," said Myra. "She makes me giddy. She doesn't understand the simplest conventions."

"She's just a young goose. I'll tell Miss Magna to teach her the elements. But better would be to lose her. It's Gus who's mothering her."

"How old is she?"

"Eighteen."

"She's very immature. But her father keeps her a prisoner."

"Myra, that's not our affair."

"Oh, you're right. But she's touching."

Debrett was a married bachelor. After work he walked the streets, went to a political club, a friend's house, or chess café on Second Avenue, to talk politics and have a cup of coffee. He never drank anything else and ate little. He did not play chess, but there was talk there and a man could sit there the whole evening for only one or two cups of coffee and need not buy a sandwich. A middle-aged woman living on the ground floor of his apartment building, lent him her daily help for half an hour a day to tidy his apartment.

16

It was never untidy. Debrett was only at home in the evening at times prearranged with a New Jersey friend, born to the name of Goldentopf, recently changed to Seymour. Seymour was a tall, thin, fair North German type who thought he looked English. He was still living at home with his father, a wholesale butcher who made money; but he despised him, his brothers and sisters, the State of New Jersey and also the United States. "There are natural aristocrats and natural butchers," he said. He kept his gramophone and a large collection of records at Debrett's in New York and often went there to hear new music, and to conduct orchestral records with a baton. He greatly admired Beatrice Debrett and Debrett admired Seymour. Seymour's evenings excepted, Debrett did not return to his apartment till eleven o'clock, or after. There, he would walk up and down working out financial and political problems till very late and then fall into bed. For the newborn child, they had moved out to a street high-banked and bristling with new apartment houses, near the Grand Concourse, in the Bronx. He had to leave his home at half past seven to get to his working place at nine; and an evening appointment brought him home after his wife was in bed. She was an early sleeper, early riser. He ate out, or got himself a bit of bread and cheese when he returned. Now that his wife was away, he telephoned her every day at her Morristown home; or sent daily letters from the office, a husband's love letters, consoling and pleading. If he called at a friend's house, he would take some coffee, talk for several hours, and afterwards, he might walk many blocks uptown, thinking and talking excitedly to himself under his breath.

He did not like to have his letters to his wife typed by these earthy girls in the office, and so he dictated them to Miss Lawrence, to whom he could explain everything. Through these letters and talks she knew of his great love for his wife and it seemed to Debrett that they could all be friends. He wondered about her life; she must be lonely. Sometimes he gave her a long look, but there was no response in her eyes. "She is certainly not interested in anyone here. She must be thinking of her talks in the Village with her artist friends." He walked around the Village, too, now, looking in at windows of studios and coffee shops, thinking he might see her; just to add a faint human interest to his evening.

One evening, reaching his street in the Bronx at eleven thirty, he was surprised to see the lights on in his fifth-floor apartment. He thought that his wife had returned. In the elevator he had a glad and disturbed face; had his letters brought her home too soon? He had hinted at his loneliness recently. Was it right, when she came home only to his late hours and the distance from the centre? She did not make friends easily; she disliked the district. She was the kind of woman who trusted only women; and even those were friends from high-school days, mostly women who had not married. She found comfort in them and their courageous struggle.

When he opened the door, Miss Lawrence walked out of the living-room into the small, square hall. "What are you doing here?" he called out. "What is wrong?" "I thought your wife was coming and I wanted to see her." "But she isn't coming tonight. How will you get home now?" "I thought she was coming tonight," she said sadly. "It doesn't matter: good night," and she held out her hand. He detained her. "How did you get in?" "A man was here and let me in." "What man?" "I don't know. He was playing records; I sat in the other room." "Have you had anything to eat since you left the office?" "No." He was hungry himself and asked her to eat something with him. She refused. "Have you money for the subway?" She began to walk towards the stairs without answering, her head lowered in thought. At the turn of the staircase, she waved her hand. He ran after her. "Where are you going? Come back. You can't walk home." "I could stay here," she said, raising innocent eyes to him. "With me?" "Yes." "My dear girl—you must take a taxi home." She took the money indifferently. When he got in again, he telephoned Seymour, a dry, unforgiving and ribald bachelor, at the moment sour with disapproval. "I never thought you would do that to Beatie, Gus. It's unworthy of you both. A typist—a typist today is like a servant girl in your father's time. I'd watch my step, if I were you. You would forfeit my entire respect." It was hard to explain to a stick like Seymour. Gus explained a little and then said he was tired. "Has she gone?" Seymour persisted. "I must get to bed, Alec. I'm tired out. She came to see Beatrice. She's a very strange girl. I don't understand her myself, but I think she needs help." At this, Seymour laughed drily, told a dirty joke; Debrett laughed and said good-bye.

"In any case," said Seymour, "Beatrice will be home in a day or two, perhaps tomorrow. I telephoned her from your place, while the girl was there and told her she ought to be here." "Perhaps she should, but that's up to her. I don't want her made anxious when she's recovering. She's not very happy and this has been her chance to recover." "If I thought you weren't good to her, I'd have a very low opinion of you," said the bachelor. "I do my best, but happiness is a mystery. One can't manufacture happiness for another human being, especially a sensitive lonely soul like Beatrice."

At the office the next day, he sent for the girl. "What time did you get home last night?" "I don't know. The door was locked. I slept on the landing until early this morning, when a neighbour took me in, and I got washed." "That is terrible, terrible." She said nothing; looked around. "What did you want to see my wife about?" "Just something private." She seemed as on other days; and he wondered what other nights she had spent on the landing, at a neighbour's. When he reached his street that night about eleven, again he saw his lights on. He walked about anxiously for some minutes, then went upstairs. His wife was sitting in an armchair in the living room wearing a handsome blue dressing gown. She was beautiful, but to him, unlike herself.

"Augustus!" she checked herself; "I have been sitting here, waiting for you for hours." "Why didn't you let me know you were coming?" he cried gladly, rushed over, hugged her. "Did you miss me?" she said, with her usual coolness; but she laughed a trifle and made advances, unlike her and which chilled him. "You know I can't live without you." "Lonely is as lonely does," she said, with pathetic wit. She had no sense of humour. "I'd better go to the kitchen and get a bite; I haven't eaten yet." "I made something for you." "Did you, Beatrice? That was very kind. You are tired. I know this is late for you. But I'm glad you stayed up." He was very glad.

The next day he sent for Miss Lawrence for some letters. "But no more for my wife," he said laughing. "Do you know why? You were remarkably close to the truth. She came home last night unexpectedly. You must go and see her in a few days, when she's a bit more settled. You'll like her. Women like her; she's very good and understanding."

And one evening the following week, when he got home at ten, his wife was again waiting for him. Presently she said, "Your secretary was here." "Who?" "Miss Lawrence, your secretary." "She was here? I remember—she asked for time off. She said she had an appointment." "And of course what Miss Lawrence wants, she gets," she said pertly. "She's been wanting to talk to you for over a week." "Over a week! You told her to come and see me. Or she seemed to think you did." "Let's not have a misunderstanding over the poor girl." "Let's go to the kitchen and you have your sandwich." "Oh, is there a sandwich? Thank you."

While eating, he searched her face hungrily. "Well, Beatrice, why don't you say what you have to say? What was the problem? I'm interested." She rose. "Frankly, I don't know. I don't know why this insistence. I gather she was here before. Because I know Seymour let her in. Oh, I grant that she wasn't expected. I credit you with that."

He said, "We don't have to spar with each other." "Still, out of all the women in New York she chose me." "You're wrong there: she's been to see Myra and Good's wife." They were standing in the sitting room. "You haven't asked about David." "How is he?" "I think he's better off here than at mother's." "Perhaps he is. But are you? You have all the work to do here. You can rest there." "Oh, you know how her vulgarity horrifies me: she's a noisy dictator. She has her slaves and maids and her truckling friends and even boy friends. Essentially, I married you to get away from it; and you keep suggesting I should go back. Why?" "Well, Beatie, so you're glad to be home?" "Yes, I am. It's lonely and miserable and isolated here and I never see you; but I'm not surrounded by drinking, card-playing barbarians screaming like hyenas at dirty jokes, all night." He sat in thought for a moment and then began to read a political weekly which had come by the morning post. He cheered up and presently said, "There's an excellent article here on Brazil."

Much later, she told him about the girl. "She walked in as if expected, said she had been waiting for me to come home and she wanted to talk to me. I was unprepared and didn't know what to expect. I was frightened, I think." She laughed a little. "Why frightened? Did you think she was going to attack you?" "Attack me?" She thought it over. "No. Why should she? Is she paranoiac?" "She's perfectly normal." "Is she? Well, who is? She began to talk and I gathered she was in trouble, but she couldn't come out with it; she was roundabout, hesitant, repressed. She seemed to want to appear too ladylike to say anything definite. At last, I realized that they were overcrowded at home, that she had no money and that she needed clothes." "Did you give her some?" he asked. "You have very few clothes yourself."

"No, not yet. At any rate, I was obliged to ask her to dinner. I just hinted and she took me up on it. She's coming to dinner on Tuesday night." She laughed. "I expect you will be able to make it by eight that night." "Tuesday? Yes, of course I will. I should like you to become friends."

After a silence, she burst out, "Oh, this is intolerable. I can't stand it. I can't stand the problems, the uncertainties. It suffocates me. If only I could die, tonight, and not have to go through with it."

"What is the trouble, my dear? You know I love you and never loved anyone else and that I live for you and I couldn't live without you."

"I don't want it, I don't want it, I don't want it."

"I don't understand, I don't understand."

"It's the intolerable anguish of living, the intolerable doubt about everything."

"Surely you don't mean Miss Lawrence?"

"Oh, no, of course not," she said scornfully. "You don't suppose I suspect you?"

"There is no reason to."

When he got home at seven that Tuesday evening, his wife took him into the bedroom and said, "I thought you'd come together. She's been here while I've been putting the baby to bed and I've not had time to prepare anything: just sitting there. She won't take a drink—"

"She's a teetotaler," said Debrett proudly.

"—and she has no conversation."

"You should have talked to her about art—she considers that the only subject fit for a human being."

"What do I know of art?"

"Well, she seems to think you're a kindred spirit," he said, with pleasure.

"You go and entertain her; she's probably used to you. I have nothing for dinner. I felt too unhappy to go out and shop."

But though the girl behaved with ladylike gravity, then and throughout the meal, she never once looked at Debrett, turning her head always to Beatrice, hanging on her words, smiling and bending her head to her plate, glancing critically at the pictures or curtains, or even at the table service. She smiled at the wife's few jokes and, when Beatrice got to her feet, Miss Lawrence jumped up and helped her silently. The meal did not take long. Beatrice had opened a can of salmon and had made some salad. Miss Lawrence had never eaten salmon; instead she ate a boiled egg with relish.

"Do you like boiled eggs?" asked Beatrice.

"I haven't had a boiled egg for years, since mother was there; but I like them."

"What do you like to eat?" said Beatrice with curiosity.

"We have vegetables—oatmeal, cheese," she said, musing as if she had never considered it.

"Are you vegetarians, also?" Beatrice said with a smile.

The girl looked at her, puzzled.

"No meat or fish, I mean."

"No."

"You have many principles, haven't you?" said Debrett.

She looked at his wife, questioning.

"But you eat dessert?" said Beatrice. "Milk puddings, I suppose? I'm afraid I only have ice cream."

"Oh," she exclaimed, delighted, "I've never had ice cream."

She left immediately after the plates were cleared. When she was going, Beatrice offered her some clothes she had set aside. The girl went through them carefully, selected a blouse, left the other things lying there, said good-bye suddenly and left, with the blouse in her hand.

Beatrice herself spoke as if she were musing all the time and her words were the product of serious thought; it had always attracted him. But Beatrice objected to the girl's slow-spokenness: "Why does she pull each word off her teeth as if it were taffy?"

Debrett had not liked the blouse being given away, it was Beatrice's. He spoke to Tom Zero about raising the girl's wages. He began wondering if he could spare her a little out of his own salary. Impossible. He gave all but a few dollars for lunches to his wife; and indeed, they were beginning to need more money at home. He had worries. The firm had begun honest and gained repute, but was taking a short cut to riches, selling its stock and increasing the stock when necessary. It had entered upon fraud. Farmers, investors, small-towners, countryfolk who had invested in the firm, bought the stock and could not sell it back; this was illegal. But the company paid good dividends, kept straight accounts, and the legal situation, handled by Tom Zero and Saul Scott, was always unassailable. All these talented young men could have made money honestly; crooked money seemed gayer and cleverer. Debrett had no heart for it. He did not care for money at all. He could make money for others, invent schemes of any colour, but never for himself. "The firm's making money; if you hang on, you bunch of crooks, you can sell out for a big price to the Chicago Farmers' Supplies," he said, with a laugh. But they hung on for quick profit and an early bankruptcy. He had no stomach for fraud or financial investigators; he decided to move. He was looking about, both for a new job with good pay and a new home downtown, so that he could see his family early in the evening. Beatrice was very unhappy.

When he had decided to move he realized that he would be leaving Miss Lawrence on her own. He took her to lunch to try to work out her problems and give her some advice. Not to be misconstrued, he mentioned it to Tom Zero. He went to a lunch-room pleasing to New York women, intending to spend more money than he ever did for himself. There was a lofty room with decorated walls, menus, flowers, a lot of small tables and he expected her to be delighted. But she looked about slightly in her dignified way; and he admired her, though he was disappointed. Halfway through the meal, which he selected to suit her limited tastes, he was greeted by a woman passing close to the table; it was Beatrice. Miss Lawrence looked up, smiled and put out her hand, "Oh, I am so glad you came, too." Beatrice behaved with the good and distant manners he admired, greeted them both and walked out. When he got home, she said, "Augustus, I would not do that again, if I were you." "Beatrice, you must understand—" "Let us say no more about it." For days he did not ask for Miss Lawrence.

She had been there nearly a year: it was August. She had refused her holiday, asking to be allowed to work during the fort-night. "And you can pay me the money extra." Debrett was also working, his wife having gone to Morristown to her mother's. Three engineers arrived from the Middle West to test a new piece of apparatus, a gas generator, which the firm wanted to market. Two of them were busy in town; the third, hanging about the office, found the young filing clerk interesting. He was nearly sixty, had a long soft red nose, and often he would sit down at one of the empty desks and begin designing a piece of apparatus. "And what do you do?" "I file the letters, I fill in at the switchboard, I type personal letters." "You're new, aren't you?" "I've been here since November." "I'm going to a little restaurant near here for a bite of lunch. Would you like to go with me?" "Yes, thank you." "What time do they let you out?" "What do you mean?" She seemed hurt. "What time do you lunch?" "Half past twelve." He took her to a large old-fashioned restaurant on the ground floor of a ware-house. "Oysters?" "What is that?" "Tomato juice?" "Yes, please." "Chicken a la king?" "What is that?" "You don't get around much, do you?" "Oh, I go around a lot; but I eat with friends, at their homes." "You have a lot of friends, then. Boy friends, too, I expect." "Boys? I don't like boys. I like men. I have a lot of men friends." "It

24

doesn't surprise me." He touched the hair on her shoulder; and she gave a loud cry and bounded out of her chair. "Good grief, don't do that! What did I do?" he said, looking about. "I don't want men to touch me." He was frightened. "I didn't mean any harm; don't you understand? I admire you. I respect you." She was very sweet. "I forgive you. I know you didn't mean any harm." He said, "I'm a real honest man, girlie; if you scream at me again because I happen to touch your arm I think I'd fall through the floor. I don't go out with girls. I just like to talk." And he went on to talk. He told her about Celinda, his wife, a farm girl who was a good bit younger than himself, a fine wife and mother, and could do anything. She ran the farm and had the children obedient and doing the chores. He talked about his children, two girls and a boy; and his well-managed little farm, ten acres, with fruit, poultry and vegetables, a tractor, horse and cow, near Hamilton, an Ohio village, some distance from Cincinnati. "My wife's as good as two hired men." He had to travel about the country; his wife put up with it and was good to him, very good. "I wish you knew her; you'd like her and she'd like you. But this is all about me."

She told him what she was interested in: modern painting, painters, new trends in poetry. "That's very unusual and advanced for a filing clerk." "I won't be there long. It's temporary. I'm looking for the right place for me." "Aren't they good to you there?" "Yes, they're good to me, but it means nothing. It's an ugly dreadful life."

"You're a country girl, I suppose." She did not answer. "Well, if you're a country girl, I know how you feel. When you look up at all those tall buildings, you think, but in what corner do they grow the corn and the potatoes; and where do they keep the hens?"

On the way back to the office he said he'd like to buy her a little gift, what would she like? She said, a book about Gauguin, small and comparatively cheap. "You meet me at Brentano's, and I'll give it to you; no strings to it. I think a lot of you. You remind me of my wife."

The next day, a Saturday, the office was working overtime again. There was an unpredicted storm, with a fiery sky; a fireball bumped over the skyscrapers into the street. No one had a raincoat.

They sent the office boy out for coffee and sandwiches; but Miss Lawrence went out into the downpour. She said she had an important appointment. She returned at the end of lunch-hour, drenched, her wet face absorbed. They got her partly dry; they fussed around her, asked, laughing, "How was your appointment? How did it turn out?" She did not answer. A new job, a boy, a runaway match? She did not come to work the next Monday, nor during the week. She was not seen again in the Farmers' Utilities Corporation.

During the week, Walter Lawrence, her brother, telephoned and when he heard she was no longer working for them, he seemed relieved. "That's good, then." "It's good?" said Tom Zero, surprised. "I mean, I know where to look." But on the following Monday a worn-out bent old man asked to see Mr. Zero. His name was Tommaseo. Miss Magna sent him to Mr. Debrett. "An old man here insists that his daughter works for us. He hardly speaks any English and I don't understand him," she said proudly, for she was the daughter of an Italian immigrant and spoke no Italian. Debrett knew no Italian but his sympathy with strange human beings enabled him to understand that Mr. Tommaseo bought fruit and vegetables early in the morning in the Gansevoort Market, east of Twentieth Avenue, and took them to a small shop he had near Bleecker Street, where he had a cut-rate trade. His daughter had stolen money from him and run away to the streets; his wife, son and other daughter had also taken money from him and never paid him back. Now he had nothing but debts and nothing to look forward to. The firm, the Farmers' Utilities, owed him money, his daughter's pay, which was his, because of what she owed him. Debrett explained that his daughter had never worked for him. "She did, she did, and you owe me her wages," cried the old man. Debrett was ashamed to call for the bouncer and eventually persuaded Tommaseo to leave; but he left, crying bitterly and exclaiming, "All thieves, all cheats." Debrett turned back shaking his head. "Crazed poverty; it tears your heart," he said to Tom Zero who was looking at this scene.

"Gus, you'll never be rich," said Zero. "I hope not," said Debrett. "That is a wish always granted," said Zero, without smiling. "But he did know something about us," said Maria Magna; "though he got all the names wrong. He's an old crook, I think; wanted to frighten you, pretend you'd stolen his daughter. The old men think up all sorts of tricks. I know them." "Why say that, Maria? All he said to me was, I've always worked hard and starved." And as he walked home that night, Debrett wished he had given five dollars to the old man, bent, grasping, perhaps a crook or deluded, casting his eyes about furiously, calling out names, "Dibretti, Seer, Scotti, I know, I know—" Debrett, Zero and Scott, names on the door-plate.

Later, Walter Lawrence called to see Debrett. His name and his sister's was Tommaseo; they had changed to Lawrence. Their father was an Italian immigrant, at home a mason, here a man with fruit and vegetables on a barrow, who by hard work and cruel pinching had been able to rent a small store, where he sold seconds and rejects. This man had become a miser, a man who watched every bite they took, and shrieked, "You're killing me, you're ruining me, don't eat so much"; horrible scenes, frightful gestures. When he went out he took the key with him and they waited for his return; either on the staircase or in neighbours' apartments. They scarcely ever bought anything. They dressed in the cast-offs of tenement neighbours. It was not only that he would not give the money, it was the unbearable scenes he made on a shopping expedition. He would trudge ahead, muttering, even shouting at them. If they stopped at a window, he would slowly come back, look in, say, "Why are you stopping here? Is there anything else you can think of to ruin me? What else do you want?" When they reached the store, no one, not even the storekeepers and assistants, though they were used to haggling, could stand the horror of his cries and insults. "I know it was poverty, but every slum father does not do that; I simply can't forgive him. My mother put up with it. My mother was afraid we would die of exposure to hunger and cold; and when the last of us could earn a living, she put an end to it. He had to pay for the gas she used then. He sold the stove and all their cooking was done on a gas ring. My sister Honor's name was Rosina. She never had any clothing till she went to school. She was wrapped up in a shawl or

27

a skirt. She actually does not know even now, I think, what it is to go into a shop and buy something for herself. As for hair, face, any feminine thing, she knows they exist, but does not think they are for her. It doesn't matter much yet. She's not sixteen yet; and in spite of the life she's led, or because of it, she's austere, pure and high-minded. She believes in what she says."

"But where is the child?" cried Debrett.

"In a way, I don't care; anywhere is better than that inferno. But I expect she will knock at my door in a day or two."

"You take it very calmly. I can't be so cool. I'm worried about a girl of fifteen—you say she's not sixteen?—alone all night in the streets."

"Oh, I know Honor. She's found herself some hole or corner. She's a surprising girl. She has a memory as long as your arm for people and addresses. She may even be with one of our neighbours up at home. But I know she will come to no harm—of the sort you mean—she's as safe as a saint; she's quite a rare human being."

"I wouldn't be so calm if it were my sister. I had a sister once. She died of tenement life; and I've never forgotten it. It haunts me."

"I know she'll come to me," said the brother. "I know she will be all right."

Not long after this, Farmers' Utilities began to break up. Debrett was the first to go. He found a job in Wall Street and was able to move his family downtown. Tom Zero quit and set up his own law firm. Scott went to work with a judge. Palmer, the old engineer, was in Chicago doing business with his old firm, when he got a letter from his wife Celinda, on the farm near Hamilton, Ohio. "A slip of a girl, not more than sixteen, I am sure, has come to stay with me here. She says she worked for you in New York and that you raved about me and said she should live on a farm. She had not eaten or slept decently for five days, but I cannot get out of her how she got here. She has no money. She said, I thought I'd like to forget everything; but she had no object, just to wander, and she found out in a day or two that she is not strong enough for the hobo life, so she came to the nearest home."

Celinda, a strong smooth-boned girl with thick bronze hair, who looked ten years younger than she was and was twenty years younger than her husband, accepted the visitor with curiosity. "My husband says you have a family and a job in New York." "I can't go back there." "Why?" "My father shut me out—I got home late." "Where had you been?" "To see—a friend of mine, for dinner; and I had to walk home." "What sort is your father?" She was apparently thinking it over. "Well—your father?" "I don't know," she said at last, sitting in her chair serenely and as if amused. "What does he do?" "He sells things, I suppose, things like you have here, vegetables." "Well, and where were you working?" But there the visitor was quite clear. She gave the name of the office, the address, the private addresses of all the partners and senior employees, the salesmen on both sides of the house (that is, for goods and for stock); and very vivaciously, she gave the names of the various firms Celinda's husband, Palmer, worked for. "What a wonderful memory you have!" The girl was startled and became quiet. "How do you remember all that?" "I don't remember them—they were in the files and the telephone book." "And you can't go back there?" "Where?" "To the firm, Farmers' Utilities." For a long time she was silent, pondering. "Did something happen there?" "Where?" "In the firm? Did something happen to you? Were they disagreeable to you? Did someone hurt your feelings?" "I don't think about them." No matter how much Celinda questioned her, she got this kind of answer.

At first Honor did nothing and Celinda thought her too weak to work. She very rarely spoke about herself, but she would volunteer remarks suddenly, such as, "My brother is not as fine as he thinks; there are other painters too." "Is he a painter?" "I suppose he is. Yes, he is. But he's overrated, particularly by himself. He's an architect of his own fame, the same kind of architect as a woodworm." After such tart, unexpected sentences, she would retire into herself, sit peacefully. And as suddenly, "My brother is a mean, slobbery little man. I don't like him at all. He is all for himself. He left my father. He never paid him back the money he owed him for his keep." "Did he owe him money?" "My father paid for his food

29

and rent when he was a child." Once or twice, sitting in the chair Mrs. Palmer had put out for her under an apple-tree in the rough grass at the side of the house, she spoke about herself. "I have finer perceptions than my brother. He will use anyone. I won't have anything to do with stupid people. My senses are delicate. I'm an artist by nature, but I haven't the means, my brother says. He says it's a complex type of human being. People worry me. I need this country quiet. I feel better than I ever did in my life. Your husband said I was to stay here and forget the city, see where the corn grows. I'll never go home again."

The farmhouse in Ohio suited her and she was going to stay with them a long time, she said. "Don't you think you should help me with the chores to cover your keep?" Honor stared at the woman. "Are you like my father?" The Ohio wife wrote again to her husband and waited. Here was a young unfortunate, she thought; so young that she could not send her out on to the roads. She measured her hospitality, but was not unkind. Honor did almost no work in the house or farm. She sat on the dry grass or the veranda, moping. She ate sparingly, drank water and milk and had her share of things that were quite different, she said, from any she had had before; fruit, vegetables, eggs. She did not want to be a nuisance and insisted upon sleeping rolled up in a quilt on the floor. "I'm used to it; and I read somewhere that it is good for the nerves." She played with the children and told them stories of town life.

"My brother stabbed himself in the foot with a railing and nearly died. In our house was a little boy who lived by himself in the daytime. His parents went to work. He climbed up and down the stairs all day, rubbing his hands on the wood and crying. My father nailed up the windows in our room so that the sparrows could not get the crumbs we put out. One day I got a prize at school and my father sold it for two dollars. My brother kept a rat in a can in the yard; but a dog got it. My mother and my brother and I used to sit on the landing and my mother told us stories about her home. It was very cold in winter and hot in summer and there were miles of stone arches to keep the sun and snow off you. Arcades they are. And in the arcades are stores with lace, and diamonds and money, stores with money in the windows, you can go in and get it; and cakes and things like that; roast chickens, too, and shoes, with red and green stripes and leather lace on them. My mother said if she ever had the money she would take us home with her. If she had had the money we would be there now. But I'll go one day."

In this way, Honor stayed till autumn. The husband returned home once. The day before he returned, Honor went away; she returned after he left, without saying where she had been, or how she knew he had gone. The second time, he was coming home for a longer stay. This time she went and did not return. She did not say good-bye, or thanks, and they never heard of her again. In the spring, they found traces of her in a shed full of lumber; but they did not know when she had stayed there. No one in the east heard of Honor again for two years or more, that is till she was nearly eighteen.

It was then that Augustus Debrett received a message in his Wall Street office that a woman wanted to see him in the waiting room. "No, not your wife." At first glance she seemed as before, the sweet sober face, the swinging skirt and then he saw that she was older; she was thin and nervous. She held herself withdrawn, standing as usual away from the centre, using the shadow for her mystery. She was dressed with taste. "Miss Lawrence!" She looked at the people doing business in the outer office, at the machine, through the half-glazed partitions. "Not here! Can you meet me in the front hall of the New York Public Library, where we used to meet?" "We used to? Can't you speak to me here? I'm very busy, Honor." "No, not here. I must see you. You must come." "I'm busy at lunchtime, Honor." "Well, at six then. I'll wait for you there." "All right, but are you sure there's nothing now? Have you money?" "Yes, plenty of money." They glanced at him in the office and he did not like that. He was always kind to girls, treated them as equals, made no coarse jokes, never flirted or took them to drinks after work, was devoted to his wife. But the girl attracted attention.

After work there was a summer storm and he did not have his coat. Still, he went up to the library. She was there. They walked about around the halls and staircases; and she was casual, made no excuse. "Where are you living now? With your brother?" "Oh, no, he's married. I went there"—for the first time she seemed to be complaining—"they had only one bed. I can sleep on the floor. It's good for the nerves. There was another room, a boxroom, or larder, something. I could have slept there." "And where are you now? Are you at home?" "Home?" "At your father's?" "I never see my father; he moved, I think," she said, after a pause. "But you have somewhere to stay?" Another pause. "Yes, kind people. I like it there." "Where are you then?" "At the YWCA." He was relieved. She continued, "It's too dear for me. There are other places I've heard of." With his grimy handkerchief, he had a ten-dollar bill he had borrowed from the cashier. He turned and twisted it in his pocket. The thunder and lightning continued. The city steamed and the water poured straight down, flushing the streets. "You have no coat or umbrella, Honor?" "Yes, I left it at the door with a parcel." She walked about with him confidently. He listened to the steps on the marble floor. "I like it here," said Honor. The storm began to clear; streaks of sunlight were seen. "Did you want to ask me something, Honor?" She looked straight into his eyes. "No, I am all right." He could return the ten dollars tomorrow to the cashier; but he would not mind going into debt for the girl, if she needed it. "You had no request to make?" He had these old-fashioned words, got from his immense reading of the old books, as a boy. "Oh, no. The rain's over now. Good-bye." She shook his hand, made a sort of half curtsy and ran down the steps, did not look back. He was relieved, thrust the ten dollars back into the handkerchief and went home.

An old house in Eleventh Street had been transformed into apartments. He had the ground floor, two lofty rooms separated by a sliding door; and in the back, a small kitchen and bathroom. They slept and ate in the back room, which had iron bars on its tall windows and overlooked an old garden. They would have to move again soon because of the baby.

Dinner was ready. "I'm sorry I was late. A funny thing happened. Do you remember that girl who worked in Farmers' Utilities, Honor Lawrence?" "She came back? Does she want a job?" "I don't know what she wanted. It wasn't money." "Does she look well off?" "Hard to say. Older, but quite well; you might say elegant. It isn't money spent on clothes: she wouldn't do that. It's style, a personal style." "What did she want?" "She said she had to see me. The office wouldn't do. I met her at the library." He recounted the episode fully, gaily and anxiously. "I assure you, I was as taken aback as you are now." "Oh, I'm not taken aback," said Beatrice in her hollow, soft and husky tones; "you'll see her again. If she came back after two years, you'll keep on seeing her." "I won't. What has she to do with me?" "I don't know," said the wife.

They ate and the wife began to worry. "There's no air in this apartment; the old trees cut out any light or air even when those windows are open. I owe it to David to go to Morristown in this weather, and Mother wants me there. This apartment has no air, only a through draught. The kitchen isn't hygienic; there's no real place to bathe the baby out of a draught and the sink gets stopped up because the pipes are laid so flat. There are roaches coming up the pipes."

"Well, go to Morristown, if you must."

"You know how I hate it. What do you get out of this marriage? I know you never wanted the child," she said crankily and full of doubt.

He sighed. "I don't know, Beatrice. I do my best."

"How long can we go on like this? Is this life? Oh, this is awful."

"I'm afraid you're very unhappy."

"Your only dream is to be happy!" she said in anguish. "The word makes me shriek."

Six months later, in winter, he was again called to the waiting room in his office and there was Miss Lawrence, though now she wore a dark grey coat, well cut but too large for her. "Can I see you privately?" But he was afraid of office gossip. She said, "Will you meet me in the Public Library?" "I could meet you downstairs in this building in about twenty minutes. Takes a seat and wait and I'll come." He was taken by surprise: she had come for a loan. "Enough to buy some clothes—you may be sure I'll pay you back. I met a lady in San Francisco who is interested in me and who is taking me to Italy tomorrow. You know my mother was in Italy as a girl. Italy is very interesting now, it's an age of youth. I want to study art and painting. I think I can do something real in Italy. I need twenty dollars for clothes." "Twenty dollars! Can you get clothes for that sum?" "Oh, yes, I can." Debrett had to take her upstairs, to ask the cashier for a twenty-dollar loan. People were about and two or three customers, men standing by, heard her further frank remarks. A big man said, "Twenty dollars—I'll lend you that, little lady; but what will I get for it?" He took money out of his pocket; the others began to laugh. She said gravely, "Give me a piece of notepaper, please." The man picked a sheet off a memo pad and gave it to her. "And a pencil, please." She went over to the desk, wrote and handed him the sheet of paper. He looked, looked at her, handed it to the others and burst out laughing. "Big day in my life!" She had written, "I will give you a kiss." He looked around with a big gay laugh, a popular man's man, the kind trusted to take out-of-towners around New York. He screwed up an eye, stared at her, looked her up and down, stopped laughing, turned back and pulled money out of his pocket, and handed it to her gravely, "I'll do a good deed, they can put my name in after Abou ben Adhem." She took the money and, before another word was said, ran out of the office. "Who is that?" "Debrett's friend." "Your friend, Gus?" "She worked for me once, years ago. She's only a kid." "Is she crazy or what?" "Just a nice girl." One of the salesmen showed the note-paper; "Nice girl or smart girl." Debrett took it and threw it in the trashbasket. "I know her history. For her it hasn't the implication it has for you."

An hour later, she was at Saul Scott's asking for a passport in her assumed name of Honor Lawrence. "Can I alter my birthplace? I want to make it Boston. I am going with a rich woman who likes me and she thinks I am from Boston."

Saul Scott's solid red face smiled kindly. "I'll tell you your rights. Put that money in your purse; you can't pay me. I'm too dear. And Vera Day, on your way out, will give you all the help you need. She'll fill in the forms."

But, with the forms filled in, she hurried out of the office; and then, with the news of her Italian journey, she visited Tom Zero, Arthur Good and others unknown. Zero refused to see her, but she was in his office before he knew it. He refused to lend her money, but in the end did so: "Twenty dollars to buy clothes to go to Italy." "Thank you, you will be repaid," she said and was gone in her usual way.

Tom told his wife Myra. "How did she know your address?" "I don't know. She went to see Saul Scott and others." "Gus Debrett?" "Yes, for one." "Beatrice won't like it!" "Why?" "You know how everything depresses her. Where has the girl been all this time?" "California apparently. That's where she met this woman. She's travelling with a monied woman." "How these tramps get around," said Myra. "They spend in travelling the money we spend in rent and comforts," said Tom. "Very simple." Myra telephoned Beatrice, who was very gloomy. "Of course Gus lent her money and of course she'll keep coming back. According to Gus, she's painfully honest, never told a lie. How does she create that impression?" "It's the New England look." "And she's an Italian," cried Beatrice. "Well, she's gone to Italy, Beatrice. It sounded final to me. Don't think about it any more." "Oh, she'll be back, we're haunted," said Beatrice. "We have no luck." When she turned to her husband she said sharply, "What's this trip about then?" "Search me: self-improvement, I think." "I envy her. She's free and she can get away from her local entanglements, whatever they are." "We can do it too, Beatrice. She's got the courage to go and try her luck; why not us? She hates this money world, so do we. I have been thinking about it, as I walked home. If a slip of a girl who knows no foreign language has the courage to rise out of that hard cruel poverty where she was starved and humiliated, why not us? I could find a job, France or Italy." "To Italy—" cried Beatrice. "France. Or England or Germany. I know all the chief cities as I know my own East Side." Beatrice was silent. At last, she said quietly, "If you want to go—I'll go. I must get away from Mother and the others. I can't stand family quarrels. How can people live like that? Among total strangers there must be calm." "*Calme, luxe et volupté—*," said Debrett, with a radiant expression. "Mother likes a good fight; it gives her tone and she looks radiant. I hate it. I could cut my throat. When you're there, they expect you to take part. If you don't, you're selfish. *When the whole family is at each other's throats, there you are with your nose buried in a book.* I often wanted to go and throw myself in the East River as a child." "Instead, we'll throw ourselves into the Atlantic; but we'll swim to the other side." He came towards her, "I'm so glad, I'm so happy you want to go. It will make all the difference to us. You'll see, you'll be happy over there." "You are right, perhaps. Your girl friend has no husband or child, so it's rather different; and apparently she has found someone to look after her. It was bound to come to that," she said mournfully. "What future is there for that puzzleheaded girl?" "Beatrice," said Debrett solemnly, "never mind about Honor Lawrence. She is out of our lives for good. Our lives are now in the future; and I swear you will be happy. You have me to look after you."

The following afternoon, Miss Lawrence came again to see Debrett in his office; she looked tired. "Why didn't you go to Italy?" "I couldn't go." "Has the boat sailed?" "Yes. The lady went but she took someone else." "Oh, Honor! Poor girl! She let you down." "She said I let her down." "How is that?" "I'm afraid I can't tell you here. Something dreadful happened. Can I see you alone?" "Not here, Honor." "In the Public Library tonight at six." He was put out. He telephoned his wife and explained why he would be late. The line was silent. "Beatrice, what is it?" "Oh, that girl, that gadfly—" "I thought you were sorry for her." "I'm sorry for women—for the struggle, without hope—" "Yes, so am I, Beatrice. Don't you want me to see her? I'll get a message to her somehow." "Oh, see her, see her," she said with bitter hopelessness. "I can see she's going to be with us for the rest of our lives." "Oh, no, she is not. I am going to see what is wrong, and if I can fix it up for good. I will tell her she can't keep calling upon me. You see, it's her innocence; she doesn't see it as hurtful, as a nuisance. She's in trouble; and, like a lost child, she cries out to the first person she meets." "I understand, Gus. I know you; I know you mean well." "Yes, I do."

When he met the girl he was tired. "Why didn't you go? How could you have been deceived like that? I thought you were eager to go and were great friends." "I couldn't go in such circumstances." "You'll have to be more explicit, Honor. I don't understand you."

"It was terrible. She's a dreadful woman, mad I think. She got me a room in a hotel, down there," she said vaguely. "Last night she came to call on me. She brought something to drink. I don't drink. Then she put her hand around my waist. I don't like that. I stopped that. She kept on and I slapped her. Then she turned into a fiend, her face was all screwed up, all in wrinkles, she looked like a bird and she flew at me, saying things in a little voice—and she threw me out, wouldn't let me stay in the hotel, wouldn't pay for me, she said." He waited. "What really happened, Honor?" "I don't know. I said to her, that's a nice blouse, where did you get it? What's wrong in that? She began to behave so wildly. She ground her teeth, her eyes opened, she glared at me and said in a rude voice, I made it myself; and did you make that yourself? And she pulled at my dress and tried to tear it off me. Then I knew she was mad. She was such a wonderful woman," said Honor slowly, turning her head away. She never cried. "I thought she liked me. She used to come and see me in California, when I had a little room with some friends, and she brought me presents and she took me to the art shows. People didn't like me in California and she was good to me." "People didn't like you? I thought you made friends easily." "Eva, this woman, took me everywhere, and I stayed with her. She gave a party for me; but they never spoke to me and, if I spoke to them, they'd turn their heads away pretending not to hear; or they would get up and go away. So she said, she'd take me to Italy, where people were old and civilized and hadn't little suburban ideas; and we would see new people. And I told her what I had never told anyone, all about my father and mother; and she said, she would be father and mother to me."

"Yes, now I see," said Debrett; and he asked her if she had a place for the night. She had, she said; and after a long pause, looking into his face, she touched his hand and left him. He went home and told his wife the story. "You see, I am right about her. I know her.

She is utterly innocent and unsophisticated. What do you make of it?" "Myra Zero has just telephoned me to say that your child-woman called on Tom at his office and told him she had not gone to Italy, but could never tell him why; and he gave her ten dollars for a place for the night. Of course, she is going to pay him back." "She always does, Beatrice. She is completely, painfully honest. She always tells the truth." "Perhaps she does," said Beatrice.

It was four months before Debrett heard of her again. She telephoned him at his office. "What is it this time, Honor?" "I must see you." "No, no, I'm too busy. Tell me now." "No, I can't speak about it like this; I must see you." "I can't see you, Honor." She was in the waiting room in five minutes. He heard her calling his name. He was alone; the reception clerk had gone to lunch. She had no need of money, she said at once. She looked older, even dissipated. Her dress, usually neat, was untidy. She no longer wore short skirts and high blouses and had lost some of her charm: her thick hair was uncombed. She was in disorder and even dirty; but was still grave and prudish. "I just wanted to see you, Mr. Debrett, to tell you my troubles are over. I know you worry about me. I have a home now. I tried for a job but didn't get it. I went to a business college and told them to give me a certificate, but they wouldn't give me one." "Did you study at the college?" "No. But I told them I had all the skills, they could take my word." "Well, you say you have a home, Honor?" She smiled triumphantly. "Yes, I have been invited to live as companion in the home of a lady in charge of a mental rest home." "Will that suit you?" "Oh, yes, she understands me. She says I will be a tonic to her after all those sick minds. She says I am quite unusual." She stood in front of him, upright, looking into his face and with a sweet self-pleased look, waiting for him to be pleased. "I see. And what can I do for you?" "Nothing. I just thought I ought to see you." As he turned, she put her arm around him. "I need friends," she said.

He looked at her profile. She upset him; he was puzzled. "I was just going out for a snack. Would you share a sandwich with me?" She agreed and they went to a cheap lunchroom, where he often ate. She ate greedily, but accepted only one sandwich and a glass of milk. While he paid the bill, she walked out; and when he reached the sidewalk he saw her hurrying, almost running down the street; she skipped once, twice, on the kerb. Was she just a child; or a free soul? He remembered what a friend had told him, "Once going down Eighth Street I saw a girl do the splits and then walk on as if nothing had happened." He did not call after Honor or try to follow her. She had left him in the middle of a conversation.

During the brief meal he had said, "When did you meet this woman?" "A week ago." "You want to be careful; she may be a Lesbian." "Oh, no, she's an American, she's from New England, just as I—" "You didn't understand what was wrong with that woman who was taking you to Italy, did you?" "Oh yes, she was mad." "Honor, go and see my wife. She'll explain. I'm going back to the office—" She had gone. He went back to the office where he was finishing up the week's work; and he telephoned Beatrice.

"I know," said his wife, "she's here now. I'll take her to the park with David and we'll talk."

He went home troubled and could not eat his dinner. His wife, a keen, solid but morbidly uneasy woman, rested on his face those large, gloomy, beautiful eyes which had always held him spellbound. She said at last, "Well, I saw that girl, Gus. You're worried about her, aren't you? You can't eat. Every time she comes into our lives, you don't sleep. Watch out, Gus. I can see you in a mess." "Over the poor suppliant? Don't be silly. To her I'm a kindly uncle, someone she worked for. She has a high opinion of herself and probably thinks I didn't pay her enough. I was her first job. She's not interested in men. But I am worried. Don't laugh at me, I feel she partakes of a sacred character, those the gods love, or hate: it's the same. If the suppliant demands and you don't give, you're accursed. That's an old idea. You can see the same thing in *Cuore*, by Edmondo de Amicis. At least in the old countries there is this idea that the sick and maimed are sent for your especial care."

"I know you can't resist lame ducks. I spoke to this girl in the park. That kind of talk is better done outdoors. She sat awhile watching David play. She seemed to like that. She listened to me and then she smiled, shook hands and wandered away, just as if she had not understood. I did what I could but I very soon came to the conclusion that she knows nothing at all of the physical side of love, to give it a name." "Do you think that's possible?" "It seems indefeasible," she said: her eyes searched the room anxiously. "Unlikely?" She stiffened. "It doesn't seem likely, but it's the result of a subconscious taboo. It's a real part of feminine nature, Gus. Such girls exist everywhere. I understand it. What have the coarse facts about men and women to do with nice manners, a soft voice, correct speech, polite ways, feminine delicacy? A girl is pretty and sweet and naturally chaste; people tell her she's charming. How should she know it's all a masquerade?" "But she spends her evenings in Greenwich Village." "Oh, she listens and doesn't hear. If you haven't the key! A woman doesn't want to spoil another woman's life. She may be lucky; she may never get tangled with a man. There are plenty of happy bachelor girls: it's a good life."

Debrett said nothing. Beatrice concluded, "Men can't understand it, even the best of them. Women are terrified not to get married; everyone's at them; and then they get married to eat and have a child; and so they find themselves shackled like an imbecile in a little room, with no money and no freedom." "It sounds a pretty miserable world for women," said Debrett. Beatrice sat down in an armchair with a tragic face.

Five days later, in the afternoon, the doorbell rang at the Debretts'. Beatrice went, stood back from the door, crying, "Oh!" Honor Lawrence was there, untidy, hardly decent; she looked as if she had been running through the streets. "I want to tell you something: let me come in!" She walked in, stood in the middle of the hall, looked around. "You had better sit down." "No." Beatrice looked at her without sympathy. In spite of their words about her, she thought the girl an awkward booby. It was herself she had pity for she was unhappy, in a trap. She had not wanted to marry, but to live like brother and sister with Debrett. When that became intolerable, she had agreed to an ordinary marriage, to avoid the disgrace of a break-up; but she could not endure married life, could not shut her eyes to the boredom and unfairness. "You don't like me," said the girl, "but that is nothing. Your husband is kind to me and is my friend; and I want you to tell him what happened to me. He warned me." "Well, go and tell him yourself," said Beatrice. "I'm sorry you find me so unresponsive, but I have my own troubles; I am not as absorbed in your problems as you are." "Surely, you must be a very selfish woman," said Honor, "but you can't imagine what happened to me, or you would want to help me. Don't you know that things are happening all the time that are never mentioned anywhere? All newspapers and all written things are lies, because they don't tell what really happens." "Well, sit down and tell me. I suppose I must listen. I don't sleep. I'm exhausted. I'm walking in a dream; but I know I can't escape this story of yours. Sit down, sit down." The woman who was to help her had treated Honor as a mad woman, and more cruelly, perhaps, than she dared to treat the patients. Honor had escaped by her suddenness, simply running out of the room in the state she was in; and had fixed herself up somehow on the way to town.

"Where did you get the clothes?"

"I took some clothes out of the nurses' room." Near the end of her tale, Honor seemed overcome by her sufferings. She got up. "Let me go now; I can't stay here any longer." Beatrice tried to keep her; she gave her a half-worn coat. The girl set out, doubtless on one of her long inexplicable wanderings, her multitude of painful visits to all the strangers she called her friends. "I suppose she calls me her friend, too," said Beatrice to herself; "I ought to be; I am. I wish I had her naiveté."

At home, that night, the wife slightly warmed now by thinking over Honor's miseries, retold the story. "I'm not surprised. The matron is a sadist who thought she had to do with a weak shade of lunatic; and I think she is one," said Debrett. "Saul Scott was always very sweet and tender with her because he held she was insane. Let's not worry about her. She's unfortunate; and in the end they'll have to gather her in." "That remark isn't like you and should never be made. She is just a repressed girl who is hunted by lechers, criminals and hags. And the only protection she has from life is that in herself she concentrates all the horror and misery which is life itself. She frightens off the dark side of life." "That is a morbid view, Beatrice." "I am morbid because I see." "I can't see life like that: I can see hope, especially for us."

Honor was at the Wall Street office the next day. Still untidy and unclean, she brushed past people in the outer office to see the president of the firm, a man she did not know. He was indignant and wanted to force her out. She did not resist it. She said in a low purring voice, "I came to see Mr. Debrett, but he can't give me advice; he hasn't the information; and I thought you could help me." She smiled at him. He was a kindly man who did not mind those who did not get in his way. "Is it about an account?" "Oh, no, nothing to do with money. I don't need money. I have plenty." He was disarmed. "Come here, sit down and tell me what I can do for you." "No, there is nothing you can do for me. I am going now." She shook hands; and she went. A week later, Tom Zero met her on 42nd Street. She was flushed, her frayed skirt slipping, and buttons missing from her blouse. Zero was a clean, ultra-fashionable dresser. This looked like utter distress and abandon. "When did you get back from Italy?" She muttered something of her story. "I don't know what to do. I never guessed women were so horrible." "Didn't you know? I thought you always knew," and he laughed a little. She turned to run. He took a step and came close without touching her. "Be a sensible girl; I'll help you, but be sensible." "Oh, that word: sensible! She said that; be sensible. Everyone says it to me. Why? What do they mean? I don't know what they mean." She put a hand up to her face—real tears had started. She left him, went on her wanderings, and the time passed.

Debrett sent his wife and child to Nice, where they lived in a poor *pension*; and when he had the money, he himself started for Europe, living at first on milk and cheese dishes, to save. His mother and a cousin, hearing of his move, also wished him to bring them abroad. Debrett worked in London and then in Berlin. He was at the Hotel Adlon and in his lonely style was walking up and down the room, working out business problems, when he received a late long-distance call from his correspondent in London, from a certain Abraham Duncan, born in the East End and now, by his own efforts, a rich man. "How in the world did you know I was here, Duncan? Even my wife has not got my address yet." "Listen, dear boy, time's short; there's a Mrs. Hewett here: she says you know her very well." The voice was discreet, peremptory, a little gay. "She says she's living in a room in Islington—that's a poor district—" "Yes, yes, I know." "She says she's starving and, by gum, she looks it; she wants ten pounds and she says you'll guarantee her. What shall I do, my boy?" "Hewett? Is she a woman about fifty: there was one had a ground-floor apartment in my house in New York—" "No, no, this one's maybe twenty-five, thirty, hard to tell: looks downtrodden, beat. Here, she says her name was Lawrence." "Honor Lawrence!" "Hurry up, my boy: you do know her? What shall I do?" "My goodness, I suppose give her the money. Ask her how she traced me." "No time now. All right. I'll call you at the office tomorrow. Lucky I was in the office—she got here at ten at night!" "That certainly is Honor Lawrence." Debrett sat down and sweated a cold salt sweat. He started to write to his wife and changed his mind. "The gadfly of fate," she had said once, an unimaginative woman, too; but an oppressed and persecuted woman, hunted by fate, or so she felt. She was now unhappy in her *pension*, the child boarded out, Beatrice leading an aimless, poor life. "Mrs. Hewett?" He thought she must have found out his old house, simply borrowed the name of the ground-floor tenant. Mrs. Hewett had sent her maid to clean his rooms when Beatrice was away at Morristown; and had kept his keys. He told Beatrice nothing about it.

When he returned to London, his first call was on Duncan and, after business was settled, he asked for the ten pounds to be put on his account. "I've sent everything to Nice." Duncan said, "I was very curious, in fact, inquisitive, my boy. It was late at night, a Saturday. I was working late, nearly ten. And she called on that day at that hour at a business office in the City. I was just going home. I don't know how she found her way through the City at that time of night; no one about. My word, she looked bad; hungry and poor. She wouldn't tell me where she lived and set off to walk home. I followed her, offered her a ride. Nothing doing. I lost her at Kensal Green, near the cemetery." He laughed. "My word! I'm not superstitious, not very; but she went into the cemetery." "You're joking!" "No—there I lost her. Made me think of the ghosts of the city of Prague; ghouls. But ghouls don't take money; proved she was human." They burst out laughing, but uneasily. "What did you think of her?" said Debrett. "Thought she must be—someone—you knew in the States; but then I saw—wasn't sex: touchy girl. Something you know at once. Or I know," he said with a warm troubled laugh. "Saw she was a Presbyterian." "She isn't." "Puritan," he amended; "if you hadn't said to give the money, I should have given it. She looked so miserable. A good deed." "I am worried about her," said Debrett; "she's such a miserable wanderer, a sort of wraith. She gives Beatrice the willies. She worked for me once. But Beatrice understands." "There's a letter for you she left." Debrett took it, looking at the envelope. "The Piccadilly Hotel! Was she staying there?" He read:

Dear Mr. Debrett

I had no notepaper and so I walked into this hotel to get some. I wish I could stay in a place like this. It is warm here and they have good clothes and are having food. This place is not for me. I am sorry to be going to do what I am. I know I owe you twenty dollars. But I am reduced to beggary and need ten pounds, not for myself. I am now Mrs. Hewett. I married Jay Hewett, who was at school with me. I wanted to come to Europe. So did he. He pretended he loved me and I married him; but he didn't love me. I found that out now. I can't imagine what his motives were. He's a dreadful person. Do not speak to him if he comes to see you. I think he must be partly mad. I am afraid a lot of people are mad. I trust you, but I could never speak about this madness. I am afraid to tell what I have found out about people; I won't be believed. They will think I am lying or even worse. I am in a terrible position. Don't try to see me. I don't know what I'll do. It was a dream, a lie; the

44

reality is monstrous; perhaps all things are monstrous. Perhaps this is hell.

Honor Lawrence

Duncan read the letter, asked her age and said, "It's the marriage shock, she means. She looked innocent. If a woman doesn't know, it must be an awful shock. I can understand a girl going out of her mind over it. We don't think; it means nothing to us. She looked distraught. She told me she had just married. Who is she? Looked a nice enough girl."

Debrett told him about her. "Is her story true, do you think?" Duncan asked. "I've never known her to lie." Duncan glanced at him, said, "Well, some girls don't. Hard for them. Hard is life for those who can't eat dirt."

Perhaps five years later, Debrett saw her one afternoon walking along the Boulevard du Montparnasse at some distance. She looked well and was stylishly dressed in a velvet dress, her hair loose and shining. She had a youthful figure and style.

"Let's go down the Rue Vavin," he said to the woman he was with; "there is Honor Lawrence, a girl who used to work for me and who married and came to Europe when I did; but she may need money and I am short at present."

Debrett had now left his wife for this woman, a grey-eyed woman with loose brown hair: her name was Mari. "Astonishing how she keeps her youth and girlish beauty," said Debrett. Mari looked and saw a plump, dark-haired woman, rakishly and care-lessly dressed in green material, the blouse pulled down tightly between her full breasts, the skirt untidy. Mari had once been married to a dark thin young man who had led her a dance and in the end deserted her for an old school friend of his, who looked not unlike the woman in green. This woman in green, prancing and bounding along the pavement, looked a little mad, self-satisfied and singing to herself. "I heard that she married again and went to South Africa," said Debrett. "I don't know if it's true. She came to Beatrice one afternoon some years ago. She found her out in Nice and when the door was opened, she threw twenty dollars at her, so that they lay inside the door. She said she owed it to me; so she did. I don't want it, said Beatrice, why do you haunt me now? He's left me, as you knew he would." "Why did she say that?" "Beatrice never understood Honor's simplicity and straightforward ways. She saw something eerie in them. She is honest herself, but never believed that Honor was truthful and pure."

A few years later Debrett and Mari were living in one room in a building in London let out in what are called one-room flats. Downstairs lived the busy, noisy, greedy but kindhearted landlady who was putting her three children through Oxford and Cambridge on her slum rents. Naturally generous, she would at times think of the condition of her tenants and try to fatten them up with a can of tomatoes, soup or oil bought wholesale.

For some time she had a stout, dark, stormy woman tenant who went in and out at odd hours, morosely; and at the end left quietly, owing four weeks' rent. "She was hard up and looking for a job," explained the landlady. "It is the first time I have let anyone run on like that; and see what has happened." There was some talk about the defaulting lodger. "I often noticed her," said Debrett to Mari, "because she reminded me of someone you don't know; Honor Lawrence, a girl who worked for me." "But I noticed her too, and she reminded me of your wife Beatrice." "No, no, Honor Lawrence."

At the end of five weeks, the dark woman brought the rent. "I owe it to you and you must have it." "You see, I knew," said Debrett. "She is exactly like Honor Lawrence, the same woman, you might say."

And five years later, when they were living in the country, a visitor came to see them, Mari's cousin Alice, a demure, self-contained girl of twenty-one, with long fair hair and a velvet skirt, who sat all day doing nothing and answered all questions after a pause. She was out of a job and looking for one. "If you had had a bed I could have stayed here, had a few days in the country," she said looking around; "it would suit me. You see I have a job offered me in town, but I can't take it; they want me to bind myself for three months. I could never do that. I must be free."

"I hope," said Debrett, "that you won't invite that girl Alice to stay with us. When I saw her coming up the stairs, I felt the hairs rise along my spine. She is so exactly like Honor Lawrence; it is the same girl. If she ever got in here, she'd never leave. I don't want her here; let her go. Never invite her."

And Mari became uneasy, and discouraged the odd, charming, long-haired girl with the soft wooden face in which was a dimple.

It was more than three years later than that, that Debrett was on a business visit to New York; and having half an hour to put in, he went towards the 42nd Street Public Library, which he had visited every afternoon in his youth and remembered fondly. On the first steps below the portico someone pulled his sleeve—Honor, the real Honor. She was now about thirty. But she looked much younger, he thought. Were his eyes getting worse? And he saw now that the others, the one on the Boulevard du Montparnasse, the one in the slum, and the young one, had not looked like her. Was she real, he thought for a moment. Did she shuttle between youth and age, inhabit and divest herself of other women's forms? "The ghouls of the city of Prague."

"Mr. Debrett! I thought I would see you here."

"It's almost a miracle that you do, Honor. I've just come back after many years away. I've come from London. You were the last person I expected to see. How are you? Where are you living?"

"I don't know," she replied quietly. "I have just come back from South Africa. I married a South African I met in an art gallery in Europe and went out with him."

"So you divorced Jay Hewett?"

"I was never married to Jay Hewett. It was no marriage and I didn't consider it one." She still had charm, her self-centred, stiff-necked enigmatic manner, but she seemed less inhuman; no ghoul.

"Would you like a cup of coffee, Honor?"

"I should be glad of a sandwich and coffee. I've had nothing to eat all day. I have no money and no home yet. If you could lend me ten dollars I will pay it as soon as I get money from Derek."

"Where is your husband?" She did not answer. "Don't tell me about your husband, if you don't wish to."

In the cafeteria he brought her the food he knew she preferred. "I wrote you a letter in London," she said; and told him his European addresses, those of his partners and of his wife. She continued, "I told you about Jay. I was unfair to Jay. It was all my fault. What he tried to do was natural; that's what marriage is. One day I met a man in an art gallery. I was waiting for you there. I thought you'd be sure to know where I was. This man took me to lunch and gave me wine to drink. Then he took me to his hotel. I had more to drink and something happened. We went out to dinner and I had more to drink and we went back again, and I woke up the next morning with him and then I suddenly knew that that was marriage." She looked into Debrett's face. "So I was married to him. I went out to South Africa with him and I had his child, my child. It's still there, but I don't know where. The family wouldn't have me. They deported me. They gave the child to an orphanage. They wouldn't tell me where it was; and I went around everywhere knocking at doors. They had taken it away. They said it was a coloured child." "Eh?" "They said that to get me deported. They were rich. They could do anything they liked. I was quite wrong about Jay. I thought we would get married and study modern art."

"Did you get a divorce from Jay? That was quick."

"Oh, I never told Derek anything about Jay. We weren't married, were we?"

"You mean you married Derek bigamously?"

She looked puzzled, "That was years ago."

"And what now, Honor?"

"I must find someone and get some money for the trip back. Derek loves me. He will meet me and convince his family. Will you take me to Pennsylvania Station? I must get a train to the country, to a woman who will be kind to me."

"Honor, what woman?"

"Come with me," she said; and he went; anxiously and unwillingly.

When they reached the environs of Pennsylvania Station she said, "Won't you come and see me in my present home, it's a room near by. We can have coffee there."

It was a small dark room with upholstered chairs and a blue-covered divan, of good appearance. She sat there in the half-dark on the divan quietly telling him her story; how she had gone to Europe with Jay, each of them travelling steerage in a six-berth cabin, men and women separated; how they landed in London, where she expected to find Debrett; they had only a few dollars and they had gone to a shelter suggested by the American Embassy. There in a miserable room without even a washbasin, and with an iron cot, there had been a horrifying scene. She and then Jay had run out into the streets. From then on they had lived in the streets, under bridges, in parks, even in a cemetery for a night or two. "I never used the money you gave me, I gave it to Jay to go away. He followed me about. And then I found Derek and I never saw Jay again. Besides, I know you will always be not far from me."

Debrett looked at her uneasily. She went on calmly, "I am ill, I can never be intimate with a man. Derek made me ill. They said it was I who did it. You must go now. I had to see you to tell you the whole story, but you must go now. I cannot have men in my room; it's not allowed. Of course, if Derek doesn't send me money, I will be put out of here. Where will I go? Give me your address." But Debrett, though he was very much upset, did not give the address. He said he was leaving town.

It was a few months later that he walked into a coffee shop near Central Park Plaza. There sat a woman who looked fifty, in clothes dirty and unbuttoned, grey-haired, face creased and yet with a self-possession and simpering, and the tender smile of former beauty. She came over to Debrett and said her name, "I have been waiting for you here. I knew you would come."

He drew back. "I had no intention of coming here; you couldn't have known." He looked at her with dislike.

"I know, Augustus Debrett; I have ways of knowing."

"You just wait, don't you, and then say things like that?"

"That's not it. It's you. I know where you will be."

She was about thirty-one, not older; but she smiled like an aged prostitute, cunningly and coarsely using the remains of once potent charm to get some last hesitant customer. She handed him a piece of paper. "Read it." On it was written, "I feel that Mr. Augustus Debrett will be at 57th Street this afternoon."

"I suppose you saw me come in and wrote it," he said, handing back the paper.

"No! Don't you know I always know where you are?"

"I don't believe in things like that, Honor. I suppose you know a lot of people and you wait till you see them."

"I went back to Capetown, but the immigration authorities kept me out. Someone had sent a letter against me, saying I had married an African, a black African."

"Had you?"

"It was Derek's family said that, because he would never do anything like that to me. And they won't let him answer me; and now I have no money."

"Here's some money," he said, getting up hastily and putting the money into her dirty hand. She opened a handbag and put it in. "I found this handbag on the street," she said; "I was not waiting for money. I wanted to tell someone my story."

He hurried into the street. A few days elapsed. He was at an art show, a Walter Lawrence exhibition in a midtown gallery, with Mari, when he stopped her in front of a drawing and said, "Look there! Do you recognize that? You've seen her: that's Honor Lawrence; that pencil sketch." "Is that Honor Lawrence? Well, it's not like the women you've pointed out several times." "Yes, yes, you've forgotten. I know who it is. No one who knew her could ever forget her."

A slight dark man of about thirty-five, with thinning hair, wearing glasses and poorly dressed, turned around and said, "Who are you? You're Debrett, aren't you? Do you know who I am? I'm Jay Hewett, Honor's husband. Can I speak to you alone for a minute? I know that she went to South Africa, but I consider myself her husband. I know that you had an appointment with her a few days ago, in a coffee shop." Debrett described what happened. "I know businessmen. I know she worked for you. I know you influenced her and she idealized you. I know she followed you to Europe." "What are you saying? Let's sit down; and then you talk like a rational man." Mari had moved on around the exhibition. "Who is that?" "That's Mari, my wife." "You met Honor in Europe and you introduced her to that South American who made such a mess of her life." "Hold on there; you've got a lot of stories tangled. I didn't introduce her and it wasn't a South American." "I know what Honor told me and she never lies."

Debrett stared at Jay Hewett with a soft open mouth. Jay continued, "I know what she told me and Honor never lies: she's incapable of it. She doesn't know why one should."

"You are quite wrong, I assure you, about following me to Europe. Why, you were married here, weren't you, and went to England together?" "I just want to say something to you. I can sense that you don't care for Honor any more. I've got to explain things to you. I've got to tell you the whole story. I knew Honor when she was thirteen, when she was telling people she was fifteen or eighteen; to protect her own childhood, she did it. I was seventeen and I loved her. I hardly had a decent night's sleep then. She was so young and innocent, untouchable innocence, such an austere fragility, such a child. She behaved like a coquette and tease, but I knew she was really a naive child. You see, I knew all about her, I have always known. I've hardly had a whole night's sleep in my life, or at least since I knew her. I wake up at four or five and begin to wonder about her. She's my joy, I rejoice in her; and I've learned you don't need much sleep. But I've had night jobs, too. I have discipline. I don't coddle myself. I've learned to like work; so I wake up and think of my work. I've done all kinds of things. I went out west. I got a job in a pool parlour. Anything real, you see, to meet people. I went on the stage in a road company, painted scenery, did all kinds of jobs. I enjoyed overcoming the difficulties. I made myself meet all kinds of women; no fretting and mooning, you see. But all the time I knew I was going to marry Honor; she must have known too, although for years she treated me like dirt—why use such an expression? She didn't know what she was doing. You don't say a bird or a cat treats you like dirt. It was just a sort of innocent and ignorant wildness. She used to go about with other boys, and men, but she never even kissed them. I know that. They talked about it.

But only I understood why. She'd leave a boy suddenly, while they were walking down the street. She could not bear to be touched. I knew this; I never touched her, so she got to trust me. She always knew where I was. And one day she called on me: just knocked at the door and walked in and said to me, Jay, today I think we'd better get married; I want to go to England and I think we'd better go. You see, she knew a lot about me; she knew my whole life. I had nothing to hide ever. I had always lived for her; so I felt it was a natural development. I knew she couldn't marry till she was ready; and I thought she was ready. Anything that happened was my fault, because I was the only one who understood her; and I didn't question her; I allowed my feelings to take over. She knew I had been writing to painters in Paris and London and was quite friendly with them; I had very good letters from them, not the usual brush-off letters. She knew all about this. So I was glad, and thought she was thinking of me. I was living for it; and it happened. How wonderful it was! That day paid for all. She understood me and others in an extraordinary way. She was inspired; she is inspired. You would not credit what shrewd, keen and inspired observations she makes about people. There are people with great gifts who want to create, but are not self-centred enough. The glory of creation is in them. They end by creating themselves; and they are miraculous creatures. People fall in love with them, because they've made something new. I don't blame you, Debrett—" he broke off, "not really."

"I sympathize with all you say; but let me set your mind at rest. I was never in love with Honor."

"Yes, you couldn't understand Honor as I could. Because she was a work of art I was born to understand: for others, the misunderstood masterpiece. I nearly called on you several times. I just wanted to clarify your relations to Honor. At first, in London, I blamed you for what happened."

"How could you?" said Debrett, with cross patience.

Hewett rested for a while. They walked along the lines of drawings and paintings. He had an unpleasant colour, earthy, and an unpleasant attitude, aggressive with a grating voice; so that, though his words carried conviction, Debrett felt no sympathy.

Debrett's eyes stared at him, wide open, his mouth too was slightly open; his breathing could be heard. His hands were cold.

Hewett said, "Life's very short, isn't it? We don't understand many people in a lifetime. We don't love many people in a lifetime. It's a dreadful thought. Life rushing past, populations of people and we're indifferent, blind; we might be asleep or dead. We are dead when we don't love. I am sure there are people who don't understand one human being in a lifetime. A lifetime! What a word! What it means! Think of the people, towns, plains, forests—it fills me with love to think of it. But for some, just habits and quirks. I suppose she borrowed money from you, too, the other day?"

"Eh?" said Debrett.

"It doesn't matter. If she owes you anything I'll pay it back. I assure you, you never meant anything to her; only one man ever did." He smiled. "Don't look so sympathetic; it wasn't me."

"I never actually spoke to Honor in Europe."

"She got money from you and gave it all to me. That was like her. She never thought of herself. If she goes about like a beggar and a tramp, with her stockings around her ankles, it's because she doesn't understand the conventional life of a woman. She's a spirit in a dress of rags. I understand poor wandering women now; I cry for them, not laugh at them. Do you know the Spanish never laugh at monsters, idiots and poor creatures? They call them creatures of God like everyone else, more so, they think. What wonderful people the Spanish are; that is love. I don't believe in God, but their heart is great. Honor told me she went to Europe to pay you back some money she borrowed from you. Isn't that incredible? And yet I believe it."

"How did you think you would live in Europe? How could you take her into that unspeakable misery? What way out was there?"

"Yes, the man of accounts! You wouldn't understand! I was too crazed with happiness to think. I thought the road was up, from there. I remember sitting in the subway and looking at some faces opposite, I've forgotten them now, and I was thinking, Well, that's something accomplished, that's done. One can't say that, I know now; especially about another human being. One must leave them free. She had despised and insulted me for years—terribly insulted; been cruel to me, and then without being asked she came and said, We'll marry. It was a reward for all those years. My fault. I thought of her as a reward." After a slight pause, he said, "It was all misery; but that is the story of my happiness and joy. Some people haven't had so much."

"Do you know where she is now, then?"

"Yes, I have an appointment with her this afternoon. I was at this exhibition yesterday. I saw the head of her and I found out from the artist where she is."

And it was from Walter Lawrence, who was beginning to fall in love with Mari, that they heard the rest.

In the afternoon, Jay met her in the Square.

"You said you wanted to see me," she said, politely offering her hand. She looked tired and old.

He had a few words with her, about where she was living, about helping her. She said, "Could we go and have some milk? I wish there were milk bars here as there are in London. I used to walk along the street looking at the milk bars, beautiful places with white tiles and clean glass, so healthy and pure. I used to go into as many as I could. Milk is good for you, you know. You oughtn't to drink beer and whisky, Jay."

"I haven't drunk beer or whisky for years. I have no money for such things. I have a job that enables me to pay the rent of a hall bedroom; and I could manage for us both if you were willing."

"I had a baby," she said quickly; "and I drank milk for the baby's sake. His family sent my baby to an orphan asylum and I went everywhere asking for it, but they said I had no proof. I was its mother, but there were no papers. And he divorced me; he told me to leave. I can never go back and I don't know if my child is alive or dead."

"You look very sick to me, Honor. Let me look after you. Never mind the past."

"No one wants me now. You don't want me. I am very sick. I can't do anything for you. I know what you want."

"Oh, Honor, Honor—you know me—" He took her arm.

"I'll take care of you. I will. I am yours. I don't want your love, or anything you could never give me. But I'd rather die than live without you; you are life. It's quite simple; you're so real. What's there in me, if not you? Your terrible sorrows are real. It's that, and the beauty of your mind and sorrows that I care for. They're my hope, my fire, my salvation. I love you."

She pushed him away roughly and spat. "Love! I spit, I spit it out," she cried out. "It was all lies. It kills you. It's to get you. There's no love at all."

She got up and he got up. "Don't come near me again and don't follow me." She went down Washington Place, disappeared into a large apartment house. She probably went out again through a courtyard, for he could not find her. She knew the city like a beggar, like a small boy.

It was three years later that he heard of her death in winter, in a half-covered doorway, up three steps, of a loft building not far from Union Square. And he too disappeared. Perhaps he died. No one asked after him, for he had never made an impression. It was only when people mentioned Honor's name, later, "Walter's sister," that it was sometimes said, "Did you know that she was actually married to a man named Hewett? But they said it was not a real marriage."

Debrett thought he saw her from time to time, but as a young woman. "Is she eternally young?" he said to himself. Then he heard of her death. "But I don't really believe it," he said to Mari. "It's too *faits-divers*. It's not like her. I expect she's turning up some-where at this moment, asking for help. She's a wraith, a wanderer. What is she?" "She's the ragged, wayward heart of woman that doesn't want to be caught and hasn't been caught," said Mari, in her beautiful metallic voice. "She never was in love." He looked at her in doubt. "She never loved anyone," said Mari. Debrett thought of this. He did not believe it, but walking up and down under the trees in someone's garden, he bent his head a little, saw nothing, wiped his eyes with his hands.

The Dianas

The balcony of Lydia's room in the green and white boulevard hotel looked over the treetops. The hotel was at the top of a long rise from the Seine, in Montparnasse. The sun beat into the carpeted, curtained room so strongly in the mornings that the shutters were kept shut till after midday. Lydia got in late every night, slept restlessly. From two to four in the morning, heavy army units and market trucks went past, shaking the whole house. About four Lydia would notice the early summer morning on the ceiling.

She had breakfast in her room and did not dress for a time. For aunts and cousins, friends, and her mother in New York, she had bought all at once, in an hour or two, four pairs of kid gloves, four bottles of perfume, a brooch, some Swiss handkerchiefs, some scarves and a handbag, all cheap and tasteless, and not at all what foreigners mean by French. She had gone into a large ordinary department store which she had laughed at in the days when she had been living in Paris in a small apartment with her mother. The articles now stood in their boxes and papers on the bed she had slept in and on the chairs. She had bought nothing for herself in Paris, but wore what she had worn in New York the summer before, a black chiffon dinner dress, bought on Fifth Avenue and imported from France, a green and white striped silk, some prints. She had brought with her for the summer in Paris, two steamer trunks and four valises. Most of her things she had never unpacked. They stood there locked for a while. Then it occurred to her that the maid might think she was afraid of theft, and she unlocked them. They stood there; and sometimes she lifted the lids, looked at what lay there, closed the lids again.

The little rosy-perfumed room with her things strewn about had an air of comfort, waste, expense, juvenile gaiety, as if she were always getting ready for a party: it was captivating. She had several bottles of perfume standing about, pots of cream and powder, open jewel boxes, all the needs of a coquette and a beauty.

She ran about barefoot, sighed, put on her pink satin mules, and telephoned her American friends staying in the hotel. She had telegraphed three hotels in Paris before coming, because she had friends in each; and then she had picked this one, where her friend Tamara lived, because her mother's friends, Peggy and Anton, had just arrived here from Switzerland. And because of her, other Americans had come to the hotel. It was the usual thing in Paris in summer.

After she was up, in her slip, dressing-gown and slippers, she would run in to see one or other of them, gossip with them, read her mother's letters, bring some woman to her room. She lit one cigarette after another, talked about her affairs with men, drank her coffee; and when one friend left for lunch, she telephoned another. Her friend Tamara, who worked in Paris, was divorced and was awaiting her man's divorce to remarry. Peggy and Anton were twenty and more years older than Lydia and had known her when she was a little child in Paris with her mother, just after the death of her father and younger sister.

At lunchtime, Lydia, if not invited to lunch, went to one of the expensive Montparnasse restaurant-cafés to have a sandwich or an omelet and coffee. It cost her as much as a real meal, but she enjoyed picking and choosing; she liked the strangeness of being a pretty girl eating lunch alone; she liked the silence, the elegant unpopularity of the hour or café she chose. There was one frequented by girlish young men: it was always quiet at lunchtime. If she went down to the washroom, she might find a fair-haired young fellow in front of the mirror; he would make room for her gracefully, give her a sweet look. There was another café, with good cooking and wine, decorated with paintings by local artists, in which neat, stylish prostitutes had their frugal lunch, like hers: an omelet, a chop, a salad, tonic water, one glass of wine. And there, well-known people, some of them of world-wide fame, local artists and writers, ate too, at ease as if in their own kitchens, good-humoured and among friends; and when she came in the second time, she was a friend too, though she said nothing but good day, good-bye. There was a little painter, all white and dressed in white, like a baker covered with flour. "I am on a diet," he explained to two other painters, one resembling a crocodile and the other a sea-elephant, and to her at her table; it was because he had ordered an omelet. "The doctor said, Diet! I am dieting for lunch just to see, but of course, this evening and tomorrow I won't diet. It's not healthy." He knew he was comical to look at; with an angelic childishness he smiled at everyone. She smiled. She, too, was friendly and simple with everyone when she was alone and unhurt in this safe harbour.

On a Friday, weary, yawning, she got up early, telephoned a few people, saw Tamara and Peggy before they went out, running up and downstairs to their rooms, in her rose slippers, her flowered white dressing-gown, pink ribbons in her long black braids and a confiding happy smile on her face. She looked about eighteen or twenty. Then she went back to her room with Peggy and discontent-edly pulled her things about.

"Last night, Peggy, I asked your advice about whether I should accept this invitation to lunch. I don't remember what you said."

"I didn't say anything; there was such a noise. Besides, you ought to know, Lydia."

Lydia explained. She was to go out to lunch with a middle-aged French baron, to call first at his apartment; and after lunching there, to go to the races at Auteuil. "But he says he's engaged for the evening; it's impolite," said Lydia.

"Do as you like. But if a man takes you to the races, he's supposed to bet for you; and beginners often win. It's fashionable to go and it's such nice weather."

Peggy was sitting on the one disengaged chair, while Lydia filled the room with smoke and ran about in skin-tight black nylon pants and bra, with her horsetail of India-ink hair down her back, and tried on one thing after another. She said, "Oh, why should I go at all? What a bore! How do I look in this? Why don't I telephone and call it off? No? Should I wear a light flannel suit? Or this white and green thing? The white coat goes over it."

She was a vanilla brunette with long oval deep-lashed eyes, ringed with black. There was a nervous rash on her back which limited her choice of clothes. She was often invited out swimming and could not go. She had a close, strong, small figure, rounded and beautiful in detail, with high-arched small feet which slipped in and out of her black slippers. Impatiently, she put some beads around her neck, some white earrings in her ears, took them off, drew out the black chiffon dress. "What about that? No, I suppose." She laughed; the kind of laugh that comes from a good-natured fat woman, her mother's laugh. "Do you know what happened to that green and black thing? I went up to Montmartre with an Englishman, Emory, and I went into one of those stand-up toilets. I didn't think and when I pulled the chain, the water flushed my skirts. I came out dripping. I was embarrassed; I didn't know what to say. He laughed nicely."

"You don't see anything."

"No, it was plain water." She laughed. "I think it's all right. Oh, perhaps I'll wear it tomorrow with the blind date. He's a UNESCO boy. I told him on the phone I wanted to go to the theatre and I wanted a job in UNESCO. I don't. It was just something to say. I had another boy to take me tomorrow, but—oh, Peggy, he's such a dope! Anyway, why should I dress up for a blind date? Should I wear this? Isn't that stupid? He means nothing to me, this baron. Why should I go? It's only a light lunch in his apartment and just this afternoon. That means I must get someone for this evening and there's no time."

But she decided to go. She suddenly, expertly, got into her tight black lace slip, put on a black and white dress and in a moment had twisted her horsetail into a loop, so that it shone like satin, and fixed it with heavy gold hairpins. Now she looked Spanish and older; but the sleepless circles round her eyes had faded into the dark make-up and powder. She had a matt skin, with a voluptuously creased neck, her shoulders and legs one bronze. She had a fleet motion, always as if running, with the feet arched, slightly bent forward. Worn out by indecisions, she now dropped on the bed. "Oh, Peg, isn't it stupid? No, I won't go."

But she continued to dress, sought among her earrings, rings, necklaces, scarves, put them all aside, put on gold, chose a green chiffon scarf, discarded them, went out in the end with only a string of small white shells around her neck. She was late, wanted to take a bus, but didn't know what route to take, nor where to change.

"Why should I take a taxi for him? I don't know him. I mightn't like it. Oh, should I take a taxi? But what does it matter? I'll be only half an hour late. Well, his lunch will be cold."

"But why keep the man waiting?"

"Oh, shouldn't I?"

"They hate it."

"H'mm, that's funny. Do they? I always do. I thought it was better. I don't care though."

She sped off to the corner, got a taxi.

She came home laughing. Tamara was home from work. She had a headache and was lying with her shoes off. She had got more bad news; her remarriage would be postponed at least six months. Neither of them had saved a penny; the divorce was taking all they had.

"Oh, Tamara, I heard someone crying in the night. When I thought it was finished, it started again. Was it you? It was on this side of the hotel. I nearly came up."

Tamara was thirty-six, a brunette, with a Javanese face, who wore dark clothes. She was almost an invalid, often ill, but a hard worker, working in three languages in an export office, in manner dry and precise, sweet and self-contained; and troubled, half mad with her worries.

Lydia sat by her and began bubbling over, falling over herself like water in a jet, leaping and shining.

"Oh, I went out with the baron. It was interesting at Auteuil. But do you know, the baron himself is a funny man. He was so careful not to touch me. If he touched me, walking about the paddock, he at once drew away. In the car, I sat next to him, but he was nervous if my coat touched him and he arranged it straightly over my knees for me. And he's as bald as an ostrich egg, just a fringe of hair; and so dull. All he says is, Should you like to do this? If you prefer that, tell me. I felt like a fifteen-year-old convent girl being escorted by a respectable cavalier drafted for the occasion and who's been told, Don't touch."

"Are you seeing him again?"

"Oh, he said he'd call, but why should I bother? He doesn't mean anything to me; and then he's so dull. I couldn't marry him. He's dull, prissy, peculiar, an old bachelor. He's at the same time unbending and a mollycoddle. Besides, he can't teach me anything. Oh, glasses and wines and table-linen—but I know that. And if he knows more than I do, I don't care. I could never marry a man like that."

Tamara sat up and looked at her friend. Lydia was thirty but looked much younger, even now when she was tired and discontented. "You are hard to please, Lydia."

"But I want perfection. I want a man to look up to and who will teach me."

"Won't you teach him? Marriage is give and take."

"Oh, no, no," cried Lydia. "It must be all give, he must give. I won't give. A man must be a light to a woman and guide her whole life and she must lean on him and have nothing more to think of. How could that be with any of the men I've met?"

"Because it isn't so," said Tamara sharply. "You must bring something to marriage."

"I bring twenty thousand dollars and a grand piano," said Lydia with a soft breaking laugh. "When I was sixteen I had my first offer of marriage from a preacher's son who was nineteen. He went to Mother first and then to me. We just sat there looking at each other. He didn't know what to say and I didn't either! When he asked me, I said, Do you really want to marry me? It seemed so funny. Then he said, Do the carpet and the grand piano really go with you? You've never seen our place in New York. It's a railroad flat over a stable. In my room, which is the sitting-room, too, there are all sorts of cabinets and a couple of carpets and my bed is behind the grand piano. I burst out laughing. He was embarrassed and said, because, if we couldn't live with Mother, we could have a couple of rooms in his father's house, but he would like to show his parents my furniture. Then he moved a bit nearer and said, I'm sitting close to you, aren't I? And I said, Yes, you are, aren't you? And he suddenly moved; and frankly, I thought he was going to hit me or push me, I didn't know which, but he kissed me awkwardly between my nose and my lip and he pushed my upper lip between my teeth. I nearly died laughing. I simply rolled on the couch, giggling. He was offended. Naturally. But he had his story and went on with it. He said we would not have children at first, because he would not be earning and I should have to finish college and get my MA so that I could get a good job afterwards while he was studying. Oh, it really is funny, Tamara. And he said he wanted a second-hand set of volumes, an encyclopaedia, fifteen volumes, which would cost about fifty dollars. He wanted to read it through and be competent in various subjects. So that was why I was to keep on working. Ha-ha-ha!"

"Well, he would have been able to teach you in the end."

"Oh, Tamara, why are men so funny? The second man who wanted to marry me was a drunk, the third wasn't divorced yet, and the next one was a poet with doughy hands. Oh, my wonderful ideal, he called me. He kissed my hand when he went. Good-bye, my beautiful ideal. He really smelled. Tamara, can you love a man who is gluey and smells like fresh-dead fish? After all, marriage is physical, isn't it? Several times I felt I had to let him kiss me and I felt my hands and lips just sinking into him like dough: he felt wet. I expected him to glisten. I used to look at him sideways at night, for he loved the dark streets, to see if he had a blue light like a fungus. And he so-o lo-oved me! And then—oh, I suppose I should go and get dressed? Emory, this Englishman, is calling for me at seven. I don't want to see him. I don't know why I got myself into it. I hate to get involved. Should I put him off? Let's spend the evening together. I'd much rather."

But Tamara had letters to write. Her intended husband worked in Rome and could get up only about once a month. She had been to see their lawyer in Paris. The wife had changed her mind and decided to fight the divorce; she wanted eighty per cent of his pay; and still was to fight it. She would ruin them, she said. When they married, they would be paupers. Morrie, the husband, did not like the prospect. Tamara was afraid he would give in; he was very tired, sick at heart. And Tamara's health was worse. She would always need treatment. He had parents to keep. Perhaps her wages would be all they would have to live on. He would have to give up his car; he would have to pay the train fare now from Rome. It needed thinking over. "Perhaps we are both thinking it over. He is so harassed, so worn down."

"Well, I will leave you to think it over," said Lydia with her clear chiming laugh, and kissed her friend. "And do you know what I must think over? Whether to live with this Englishman for a week! He begged me the night before last. He got to the point of tears in his eyes. He doesn't love me, but he likes me and it might lead to love. Ha-ha-ha-ha! What gentlemen! I shall say no. I thought it over, too. No, no. But he was so kind, so sweet, so gentle. In a way," she said suddenly, thoughtfully, "he's the sweetest of all the men. But—why should I get involved? What for?"

"Of course, you can't do it," said Tamara.

"Oh, it's just a silly proposition. Must I give up my comfortable room here and put my bags I don't know where and move into his hotel room in the Passage for a week, without knowing if I'll be able to touch him after one night? Ha-ha-ha! Does he wash? He probably has a frying-pan on a gas ring in the corner. Men are so strange, aren't they? Aren't they? He begs and pleads with me," she said, getting up and clasping her hands, her manner serious, urgent. "He will treat me with respect." Her voice became strident. "But what's it all for? I go back to New York in a few days and then I'm involved, without any reason."

"Not if you just wrote letters."

"That would be involvement. Letters about nothing. Sweet nothing. I can't stand the mere idea," she said, shrugging. She turned and glanced quickly at her friend. She smiled a sweet smile. "I'm so silly, Tamara, advise me. It's no, isn't it? Oh, of course, it's no."

"You are too sweet for that; you're not the kind."

"No. But what am I to do? Tamara? What am I to do? I can't get on any longer without a man. I must have a man. This is my chance in a way, isn't it? Just a week and—snip-snip! Just a day!"

"Yes."

"Oh, no," she said decidedly. "Then he would think he owned me. He would expect affection from me. Why? What nonsense. I'll tell him, Go away, no!"

She began again mirthfully. "And he's been waiting—ha-ha —imagine—since three or four days when he first began it— ha-ha-ho—it's funny though. He's been waiting for me to say yes. And now he's downstairs, I suppose, waiting already."

Smiling with her little white teeth between her half-closed lips, kissing Tamara, twisting her loose hair, she thrust her feet into the black slippers and ran off. "I'll call you in the morning, Tamara; I'll tell you what happened. Oh, but Tamara, I ought to spend the evening with you. You're lonely. Oh, it reminds me of home. I never know whether to go out or stay with Mommy. Then the telephone rings and she says, Go out with him, my chick, go out, my darling. Then I say, You go out with him. Then we stay at home and laugh and laugh. Oh, Tamara, I do love you; but suppose I must go."

When she reached her room, it was seven o'clock. She threw off her clothes, bathed, half-dressed, telephoned an American girl she had been out with two days before and chattered eagerly and with bursts of laughter about their adventure. They had picked up two French interns who had invited them to pass the night in their rooms at the hospital. "We're not serious, of course, but all for fun and you'll never regret it." The girls agreed and at the last minute Lydia had refused. "I'm not plucky." "You have nothing to be afraid of, we're doctors." "No, no, I just don't dare," Lydia had said smiling and shaking her head. The other girl said to Lydia, "You're so pretty, but I don't see what you get out of it: what do you get out of life? Soon you'll be on the boat going home to mother. Here are two nice Frenchmen and you turn them down." The other girl had gone to the hospital and Lydia had gone home. Now Lydia excitedly asked her about her experiences. "Oh, perhaps I should have gone. Oh, what a coward I am," she cried. The other girl raved about her happiness. "You'll never know what love is, if you take no chances," she repeated. "But what am I to do, I can never make up my mind," said Lydia. The girls talked for a long time eagerly. "Oh, my goodness," said Lydia, "a young man has been waiting for me downstairs for at least half an hour." When she put down the receiver, the phone rang from downstairs. It was the UNESCO boy, Sam, the blind date. "Oh, I thought you were coming tomorrow."

"Maybe I got it wrong: tonight, I thought."

"Well, I'm not nearly ready. I wasn't expecting anyone. I just came in. I spent the afternoon with a French baron at Auteuil. Oh, it was a bore." Her voice broke and she laughed warmly. "Yes? Can you take a walk? What do you look like? Well, never mind, take a walk and I'll be down in twenty minutes."

"Well, I've been waiting half an hour, but okay," he said. He had a dull New York voice with thickened consonants. She looked over the balcony and saw a middle-sized man with thick black hair and an unpressed double-breasted blue suit. He slouched off. He turned and looked up, at the hotel. She bent double over the balustrade, laughing and waving her hand. "Is it you?" "Yes," she said, bursting with laughter. He smiled. "Hurry up, I can't wait." "But I can," she called out.

She went inside and sat down in the comfortable warm room, consoling in its feminine untidiness. She put on her frock, examined her complexion, took the frock off and tried on a light dress with a big flowered design, a summer dancing dress, low in front, high in the back. She peeped over the balcony again and now she saw Emory, the Englishman, hanging about near one of the trees. She ducked her head in, hurried to the long mirror and then to the brightly lighted bathroom mirror. Her skin looked sallow against the light dress. She took it off and tried on the black and green stripe. "But I'm so sick of it. It won't do." She telephoned her mother's friend, Peggy, a quiet, patient woman, to come to her. "Oh, Peggy, I can't make up my mind and he's there waiting for me, my Englishman, you know." When Peggy arrived, Lydia nervously showed her three dresses which she had put out. She also held out a flame-coloured dress. "But that's tartish, isn't it?" Peggy considered. They chose the white and flowered. Lydia hesitated, as usual, over all the details, but at last she was ready, in her customary elegant simplicity and she ran out of the room leaving it a flowering disorder.

Across the sidewalk, beyond the trees, she saw Emory, who began softly to move forward towards the door. She looked nervously aside and saw there, through the glass-paned doors, in the small, brightly lighted hotel sitting-room someone she recognized, a middle-aged American with a half-bald sandy head and fat sandy face, an upstate professor of psychology, for a long time her mother's friend. Lydia's mother, Hester, a dumpy profuse gay little woman had had an extraordinarily varied life. She had been a governess abroad, had trained as a nurse, nursed men in war hospitals, worked later in a hospital laboratory; but she knew nothing about men. Since her husband's death many years before, she had had one or two silly flirtations with middle-aged drifters. The upstate professor was one of them. Lydia knew all about these affairs. The two women would tease each other; Hester would tell all that had happened and say, "Why did he do that? What did he mean by that?" They would giggle, and ridicule the men. "His waistcoat was open all the way down and he had a stain on his shirt. He sat on the divan and put his arm round me, but I could feel his armband sticking into me; and he kept pressing harder, so I had to ask him to stop." Then, what gales of laughter.

The professor's name was Russell. He was a great flirt, gossip and backbiter. One snowy evening he had come to Hester's apartment and stayed till the guests had gone, till one o'clock in the morning. Then, when she took him to the door, he said, eyeing her hard, "Don't you want me to stay?" "But I don't know you very well, Russell!" "You'll know me better by morning."

"No!" Hester burst out laughing; "why it's crazy, kiddo. You never said you loved me."

"You're naive," he said, annoyed. "I thought you were a woman of the world."

"You're naive, kiddo," her mother replied mirthfully, "to think I was a woman of the world."

When Russell went, discomfited and annoyed, Hester ran into Lydia's room with her handkerchief to her mouth, panting with excitement and gaiety. They both shrieked with laughter for a long time. They went over all the details. "And what expression did he have when you said—?" Russell was married. His wife Myra was Hester's friend. Hester could never get over this and gaily reminded him of it. "What would Myra say if she saw you sitting on the couch with me like this? Myra would think you were one heck of a wolf, if she knew, wouldn't she? What the hell, kiddo, do you do that to Myra?"

Hester, of foreign birth, had received a good education as a girl; but the English she had picked up later in New York was stuffed with incongruities.

"Russell!" cried Lydia now, skipping into the hotel room. "What are you doing here?"

"Your mother told me you were staying here and to look you up."

"Oh, what fun! How is Mother?" cried Lydia, beside herself with real and assumed excitement. She flung herself down on a chair and flashing a glance towards the heavy lace curtain and row of plants at the window, she observed Emory looking in. She became effusive, kissed Russell's cheek, patted his arm, smiled into his eyes. "Oh, Russell, how wonderful to see you," she repeated in a high, rapid, hysterical voice.

The professor of psychology was going away the next afternoon on a weekend trip to Chartres.

"Oh, goodness," said Lydia, "and I've been here six weeks, Russell. I intended to visit England, Italy, Spain, Germany, and I've spent the entire six weeks in this hotel, yet I've been on the go all the time. I've hardly spent an hour here except to sleep. I met so many people here. There are so many Americans in Paris. And I've been looking for a Frenchman to marry, but I've scarcely met one—only a baron and that was today. Don't you think I'd make a good French wife? Oh, I think so. Oh, I wish I could go with you and forget all about this. Paris is such a fever, such a torment, and I don't know how to get out of it."

"Well, come along with me tomorrow," said Russell, in his plain way. "I'll take you along. I've got no travelling companion. Haven't you been to Chartres?"

"Oh, no," said Lydia. "Yes! We'll go fifty-fifty and on the up-and-up. On condition that you leave by five tomorrow afternoon. I have an appointment—with a man—that I must avoid—tomorrow evening. Such a nice man—" she began to explode in mirth "—and I don't want to hurt him too much. Look, I must fly. He's out there now—do you see someone doing sentry duty among the trees?" She pointed, laughing. "You see! I'm telling the truth. Well, all right for tomorrow?"

"Yes, I'll meet you here at three."

"Yes. You have a car?"

"No. We'll go by train."

"Oh, bother! Can't you hire a car? Well, all right. At three sharp, not a minute later," she said decisively. "Oh, Russell, it's so good to see you. Let me kiss you, that's for Mommy." She kissed him on the forehead and cheek before she rushed out to Emory. She was trembling.

When she met Emory, she made him walk two hundred yards up the boulevard, then allowed him to kiss her. She put her arms on his shoulders, raised herself and kissed him again. Then she said nervously, almost crying, "Oh, Emory, you are the right man for me, but I am a virgin and it is a terrible thing for me. I am sure to get involved with you. I can't risk my whole future on this. Can I? Can I, Emory? Let's take a walk. Just walk up and down, let's turn the corner, not in view of the hotel because my mother's friend Russell is there, what a nuisance—he's come to take me to dinner! Mother might have known better; but she doesn't; I don't want to talk to that old bore all night. He's so silly, Emory, he's so silly. He's so portentous about sleeping with you. With girls. A professor, you know the sort. And my friend Tamara's room, too, is on the front, right in view. You'd love Tamara. You must meet her."

"Why mustn't they see me?"

"Oh, only that—I don't want to explain things—I want to be free."

"You can't be free forever, of some things."

"Do you forgive me, do you understand? You do, don't you, Emory?" she said rapidly. "I am so nervous, so confused. I don't know what to say. I thought to myself, he understands me, he is so good. You must let me go until tomorrow. I promise tomorrow evening, when you call for me—at seven —I'll give you my answer. I'm desperate, Emory." She laughed lightly, fluttering. "Oh, I am silly, I know. Oh, I ought to do it. You see, I can't bring myself to. It is stupid, isn't it?"

"No," he said, "but really, tomorrow, it must be yes. How can I go on like this? And it seems so natural with you. You're not like the other American girls. You're independent, but you're so fresh, really lovely," he said in a low voice.

"I'm old-fashioned, aren't I?" she said, trembling and giving the impression that she was caught. "Mother and I are dreadfully old-fashioned."

"You're very different from the others I've met."

"I'm afraid I'm too different," she said in a low strained voice, "too different. What does it show, never to be able to come to a decision?"

"You're as decisive as a humming bird," he said cheerfully, "but you go too fast. You dart here and there and don't get any rest. That's your charm, too."

"Yes, you understand me; I don't get any rest."

"Well, let's go to dinner."

"No, no. I simply have to spend the evening with my mother's friend Russell. And then I must see Tamara. She is going to marry a man who is getting a divorce, but the divorce will take six months longer than they expected and poor Tamara cried all night. I heard her. I know you will let me go."

"I am very disappointed," said Emory, rather stiffly.

"Tamara and I worked for the Free French during the war and we worked here in an office after the war and we've been together so long."

"What is she to you?"

"She gets into such messes and she has to confide in me. She talks so much and everything is so gloomy, I get quite hysterical. I want to laugh and I have to break in with my affairs and pretend I'm laughing at them. And she's so sick."

"And will she be sick tomorrow?"

"Oh, no, let me go, Emory dear"—she reached up to him and kissed his ear—"Let me go, I must go. You know what it is to live forever in a hotel room waiting for someone."

"Yes, I know," he said flatly. But he accompanied her to the door and left her, not noticing the UNESCO man who had returned and for some time had been watching them, himself keeping under the trees. She changed her mind at the door, walked past the hotel with him to the corner. When he rounded the corner she tripped back to the UNESCO man.

"Oh, I am so sorry to keep you waiting," she said, beginning to laugh; "but this Englishman keeps coming here and wants me to sleep with him, but I can't do it. How can I? He's an Englishman and I'm going back to New York in a few days. Isn't it impossible?"

The evening with her blind date was a dreary joke. He walked her to a small restaurant on a side street. She never went there, because it was full of poor, young Americans living in Paris, men who had been on the GI Bill of Rights and stayed on, others self-exiled, artists and their poor, young, thin unfashionable wives. Some of them took just soup and bread, others had stuffed tomatoes, or, if richer, hamburgers. The menu was scribbled in chalk on a slate, high on the wall. They always had stuffed tomatoes and hamburgers. Sometimes someone who had received a cheque would talk gloriously. The UNESCO man, Sam, always dined here. He told her it was a very good place, a find of his. They ate some mussels, and then he said, "What dessert would you like? Are you having a dessert or are you on a diet, like all the girls?" They had strawberries and cream and coffee. A few minutes afterwards, she felt uneasy. Hives came out on her legs; she scratched at them, at first secretly and then openly, saying to Sam, "It must be the strawberries! Or was it the mussels?"

He was a worn-out, dusty, bored New Yorker of about thirty, her own age; and this closeness of their ages seemed very dreary to them both. It all seemed dreary; that they came from New York, had worked in a Paris office, that they were blind dates; and now the restaurant full of hungry poor Americans, some of them enthusiastic but only for art, seemed dreary, also. She nagged him about working in a Paris office. "What are we Americans doing loafing abroad?" she said. "There are seventeen thousand of us here speaking bad French. Why would they want us here? We don't belong here."

"I couldn't care less. That's what the English say, isn't it?"

"That's a fine way to live your life: I couldn't care less," she nagged him. He returned her to the hotel by a quarter past nine and dragged himself off.

Lydia went up and telephoned her friend Camilla, Cammie, the American girl who had gone with the French intern, but she was out. Lydia went straight out again to look for her; and after visiting two or three cafés, she found her with a Fulbright scholar who was studying art in Paris. While they were sitting there, other Americans drifted in, among them a curly-headed young man, neat, pale, big-eyed. Camilla was small, with the complexion of unpainted pine, a long soft cheek and neck, long, soft, colourless hair, thin bare ankles. She wore light-coloured silk on her hair and a skirt she had made herself out of bright material gathered around her thin waist and flat body. She had the fresh damp purity of flowing water, and a strange self-regard which looked like innocence. She left with her companion, a tall fair girl with a tall fair man: the pair out of proportion and out of place as legendary figures.

When they had gone, the new man, Roger, said to Lydia. "That clears the atmosphere. Now you're going to have some wine with me."

"I just had dinner and I'm ill; mussels, strawberries and cold water. Brr!"

"You ought to be ill. Is that your idea of French eating? Only Americans think cold water is digestible."

She told him all about it, laughing and disgusted. She had given up an evening to a real romantic who couldn't care less and was washed up at nine-fifteen.

Roger said, "What's the matter with him—or you?"

The little fair-haired man posed as untouchable, superior. She flirted nervously at moments, and at others looked around the café. There were some attractive American boys she would have liked to talk to. One was showing a new small camera got in Germany; it was about three inches by one and looked like a wrist watch in a case. She leaned towards them, two tables away, went and sat by them, asked them about the watch, a hundred questions, not listening to the answers, asking the same questions again. "And you say this is a—what did you say? Oh, you're not at all clear. Oh, that isn't an explanation," and her chiming, breaking laugh. The owner of the watch became tired. "But I've explained that to you ten times—" She was looking older. She returned to the fair man. He kept the conversation going in an undertone, keeping at her as if sharpening a knife on her. Lydia said she was tired; she had a sick friend upstairs and she was expecting a call. She didn't know whether to stay in the café or not.

"There's me; you can stay for me," he said with frigid vanity, looking at her.

"I don't mean a thing to you."

"I'll find it hard to come back to this café. I'll think it over, I tell you, because now I've met you here," he said in a cold, insulting tone.

She scarcely laughed, looked idly around, then bent forward, tracing on the table. "That cuts no ice with me, Roger. If you want to cut ice. I don't know what to do. I'm looking for direction. You haven't got a message for me." She laughed, high and sharp.

"Well, there's just being with me. That could be something if you knew how to take me. I'm an experience. I'm a rare American. Something you won't meet again. It's my quality."

She laughed outright, interested. "Oh, how funny you are. You don't mean that. What could I get out of you?"

"You'd have had me."

She laughed and shivered. "There's a breeze! Why are your eyes so red? Have you been crying or drinking?"

He turned quickly to look at himself in the café mirror behind him. She lent him her little mirror. "Just look!" She continued, "I've made an application to UNESCO to get a job here. Double-talk, French-English translator."

"You've only been in Paris six weeks and you expect to get jobs of that sort?"

"Oh, I was brought up in Paris. Part of the time. I ought to get back to my friend Tamara. She's a charming woman."

"Charming! That's a word I haven't heard since I left America. My mother always says it. It doesn't fit you. It seems to belong to her more than to you. She has quality."

"Still," said Lydia, unvexed, "it's a word often used. Tamara wants me to stay here and get a job; and there is the problem of my mother, who is alone. I had a sister who died years ago. I ought to get home to her. She's ill; heart trouble."

"Nothing but ailing women in your life."

"Oh, how complicated you are," she said, beginning to laugh.

"Yes, I am complicated. That might be good for you. A little drama might wake you up."

She looked at him, bored, horrified.

"What? I was here just after the war, working with people from concentration camps," she said.

He did not catch her drift. He pursued, "Have you ever been in love?"

"I've never been let."

"Somebody ought to let you."

"To tell you the truth—"

"If you can," he murmured swiftly. "Have you ever been analysed?"

"No, I'm waiting till I'm old and rich and full of lies."

He analysed her depressingly.

"That's not the way out," she said.

"I might be the revelation," said he.

"You see, Roger, there's a curse on me," she said seriously. "My mother has an older sister, named Diana, my aunt, of course. Diana thought my father was in love with her; instead, he married Mother, who seemed like a girl always, thoughtless, heedless, though she's really a very earnest woman; she's a pharmacist. My aunt Diana was much older, supposed to be the intellectual one, a political force, a union worker, head of department; and she writes textbooks. She has the men coming round to talk about things. Mother was supposed to be silly, she laughed so much. Mother's full of fun, generous, she loves music and she's crazy as a goose. When she was a girl she went as a nurse to Berlin and even to Moscow and thought nothing of it; that's the way she is. That was after the first war. People hear of it, but it doesn't make any impression. But Diana told my father all about it before the marriage and said Hester, my mother, was a libertine and had been with all the soldiers and tramps in Europe and that she had probably caught something."

Lydia's hysterical voice broke into laughter. "If a man comes into the room Mother fluffs out like a kitten or a bird and gets touchy, skittish and begins to laugh: she's just an ingenue. Then combined with her *charming* silliness, there are her simply impossible stories of her life abroad as a young girl. They're heroic. No one believes them. And yet if you fit them together, they match and they're all true. Well, my father was a doctor, so he wasn't much frightened; he probably thought Aunt Di was a crazy old maid. But Mother was frightened of men and she thought Father wouldn't respect her if he slept with her, so for months after they married she remained a virgin; and she was an idealist too."

Lydia laughed again. "So of course Aunt Di wrote letters to Father, saying it all proved what she had said was true and she wanted Father to leave Mother. Well, of course, it turned out not to be true and one morning Father said to Mother that he had wronged her dreadfully, he would never be able to make it up to her. He spoiled her; he adored us too. She never learned anything while she was married. Then one awful New York winter Father died and the young one too; and I was left alone with Mother; and I was a hot-tempered, bitter, sharp little girl. Adults seemed mad and coarse to me. Just after the last funeral, of my sister, who was eight years old, Aunt Diana wrote Mother a cruel terrible letter saying that her wild life with the soldiers before her marriage had caused those deaths. Aunt Diana was a mad woman, I assure you. If it's not madness, what is it? And everyone thinks the world of her; she's on committees. And she didn't marry. I think she remained in love with my father."

Lydia began laughing maliciously, "You see, if it's chastity that worries you, we're all problem women."

"Your Aunt Diana is quite a woman, she has strength of character. And what about you, does she say you're degenerate too?" said the sour little man.

"Oh, no. She once told me she'd leave me her money if I agreed to live apart from Mother. I didn't, so I suppose she hates me now."

"How much money has she?"

"How much can she have? She earned it all herself. You don't make money by earning. I have money myself, but she doesn't know; it's a trust fund."

"Ah, that accounts for it all," he said, leaning back and speaking coolly. "You've a father fixation and identification with the most forcible personality in your family, who happens to be unmarried. You rely on your money for defence and fulfilment, and for vengeance; just as she does. It's castration by money."

"You mean I'm a miser," she said with a tender laugh. "Oh, perhaps I am. At least, you see, I must marry someone who can

78

give me what I want. Why should I spoil my life? I don't want to get involved and then give some man twenty thousand dollars because I'm involved as a woman."

"You'll never get married; you'll just drift on and on. And will you get something from your mother?"

"Oh, she hasn't a red cent," she said, laughing again. "She spent everything my father left. She didn't know. She just kept giving everyone cheques. Then she just had enough to go to college and learn pharmacy."

He kept teasing her in his disagreeable way; but he accompanied her home and warned her again about losing him. The woman at the desk smiled at him, seeing a sweet-faced youth with good manners, and congratulated Lydia on her choice, with a gentle smile.

Lydia ran upstairs to Tamara's room and gossiped with her for a while. Tamara told her all her troubles; how their life would be a life of struggle and poverty; could their affection hold out under the wife's attacks? "Living in a hotel room as I've done for years and just going to the office and coming back to headaches, is a miserable inhuman life."

"But you love each other," cried Lydia.

"Oh, love—yes, I can live with him: that's the principal thing."

"What a compromise, Tamara!" said Lydia, bursting out laughing, but embracing her friend and kissing her on both cheeks, bouncing about her with kisses, puppyishly. She giggled and lay down on the bed. "You're a mother to me, Tamara. Oh, I miss dear darling Mommy. What a nuisance I am to her. I'm the plague of her life. She has ruined me, I think. What man will give me the love and patience and care she gives me? But Tamara—I must have love! I must love, to marry I must love. Supposing Diana dies and leaves me all or some of her money? Of course, she won't; that's ridiculous! She thinks I'm mad. But supposing she does. If I gave up my father's name and took hers, she would. If I did, I would have no need to marry till I love, then. I want a man that's perfect, Tamara—Mother said my father was absolutely perfect. No substitutes, no compromises. He must adore me. Why shouldn't

I have everything? I can get married whenever I want to—to a hundred different men. That puts me off. It's like sitting in a bus— a hundred different passengers." She shrieked with laughter. "How boring! No, I prefer to wait."

Tamara had a headache, and Lydia went away. Shifting some of the bundles of clothing and other things, she went to bed. She fell asleep and, as usual, awakened after only an hour or two. Everything was quiet; no noise had awakened her. Her heart beat hard. She impatiently unbraided her two long thick plaits, thinking that they were hard to lie on; and then, feeling hot in her hair, braided them again. She put on the light and put it out, listened. It was the hives that had awakened her. She scratched them and tried to remember what she had eaten for lunch. With whom had she passed the day? She had almost forgotten Roger, who was last of all. Should she have gone with Emory; been, even now, in his room with him? She began to laugh, thinking of ridiculous endearments, postures.

She had been close to many men. She tossed and pondered; she had taken awful risks. An old man in a big house in Long Island, where she had worked during college holidays—she had been engaged by his broken-hearted, broken-faced wife. A dark young man with his eyes popping from his head, with whom she had gone to a shack over the weekend—she had beaten him off, like beating off insects, laughing and beating. Coming home from college, from work in the dark streets of the city in the evening; a man who stood in a dark doorway and urinated as she passed; a young man who cried, "What time is it? Four o'clock? Five? Half-past five? Six?" Six dollars! She rolled about on the bed laughing. She never passed that place in Sixth Avenue, a deserted row of shanty buildings, without smiling.

She did not sleep and it seemed to her a voice was saying, *Macbeth hath murdered sleep,* as if it helped her. She rose early in the morning and started out on her little errands. She took her suede slippers to a man around the block who would glass-paper them. Then she took a coloured dress to a laundry which refused it and then to the dry-cleaner's. She went to a little shop to match a button. When she returned there was a letter from the Englishman, brought by hand, a passionate barefaced letter. She copied part of it out, and put it in her purse; then she burned the letter with a match, in her *cabinet de toilette*. She put a little valise on the bed and began to pack for Chartres.

After putting in two or three things, she telephoned and ran upstairs to Peggy, with a housecoat over her chiffon underwear and Italian rainbow-striped slippers. She told her the whole story of yesterday. "I must have your advice, Peggy; what shall I do? Oh, what shall I do? I can't go back to New York without doing something. You've known me so long. Give me the right advice!"

"Well, go with Emory then," said her mother's friend, baffled, irritated, worried by the girl's frantic mood.

"Oh, no, I can't, I won't, I don't want to. It's awful to go to a man who wants you. It's degrading. He can keep me, jail me. Real passion is awful, unless I feel it too. I couldn't stand it."

Peggy, a long-faced, irritable woman, herself tormented by men, tried to get her to go.

"Oh, come down with me, Peggy, come down with me and help me choose the clothes to take. It's only a silly weekend with a friend of Mother's. What do I care? He's dull and goatish. I'll just throw anything in. But do come down and help me."

Peggy went down but, when she got there, Lydia did nothing but shift through the piles of clothing. She kept trying on pretty things and asking advice about these and her skin troubles, and all kinds of things; talking fast with her innumerable hysterical sweet laughs.

Towards three o'clock Lydia became very nervous, fearing the professor might be late and Emory come too soon. For once, she was packed and ready before time. When she saw the professor on the other side of the street, she ran across to him, tilting forward on her high heels, dashing between the cars.

"Oh, Russell, let's get a taxi. Come and get my valise!"

"Well, I have my own—"

Without a murmur, she herself brought her valise and coat and put them in a taxi which she hailed. The professor objected to the taxi, saying he had little money with him. He had only just received a cheque from his wife, late in coming and he could not cash it at the American Express before Monday.

"Oh, never mind, I've plenty of money. I'll pay everything for both and you pay me back on Monday, or any day," she said glibly, getting into the taxi and pulling the professor by the sleeve. "Oh, let's get going and shake this town off. I've seen too much of it, I'm sick of it. Oh, what an obsession! What do people come here for? Don't you think the world's the same everywhere? Especially now." And so, talking feverishly, she got him away from the boulevard. She had left no message at the hotel.

She calmed down, breathed and began to laugh joyously. Her demonstrative relief seemed like interest and affection. She talked about her mother and she beamed at him. She laid her hand on his coat, ducked back and forth, leaned back and burst out laughing at all kinds of ordinary sights and sounds in the streets. She took a roll of bills out of her black suede purse, took her own luggage, paid the taxi-driver like an eager schoolgirl, out for her uncle's birthday. She asked the professor a dozen questions, began eagerly to listen; another question tripped over the heels of his explanation. She flattered him, tried to attract him.

"Oh, what a relief, Russell, to meet you, to be with you. Oh, it's like home."

She proceeded to tell him some of her adventures, a tangle of relations she had with men; about the baron, stiff and ignorant, who never touched her hand; and about Emory, who even then, "even now at this moment, imagine," was at the hotel, astounded, hurt that there was no sign, no word.

"He'll understand, I suppose, that I've fled before him, gone with the wind, oh, dear, oh, dear. Ha-ha. He'll think that the disgraceful frank letter he sent me frightened me off. Because I am a virgin, you know, Russ, I am a virgin. Do you believe me? That will teach him a lesson. I put the blame on that, if he sees me again. Oh, but when I come back it will be close to sailing and there'll be no question of being involved. He'll give me up. Oh, what the hell," she said, belching one of her mother's ribald phrases, and again she laughed heartbreakingly. "Oh, Russell, advise me! Shall I come here to live and work? But then I must bring Mother. What shall I do? Ought I to marry? But Mother will be all alone. Go out from a room and work and come back to a room. But Russ, I can't keep on living faster, faster, faster and getting nowhere, can I?"

In the evening light of Paris, in the half-light of the cab and station, taking off her jacket and scarf, arranging them, saying, "Russell! Shall I wear it or not? Does it suit me?" quickly twisting a stray lock of her black hair, fixing a jewelled clasp, making up her black oval eyes and brilliant red lips, and turning herself out, in the end, simple, girlish and yet like a dark flower, alive and with disturbing fleshy perfume, a low-growing solitary and strange flower, she wove her rhythms around the sandy middle-aged professor.

"Oh, it's all right about this Englishman, never mind about him. I like to be with you. I can be friends with you; I can be entirely myself. You do understand, don't you, what I feel about you? I can have two or three days absolutely without a hitch and without thinking of anything. You're a friend of Mother's and we know each other. It's such fun, Russell. I feel so happy, so free, for with you, Russell, it's like being with an uncle. Oh, Russell, it's so funny with you!" She put her hand behind her heavy knotted hair and gave a crow of amusement. "Oh, Russell, you don't know me! Men don't know me. When I'm with girls I have such fun. Do you know in the office, after the war, when I was here with Tamara, we used to go into shrieks of laughter. I am always tossing off my shoes. One day, they hid one of my shoes, and when the boss rang for me I had to hop in with just one shoe and one bare foot. Oh, we went into gales of laughter! Oh, it was all so charming. Why aren't you men so charming? It isn't fun with you, is it? Don't you have an awful boring time with each other? Confess, Russell, that you are deadly boring, so stuffy? Of course, that is why you need girls. Ha-ha-ha." She said, sitting opposite him at the window in the railway carriage and looking at the landscape passing, "The country! Now I can be free. Oh, Paris is an obsession; I feel it like paprika. And then the men fluttering round, so aimless and asking you to decide. Oh, Russell, I can't stand the idea of Emory standing there, pleading with me, hovering round the hotel. Where's the satisfaction? Oh, of course I have got to live with a man eventually, to find out what it's like, because I can't sleep, I'm on fire. The world has narrowed down so, I don't even see Paris, except as a décor for a man. And that's the way they see it and I despise it. And then, though I've had fun, it's light fun, the food's poor and the trips are uninteresting, just because they don't give me what I want. It's there for me to take, but I can't get involved for a night's play. And then how do I know if I'd be glad? Is it worth it, is it worth it? Oh, I'm stupid, Russell; I think you're Mother; I treat you like Mother. You're a man, aren't you? Oh, yes, you're a man, I suppose. With you, I'm different. I don't know, perhaps I'm wilder. It's because I'm safe, with you," she said, and her voice, pure, girlish, bewildering, broke strangely. "Oh, Russell, what shall I do? It's like being delirious and yet clear-minded. I think of nothing else, nothing else; but I don't want a man when I see him. I'm a fool, I suppose. Am I wasting my time? What am I to do? Men are a terrible aphrodisiac, and yet I don't want them. They're so much trouble."

She gave him a quick slippery smile and looked out the window at the country.

"If it's on your mind so much, you'd better go with a man," said the professor.

"Yes, oh, yes. If only I could, Russell. But I always laugh too soon. One I know in New York, he has a fat back and a shine. He put his hand on my thigh, on my leg—ha-ha—and put my hand on his. Oh! You'd think he has no bones at all. And there he sits lamping me with those foggy big eyes, and he says, Perhaps a trial marriage would be a good thing for you. I laugh. He says, You're wicked, you're wicked. I laugh and laugh. I nearly died of laughing. He went out of the door looking backward and says, I want to bring a lady friend of mine to see you, she's a poetess. I had to keep both hands on my stomach not to fall down laughing. I sit in the library and think of you, he says. Ah-ah-ah! You are complicated, you understand evil! Ah-ah-ah! His kiss is deep warm, like a mealbag.

His face is pale and pearish and he has a seeking mouth like a baby looking for the nipple. Oh, I suppose you must put up with things to get married? Perhaps there's something about me that attracts peculiar men? I ought to be grateful, I know. They take me out and I think about it at night and make up my mind; next time I'll let him kiss me, it's only right. And then I do it gingerly with the tips of my teeth: slobber, smack, drip. Like a wet rag on the floor. Oh, why are men so awful? I guess I'm crazy, eh, Russell? I can't interest myself in other things, though. This fat one took me to concerts. They go year after year, all their lives. It's awful to be trampled down by a stamping herd of true believers, at a violin concert. And there is Aunt Di running off to Madison Square Garden to roar with the other frogs. Seriously, is that a substitute? You're a professor of psychology. You can't seriously believe it is?"

He talked to her about it. When they got to Chartres, she said vivaciously, "Oh, I know a good restaurant here, it's in a hotel. Let's go there first and then find a place. Perhaps we can stay there; it's a good hotel. I've stayed there. It'll be early for hours. I just want to walk about in the air, just to be free." The words tripped out of her mouth, falling over the laughter. "Oh, poor things, I shouldn't do it. I have completely forgotten already about poor Emory, and really it was to avoid making a decision and avoid a scene that I came away with you, Russell. Oh, Russell, I love you so, you're so safe. Ah-ah-ah! What a pity you're married. I'd be so safe with you." Laughter and excitement rippled out of her little nut-brown face. She took his arm and stepped along briskly, "Come along! Have you enough money to pay for dinner for yourself at least, Russell?" Over dinner, she told him her various troubles and about the interns.

There were not many people in the big old hotel which she knew, but she wouldn't stop there. She insisted upon looking for a small hotel. "Just an auberge, there is one. Oh, how nice to be with you, Russell. But you see, I was at the other hotel with Mother."

At the little hotel they asked for two rooms; but found that only a double room was vacant. She said impatiently that they would take this; and they moved in. They walked out, saw the front of the cathedral by moonlight, went back and went to bed. Lydia asked Russell to go into the bathroom while she undressed and got into bed. He did so; and he was nice enough to her, did not bother her when she said she was tired.

She wanted to move to another hotel in the morning. She helped him with the bill. He was a clumsy, dogged man without pleasing ways of doing things; and he was used to being looked after by his wife. He would look at things put before him on the table with intense interest, but without saying thank you. He drank his coffee without pouring out hers; he ate more than his share. She laughed and grabbed her food from under his spreading paw.

"Oh, you are so funny, Russell," she said, breaking away from him, as he maritally put his big hand on hers. "You're just a big lunk. You're no Romeo, are you? What would Myra say if she saw us sitting here together half-dressed and so greedily snatching food from one another?"

"Myra doesn't come into the picture."

They paid the bill and set out for a walk and to look for another hotel. Now Lydia wanted to go back to the big one she had stayed in as a girl. They spent some time in the cathedral, went down to the river, walked about and were bored. At lunch-time they moved to the big hotel, where they also lunched. They spent the afternoon traipsing and complaining. Lydia had got one large room for both. She used her own name and told the proprietor she had been there with her mother. This time the washbasin was in the room behind a screen; so Lydia asked Russell to go into the corridor while she undressed and washed. She then got into bed and turned her back. Russell presently returned, made ready for bed and, when he got in, took hold of her.

"You're surely not going to refuse?" said he.

"You're surely not going to force yourself on me?" she said. "We're travelling together, my dear Russell, but we're not intimate. We're comrades, remember; we scarcely know each other though you're my mother's friend."

"Are you kidding me?" he said. "What do you think I came away with you for?"

"You're not going to get near me, you big ape," she shrilled; and she was such a shrew that Russell quailed. He went out into the corridor and did not return for a long time. One of the maids became alarmed and the manager came upstairs. "Are you the American who's walking up and down?"

"You bet your nose I am; my girl friend won't let me go to sleep."

When he came back, she seemed asleep; but was not, watching him angrily and crouched like a kitten that has been too much set upon by boys and dogs. Russell tried to make a conquest in the night, but she ordered him out; and the next morning found him crouching against the head of the sofa. She ordered their breakfasts downstairs. They went out to the cathedral during Mass. There was a light unpleasant wind. At lunch and in the afternoon, he made attempts to flirt with her. In the evening, as soon as they entered the hotel, she marched to the desk and asked the manager to find her another room.

"I accepted this room," she explained, "because I thought you might be short of accommodation. There are so many American cars about. But this man here is nothing to me; he's my mother's friend and his lack of gallantry is disgraceful. I can't even bear his presence. He attempted to make love to me, not that he's really capable; he's only an American boor. Kindly find me another room. Please do what I say, because I'm paying. He has no money on him."

Russell did not understand so much French, but he refused to move out of the big bedroom. "You can stay with me if you want to. You know very well why you came away with me. I'm not going to pay for all that cheating. Stay or go. I don't care."

"Well," said Lydia, laughing spitefully, to the manager, "he cannot pay and he will not move. So I must move. Unless you are prepared to throw him out. I realize that would cause a scandal. I have the money for everything, so kindly do what I say. Oh, please do what I say, sir. I made a great mistake when I came away. I am foolish, I suppose. To spare any scandal I myself will move, but he must bring the bags." Then she said to him in French, which he understood with difficulty, "I will now meet you at meal times. You

87

will have to meet me for dinner, since you have no money. I have you at my mercy because you have no money, no sense and no French."

She dressed delightfully as usual. Everyone in the dining room looked at her. She had now dressed her hair in a Spanish style. She was perfectly at ease, with smiling gravity. After a considerable time, Russell appeared. He was a big hungry man. However, at the table, he turned his back on her and took no notice when she asked for the salt and pepper. She called the waiter, who offered them and cast indignant looks at the man.

"Haven't you any manners?" she scolded Russell in French. "Fortunately, I should never think of marrying you." Her voice, though light, amusing, had a sort of scream in it. "Pass the things! If you are not a man in any other way, can't you have the manners of a man?"

He kept his back turned and ate, leaning over his plate. She reached for the bread herself. When she had taken a piece, she placed the basket in front of him and said, "Here, put it back! What will they think of you? You need not show in public that you are impotent."

He turned around at this, "What do you mean by that?"

"It's social impotence, not to know how to behave with women. It's impotence to treat women badly and to sulk. It's impotence to go away with them without the right money; that's financial impotence and you may be physically, for all I know. I know nothing to the contrary. But why lead people to suspect it? And then you are in the wrong. Very much in the wrong. We are in France, not Keokuk."

He sat there eating his meal. At lunch, out of shame, he had eaten very little. She said, "Well, I've waited long enough. Are you ordering wine?"

"I don't drink wine," he said.

She hailed the wine-waiter and ordered. "I'm taking it, I'm used to it. Must you behave like a hick, you fat porky hick? Just because you come from a fresh-water college you can't order wine?"

In the night he tried to enter her room. She had left the door unlocked. She was waiting for him. She sprang from her bed and rushed out into the corridor calling for help. When the night-porter came, a squat man in pyjamas and a faded dressing-gown, with dyed hair and whiskers, she asked him to conduct Russell back to his room and to lock him in if he could.

However, she insisted upon having breakfast with Russell in his room, for the sake, perhaps, of confusing the staff and irritating him further. He said at length, "Lydia, you don't like me; you'd better go home. Leave me here. I don't care what becomes of me. Go on, leave me."

She thought it over and then said she could not. "I got you here with a promise to look after you. I thought of going back on Friday when we got here but how can I leave you adrift? You're so helpless. You're like a little boy. You're like a baby. When you're asleep, your face is pinched up and I say to myself: why does he look like that, what does he want? No, no, Russell, I've got to see you through."

"Well, let's both go back at once."

"No, no. I'm sick of this hotel. We'll go to another hotel and I'll see what I think. I shouldn't have come to this hotel where I stayed with Mother. Oh, Russ, I thought I'd have some fun. I haven't enjoyed myself at all. What's the matter with you, Russ? I ought to revenge myself upon you, but I can't. I've got to go through with it. Let's get out of Chartres. It's a dismal place. We'll go somewhere else."

She settled up, asked the manager's advice. He was plainly taken with her and advised her to leave this gentleman and to go back to Paris. "Oh, yes," she said nervously, "I should marry a Frenchman, don't you think so? That is why I came over. I have always thought so. But Mommy loves New York; and then I should lose my citizenship, you see?"

"But no; you don't have to lose it now, mademoiselle."

She got tickets and they went by bus to a place suggested by the manager. Here they walked about, ate and went up to their room; for once more she had asked for a double room for herself and her friend. Russell this time took no notice of her, turned his back while undressing, while she merrily mocked him for his underwear, his heavy body, his hairy arms. "Oh, you men, such dreadful creatures!" She got into bed with him, however, and each turned his back and stretched out on the extreme edge of the mattress. "You see," she said as soon as she thought he was dozing, "if you really only came away to sleep with me, well, in a way you are sleeping with me." He lay awake and silent. Presently, the bed began to shake with her laughter. He said nothing. She laughed more and more and presently out loud.

"Oh, Russ, oh, Russ! If Mother only knew that here we were in bed together! Mother thinks you're such a nice man! Funny things happen, don't they, Russ?" She turned around and clasped his arm, "Don't you think you're going off to gulp and snore when I'm here. You may be weak, you may need a tonic, but to snore away when I'm here is too much." She kept him awake for some time, when she herself suddenly fell asleep.

In the morning she said to the chambermaid, with whom she was friendly, "Don't hesitate to come in. Our relations are pure, you know. He's oh such a sweet man; he lives with a woman like a brother."

She was so quaintly bewitching that the chambermaid could not help smiling. "Madame," said she.

"Oh, I am mademoiselle and shall be till the cows come home, if it depends on the anchorite here," said Lydia, beginning to shake with mirth. The chambermaid could not repress a slight friendly smile. Lydia in her rose-sprigged white gown, pink slippers and ribbons looked like a schoolgirl. "Mademoiselle," said the chambermaid.

"Why do you do that?" he asked. He had brought no dressing-gown and sat in his loose-cut pyjamas, looking his worst.

"I wouldn't mind you looking goatish if you behaved like a goat."

"You have no call to say that to me," he said miserably.

On the way in to Paris, she was shrill, uneasy, bitter. The man half groaned as he said, "I had no idea you were such a spitfire. You never gave any sign of it. You looked so sweet."

"I had no idea you came from the barnyard! A capon from the barnyard. When you dip a fowl in hot water to get its feathers off—that's what you look like."

They parted at the station without a word, although she offered to take him to his hotel in a taxi. He appeared at her hotel about lunchtime and said, "Here is all I owe you," and immediately went away again.

Lydia sat in her room feverishly pulling over her goods, looking at herself every few minutes in the mirror and saying, "How awful I look! Like an old hen." She tried on all her shoes, studied the hem of the dress that had been splashed and remembered that Emory had been sorry for her. She pulled a jacket on over the flowered and not too clean dress she had on at the moment and ran out with bare legs to the dyers' and the laundry. Her things were not ready, and in a jolly scolding way she told them she had to sail within a few days. She telephoned one or two friends, made an appointment with a man; and because Tamara would not be home till five-thirty or six, she went and sat on the terrace of the next-door café drinking a lemonade. Sitting there with her hair hanging down her back, uncombed, for the first time snarled and wispy, her face pale and indignant, she looked ailing and almost plain. Emory saw her there and came over to her. She began to tell him about her wretched weekend, but almost at once, saw Tamara going home from work, and called her over.

Tamara's curly wiry hair was blown loose, her face was tired; she had a headache. There was no end to the legal papers to be copied, witnessed, restamped and paid for. There was no way of telling when the case would come up now. The lots had been drawn and she had had no luck; it would not come up before the law vacation.

"I'll come upstairs with you," said Lydia eagerly. "I have so much to tell you. Oh, Tamara, this is my English friend. I told you about him. But I must tell you what happened this weekend! It was horrible, awful. I must tell you. Oh, lord, what a fool I am."

"You were telling me; do tell me," said the Englishman. Tamara did not want to stay with them.

"Oh, I oughtn't to talk about it. I had the worst time of my life, I think." Looking again pale, undone, wretched, tossing back her untidy hair with one hand and with the other on Tamara's arm, she said, "Oh, I'm tired. I could die. I'll come upstairs in a minute, Tamara."

"I'm going to take an aspirin and lie down; don't wake me if I'm asleep," said Tamara.

"How pale your friend looks," said Emory.

"Yes, this divorce will kill them both, if it doesn't separate them. Oh, there are hundreds of these official Americans in these messes abroad now. And then they're afraid they'll be called home: they have no security and of course none of them has any money. Oh, listen, Emory: I am sorry I went away. I was punished. Men are such wreckage. What we are supposed to put up with, because we are women, because he is a man! It's funny, isn't it? We're supposed to be so delicate!"

She told him the story of the weekend, leaving out no detail, but without embroidery. She trembled and laughed. "Oh, what should I do? My last opportunity has gone. I've got to sail in a few days. I saw nothing. I didn't even see Chartres. I've seen Chartres a dozen times; it doesn't matter; but it was as nasty as walking round in a wet bathing suit in an east wind. What is your advice, Emory? Soon I'll be back with Mother and I can't torment her again with my shillyshally. Shall I come to live in Paris? I expect so. I'm sure I can only be happy here. Frenchmen and Englishman are so much better than Americans; Americans are mere boys. But then I must bring Mother; and it will be the same. I am so worn out with teasing and tormenting Mother. Poor Mother. Well, I will come back next year. That is all that happens to Americans when they come to Paris—they come back next year."

She packed and suddenly was gone, rolling over the waves, her head and body burning, her tongue running on, laughing, asking; and at night she thought of curious things. It bored her to fancy anything; but she had a fancy, that she would like to jump into the dark sea's water and swim. It was a long time since she had had a good swim, because of the rash on her back; but in the dark, in the wave, who could see? She would be alone, free, borne up, delighted.

"What have I done? What is the matter with me?"

And in her mind she returned with weariness to the hideous

fever of the man-woman struggle in New York, necessary, terrifying, endless, ugly. She had to take part again because she was a desirable girl, in the insatiable checked licence, checked by cunning and calculation; in the lascivious longing, squalid fun; go back to dissatisfaction and cynicism, horror and fear, doubting; every hour the prey of a mad Venus, cruel with delay.

"Well, Mommy, here I am again, come back to plague you. Do you think we should go and live in Paris? You used to study music there. You would get young again. I thought of you all the time; and I thought how selfish I am. Oh, no, I didn't get engaged; I didn't even look for the Frenchman I told you about; I didn't go near his office. The French take love so seriously, I should have been involved. I had no time anyway. I saw nothing. I can't tell you what the streets looked like. But I had such a good time and went out with plenty of people; so many beaux, Mommy, it was exhausting. Oh, what's the news, the good old news?"

"Your Aunt Di's in hospital. Oh, I feel terrible. She was in a car crash in New Jersey and they've brought her in. Do you think we ought to go and see her? I must go and ask after my own sister."

Lydia said she thought it was no use and she didn't care about Aunt Diana; but her mother worried about it so much that the next day they both went to the Second Avenue hospital and sent in their names on a slip of paper. A nurse came back almost at once; the sick woman said she didn't know the name, didn't know them.

"But she is my sister, my elder sister; I must see her. You see, we quarrelled and she is bitter, but I know she's very ill and I want so much to make it up."

Hester was a sparkling black and white and rosy little woman; she breathed generosity and affection. The nurse went and returned; but this time she was stiff and sharp. The patient said she did not know them and would be annoyed by strangers who thought she had a will to make: "I suppose they read it in the papers."

"I can't believe it! How could she say it? What were her words, Nurse? I have been a nurse myself, I know that patients can be very cantankerous and queer when they've had a severe shock."

The nurse unbent a little, a faint doubt in her face. "Oh, Nurse, what did Aunt Di say?"

"She said you were impostors who know she has money to leave. You must not insist; the patient won't see you."

Diana was on the danger list; then she died. In her will, she left five thousand dollars to her niece if Lydia would leave her mother's home. Hester was not to attend the funeral. The rest of the money—more than they expected, for she had done well in the stock market, she left to a doctor in the hospital. "He is the only person I have been able to trust since I was four years old; he taught me to trust people again."

"Five thousand dollars left to me! I can't believe it. Oh, it's so ridiculous. People are so ridiculous. Did she think I'd leave you, Mommy? People are crazy."

"She said I was not to go to the funeral and I did not go, but it looked funny. People will think I bore her a grudge. It looked so cruel. My only sister. She has got people believing that I ruined her life. I took her sweetheart and then I took his life and the life of my own child. Do you know, kiddo, I never hurt a fly. But I don't cut any ice with people. Diana had so much character."

"All strong characters are bad. You're not, you're a failure, Mommy." They laughed nervously. "What an idea! Creeping up the fire-escape to see my own Mommy. The midnight visitor. Don't worry, Mommy."

"Well, darling, it's a lot of money and I have to leave you soon; it might be any day. I think you'll get married when I die. It's me keeping you from getting married. You ought to live alone. You bring men here, and I can't go out and leave the place free for you; it doesn't look nice. I lived abroad all those years, but I was old-fashioned. Diana was a modern woman always."

"Oh, baloney! If she thinks she is going to do this to us—the claw from the grisly grave. Ah-ha-ha! Whew! It's gruesome. It's funny. Oh, I probably won't marry anyway." She was silent for a long while, then said, "Do you know, Mommy, I am going to that hospital and I'm going to see that doctor."

Hester looked frightened. "Oh, no, darling."

"I want to see the kind of man."

Lydia went to the hospital and saw the doctor, a tall, burly, dark, middle-aged man, with glasses, eagerly energetic, imposing, with an amusing street style. While they talked, she was looking at him, musing; her fierce, independent aunt, on her deathbed, had loved this man. How funny he was! "Your aunt had energy; what a worker she was! She was full of fun! She thought I would cure her; I didn't," he said, in a gentle, simple way. The doctor walked her to the door. "Of course I'll give the money to the hospital," he said.

She came away very thoughtful.

"What was he like, darling?"

"I don't know. I can't really tell you."

"I thought we'd have a good laugh over him," said her mother mirthfully. "What must he be like for Di to fall for him! A squib; she liked to dominate."

At last she said, "Mommy, he was a nice man; very kind. Aunt Di was right. And he admired Aunt Di; he said she was full of fun."

"I can't believe it."

"Mommy, we laugh too much, don't we?"

"We have to laugh, kiddo. I cried for years after they died. At first I stayed up all night playing patience; I couldn't sleep at all. Then I would sleep and dream I was talking to your father, that our family life went on. I would wake up and find he had gone, they had all gone but you. And you were very sad, you were such a doleful thing, a wet blanket." She suddenly laughed. "So, kiddo, I had to start; and I knew nothing."

"Mommy! I am going to find a man I can give all my money to, like Aunt Di did. We thought she was a stick; a ridiculous old scarecrow, didn't we?" They both began to laugh. "I am a stick, Mommy, oh, I am such a stick."

Her mother gave musical evenings; they invited their friends and young men. They prepared a variety of rich dishes, both being good cooks. The guests could look at the pieces of rare furniture and a cabinet of old china and jewellery which they had kept from Hester's marriage. The year passed. They heard that Tamara had committed suicide and that her lover and his wife had made it up.

"The money had given out," said Lydia. Spring came. Lydia was very tired. Her mother could not get away from her work; so Lydia went alone to Saint Augustine, Florida, a place that Peggy had raved about, when they were in Paris. She was very disappointed: the hotel was empty. There were no noisy visitors, lively crowds. She tapped along in her New York clothes, and she knew that at sunset it looked like a town in the *Arabian Nights*, but she did not care for sights; and when she walked along one of the roads, she heard noises. "What's that?" she asked a passing man. "Rattlesnakes." She hurried back to the hotel.

There was a long strip of fine beach, no one on it but an eagle with feathered boots looking at a sand-dollar. She walked from it back to the hotel.

After a few days, she decided that Miami was the place she really wanted. She walked out on her last evening towards the St. John's River, where the bridge crosses to a small sandy island. Walking about lonely was a stately young man of athletic build, fair haired and well dressed. After a few paces, she called to him and they walked along together; but she did not chatter in her usual way. She was quite serious and somewhat plaintive. She stayed on and they passed several days together. He found out her age and said, startled: "But why aren't you married? I can't understand it, a beautiful girl like you." He walked along for a time without saying anything more; and at last, "How do you explain it?" He already knew her family history, that she had some money, a good job, that she was well educated.

"I have never been able to trust a man. It is very foolish of me," she said. "I want a man I can trust always. I want to rest with him and never to be anxious again. Oh, I have had such a wretched life; perhaps I don't understand men."

"Have you ever been ill, nervously ill?"

She laughed. "You mean am I crazy? Oh, no, Arthur; oh, how ridiculous!"

"I can't understand it then."

She was at her ease with him, looked forward to seeing him and was not in a fever. They took the same train back to New York.

But she did not hear from him. She told her mother about him, adding, "He probably thinks I'm crazy or there's something wrong with me. Otherwise I should have been snapped up long ago." She began to laugh hysterically.

Two months later, he telephoned her in the evening. "Will you have dinner with me?" She had meant to turn him down, if ever he telephoned, but instead she said, "Yes." She went straight to the restaurant and they spent a quiet evening. He did not ask about her mother. In the weekend, he took her out to his home, a house on Long Island. He was a bachelor, aged thirty-eight, who collected art treasures and studied the 'cello. He played for her: he was an artist. "Sometimes I have a few friends here; we make up a quartet." "Do you go to concerts?" "No; sometimes I get an orchestra to come here." She saw that he was very rich; and the quiet house with the servants, his own independent, eccentric absorption pleased her. He was quite amusing when alone with her. He took her home but would not go in to see her mother. "I think I know your mother now," he said. She did not expect to hear from him again; and even this, though she felt disappointment, left her with a feeling of calm. For the first time, she was resigned to her life. "What a funny man not to want to see your Mommy! Did you quarrel?" "No." "What's he like, kiddo? Come, tell me, and we'll have a good laugh." "I don't want to talk about him, Mommy. Supposing he never telephones again? More water under the bridge! I wish I could go swimming. I couldn't go at Saint Augustine: it was too cold and I couldn't go swimming on that lonely beach. It is so quiet out there at his place; and it's by the Sound. I could swim there." "Well, some day in summer he'll ask you out."

The following week he telephoned again. They met in the same restaurant; and as soon as they sat down, he asked her to marry him. "I've thought about it for two months and I couldn't believe it; but I feel sure. I couldn't understand why you weren't married. I thought there must be something wrong with you. I was looking for a woman when I met you; but I never imagined I'd meet you."

She said yes, at once.

"I've thought about you and your life and I've made up my mind what I am going to do."

She listened and did not laugh. It seemed to her that he had found the solution; what he said was quite right. She was going to be happy. Her mother was invited to the engagement party which he gave; but he did not speak to her. "I don't understand it: why couldn't he say he was glad to know me, that he was grateful to me for bringing him his wife? He needn't have meant it; but it would have been a few words I would have been glad to hear." And little by little, patiently but with determination, he met her old friends, was good to them and discarded them. Presently it was as if her old life had never been; and she had grown up in his house; and it was many years before she thought about their union or found anything in it extraordinary.

The Rightangled Creek

A SORT OF GHOST STORY

The road rises steeply from Lambertville on the Delaware, into hill country, bared for planting and grazing, with small old white villages in trees and unpainted farmhouses high on the ridges. The road follows the uplands. Several miles along, entering Newbold Township, a track turns right and down by Will Newbold's red barn, a landmark. The track drops between Newbold's home patch and the pasture for their famous red and white herd; and, on the other side, some acres of corn and alfalfa. It drops into trees between stony ridges on which live poor Austrian and German farmers, down to a narrow creek. This tiny creek first appears as a meander in a wet place, and then as a wallow, where a broad soft meadow declines into swamp, where Sobieski's black and white cattle lounge all day in a hemicycle of trees, till they are called in the evening, Cow, cow, cow, by Sobieski's little boys. Above, it becomes a creek, falling from a series of rocky saucers from which the transparent water drips between banks of poison ivy, elder and tiger lilies. In the saucers are elvers and other small fish; and where the track and the creek together make a rightangled turn and go east, a trickle from the Strassers' rocky infertile ridge has made a deep cut, passing under a strong wooden bridge in which there is a loose plank. This plank is kept loose at one end to tell who is passing: a footstep, *lunk!* a car, *lonk-lonk!* It is heard in the daytime in the fields; at night, much louder, it wakes from sleep: "Who is that, so late?" But it is above this thin trickle from the hill and going higher and eastward that the creek broadens to several feet, deepens to eighteen inches and more, and threaded with current, planted with waterweed is lively with eels, fish and watersnake. Now, with a wooded ridge on the right hand, on the left it has turned around a small patch of cleared bottomland, on which stands a double cottage, Pennsylvania style, and a big barn. A solid wooden bridge crosses from the road into this clearing, under a magnificent pin-oak and a few other trees, beside the barn; and this clearing of not more than two acres of bottomland, fenced off from Sobieski's rising rounded meadows, with the right angling creek, coming along a panhandle from Sobieski's cattle-wallow and running east suddenly along another panhandle, turning all around Sobieski's hill, getting deeper and wider under heavier and more tangled bushes, is Dilley's place. For some strange reason, the whole creek in this corner belongs to a piece of land too small to farm; and on this tiny piece of land stands a new barn large enough for a tractor and farm machinery and the well-built house, part stone, with stone cellar and attic, part wood with double porches and upper storey.

"That's it," said the taxi-driver to his one passenger, a stubby dark man with bright blue eyes. They passed the cattle-wallow, the car hobbling over ruts and stones, they entered a passage of tall trees, not disturbing two immense affable ravens on the first half-dead, sky-searching bough. Low set in the green, below the pouring ivy and lightblow of tiger lilies, ahead through thick leaves, was the cottage, with a set of shining windows. All the other farmhouses bare on the hilltop were blistered and weathered bone-white or raw; this one was fresh in buff and red. Ringed with high fields, waters, trees and overgrown ridges, with its lines flowing towards the brook, low set and like a pumpkin flower, the cottage was spellbinding. The April afternoon was rather quiet. A flock of gold canaries flew through tall weeds. Between the weeds and the creek

102

a lanky soft-moulded woman in turban and trousers, with a heavy fork was trying to turn the sods, in an irregular vegetable patch: a fine day, a west wind, a paper-chase of torn cloud blowing over, and coolness with the shadows. The house had two porches, two pitched roofs and, at the back two tall stone chimneys. The spring sun with the birds bathing in it lay on the track. They passed the warning plank, and a large mail box on a post with the name: Laban Davies.

Said the passenger: "Put me down here. I'll give them a surprise. I came straight here from Paris. They don't know I'm in America. I knew Mr. and Mrs. Davies in Paris. We're old friends. They'll be glad to see me. My name's Sam Parsons. If I stay here, you'll see me around, my friend."

"I see Mr. Davies often in Lambertville when he goes to mail his packages," said the taxi-driver. "My name's Newbold."

Parsons crossed the bridge, which was the only entrance into the place, crossed the tussocks and stones, dropped his little valise by the open kitchen door, went around the house, creekside; but the woman in the vegetable patch, her tired face turned away, did not hear him above the wind and water. Parsons approached smiling, waited, came closer, walked up to the edge of the fresh sods. The woman went on pushing the fork with her sandalled foot, she stooped to pick out a vineroot, threw it on the burning pile.

"Hello, Ruth, hello!"

With her foot on the fork, she looked up, looked into his face with dull anxiety. He was a dark mass against the sun. She took off her spectacles.

"Sam! Oh, my stars! How did you get here?" She began to laugh, showing her strong white teeth.

"I thought you were in Europe! Oh, wait till Laban sees you! Oh, Sam, oh, my brother."

Sam laughed and waved his hands, his wide mouth opened, showing his buck teeth, creamy and broad, and his wide throat: his blue eyes opened and shut.

She was pumping his hand and beginning to weep. He kissed her.

"Here I am, yes, here I am! Not there, here! Ruth, my sister. Ha-ha-ha. What's the matter, old girl?"

"Oh, Sam, you helped us, you helped us. We've never forgotten."

"It was nothing. I was broke that time and couldn't help you much."

"Oh, Frankie has never forgotten. He wanted to stay in Paris, with the man with the money, you remember, the man with the money?"

"The man with all the money—ha-ha!"

"Excuse me calling you my brother, Sam; I feel like that."

"Ha-ha-ha—I feel as if you're my sister. Ha-ha."

"How did you find us? No one knows we're here."

"Don't you remember you sent us a Christmas card last Christmas?"

"Did I? It was a hard winter, Sam," said she. "Where's Clare, but where's Clare?" she continued suddenly looking everywhere, to the porch, the tall weeds. "Oh, she's hiding! Oh, what a surprise," and she began to laugh.

"Clare's in New York: she'll be down. I don't leave my wife behind when I travel."

"Some do, but you wouldn't," said Ruth.

They entered the framehouse by the downstream porch.

"This is a typical way of building round here," said the woman. "A farmer builds himself a framehouse and when the son grows up, he builds on a stone one for the young couple. You see it more across the river in Pennsylvania than here."

In the wooden house there was only one room downstairs, the big farm kitchen with its two doors, two porches, a long range of windows warm with the sun and warm with the big wood-and-coal stove with its double oven, standing in the centre. There was a table, a few chairs, some tubs, a sink and a pump beside it. "We save money here, I do everything," she said in her warm round voice in which there was a strident note. On the stove was a white enamel coffee pot; on the table a thick white cup half full of cold black coffee. There was also a closet; but this turned out to contain a staircase leading to the second-storey rooms in the wooden house. Ruth called and explained pleasantly.

"Laban, it's Sam!"

Footsteps irregularly came down the stairs somewhere in the house, though there was no one there. "There's another staircase; it's in the stone house." They went up a step into the stone house.

The sitting-room there had only two small windows and was dark. Laban stood there, a couple of yards from the doorway, looking at them; and then rushed forward with his big hands outstretched, crying, "Sam!" and kissed Sam on both cheeks.

"I couldn't think who Sam was! I'm working and not to be disturbed. Company's not good for me. I mean some company; the sort we're likely to get."

He was a tall thin countryman, in slippers, bare elbows, spectacles, a home-knit waistcoat. His fair hair was thin and turning grey, the large hollow eyes were a transparent blue; he had a knife-edged nose and hollow cheeks. A horrible scar ran from below the ear on the left side of his face up into the scalp, which was bare at that place. The flesh had knitted roughly in the old wound.

They sat down at the table and drank black coffee from the white enamel pot. It was on the stove all day for Laban, who drank three or four pots a day—bad for his heart, but it kept him at work. He was working well now. They had taken the farm for two years at twelve dollars a month, a very low rent. They had been lodging over in the artists' colony on the Delaware, New Hope on the Pennsylvania shore, and had seen this place, Dilley's place, advertised in a store. They had rented it from old Mr. Dilley who was retired, they believed, and lived in Jersey City. They lived on country produce, home-grown potatoes, little meat. If Laban's book, a history of European culture, sold, they might buy this place from old Mr. Dilley to have a home in the country for their boy, Frankie, who was now twelve years old, and who was to go to one of the big colleges.

Sam Parsons was a very lively man and had a lot to say about Paris, though Laban himself was in closer touch with literary people over there. He said in a dignified way, "You probably noticed my big mail box."

Sam had no fixed plans. He wanted to look around for a place for himself and his wife in New York City. The Davies said he must stay with them. They had plenty of room, three bedrooms upstairs, and even a small boxroom with windows that would do, when they got a couch. They bought their provisions in big quantities at the beginning of each month. Sam, who was a writer, and his wife, an illustrator, could work there. "You won't be disturbed." No one had this address but Laban's agent. "Lambertville is too near to New Hope. We never go to Lambertville, where Laban would be recognized. According to Jeroboam's wishes, Jeroboam being our twenty-dollar Ford, we shop each month in Flemington, Hopewell or even Princeton," Ruth explained.

It was to Princeton that they hoped to send Frankie, if they could buy the place and if Laban could sell enough. The only true drawback here was that Frankie had to go to the local school, eleven pupils taught by a young city girl, in a small shed. "We take him there in Jeroboam. The pupils are country boys and girls of all ages, mostly rough and backward, destined to be village gossips and wiseacres," said Laban. Frankie had easy victories: he deserved better teaching. But Laban's work came first this year. He had already completed one volume and had sent it off to Paris, asking a celebrated French scholar to write an introduction.

"With typical French negligence and improbity, a rascally, shallow nation, Lebeau, who wrote me such flattering letters in Paris, does not now even answer my letters. Naturally, if I could pay him, I would hear soon enough. But I can't pay; and I think scholars should help each other, without dirty money coming into it. He wrote me a letter recognizing me as one of the leading American cultural experts," said Laban. "Probably he flattered me, expecting me to put him over in this country."

But Laban began to smile. His spectacles shone, he became excited and went out to the barn, got out Jeroboam, took Parsons to get Frankie, all the time talking about his work, his contacts, literary life abroad. Laban was a self-taught man, a ditch-digger's son become a city desk man, turned to literature. Working with irritability, energy, spite, prejudice and vanity, and a nose for the trends, he had set up a remarkably wide circle of useful acquaintances in many countries. He brought out anthologies of writing in languages he could not read, re-translated famous works, wrote introductions to others; had built himself a solid reputation in America. These works were all potboilers; yet Laban had taste, judgment and cunning, and was a literary figure.

When Laban returned he showed his workroom, files, schedules, correspondence; and then the bedrooms. They kept all doors and windows open all the time, merely shutting the downstairs doors at night. The doors and windows all over the house commanded every part of their land; the track, the creek, the two bridges, the Sobieski cattle. "The Empress Eugenie and her court," said Laban. The cattle lounged handsomely under the trees on the grassy knoll beneath which the house lay. They were sheltered and surrounded by sweet waters and grasses.

No one had ever bothered them. Last winter had been dry and the roads easy. They had gone to distant towns for their groceries. The mailman came twice a day. They went to the Newbolds' to telephone. Frankie had friends at school, especially the fine little Sobieski boys who did all the work on the farm with their widowed mother; and the lively little Tanner boys, two Negro lads, sons of a very fine man who lived in the back streets and by hereditary right had the business of cleaning the outhouses for the whole community. Sometimes Frankie went with them to the Delaware and along to Trenton; at other times they explored the creeks and woodlands; or they got to know everyone in town; real boys.

"Frankie has got everyone tabbed," said his mother: "he knows everyone in Newbold Township as well as the doctor or the sheriff. He has political genius, Sam."

And the father said that, if his books sold, they could have two cars, one for Frankie at Princeton. "We can manage with another edition of Jeroboam."

Laban went back to work. Sam went to perambulate along the grassy track under old trees. He met Frankie with the two

Tanner boys. They were all going bird-nesting. Sam returned to the homestead with Frankie's thin hand in his short square one; and both talked politics. Frankie, last seen a big-eyed starveling of six, was unrecognizable in this self-confident stripling, with acid prattle, deliberate views. He referred to "the party line," criticized all writers of left literary bent if they deviated, as men will, from his stiff-necked views. But Sam laughed at him, the boy allowed his old charm to flash out; and they laughed, returning like a good-tempered child and a sensible man.

The days passed. The Davies were poor but would not allow their guest to provide anything. The first item in their budget was tyres and repairs to the old Ford; then, flour, potatoes, bacon, coffee, cigarettes, typewriter supplies and stamps; next, milk, eggs, and occasionally a fowl from Mrs. Sobieski on the hill. Mrs. Sobieski was Ruth's only friend in the district. The vegetable garden by the creek, with only Ruth to work in it, had not yielded. Laban went straight from bed and table to his desk. Frankie was being raised as a straight, clean American boy, with woodlore and boy's friendships; and ahead of him, his brain, his dizzying future. Ruth, the mother of them both, and now of three, cleaned, cooked and dug, worked the pump, chopped wood, brought coal, collected sticks, heated water and carried tubs, scrubbed linen, spread it and ironed it; fixed blinds, mended doors, carried food to the deep cellar. She had been a strong girl, brought up in jolly health, a success in a small town. Now she was overworked, uneasy and cranky: she saw dangers all around them. The Davies voted Democrat. Mr. Thornton, the rich farmer on the next hill, who collected their rent for the Dilleys, voted Republican. He and Will Newbold were heads of the local farmers' co-operative and charged the rate agreed, fourteen cents a quart for their pasteurized milk. They were all rich farmers, long established; some of the families went back over two hundred years in that district; some had first fraternized with the mild Leni Lenape.

Mrs. Sobieski, poor and a newcomer, like the Austrian and German farmers, did not belong to the co-operative, but sold her uninspected milk for eleven cents a quart. She was a young widow with six boys and a girl to bring up; she had to get rid of her farm produce around the neighbourhood. Ruth was preoccupied with these troubles. The farmers might use their own unpasteurized milk. The summer visitors were "typical bourgeois hygienic snobs" and would only buy pasteurized milk from the rich farmers. And there was a well-to-do German family living on the terraced ridge just below the Newbold farmers, who had plenty of water and spoke to no one, "typical Nazis." The Austrian farmers on the ridge opposite were shy, ignorant, peculiar people, too poor to get their cow serviced, so that it had bellowed all last summer rubbing its hungry flanks on the fence; you could see the hairy railings now. There were two black-eyed sulky full-grown sons, who went past without speaking and drove furiously to town on Saturday afternoons. Ruth, brought up in a town, was quite at home in all the cults and sects of any metropolitan society, and very uneasy here. Laban, bred in a farming community of the Middle West, was knowing and sarcastic about all his neighbours. Frankie learned all these opinions from his parents, and all the local news from the Tanner and Sobieski boys; and the three of them, anxious and hungry, lived in a ferment of distrust.

Sam Parsons was a great one for going to the mail box. He waited for the mailman at the other end of the track near the ravens' tree. Laban said, "If no newspaper comes and no letter, I don't worry. All I love is here. No radio, no local news, I don't care. If the cities go up in smoke, ditto. Nothing can happen to us here. Ruth is here and Frankie is here; and I am here. Ruth has no other interests but Frankie and me; and Frankie, when the time comes, will have all we can give him." Frankie, listening to this, leaned back in his chair, while his gaunt mother, in her turban and overalls, hustled between stove and table feeding the three men with toast, cereal and coffee.

"I'll have eggs this morning," said Frankie.

"Give him some eggs," said Laban.

"If he asks for them, he needs them," said she.

Frankie remarked, "I was in the post office at Ingalls yesterday with the Tanner boys, when a man came in to buy eggs. Don't buy eggs from Mrs. Smith, the postmistress here, I told him, she overcharges and she gets her eggs from the Strassers, they're Austrian dirt-farmers. Their hens come over into our farm all day and peck our grass. They're not properly fed. I'm always chasing them off. They get drowned in the creek sometimes. Those Strassers don't know how to farm and they overcharge. They belong to the Bund. Do you want to encourage Bundists, I asked him. They stick together, they cheat and they're enemies of the Republic. You must go to Lambertville, or go to Mrs. Sobieski's farm just along the road and you'll get eggs for twenty-three cents a dozen. They're not candled, but no need; she sells all she has. Mrs. Smith told me to get right out and said I had no right to spoil her trade; but I told her very plainly she had no right to cheat the public and that I wouldn't let her get away with it. I told her I'd make people aware. A friend of mine has a printing press in Lambertville, I told her that; and I said, if necessary I can have leaflets printed."

This was greeted with a silence that surprised Parsons. "How do you know the Strassers are Bundists?" he asked.

"They must be Bundists, they're Austrians and sulky bad people, too mean to spend a cent on their farm. The boys go to Lambertville every Saturday night and get drunk. You'll hear them coming home at two in the morning."

"That doesn't prove that they're Bundists," said Laban; "but they are, in fact, Bundists. I'm sure they vote Republican if they vote at all."

"I'm not going to allow Bundists round here to make a living," said the boy; "they've got to be driven out. I told Mrs. Smith I'd close her store if she kept on selling Bundist eggs. At any rate, the man was scared and he went out. Mrs. Smith said she'd make me pay for the lost sale. I said, No, indeed she wouldn't; and it wasn't the last dozen eggs I'd lose her."

Laban was leaning back looking his boy in the face and his own face was shining as if in the sun.

"Well, by gum, Frankie," said Sam, "aren't you ashamed to take the bread out of people's mouths? What crust, my lad! You're a twelve-year-old school kid and you go running about ruining people's business and uttering threats. Supposing Mrs. Smith came to the school and said, Don't teach Francis Davies, he's a numskull, I don't like his looks, put him on a stool in the corner."

Frankie laughed heartily at this. "Oh, it wouldn't work," he cried. Sam Parsons was laughing and the father smiled a little; but the poor mother did not like it. She said that the farmers in the co-op put an unjust price on the eggs, where her poor widowed friend could not get rid of all hers even at a cutthroat price. She was sabotaged; and as for the Strassers, who undersold the co-op, it was not the same thing, for they were European individualists, dirt-farmers, mean, dangerous, vindictive. Embittered by ill-luck, and their hard-won failures, they were ready to join the Bund at any moment: they formed a solid pro-Nazi bloc in spirit. If people did not stand with the Democrats, the Bundists and Mr. Thornton would turn Newbold Township into black reaction.

"But I happen to know that this section has been copperhead since the beginning; they're too durn sly to side with anyone," said Sam Parsons.

When the boy had gone out to play and they heard him hallooing innocently along the track with his friends, Ruth said kindly to Sam Parsons that they were careful not to make any attacks on Frankie's self-esteem; they wanted him to have a perfect sense of security, to be sure of their love. At school he was, of course, a prizewinner. He had a vivid imagination and he might easily have a nightmare tonight at the scene of disgrace evoked by Sam. "Supposing he dreamed of failure!"

"Surely no boy is as brittle as that!" said Parsons.

But the parents explained that Frankie was not like other boys, but a genius; and all his idiosyncrasy was only that of genius of a high order. He slept feverishly and often called out in his sleep; he dreamed about political enemies, thought he was making speeches. He had a particular ferocity against the "half-savage backward and medieval individualists" of this part of the country. This phrase Laban read from a diary which he kept of his son's remarks.

At each meal, the conversation turned to political matters; and while Laban listened and interjected, both men argued and the boy laid down the law, the mother, always on her feet, hurried from stove to table serving. The child developed his ideas. He listened in silent satisfaction, however, when his parents spoke about his future; but the reality of his genius, the certainty of his eminent future, was so often discussed and as a matter of course, that he had no fatuity. His future was a rather important fact in the future history of the country; he would possibly be President. Afterwards he ran about with the children of the hereditary outhouse cleaner and the Polish widow's sons, while the parents listened to his distant voice and yearned after the thin child running like a rabbit in the hills.

Laban said, "We don't feel any sacrifice is too great; we don't need anything ourselves; we have each other."

"You see," said the mother, hastily cleaning up the table and setting a fresh pot of black coffee between the men, "a boy like that especially must not be frustrated in any normal desire or deprived of any normal object. Satisfaction is release of energy, it is victory. That's why we want a good car for him, too. Here it's the symbol of achievement, it's the normal means of personal expression in this country; it's release of power for every individual; it means normal living. We were brought up with older symbols, symbols of poverty. But he must be normal in this age."

"Yes, in a few years Frankie will live in rooms in Princeton or Harvard and have his car and spend money. I would walk to Princeton or hitch-hike to Harvard to see him; and if, when I got there, I saw his car parked there and him in good clothes, a leader in his society, I would know that I was right in denying him nothing."

"You see, Laban knew what deprivation was. It didn't do him any good. It doesn't do any of us any good," she said, beginning to weep suddenly, but still hurrying with her work. "We blame Laban's troubles on his early frustrations: the struggle is too hard, too hard." She turned her back to them and began vigorously washing pot and pans.

"And for you," said Parsons, "why don't you go back to town? You mean—the rent?"

"It's for Laban: he's on the wagon," said Ruth, now cheerful again. "Back in town he gets into that drinking set. He wants to get his books done. He needs success: he needs fulfilment. Adversity was always bad for him. He needs recognition. No one knows where we are: and when we come out of the woods, Laban will have his reputation made. That's why we're so glad to see you. Laban has an intellectual equal in the house; and you never touch the booze."

Sam was very happy at this and talked for some time about how much coffee he drank and how it had been in his boyhood; as much coffee as you could drink at Child's, for a nickel; and how he almost bankrupted the place; and probably because of him they had changed the rule; and how, after meetings, when he was a boy, they had all gone to a Greek baker's, and over only one cup of coffee for a nickel, and perhaps a roll, they had talked till two or three in the morning. They could see that though he had been very poor, he had been happy and had had fulfilment.

In between his working-spells, Laban with Sam, in Jeroboam, scoured the low Jersey hills, past cornfields and barleyfields, lost farms where the cattle and farmers watered at an outdoor trough, where nothing was to be seen but low long fences, a big barn some-times broken, a shaky hovel surrounded by children, pigs, dogs. The river was now fat, the tasselled maize turned red, the wheat yellow, the wind blew dry, strong, the air was full of dust, pollen and mites. Laban would often stop halfway in a winding rutted track in a place free of trees in a yellow land, and snuff it up. In the distance, perhaps, would be the Delaware and the Pennsylvania hills turned yellow and red. Laban had then more of the hobbledehoy; he was full of shouting and joy; and in these days he brought out an old manuscript which he had written as a farm labourer. He then wrote of trees, moons, moonlit cornfields, long open stretches of bearing soil where he worked and grew dry; a man, a farm labourer lying dead drunk by the fence, in the silver, in the moon.

The two men would wait for young Frankie outside the school. In the morning, they would wait for Newbold the mailman, walking up and down the sunny track. "See the humming birds sitting on the twig: he's off and back quicker than the speed of sight," said Laban. Sam could not see so fast. Sometimes, they were off somewhere when the mailman sounded his horn for Laban's registered letters. One day when Sam returned from one of his walks, which always lay along the green tracks where the careless rabbits sat in the ruts, he found the Davies couple very nervous. Laban was drinking black coffee in a determined manner, and Ruth was sitting at the table rucking up the tablecloth with her fingers and talking hurriedly.

"Read it," said Laban, pushing a letter across the table to Sam. It was a scribble saying:

> *Ha, old Laban, you old horsethief! We just found out your hideaway from someone New Hope way who saw you scorching up the Jersey hills. We made enquiries of your mailman. We hear you're on the wagon; well we're coming to drag you off it. Expect us: we're on our way. The Rosses are throwing a big shindig Saturday: we all want you there! Tell the good grey mare we're coming to get you off the chain. Nuts to Ruth. What's the idea, chaining up the best drunk in the USA? Nuts. The Old Bunch.*

There followed a dozen signatures.

"I felt something impending," said Laban. "I felt anxiety."
"If you could go out and dig the potato patch," said his wife, "you might work it off; it's the mental concentration."

"I hate digging; I'm an ex-farmboy. If I stop writing and do physical work, I become what I was, as a boy on the farm in Illinois, anxious, troubled, a sort of black sterile perpetual insomnia in the daytime. My mind is awake; the back of your mind, which sleeps normally, wakes up in insomnia, is then awake all the time. There's anxiety and a sort of sinister grin too. *I know more than I let on.* Well, you want to drink to shut that terrible eye. They're right in one thing. I know the danger of cutting yourself off from men and living among the *ragged rocks and shivering shocks* of Nature. And society and work go together. Without communication I lose my working ability. The contrast between the world I've seen and those self-satisfied copperhead farmers and the clods on the ridges is too great. I have to shut my eyes to it. Every psychopathic drunk like me is an intensely dissatisfied and yearning man. He can trust no one and he longs for the simple rest a child or a woman or a dog has. People who can rest, sleep, as they innocently call it, are never fully awake even in the daytime. And life here is vegetation. A man wants more, much more. I have the will power to live as a recluse in this green prison, but I know what I am missing. The life of cities. The mind is like a city; it isn't like a clod. You don't know the agony of living by will power. What will power do you or Ruth need to stay off drink? I don't want to make out that I'm a moral hero. There's the physical and mental sickness to help you, the awful paralyzing weakness, the feeling, How can I ever get back to shore? I'm in the shallows only a few yards from shore, where I could lie down and drink in strength from the sun, but I can't get there; I'll never make it. If I ever get there, I'll do anything, live on bread and water for the rest of my life. And then there's the hate of drink! I loathe it. I must smoke," he continued stridently, "and smoking dries your throat and turns your tongue to pemmican; and I drown all that in black coffee. A man must turn out work, living like that. And we're eating badly now, saving for the boy. That's another reason I mustn't drink. Drink's a matter of physical need, that's what you don't know. You have a certain temperament, high strung, hungry, and your cells, your enzymes, I don't know what, are crying out for the one thing that will satisfy the one desire; and we haven't even enough food."

Sam Parsons, exceedingly embarrassed, said he ought to go to New York and look for a place for himself and his wife, see about getting some work; he oughtn't to be there. They had a little money still which they must not waste, but keep in reserve.

Laban hectored him, "Sam, you stay here and keep me from thinking about New York. I get the idea at times that they are all drinking and kidding around there and calling me names, saying I'm tied to apron-strings; and so I am, but I bless them for tying me." He paused, got up and kissed his wife. "My blessed chains. I bless you." He turned to Sam. "That's what they're saying when I'm here. They insult Ruth and I'm too cowardly to defend her. I agree with them; 'damn cow likes to graze.' They're a lousy lot. But I fool myself into thinking that if I were there I could sit on them, stop their sneering. This is a refuge, an asylum in both senses. I'm always glad when I get into hospital after a bout; I wish I could live in one. Once I wrote to an asylum to take me in; they wouldn't.

"The country is so damned dull with their quarrels and animosities over five cents, and who's a Republican. Who cares? Ruth and Frankie are getting sucked into it, too. That young fellow up at Strassers' skulking round that dry rock farm often looks as if he's going crazy. If I went to town I would worry about leaving Ruth here alone. He might go nuts in the middle of the week and start burning our house down. I know what's passing in his mind; it passed in mine. You know they've got no water. We're hogging it. All the water they use must come from that spring house that drips across the track back into our creek. I've dreamed that I've seen this place in flames, a fiery honeycomb," he said, exalted; "all we have is a leaky pump, although we own three-quarters of a mile of creek. It's the inconsistencies, stupidities, the smug imbecility of the country that gets an intelligent man down. It's all right for women and children if they've got a defence. I often thought of getting a big dog here to defend Ruth and Frankie; but if I did so, do you know what," he said with a bright smile, "I might go off to town. This way I stay here to look after them. That's what irritates me about Ruth's attitude. She quite openly thinks that I'm straining to get off the string. She doesn't understand that I'm thinking of her and Frankie day and night. She doesn't realize that no decent man would go away and leave them in a place like this, without a gate or fence, with all those doors and windows; with the crazy Strasser boys and trucks full of farm workers going about on the road and the hot summer coming. The other day a truck full of boys about seventeen, eighteen, sex-crazy youngsters, stopped by our bridge and three of them walked right into our kitchen and took a drink of water. They stood there by the sink pumping water and drinking pints of it, pouring it down their throats. I was on the track, Frankie was at school, Ruth was upstairs making the beds.

You know Ruth. She's not afraid of men, used to be a good-time gal. But she was afraid. She came down and asked them what they were doing there. They looked her over for a long minute, and they walked out without saying a word. When I came home she cried on my chest. Ruth!"

"Well, I have to hang out the washing," said Ruth; and she went out with the basket.

Laban laughed and said, "It would drive you to drink! It's all a worry to me. But the city's hopeless for us. I go along seven or eight months and hate the sight and sound of it; and then I backslide and hell opens. I'm a pathological drunk like Poe, you see; one glass—you think I'm weak-willed probably."

"No, I don't, Laban. I assume there's a factor unknown to me."

"I'm not an ordinary sot. It's another dimension. One glass—and I'm off on those joyrides you dream about as a child, *up the airy mountain, down the rushy glen,* in an airborne toboggan, flying, the rushing frightening joy that people buy for ten cents on the loop-the-loops. One glass of ordinary red ink and no one knows how long it will last; as long as it takes to make me a sodden, spineless, helpless imitation of a human being, unable to use his tongue or his legs, crawling about the floor like a child of two."

Sam said nervously, hearing the ring of triumph in Laban's voice, "Love of drink is a strange thing. But there must be a great joy, release, excitement in it, when you feel superior to your troubles and to other people, I suppose."

Laban's voice, metallic, hurried on, "In the beginning, as a boy doing the farm chores, I drank greedily and with a certain amount of vanity and pleasure." After a pause, he said, with an underlit smile, "You see, I don't remember many things, many weeks, many months—long periods of my life don't exist for me. If I were under oath and after due reflection, I'd probably say something incredible. I loathe alcohol and I always did. I get an infernal brutish feeling that I'm injuring everyone and everything I ought to like and love, I'm a brute; and then, to hell with it. I never had any joy or excitement or release. Maybe I did. I get to a point where I'm above all such petty considerations as decency, morality, family, fame

117

and even success. I know why they egg me on, they don't want me to succeed. I'm a comment on their living when I escape and get to work." After a moment, he looked friendly towards his wife and said more cheerfully, "I never allow Frankie to taste it. In Europe they let children have beer or watered wine, but Frankie never had it. As a child I was terribly greedy for it. I drank a whole quart of homebrew on the way home one day and was picked up after a storm, senseless, frozen, wet through. It wasn't the only time; but you only die when your time is up; I survived everything. I've been able to make something of myself even with the curse, because I read a lot as a boy and I realized that I wasn't alone. So many great men have had a hankering or lust for liquor or whatever other artificial paradise: some such terrible blemish usually goes with genius. So I'm afraid for Frankie: because of the father in his blood."

Sam Parsons said he wasn't a genius, but he had read somewhere, some Frenchman had said that genius was the control of disorders and blemishes, just as Laban himself thought.

"Well," said Laban, "you are right, that thought helped me. And I think America's a land to live for. I naturally believe in the future of men; and I believe in myself; and I have the youngster, I believe in him. So what have I to worry about, except an accident of temptation, which I avoid? And I thank God every moment for Ruth. She did more for me than my own mother."

Parsons tried to bring the conversation back to America's future; but Laban laughed poignantly, to say, "My mother's old folks were very religious people; but they took their moonshine and their Bible in equal parts. Religion wasn't my brand. I have got to believe in society, social destiny in our people. That gives me something to give Frankie. My poor father had nothing to give me. He was not much better off, and not as well regarded as Mr. Tanner in Lambertville. When he found out what a present I had got from the old folks, blood ninety per cent cornjuice, he just gave me up."

While this conversation had been going on, the men had risen from the table, and had walked up and down the track from the ravens to the rabbits.

When they returned, Ruth was looking for them, as she sat with Frankie in her lap, on the southern porch facing the rustic bridge. She beamed.

Laban kissed her and his son, and remarked, "Boaz has got his Ruth. Whither thou goest there will I go. What did I ever do, Ruth, to deserve you and Frankie? In all my dreams as a young country poet, I never thought of such a perfect afternoon as this, *so cool, so calm, so bright,* this green paradise, this home. I laboured in the stormy seas, but I got a toehold on good land at the other side: I am safe home now."

He went upstairs and began writing. Ruth walked out to dig in the vegetable garden. Parsons stood beside, watching.

Ruth said, "I am going to bake our own bread, to save money. I can manage better than I do. Laban is such a good man, such a good man! I never knew there were really good men till I met Laban. I knew there were good fellows, friends, but Laban was something else; almost a saint, I assure you, Sam. He writes me such beautiful letters when he's away. I'll get them out and show them to you. One day they'll be printed. He's never written me a cruel word."

A moment later, she said drily, referring to the time Parsons knew of, "And yet, Sam, that same summer, when you had to buy my boat-ticket home, he went to my father and borrowed six hundred dollars to bring us over; and he used up all that money in six weeks and was destitute when I found him in the hospital. I had to borrow another hundred dollars to start again. He knew, when he came over, that Frankie and I were starving in Europe, in a ruinous stone hut in a village no peasant would live in. We had not the money for eggs or milk."

The next afternoon Laban wanted to walk with Parsons to Lambertville to mail letters and get newspapers. It was a good two-mile walk, up and down, either way; they went by the back way, the green road, past Thornton's, as the bulls were then dangerous up by Newbold's and Sobieski's.

Laban broke into their usual political comments, "You asked me about the pleasure of drink only yesterday; and today I can give you a good picture of it. Last night I dreamed I had taken a glass of

119

the old poisonous slop I used to get as a boy on the farm; and the bottle was standing just out of reach, on top of the outhouse among the wild grapevines; it was the very image of desire. I held the glass in my hand. It was full and glowed like a jewel and the bottle when I looked at it with such desire, delightful, hopeful and hopeless passionate desire, glowed in blue and yellow, absinthe jewels. The drink was very real: it's real to me now. The way I am now, the mere sniff of a dirty old Third Avenue saloon with its mixed smell of sawdust, lethal alcohol and piss would send me raving with delight. Yes, delight and horror; there's delight in it and the utmost limit of horror. Most people don't know what horror is. They talk of it—the horror of the Nazis, the horror of crimes; this is loathsome, that is terrible: they simply don't know. In fact, I wonder how can you be a poet and know the just measure of words and emotions without being a drunkard—a hopeless drunkard like me. I'm glad you're here; and I'm here. As soon as I'd taken that fatal glass in my dream last night, I heard voices shouting, and hissing and singing like a thin musical saw, a saw about two inches long. I saw a cornbin on a bare hill; and this bin was done in rustic style, with a rustic railing round the porch and pieces of wood fitted together to read M—A—D; and voices were singing away over the hill, down the sky in a shouting chorus, 'In-sane, in-sane, in-sane.' I woke up and looked beside the bed and there saw a nest of fluorescent snakes coiling where Ruth had put her stockings. You know the barmen are very clever to put bottles on glass shelves with glass behind them. It's fascinating. If even a drop of water had touched my lips then, it would have turned to whisky, just from my burning desire and I should have been out raging today."

"You had the DT's just from a dream?" remonstrated Sam.

A cold bitter smile was on Laban's lips. "You people call that the DT's. As you can imagine, I'm a specialist. That's a very light hallucination. Why some bad drunks are committed to the madhouse without knowing genuine DT's. There's no imagination in the bottle that you didn't put there. Naturally, with my temperament and visions, a poet, I have very out-of-the-way hallucinosis."

"Don't let's talk about it," said Sam: "it's not good for you."

"The dream's in me: let me talk it out."

"Don't dwell on it."

Laban took his arm in a hard grip, "No, no, it drives me on. Ruth must never know I'm in this condition."

"Let us talk about literature and history. It's better for you. Try to control yourself."

Laban laughed and pointed to his scar. "Ruth told you I got this scar in the First World War. She used to believe that too. One cold Christmas I was out with a friend, from one place to another where they made their own stuff, during prohibition, and we came to a country druggist's who had a kind of general store. He had the stuff in barrels. He was always half-blind, not with liquor, but from drugs from his own store; and he loved people to come to him, he loved to destroy others. There he sat like a blind barn owl and motioned us inside. Inside was a cabinet where I knew he kept his home-made whisky. Our host couldn't move; we helped ourselves. I don't know what happened after that, but we heard howling and screaming about the countryside that night; and next day I was picked up beside a barbed-wire fence along which I had been dragged." After a pause: "Not that this is my only scar. Hard work on the farms such as I did not only as a boy younger than Frankie, but all the time I was working my way through college—and the fact that I felt obliged to drink because I soon became famous for it—well, that accounts for my obsession. It's like the obsession of a mother like Ruth with her children: I am one of them. What she has gone through for us has turned her from a normal woman into a sort of lunatic, part prison warder and part village sibyl. You know how madhouse warders are all of turned wits. And every year it grows in me, getting bigger like an oak, stronger. I want you to see what I have in me, my will power. It's abnormal, like my vice. How can a man like you who doesn't care if he never sees a drop, understand the need I have to talk about it? Mustn't a lover talk about his love?"

Sam was silent with disgust and fear.

"If I wrote down my dreams, or rather my hallucinosis," said Laban, "they would rank with the stories of Poe. I once thought

I saw my mother standing in the doorway in grave-wax, her grey and white hair around her woven into a coat and crying that I had killed her. That's hackneyed, isn't it? I once dreamed—"

"Do me a favour, Laban, and don't tell me any more of this graveyard poetry. I'm not quite the pachyderm you think. I can't take it. My mother is dead, too."

Laban smirked. Neither made an attempt to lengthen the walk, but returned straight to the house. Laban took a jugful of coffee upstairs, shouting to Ruth to put on more. They had a gay supper, and Frankie was allowed to sit up late talking politics. Everyone was happy, Laban in his best mood, penetrating, considerate, balanced. He condemned the Fascists and their "watchdogs and lapdogs of the pen," and he named names—all those who sold their pens. He showed how the ideas of the corporate state and of the brown-shirted horde were essentially incompatible with true writing. Of the four at the table, only Frankie did not know that upstairs in a velvet-lined case in a box was the jewelled cross on a ribbon; and that with it the former farmboy, following Ezra Pound to Italy, dreaming of glory, and flattered by the empty-heads around Mussolini, had acquired a title in a Fascist order. The honest radical scholar, the poor farmboy could not give up this secret jewel.

In the morning, Laban came down from his workroom with spectacles on, looking fussy and saying that his agent had written a ruinous contract, giving fifty per cent of Hollywood sales to his publisher.

"That's quite normal," said Parsons: "that is in my contract too."

Laban withered him with a glance. "These ten per cent bastards are working for the publishers, though we pay them out of our thin purses. They get into a huddle at cocktail parties, kill themselves laughing at the pretensions of authors. What chance do I stand living in the back of beyond? I am classed with the other daydreaming hicks."

"Write him a sharp note," said Ruth.

"I'll have to go to New York to straighten things out: they throw your notes into the trash basket. Author equals moron." Ruth and Laban had rancorous words. In the end Ruth won. Laban went up to Newbold's and telephoned his agent.

The next evening, a Wednesday, after dark, they were having a light meal in the kitchen, when they heard a car bumping along the track; and shouting and whistling. It was all quite clear, at a distance, in the still gully. The car stopped below Strassers', men got out and there was a lot of shouting, which sounded like "Laban! Laban Davies!" A man evidently fell into the bushes by the creek, was pulled out and the car struggled forward. "A bunch of drunks," said Parsons. Laban was sitting upright and still, his odd long round-eyed face staring at a window which faced the creek.

Ruth cried, "They've come!"

Laban remained motionless, excited, staring.

"All of you go upstairs at once," said Parsons; "I'll say you're not here." He got up, pulled down all the blinds, starting with the ones facing the creek. When they were down, the family hurried through the door into the stone house, which was dark and so up the enclosed stairway of the stone house. The house was now in midsummer screened from the road by the trees. The taxi with the visitors had to make the full turn around the rightangled creek to reach Dilley's wooden bridge, the only entrance to the property. Sam observed the car from the door. It had stopped at the very beginning of the Dilleys' place and with pocketlights the visitors were surveying the creek for an entrance. The banks were smothered with poison ivy, an effective barrier. "Sit still and don't make a sound," said Sam, shutting every door of the stone house. The car started up again and was cautiously making its way over the track, avoiding the creek. Presently it thumped over the bridge with the loose plank and the shouting went on, the voices calling for Laban, all very clear in this hollow. Laban on the way upstairs had recognized voices. There was now not a sound from upstairs, where all was dark. Parsons had no more time than to partly clear the table, leaving only one place, his own, and push away the chairs, when the car, which had taxi lights, found its way over the Dilleys' bridge, and stopped by the barn. The men, all drunk, were arguing. The taxi-driver refused to go farther. There was nothing but tussocks and holes ahead. Two of the passengers got out, and, cursing and stumbling, shouting for Laban, they made for the house. Several others milled around the car, took a few steps, saw the creek, hesitated. Parsons stood at the door.

"Put on the porch light, you so-and-so," shouted one of the drunks.

"There's no porch light," called Sam in his resonant Mid-Western voice: "what is it you want, my friend?"

"What's the matter, you damn so-and-so, who are you? Where's Laban? The taxi-driver won't come any closer. What the hell sort of a dump is this?"

"What's the matter? Whom do you want, my friend?" cried Sam.

"Shut up, it's someone else," said the man behind, not so drunk.

"Where's Laban, Laban and Ruth?" asked the first drunk, arms spread to help him over the tussocks and stopping a short way from the porch.

Cheerfully, jolly Mid-Western Sam Parsons declared: "They've gone away, my friend. I'm sorry you had the trouble. Sorry to put you out. They've been gone two days. Went to stay with Ruth's people, in Springfield, Ohio. Where are you from, my friend?"

"Took a goddamn taxi all the way from New York," answered the drunk sulkily.

"Is there anything I can do for you?" cried Sam affectionately.

"What did they go for? Why the hell didn't they stay? Who are you anyway?" said the crestfallen merrymaker. Sam kept up his out-of-date jolly style, while one drunk argued with the other and with the taxi-driver, who said he was going to turn around and get back home.

"Well," said the drunk, "have you got a drink anyway?"

"I'm sorry, my friend, I never touch liquor."

"What the hell sort of a dump," muttered the drunk to himself; but he was so fuddled that he allowed himself to be taken by the sleeve and headed back to the taxi. A cheerful drunk shouted, "Where can we get a drink round here anyway?"

"Wait till I get the lamp," shouted Parsons with overwhelming good nature, "watch out or you'll be in the creek."

"This damn creek is everywhere," said one.

Taking the storm lantern, Parsons now hurried after them, apologizing comfortably and he reached the car, where the rest of the crew, all drunk, were pushing each other into the seats. "Go to Lambertville, go to Trenton, plenty of drinks there," cried Parsons cheerfully. "Go to New Hope, lots of friends of yours there, I expect." The car began backing and filling, the taxi-driver began grumbling and cursing, doors slammed and the car hobbled towards the bridge, Sam stood gaily waving the lantern and shouting, "Good-bye, boys, good-bye: better luck next time. Mind the turn, mind the creek." They got away. This time the little red lamp went faster and winked engagingly in and out of the greenery. Parsons took his lantern, went in and locked all the doors. What luck that they had been so drunk! What luck that not one knew the house. They could have taken it by storm. What luck that his breezy, plainsman manner had thrown them off. He went up the wooden stair into the second storey and found the mother, father and child sitting hand in hand on the iron bedstead in Laban's work-room, silent, their thin stomachs tucked in, their thin forms only visible by the pale light from the summer fields.

"We did not move the whole time," said Ruth. The child was silent. They went down, ate a few scraps of food, Laban drank only one cup of coffee and for once they went to bed early and almost in silence. Saying good-night, Ruth wrung Sam's hand and kissed him on both cheeks. "My brother!" She turned in the dark doorway, on the step to the stone house, and said, "You saved our family tonight."

"They would have taken me away by force," said Laban, pallid behind her and standing in the dark; "I'm strong but there were how many of them?—five or six?"

The next afternoon he walked with Sam and talked. "Have you had any more nightmares?"

"Oh, that phase is ended. Seeing the gang last night brought it home to me."

125

In the morning of the following Saturday, that is, two days later, Laban came downstairs new-washed, shaved, in his best tailormade light grey suit, his shoes polished, his hat on and his satchel in his hand. The hat was pulled down to partly hide his scar and he had a smooth superior smile. He said he was taking the ten-thirty bus to Trenton to catch the New York train. He had to see his agent. They were not to worry. He would be back not later than six or seven. Ruth, wiping her hands on her sacking apron, looked with worry at her husband, now an attractive New Yorker. Had he money, this and that, she asked.

Ruth was quiet all day, prepared a good evening meal; and Laban did not return that night. They locked the doors, but left the blinds up, with both kitchen lights on. Next day, from Newbold's, they telephoned the New York agent. He had not seen Laban. They waited while he telephoned others: no one had seen him. "I cannot telephone that crowd," said Ruth, "and let them know he's away. He may have stopped over somewhere and be back this morning." All day, as they waited, she talked about those men who had come in the taxi; and past events. "I met Laban at his own engagement party. As soon as he saw me, he knew the other affair was off; but he used to see that girl and I didn't feel I could stop him. I had taken him away from her." She showed Sam a letter she had got in Paris, when Laban was wandering around the countryside, lost, memoryless, brainless, a dreadful raving thing, eating nothing and craving any kind of alcohol, an obscene insulting letter signed by Laban and his friends. "Why did you keep it?" "He came back from there. That was our low point." Some of the names were those of well-known New York writers, some talented men. "But they're unable to quit because they're empty and cynical and they can't let anyone else get out. They love to see Laban changing from a man to an animal and from an animal to a log. They can talk about it for months."

The letter said:

"*Dear Ruth, As Laban says, Ruth my truth, you should have been with us last night though no one missed you,*

126

*least of all your dearly beloved Laban. He was hugging
Jenny tight but as usual paying even more attention to the
bottle. As for the bottle, he had it bad. When he was going
to drink out of the bottle he groaned out that it was blood
and when he spilled it he tried to drink the blood off
the counter, my blood, Ruth, my truth's blood, he said.
How's that for a beginning? He groaned, I'm drinking
blood! Oh, boy. We all had a time. Don't be counting the
minutes baby: he's going to be good this time—"*

and more.

Pinned to this faded letter was a note from Laban written in
pencil:

*"Oh, Ruth, borrow the money and come over and save
me. I love only you and Francis but I am on a spree
and cannot stop. I am sober now, but it is not over and
I need you. You are my angel, oh, thousands of angels say
your name around me; but save me. I don't know where
I was last night. My father came through the ceiling
and walked slowly past me, looking at me with disgust
and irony. He went on moving and moved past me.
I heard sobbing and I don't know if it was I. Perhaps
it was you. There was a vague face in front of me and
I heard voices of all kinds. You see what has happened
to me because I am alone. Take no notice of what you
hear. Remember I love you and Francis."*

Ruth looked on with dry eyes as Sam read these documents and
she remarked, "You see, I know he loves me; and so do they. And
it's inhuman joy to them to take him away from us and to kill him
with drink. They know he'll die of it some day. They want to be
there when Laban Davies dies."

They waited, in all, ten days. There was no news from any
quarter. "Let me go to New York and look for him." "Don't
leave me, Sam. There's something peculiar about this place. Do

you know I have an obsession that there's someone in the attic, a huge hairy man."

"No one could live in that attic," said Sam laughing.

"It's big enough: there's a huge room up there," she said. "There's no one there!"

"When you go out for walks on the track, Sam, in the morning especially, I feel sure he's there. I feel sure I'll hear him coming down the stairs." For the enclosed staircase in the stone house, which opened by glazed doors into the first and second stories, went on up to a clean and roomy attic, a well-lighted attic. "It's foolish of me to have such fancies; I'm not the type of woman."

In ten days Ruth did not weep and Frankie, though subdued, asked no questions. She encouraged her son to go out each day with the boys. The lights in the farm-kitchen blazed all night. They sat up late, with the blinds undrawn, talking. Ruth explained that they had never seen the owner, Mr. Dilley, a man about sixty-eight, a baker in Jersey City. He had put two thousand dollars' savings into the farm and borrowed the rest from a bank; total price four thousand dollars. It had come cheap because it had been run as a berry farm for a year or two by a brother and sister and had failed. She did not know who the original farmers were who had bought the creek and the fringe of Sobieski's land and built the double house on two acres. The Davies wanted to buy the place but had not yet the money. They paid the rent to Thornton, who knew Dilley, and now considered himself the estate manager. "He's always snooping around. He takes the rent but I'm not sure he gives an account of it to poor old Mr. Dilley."

"Is he poor?"

Ruth was puzzled. "I don't really know. Someone was ill, the wife I think. They don't want the place, but they hang on to it. It's hard to give up something you've acquired with your life savings."

"Thornton's pleasant to talk to, he's a shrewd modern man. He was telling me about his ten sons, all farmers."

"Oh, yes, he's very hail-fellow-well-met," said Ruth furiously; "but he always has an object."

Sam laughed.

Ruth snapped, "There's a lofty attitude in his friendly smile. You don't know how the yokel, the clod looks at city intellectuals."

"All I know is, he's very pleasant to me."

"Besides Laban, you're the only angel I know among men," said Ruth, and suddenly began to cry.

The ten nights passed and no figure came along the track. The thicketed meadow in which they lived led a simple life of its own without terrors. It was a hot fertile summer. The fire flies walked up all the windowpanes putting their lamps on and off; and with their sparks outlined the branches. One day Parsons went to New York and returned, without having found a trace of Davies. Ruth stayed there because at any time Laban might return and she was his truth. The boy, at first oppressed, soon began to treat Parsons as a father. They walked out, hand in hand, talking eagerly. They sat up late every night; till dawn the lights streamed out to leafy creek and track.

On the morning of the eleventh day, young Newbold the mailman blew his horn. Riding with him was a boy from the bus company. A man had been riding back and forth between Trenton and Lambertville for the last ten days, sometimes getting off at Trenton, sometimes coming straight back. He had slept a few times in the Lambertville bus-barn. He kept saying, at first, that he had to get home. He had been seen yesterday morning last. The boy went down with Ruth and Sam in Jeroboam; but when they reached the big bus-garage they found only a bus-conductor. He said the man in question, who did not know his name, was dressed in a cotton shirt and grey trousers, bareheaded and barefooted now, had gone off yesterday to see old Doctor Young, "the old doc who drinks." When they called upon Dr. Young at eleven this morning, the door was opened by a strong thick-set man, amiably drunk.

Dr. Young said,

"You see I am fond of liquor myself and I recognized how ill your husband was. He told me the sidewalk was—" He checked himself and continued, "I knew he needed a little rest; and I gave him a sedative. But his spree was not over. If I'd locked him in, you see, he might have gone out of his mind. He would have been locked in with his hallucinations. I had to go to my patients and when I came back he was gone."

The next morning Ruth left with her boy for New York. After she had left Frankie with a friend, she borrowed money and set out on her search for Laban, who might be anywhere in the States or might even have left the country. Sober, he would not borrow money; drunk, he was very ingenious.

Sam Parsons closed the farmhouse and gave the keys to Farmer Thornton. On his way, he looked back at the place through the first trees. Set back beyond the great pin-oak, the grasses, the round meadows, with old trees beyond, and by the potato patch, with weeds and native flowers grown shoulder high, and flocks of birds, gold, blue, red, feeding there, folded in by green hill, deep summer trees and dripping creek, Sam thought,

"I must remember how pretty it is; it's really enchanted; it smiles: it's a dream cottage. Clare would love it."

He went along the track and into the sunny stretch beside the blackberry bushes where there were this morning seven cottontails. They waited for him to come right up to them before they scattered. He passed Thornton's heavy-headed fields along and up the hill.

The next summer Sam and Clare Parsons took the cottage from the Davies who were now living in California. Mr. Dilley offered the cottage to them for a year for $150 and this they accepted. On a sunny June morning Mr. Thornton met them in front of Dilley's farmhouse with the keys and went around the place showing them with pride how clean it was. He had gone to the expense of putting new paper shades on all the windows. He soon left, saying he had ploughing to do, but they could call on him for everything—and, if they wanted it, he had milk for them at fourteen cents. "You will find it every morning and cream, too, in the springhouse," and he showed them his duckpond, his springhouse, his chicken run. The springhouse was a fresh little cave with ferns in it. A long letter was waiting for them from Ruth Davies, asking them to take Frankie for the summer, for Laban was working on his book. They had had a very difficult winter; the boy was pale and over-excited. The next year he would go to a camp "reserved for children of leaders" but this year he was too keen on politics, he couldn't sleep for thinking of politics; and they wanted him to roam the country with the Tanner and Sobieski boys again. "Let him be a barefoot boy with face of tan." Ruth enjoined them not to have any dealings with Thornton, but to get their dairy produce and chickens from Mrs. Sobieski, who was so cheap. She had, indeed, already written to Mrs. Sobieski about it.

They went up the hill to visit Mrs. Sobieski, a young good-humoured gold-haired plump slattern; and said they would take poultry and eggs but no milk. She was sitting in her kitchen, a wooden lean-to, peeling potatoes for her boys, and the farm-lad. She remarked joyously, "Don't worry about it. Sit down, have some lemon tea. I had a letter from Ruth, but don't think about it. Take the things from Thornton: he's not so bad; he'll like it better. Ruth always wanted to help me because I'm a widow with so many boys; but I'm a happy woman with all my boys. No hard feelings with anyone. I can sell all I grow; I sell it round. You don't have to buy my chickens; perhaps you don't like chickens." They parted on excellent terms. "We'll visit you—become friends," cried Sam Parsons. "Eh! You mustn't visit me, I'm too busy," she cried standing at last in the shaky doorway and waving her hand. "If you want to see me, drop in, but I can't visit." Off they went.

Parsons said, "So we are friends of everyone; and we will be left alone. You'll be happy here. Last summer I was thinking all the time, Clare would like it here, this is a nature-lover's ideal, a house sitting on the grass, completely open but inaccessible, neighbours on every hill but invisible, trees and fields all round, and as rich in birds and animals as a Breughel painting."

Clare laughed. "A Breughel painting! Well, not only the sleep of reason, but nature breeds horrors; and this is where you feel the multitudes, the creeping and running, the anthills and wasp nests, the earth breeding at every pore, there's a sort of horror in fertility and rioting insanity in the hot season. I love it."

"Yes, it is the place for you: you will be close to nature."

"But you don't like nature?"

"Why do you say that? I've learned to look at things and recognize a few. I'm not the bookish man I was."

"What I like about the house is it's so lowset that nature comes in on all sides, you see nothing else—the track only, but it's like occasional people passing behind the scenes. We're sitting on the stage and what's happening is animal life, faint sounds, the shrieking of the birds, trees cracking; you could be thousands of miles away from people and yet fields that have been ploughed for two hundred years are a few yards off and they can hear what we say in Strassers' springhouse."

The warm spring air was thick damp and breeding. There was no wind in the hollow. Sometimes it roared over them. Occasionally a car, boy or heavy animal passed over the bridge and the plank flopped. Though they were city people they had confidence in this silent sunny spot, beautiful from all angles. "It's spellbound." "You mean you are?" "No, it is." "Spellbound." "Joy and trust breathes out of it. And it's a bird sanctuary here, they say in town. Every bird is here that's been chased out of ploughland and uprooted woodland." "It's pure happiness here."

In the evening they unpacked. Clare opened a drawer in the kitchen table for the tableware; but they found a large assortment of cutlery. She spread all this on the big kitchen table; many carving knives, and many unshapely, blunt, notched, tarnished, ill-assorted and meaningless blades. She rolled all the knives into an old red cloth, pushed them to the back of the big old bread oven and set in front of them two old iron casseroles. Then there were quite usual objects, an axe and a hatchet for chopping the wood, behind the stove, then an axe that no doubt Mr. Thornton had put on the porch for them with the new wood and a boy's jack-knife thrust into a crack in the porch. She took all these to the barn and locked them in, sticking the jack-knife into a crack in a joist. Then she locked the empty barn and ran to the sitting-room of the stone house which contained very little furniture. There was an upright piano, a small table, a short wall cupboard cut into the wall and painted to resemble a curtained window. It contained part of a dinner service, and behind a large serving dish were a carving knife, fork and steel and several dinner knives. It looked as if everyone who had used the house had come fully equipped with knives. The wife was nervous and began to hurry, to get all done before Sam came in.

He was out on the track taking his last walk of the night. He would soon be in, certainly; for the mourning dove had begun his grieving and sobbing, a desolate sound in this sunken place now quickly filling with the dark. To Sam the mourning dove was horrible. She looked everywhere now, up the chimney, in the grate, under the divan, under the piano—nothing anywhere. Sitting in the kitchen, once more, hearing how someone trod on a loose plank, hearing the mourning dove, she thought of something. She lifted the piano lid and looked in. In fact, there was a hunter's knife in its sheath; the sheath was mouldy, the knife rusted. Clare thought it might be useful, so she put it with her own to polish it. That was all. Except that a few minutes after they went to bed, she remembered that she had not looked behind the divan or behind the piano. They had locked the doors and windows. She went down, unlocked the staircase door, went into the stone house and looked. Behind the piano she found another axe. She took it out to the barn, locked it in and came back. Out of doors she had no fears; it was a cool, slightly breathing night with many powdery stars. It was three nights later that she told Sam, as a joke. Sam was untenanted by premonitions and grisly fancies and feared them the more. But to Clare they were an unrecognized part of nature, like the faint sound of a spider scuttling under leaves, or a cat's footfalls. Few heard them; they were there.

The days passed; nature thickened around them. "The grass and the weeds need a-cuttin'," said Mr. Thornton, one fine summer morning. "I'll come down later with the scythe, or send Johnson." "Oh, leave them: we're not making a garden; we like things wild," said Sam. The weeds, white, yellow, purple, wild flowers and plants were so high that Sam could walk into them and be hidden. Here the birds clung and hunted. Plenty of small things ran about the ground in the shade. There were several woodchuck families in various parts of the Dilley creek banks, especially in the long strip of wild land along the Sobieski fields. The creek still was hidden there and there boys fished and swam all hidden, and the mocking birds had their nests. There were large and small burrows opening around the Dilley house, right at the porch and farther out. There were skunks; a weasel like a big swift worm dived and doubled into his hole by the steps. The birds reared full families and started again. Under the separated planks of the bridge was a black spider so large that it could be seen from three hundred yards away. It also was far sighted. It spied the Parsons coming at a distance and it ducked under the bridge, looked out, ducked in. The creek was full of life. Along the sunny track in the fresh mornings, little green snakes took the sun on the low green branches. A dozen little rabbits, or more, played on the track. Sam Parsons walked there talking to himself and switching the dust. Up and down he tramped. It was so silent, so fertile, so safe. No vehicle passed there, but the mailman at about nine, the Tanner boys on their bikes, or children after school. Sam Parsons thought over his past business relations, books he might write, about the Spanish Inquisition, the Forty-Five, the Commune; he looked at the flowers, remembering that he ought to learn about outward things too—this was a chicory, this a goldenrod, "our national flower, I should know it." That was poison oak and this poison ivy and that poison sumach. Clare had taught him those first. "Don't touch them." He was a big city boy. He was very proud the first time a bird answered his whistle. Sometimes a friendly but puzzled bird followed him along the track. "It was talking to me, we had quite a conversation," he would report.

At night they went to bed early and sometimes slept badly. They barred the house downstairs but the second storey was lower than the hill. They could hear animals passing above them on the hill, birds lower than they were, in a tree. At times the loose-plank bridge solemnly plonked; the owls howled; and there was the restlessness of the magnificent corn nights, the very sensible restlessness of the fast springing harvest, heads weighed down; and the lowing cattle. The house must have been full of field mice. Each night a skunk and its family passed under their window. The woman was awakened each night by the pungent smell and the knowledge that

134

animals were moving around them; she loved animals. It was a lake, a deep pool of animals, a deep pool filled to the top with air and in it animals, not fish. When the skunk smell came, all the mice within the walls scampered in a multitudinous rout down or up the walls. And often in the night now there were footfalls. These footfalls came from the landing outside their door and went down the stairs, one by one, to the bottom, thoughtfully, clumsily, almost reluctantly; and later would return one by one to the top, crossing the landing. But the door at the bottom of the stair they kept locked. It led to the kitchen.

She heard these footfalls several times without waking the man; but once when she heard his waking breathing, she said, "Listen to the footfalls. Of course, it is the mice! Or rats, do you think?"

"Yes, it is like footfalls; it must be mice, mustn't it? What else could it be?"

They listened for several nights. Downstairs the doors to both stairways, all the outside doors and windows were locked. The knives and axes were put away. They had no fear at all of intruders or assassins coming to them through the woods and fields, the lonely roads; they were happy and safe. But they always, at night, felt agitated, though not lonely. And there were the dreadful doves, driving Sam in before sunset, out of the damp, into the house to light the lamp; and so the nights began too early.

The days were perfect summer and still. The tiger lilies sprang all along the creek and in patches around the house. Sam walked to town every day to shop, talk to Thornton and "the boys"—acquaintances he had made in town; they heard the farmers and their lads at work behind the thick curtains of trees. Clare at home, did her work, tried the piano with the broken keys, heard the Strassers a few feet away on the ridge, noticed the many small birds rearing broods in the porches, woodpiles, weeds and trees. The house was a shed, a roof in which they ate and slept and into which the air and sun poured. They knew the house, the deep cellar under the stone house and the stone house's high attic, full of sun and dust, with old trunks—whose?—bikewheels, rubbish, a blameless place, looking out on the Sobieski pastures. At night the skunks, the cataracts of mice, the plonking plank and the footfalls.

But where did the mice lodge, they idly asked, that went hopping downstairs every night; and what did they eat in the kitchen, where all the food was put away? Or had they some other purpose? "I believe they come out of that little locked room: they cross and recross the landing from there."

"Leave it alone," said Sam; "they do us no harm." "But listen to that thumping!" "Let's sleep." *Plonk!* "Who's coming over the bridge so late?" "It's not late."

One day when Sam was in Lambertville, Clare found a key to fit the lock of the little room. It was an engaging little room, the prettiest in the house. The roof sloped to the floor. Two small windows, set at floor-level, surveyed the sweetest part of Dilley's acres: they looked down upon the green, the weed patch, in which birds flashed; and the clear shallow saucers of the brook surrounded by orange and white flowers could be seen; all swimming in the hollow full to the top with sun and the invisible but thick and moving damp. If you are an underwater swimmer and have visited rock-cities, floated over weedy and sandy bottoms which the fish know, looked down like a fish, that is the liquid sort of scene you see. It was scarcely twelve o'clock. It was still. The world was at work, men, beasts, plants; all was well; an unforgettable hour; the smiling heart of that ineffable house.

After a while, Clare looked at the room. In the centre of the bare floor was an old-fashioned leather trunk with a domed lid, attached by leather hinges and straps. The leather was discoloured, worn and scaly with age. There was a hat tree behind the door, an old locked wardrobe and a kerosene lamp. She was going out again when she noticed a leather belt hanging on the hat tree. It was of soft leather, with notched edges, about two and a half inches wide, awkwardly hand-embroidered with red, green and yellow wool; and red, green and yellow glass jewels had been let in, in a simple design: a stage property. She tried it on and put it back. She locked the door again.

There were many insects about now and in the silence their

multifarious life could be heard: wasps scraping wood off the rough wooden seat on the porch, some insects singing perhaps in their nests, bees humming, the immense horseflies droning, the interminable whipping chatter of the house-wrens and other tiny sounds about the house, half invaded and possessed by wild life; they poured out of the sun copiously on the earth, richest in this man-idle dell. There was one other sound which now Clare heard very often in the daytime, in the sun, when she was upstairs or downstairs, or had come close to the house from the fields, a singing or faint twanging in one of the corners of the porch or in the kitchen corner. It was larger than a mosquito's voice, not much more at first, but when she became accustomed to it, it became louder and more insistent; like a brass spider twanging on its brass web. The insects were so thick and noisy that the Parsons did not trouble themselves any more about them. They no longer sat on the porches, for there was, that year, a plague of flying mites, and in the evening, the mosquitoes. So they sat without lights till the light faded, and then went indoors, while up the windows crawled thick the winking fireflies. But she came to listen for the creature singing in a corner of the house, at its work or in its nest. Now she could hear it halfway from the creek, her ear sharper and sharper for the world of beasts and leaves.

In a few days, alone in the sunny silent morning, she returned to the little room upstairs. She undid the buckles and set back the heavy leather lid. The trunk was full. On top was a leather headband to match the leather belt, with stitching and glass jewels. With it were berets, headbands, short skirts, cloche hats, fashion magazines from many years before for out-of-date bridal dresses and baby clothes; and with this a pale brown cloth tunic roughly stitched. Underneath these was a white silk dress with lace and pearl beads sewn on it, a simple net veil and pearl circlet. The brown tunic was a fancy dress, unfinished. It was slashed into fringes around the opening and skirt and the skirt was decorated with the same glass jewels. Underneath these, several large feathers dyed, a man's khaki shirt, a Sam Browne belt and other relics of war days. Clare closed the trunk and locked the room. She sat down on the porch teasing the wonderful sensitive plant that grew there. It took it but one hour to move from one side to the other, as she moved an enticing walking-stick; towards the stick its corkscrew tendrils vibrated. On one side was a skunk's hole. The sensitive plant, after only a quarter of an hour, began a slow swoop upon the walking-stick, which she held out for it. "Yes, plants too live, the Hindus are right: this plant is thinking. But here in this hot-bed, everything lives and thinks. The house itself—" Idle, fascinating days. The catbird clucked in the bushes by the creek or sat on the bare wire of the porch trying to imitate Sam's voice; a cat sneaked through the grass. In a storm a wolfish dog, mad with fear, rushed under the house and howled. The little insect in the porch-roof sang loudly.

Mr. Thornton came down bringing the milk, and placidly going backwards and forwards over the tussocks with him, Parsons talked about simple ways of improving the house. "I suppose Dilley would be glad to sell, if things are the way I've heard. Mr. Davies told me he was in financial difficulties, that he has a sick wife and daughter and he finds it hard to meet mortgage payments."

"I don't know if they're in such a hurry to sell," said Mr. Thornton. "The wife, Mrs. Dilley, thinks the daughter will get better and she wants to keep this place on for her. She thinks the country will improve her. She thinks it was a nervous breakdown. But old Mr. Dilley knows better."

"So you think he'd be prepared to sell?"

"I could ask him. I'm always a-writin' to him about the house. You see I manage for him." Thornton fetched a grass-cutter from the barn, and said he would just do a bit now and then he'd send Johnson. "The place needs a-ploughin' and a-smoothin' down first."

Clare through the kitchen window looked out and said, "Yes, then I could grow my own vegetables here and have a chicken run. If you would lend Johnson to do a bit of digging."

Mr. Thornton was silent for a while. He smiled presently and stated, "Some I-talians, brother and sister, deaf ones, had a berry farm here; but they had bad luck, the crop failed. It's not the place. They went bankrupt. It waited a while before the Dilleys took it. And after them, it waited a while—"

Clare, pumping water into the sink, said, "But what is the matter with Miss Dilley?"

"Mrs. Grace, Miss Dilley that was," he said gently. "Well, I couldn't say. I don't think she'll recover. She's a-lingerin', it's a long business."

"Is it tuberculosis?" said Clare.

"No; I don't think it was that; but it might have been. Was somethin' catchin'."

When Clare had left the sink, he said to Sam, "Come up by the barn. I'll start a-cuttin' there and I'll tell you somethin'." When there he stopped work, and standing strong and tall in his sixty years, his hand on a hoe, he said, "I wouldn't like your wife to hear this. You can tell her after, if you think it's right. I never told my wife or daughter about it; and round here with people a-comin' and a-goin' on this farm, they hardly remember anythin'. Perhaps Rudolf, that Strasser boy, remembers; but he wouldn't say."

"Is the girl dying?"

"She's a-dyin'; I don't think she's dead. I don't know. I saw her myself about eight months ago. I'm the only one knows all about it. I guess I know more than her poor mother. I never told Mr. Davies, for Mr. Davies was a sick man. Well, since you ask me, I think I can say the daughter isn't dead. I think they'd tell me if she'd died. She's right near here. And that's what the Dilleys think; that some day soon she'll be back here, a-waitin' for them; or the mother thinks. She's not far away. She's very bad. She's in the madhouse over in T. and she'll never get out. The mother thinks she's a-gettin' better, but she's a-gettin' worse. I went to see her at the request of Mr. Dilley about eight months ago and she's nothin' like herself. She didn't recognize me, though she always liked me; and she's not like a woman, she's like a sick animal or a baby, worse; and she doesn't know who she is. They haven't let the mother see her for three years.

"It all happened because of a Nevada man. Dilley was a shoemaker and sold leather goods; and durin' the war he got enough together to retire. They bought this place, which was a-goin' beggin', part paid for and part on mortgage; and thought they'd keep it for their only child Hilda for when she was married. Lambertville was better then than now, Lambertville's a half-ruined town. These factories along the Delaware closed down and the place never came back. At that time it was full of life; and the Dilleys often went in in their old car. There was a big army camp near here where they put the young men who were a-waitin' to be demobilized. This young Hilda was about twenty-two and she was full of life. She used to talk to that Strasser boy, a-callin' across the creek; but the parents on both sides didn't like it. There was this Nevada man there, a big tall fellow in a uniform who talked a lot and sang a lot and had this gui-tar.

"Well, he got her to fall in love with him at once; and she wanted to marry him. The parents always gave in to her in the end; so they married and the Nevada man thought, I guess, that he was a-goin' to live soft. He moved in here with the Dilleys and never offered to go to work. He sat round the whole livelong day, a-talkin' and a-eatin' and a-singin' to the tunes on that gui-tar. Well, he was an ignorant man and he had a disease and he gave it to Hilda. She had a baby which died and that began to turn her mind; she used to cry for it. The Nevada man wasn't cruel; he just was lazy. He'd sit up there in my kitchen many a time, a-playin' his gui-tar and a-talkin' to my wife. She liked him and he liked her; she was in the house then with our baby girl, my only daughter. He'd amuse the baby! That he liked right well; and he liked to amuse visitors; and he'd go to church and talk to the men. But he reared at work like a crazy horse. I said to him, Come on, come out with me and I'll show you how to plough; and he'd go out to the field with me; but he'd laugh and watch me plough; and he'd sit down and begin to strum and sing. The poor girl began to cry and act strange and to amuse her they took her to the movies and to the the-ayter that they had at the church hall. Well, it's a funny thing. One of those shows was about Pocahontas and Captain John Smith. Now that Nevadan said he was a captain; I don't know if he was. He said he didn't wear his ribbons because he was a-doin' of some work. I don't know if he was. But this seemed to stick in her mind; and she began to say she was Pocahontas and she was a-goin' to marry Captain John Smith. She forgot she was married sometimes.

She forgot about the baby. So they bought her a doll and she seemed to think sometimes it was a baby. It's hard to say just what she thought. Well, they didn't say anythin' to that Nevada man, because they were afraid to hurt her feelin's and he was better round the place than away. Then he went away. I don't know where. He wrote one letter and they never heard from him again. The parents hadn't thought much of him, but they set a detective after him; they wrote letters to people they knew; but he was never heard of again.

"After this Hilda was in a bad way. Her mother, who loved her, sewed her a kind of Indian dress. I've seen it myself; and she'd walk with her every day along the track, a-lettin' her wear this fancy dress and a-listenin' to her talk, which was very proud and boastful. I'd meet them very early in the mornin' sometimes when I was a-comin' back from Lambertville; and I've heard her a-talkin' high because she thought she was this Indian princess. I told Mrs. Dilley I didn't think it wise to encourage her; but the poor mother would not oppose her. She said her mind was turned with so much trouble and only kindness would bring her back. Well, there had been talk about this Nevada captain, if he was; and I myself wondered—if somethin' had gone wrong. My wife and the others too saw her, a-singin' and a-talkin' and sometimes she wore flowers and had a tomahawk or a knife and a rope. Once I was frightened to see her costume there a-lyin' on the road and I thought somethin' had happened; but I saw her a-runnin' naked along the track and a-slippin' down into the creek and she had some leaves round her neck. I thought that was no sight for the young men up at Strassers' to see, or my young men either; so I brought the girl her clothes and told her to get dressed like a good girl. I was shocked at her, I told her; and wouldn't be her friend if she misbehaved like that. I said to her like I always said, even when her mother was there, But you're not Pocahontas, my girl. It's just a joke; you're Hilda, you know. But she wouldn't have that: and I thought, maybe her mother was right.

"One morning Rudolf, the Strasser boy, the elder, came a-runnin' up the hill about nine and sang out to me, Mr. Thornton, come quick, down to the Dilleys'; it's murder down there. I said,

What is it, Rudolf? And while we were a-runnin' down he told me Hilda was out here a-throwin' things and a-screamin'; and her father and her mother couldn't get her home. Well, I wasn't too sure, because she's been funny before; and I thought the boy could get easily scared by her; but I ran down with Rudolf just the same, a-takin' a bit of rope which was a-hangin' on the fence, with me. I thought: I'll bind her up till she quiets down. They were a-shoutin' and a-hollerin' and when I got round the corner of the barn here, I see poor old Mrs. Dilley with her grey head bendin' low down over the garden path, her head nearly in the earth, and Hilda her daughter was a-throwin' knives at her. Just as I came along, Hilda flung a tomahawk which struck her poor old mother on the shoulder. Her head was already covered with blood. She collapsed into the dirt and I thought she was dead. What are you a-doin', Hilda? I shouted. She had an axe in her hands now and she was ready to heave it at her mother. I ran right up before she could think, and said, Hilda, put down that axe! What are you a-doin'? Aren't you ashamed? She looked very pale and wild; and she told me she was a-killin' her mother because her mother did things to her. She said, She takes everythin' from me. I said, Shame on you, Hilda, shame on you! Look at your poor mother, a-bleedin' there in the dirt; you've cut her on the shoulder and on the head. I am ashamed of you, Hilda! And while I was a-talkin' and she was a-lookin' to see what she had done, I grabbed the axe. She held on to it, but I got between her and the tomahawk a-lyin' on the path. Then Mrs. Dilley, who had said nothin', was groanin' a little and she started to get up. She leaned on her hands and said to me, The poor girl doesn't know what she is a-doin'! She was always so quiet.

"Well, I went on a-talkin' to her and a-pushin' her into the house: and I found her father where she had driven him with her axe into the staircase and locked him in; because she said she was a-comin' after him to kill him next. I gave her a terrible talkin' to, shamin' her for what she'd done; for her wickedness, and I talked so much, I got the rope round her and tied her to a chair. There was no place to lock her but the barn and that was full of sharp dangerous things. Upstairs she could have got to the windows and done harm. Then I sent Strasser up to my place to get them to telephone for a doctor and I waited there till he came. He fixed up the parents and went back to town to arrange for the girl. There was no doubt at all; Hilda was mad and dangerous. The doctor had given her a drug and they put her to bed and locked her in. Well, after I finished my work I went a-back there and found her awake and a-ravin' and a-shoutin', so I stayed there until two in the mornin'. But when she quietened down, I went in there and I talked to her a long, long time; for I couldn't help a-feelin' that if they hadn't given in to her and let her wear that fancy dress and have that baby doll and that tomahawk, she might not have gone mad. So I talked to her sensibly and scolded her and asked her what was the matter, until she got quite quiet.

"She said I wasn't her friend because I had tied her up with a rope; but I told her she was only like a calf or a young horse, she had to learn. I knew she wasn't a bad girl, only selfish with no thought for her poor parents. Well, we talked on nearly all through the night and she told me a lot of her strange ideas. She thought people were her enemies. When she was quiet I gave her the drug again and locked her in and went away.

"In the mornin' at eight o'clock I came with my buggy and horse and knocked on the door: Hilda, it's Mr. Thornton. I want you to come and take a ride with me. You let your mother dress you.

"After a bit I went in and said to her, Hilda, do you want to go to a square-dance? Will you come and dance with me? Then you must get dressed up in your best dress. What are you a-doin' like that, Hilda? You said you'd come dancin' with me. For she had torn her nightdress into pieces. Maybe she wanted to climb out of the window. Well, with a-beggin' and a-pleadin' and a-sayin' of fine stories to her, I got her to get dressed and I brought her downstairs. The poor parents were keepin' out of the way, as they had been told, though it was hard for them. We did not dare tell the mother where we were takin' her. I kept a-talkin' about the square-dance and a-praisin' her looks and I picked some flowers outside the door to put in her belt. But she was puzzled, too; and she said, It's early in the mornin' to go to a square-dance. I said, No, it isn't,

Hilda. We've got to go to dinner at the hotel first; and we have people to meet. I am a-drivin' you in and I want people to see you. She was pleased and put flowers in her hair too; and I said, Give me those flowers, Hilda, to keep fresh; you know what a long dusty road it is to town. She said, Why, are you ashamed of me? Is there somethin' wrong with me? I think there's somethin' wrong with me. I said, No, no, Hilda, but you are so sweet and pretty, I wanted to see you in the first figure of the square-dance the prettiest there; so keep your flowers fresh till we get to Lambertville. She looked quite pretty, though her face was pale and troubled and she had not been able to smooth her hair right, poor thing. I drove her straight down to the doctor's and he went with us to the asylum. Mr. Dilley took her things there the next day; and she's been there ever since, many years.

"Her mother kept a-cryin' to get her out and blamed the doctors for not a-curin' her; and with a-worryin' and a-blamin', she got worn and tired out herself. So I'm sorry for Mr. Dilley, too. She can't go far enough to lay the blame; one time on the farm, another time on them both for a-lettin' her marry that Nevada man with the gui-tar; and so on.

"That's the story, you see; and I'm a-lookin' after the place for Mr. Dilley because of his hard luck. Mr. Davies thought I was a-takin' of Mr. Dilley's money, I could see; but I said nothin' to Mr. Davies because he is a sick man. Yes, I saw her right here in that doorway a-throwin' axes and mad as a coot. Young Strasser could hear from the hill—on that hill they can hear everythin' you say down here if they listen. And I guess you can hear what they say, except that they never speak on this side of the hill. And young Strasser ran for me, you see, because roundabout here they run for me. Well, I'll send Johnson down to cut down your weeds."

"Oh, no, please don't, Mr. Thornton. Those weeds bring the birds and my wife loves to have them round."

"Ah, the only birds you can find for miles are in this creek run. They've been driven out everywhere else. My sons have been to agricultural college and say we need them. But we're not used to them round here. You can have too many of them."

"My wife can't have too many. I think she could live all her life here with them and not miss people."

"Well, that's not quite right for a woman: it's too lonely."

"You don't know my wife. She loves all this. She doesn't need anything else. She always wanted to live in the zoo. She'd like to have the animals, including the insects, in the house with her."

"Would she now? Well, they try to oblige her!" he said, with a kind look, and pointing to the large spider which had slipped out from its plank, viewed them and slid back. "Does she like that?"

"Well, she looks out for it from the house. She tells me, There's the spider sunning himself. He sees her, too."

The summer was fat, steamy, heavy-headed, an obsession. Sam went to town to see "the boys," and Mr. Thornton was busy. Clare was happy in the Dilleys' place. She put out food for the animals, and pulled up no plants because each plant is a shelter for some living thing. Once or twice, when alone, she herself lay down naked in the centre of the weed patch, to get all the sun, lay there drowsy thinking of fertility, surrounded by all the life and love of the beast and plant world, part of the earth life. "Why is the devil called the Lord of Flies? If he is, then we must be close to his hole." Myriads of flying insects shone, flitted, strummed, whined and in the thick air lived. "The woodchuck is quite bold now, he comes nearer the house every day observing us; only his wife hangs in the background; but she too is coming nearer." The woodchuck who lived in the bank fed in the old vegetable patch. There was a family of skunks now that came for their food by night, hundreds more mice living with them in the two houses. Two weasels flashed in and out by the porch; the house-wrens on the porch singing boldly or creeping mouse-like through the woodpiles all day sounded their rattles; there were more mourning doves making every clouded and clotted evening sky sad; the whistling whip of the sleepy thrushes, the lowing cows and their lost calves, the woodchucks nearly to the house now, the birds invading, the danger-calling catbirds, the strange insect's strumming in the house, immense flies and wasps, the increasing heat and damp, the owls, the insect rabble; and myriads multiplying in this one sacred uncleared hollow. "If we lived here long enough and everything grew thick enough and high enough we would see the world as an ant does among his grass stalks."

Clare cleaned the house and was frightened. "I was on the landing at the top of the wooden stairs and I felt myself being pushed towards the stairs, a force from that little room wanted to throw me downstairs, from the door, like a…I was afraid; I came down the stairs step by step sitting on them."

Sam Parsons then told the story of Hilda Dilley. "I forgot her married name. But that was Poky—Pocahontas—after you."

"Is she capable of such strength? The house has accumulated a great ousting power. But how can it oust me? I am for it, I am for all here."

The catbirds' catcalls and mewing ran through the bushes. Eels went downstream. Clouds of insects came from the cornfields. A large ball of soot sat watching on the bridge and bobbed down when it saw them move. At night the fireflies burned like a net of sparks through the wild plants. If they turned out the light this curtain of fire made a faint glow around them. In bed, they saw them still, for Dilley's place was an underearth, lower than all the green around; and there around them burned the world of flies, so that the distant sky-stars, obscured by night insects and waving vines and leaves as if by smoke, were unnecessary. It was a kind of infant lightning.

The air grew heavier; unusual streaked and mottled skies appeared. "I never knew we had such large flies in the USA. I thought that was for South America."

"The ants and spiders have come in everywhere. It is going to rain."

"I never lived in so much nature; I never knew I could," said Sam, laughing, tenderly, helplessly.

"Poky is singing much louder now," said Clare referring to the insect that strummed in the corner, and which they had never located. "This morning I heard it when I was near the creek; and I looked for it again."

146

"I suppose there are more of them. Whatever it is, has had a family. Everything round here has had four or five families this summer."

"I read in the Lambertville *Gazette* that this and the wood on the cliff, in the film-star's estate, is a refuge for birds and all wild things, everything driven from the farms."

The owl hooted. "That's a dreadful sound."

"Yes." To comfort him, she remarked, "Where the mice and little birds and insects are, there are owls; and mice and little birds where corn and insects are."

"Oh," said Sam Parsons, "I have gotten used to them. Not so long ago I would have taken the first train back to New York."

They listened awhile to the footsteps, which now began to go downstairs, with a heavy soft irregular tread.

"The mice must enter the kitchen where the step is worn under the door at the bottom."

Presently the footfalls came upstairs again the same slow soft way and crossed the landing.

"I suppose they get crumbs; I put away everything," said Clare, "but why do they live in the little room here?"

"Let's go to sleep," said Sam.

The plank in the bridge clonked.

"They're coming from the movies."

She heard Sam breathing faintly in sleep. The living sleeping night was all around, close, formless, rich and suffocating as a mother's breast. On the black breast of night she fell asleep, too. The footsteps passed her again; she did not hear them; the bridge gave warning; they slept. The faceless haunter of the stone house moved slightly through the open attic door and down the closed stairs; with the strength of water behind glass, without shape and ready to pour through, it mixed with the moonlight at the locked glass door, mixing as blood with water, smoking, turning. But there was peace in the bedroom; until the skunks came for the liver laid out at the back door, when, at the musky stench, there was a great rain of mice and Clare awoke, listening, delighted. "There you are, friends, animals, children," she thought; and heard many small real footfalls, squeaks and movements.

In mid-July the skies began to cloud. The air thickened and darkened. All day long the wren's wearying clackers rang. Awfully mournful in these oppressive days, was the late and early sobbing of the doves; fateful, the sound of the thrush retiring last in the woods. The ants marched thick along their routes. When would the rain come?

Every evening and morning now the Parsons walked out of the brooding hollow, where the Lord of Flies surely sat spinning his flies; and they walked on the upper roads and tracks. Higher up, where the Dilleys' creek parted from the river, was a bridge; brilliant birds, tanagers, orioles, canaries and even bluebirds flew and sat freely here.

One evening they were upon the township road winding around the meadowy hill above the Sobieskis'. Below lay their hollow, the thick trees surging over their red roofs. They were now higher than the Strassers' ridge and the sun was setting over it. There was trouble somewhere, a warning. Something not yet unwound but waiting lay complete under the green stuff in the valley bottom. On this upland the air was easy to breathe; there was still golden light. They started back again, almost with regret. A dead swallow, which had been for weeks dangling in the telephone wires, had now turned to skeleton and hung still. The descending road turned south and caught the Dilleys' track which turned west. The sky was sapphire. Looking at it before they went down to their burrow, they saw one cloud forming, one cloud only in the whole sky, in the west directly over the sun going down. It came out in flecks and wisps, became suddenly one curled gold feather, and so stayed, as if beaten out of metal; marvellous, and the only thing in the sky and like an eyebrow right over the sun in the green sky.

"Down came the hurricane," said Clare as the first cold air caught them.

"You would say that is a hurricane cloud?"

"Oh, but it is so still; and the sky is clear. No; that is from the 'Ballad of Carmilhan': the Captain up and down the deck—"

148

They came down into their trees. It was nearly dark there. There were the solitary liquid notes of the woodthrush beginning to be heard in the brush by the track. "Birds understand music and natural beauty." And then began, miserable, intolerable in this air, the dove who nested by the bridge. For a long time he sobbed; and the birds were restless in the fever of midsummer.

They ate and looked through a book they found on the top shelf of the window-closet in the stone house. They never used the sitting-room of the stone house, preferring the stove, the porches and fiery windows of the farm kitchen. But tonight for the first time they sat there, and read the fat, heavy volume, a farmers' encyclopaedia, of the sort once sold at country fairs, miscellaneous reading, advice on farming, cooking, sewing, illnesses. A nineteenth-century gingerbread murder castle: "But how could you calculate all the unaccounted-for space in a gingerbread house?" An account of John Wesley and his diary: "You know when he says he gave up smoking, I believe he meant something else."

The lightning was now forking from opposite the sunset, stabbing high; and then the sky-creature's blue nervous system, its brain, its lungs and its nerves like trees lighted up all around, on high, turning the trees into a black huddle, a pressed herd. Now they did not seem to be lost in a lowland, but the lowland was heaved up to light and the hills flattened by the pallid shine.

The rain began, at first only a few drops; and it remained almost dry all night. Soon they locked everything and went to bed. It was cooler. The entire sky now quivered with pale light. As well as the perpetual quivering everywhere and the faint sound, another lightning now rolled over the sky from east to west in long pale corrugations and thunder followed its rolling. There was no darkness and no silence. Such a strange storm they had never seen. They did not sleep; and it was not the storm, not the light, not the noise, so much as the strangeness. At length, Clare came and sat on Sam's side of the bed and held his hand; and the two of them sat all night huddled up, looking with astonishment at a night they had never seen, the combers of light, the continuous irregular rush, murmur and roar.

The next day it rained. The thin glassy creek thickened and washed from saucer to saucer. In the evening, it could be heard slapping down, in the night it was gushing. What would the woodchucks do? But Mr. Thornton had already told them about the good sense of woodchucks. Old man woodchuck had a dryland exit somewhere up the bank; he would doubtless save his family. In the morning, with the rain continuing, the creek had risen yellow; it poured and curdled along. The mailman blew his horn. They hurried out. "Are you all right?" At this they laughed. "Right as rain." In the afternoon, Riondo, the Lambertville butcher, came along in his car and shouted, "Are you all right?" "What are those planes?" The planes, which had been above them all day, were army bombers looking out for marooned farmers. The Delaware had risen; those nearest to it in Lambertville were in danger; they had drawn all boats out of the river. It was exciting. The birds made little sound except for the house-wrens and the dove. It was still warm. In the afternoon, when the rain ceased, the insects and birds began again; but the woodchuck and his wife did not come to the vegetable patch. It was still raining elsewhere. The creek had risen again and was a yellow pouring in which no life was visible; only the rubbish from the banks and woods. The rain came again at night. Through it, they heard their creek as it tore through the vines and roots. Then it grew quieter and then ceased. In the morning, the rain had ceased and Clare getting up saw that they were surrounded by a grey standing fog, for from all the floor-level windows she could see grey only; but when this grey fog moved slightly, carrying sticks, then she saw it was flood; Dilley's place was under water. The water had not yet entered the house and it had stopped raining. They took all movables upstairs and prepared to leave. The water spread out over the two acres was smooth and moving slowly; but it rushed and foamed out of the long narrow gorge beyond, where the boys bathed, and had risen to the top rail of the bridge; the spider, the ball of soot, was no more. They waded through the hip-high water at the bridge, climbed the hill and asked Mr. Thornton to get them to town.

His fat fair wife and her fat fair daughter were sitting in

rocking-chairs in the kitchen in a jolly mood. They had just received a three-burner kerosene stove from town; they had used a big farm stove like the Dilleys'. Up to this moment they had spent money only on necessary farm improvements and on a small radio. They were not like the Newbolds, who had every new electrical improvement.

"My daughter is going to have the money when she marries. When she goes to church on Sundays, all the boys look at her, don't they, Maureen?"

The girl laughed, rocked back and forth. "Maureen is the catch of this township," said the mother, looking back from the stove on which her eyes rested. "We thought you'd be getting flooded out," said Mrs. Thornton laughing and rocking. "Mr. Thornton was saying, They'll have water through the kitchen by this time; that cellar is always full of water in winter."

The daughter laughed and rocked. They talked about her sow which had farrowed three times in a year. Last time it had had seventeen piglets of which it had eaten two and smothered one; but that still made thirty-six living piglets in a year.

"And they're all Maureen's," said Mrs. Thornton. "The sow's hers; she looks after it and they're all her pigs. She sells them and the money's hers."

The fat, small-eyed daughter grinned.

They had sent the boy Johnson, a white-skinned lad of heroic build, for Mr. Thornton, who now arrived, very gay.

Said he, "We've not a drop of water in here; all watertight."

"I always wondered myself why all the houses were built on top of these hills where the lightning can strike," said Clare.

"That house down there is always the same, winter it's water-bound," said the farmer.

"In winter, all you have to do is lean out of the kitchen window and dip in the pail," said Mrs. Thornton.

"Always twenty foot of water in the cellar," said the daughter. "You know that hailstorm we had? Came right up to our fence and turned back, didn't touch a blade nor an ear. Laid everything in Strassers' flat and they're poor, haven't a cent. Everything that side, laid flat. Stopped right at our fence. I wish I had shown you, to see."

They looked brightly at each other.

"You have to have luck," said Mrs. Thornton. "The berry farm failed. I knew it would. One of them got sick; and then the Dilleys had their daughter get sick with the lung-sickness, that's the damp; and then the Davies came. You could see right through that boy when he came and the father's a very weak-looking man," she chuckled, "and the bottle didn't help."

"Mother," said Mr. Thornton, "that's Mr. Parsons' friend."

"Oh, excuse me. Mr. Thornton looks after the house; well— and the—" She began to laugh and poked her daughter in the arm; they both laughed. The daughter could not take her eyes off the visitors. She laughed in a vain way and at the same time her eyes devoured their valises, their town shoes and Clare's light coat.

Mr. Thornton sobered down and said, "There's nothin' to be done with that house. You might as well pull it down and move it farther up into Sobieski's fields. But Mrs. Sobieski wanted money and she sold off that bottom bit of the field that is no good and all the long bit of creek the cows could fall into. It's not much more than a water-meadow. And it was a crazy idea to build that deep cellar; it's just a watertrap. Keep fish there."

At this amusing idea, the mother and daughter went into a gale of laughter. "Yes, fish."

"Couldn't it easily be fixed up?" said Parsons. "There must be a local engineer who could build a dam and there are new ways of treating walls for seepage. Deepen, widen, dam the creek, get permission."

Mr. Thornton thought it might easily cost $10,000. He'd talked to engineers, had one over. "The house and ground is worthless as it stands."

"Well, that wooden bridge stood up to the flood the last three days and is as firm as a rock," said Clare.

"Do you mean to say we can build TVA and not fix a little thing like that," said Sam Parsons.

Mr. Thornton became very intent. He'd had it studied; it couldn't be done. Mr. Parsons, surprised, said that the whole fault lay in the narrow gorge the creek ran through in the panhandle

152

part of Dilley's and the sharp right angle it turned. Mr. Thornton argued emphatically, while the mother and daughter looked on with rounder eyes, ready to laugh, but aware that Thornton was upset. "It catches all the water from all these hills and you'd need to pull down the house and make the whole place a dam."

He presently took them off in his car. At parting Clare told the Thorntons she would see them in a few days.

"Oh, are you a-comin' back?"

"Oh, yes. We've rented it till the end of October."

Staring, the Thornton women watched them and their valises into the car; and then suddenly again were overcome with fun.

"Well, just send me a line when you're a-comin' back and I'll open up the place for you," said Thornton placably, as he saw them off at Flemington station.

It blew, it rained for two weeks; and in three weeks they returned. As they approached they saw the cottage radiant through the trees. Mr. Thornton was waiting for them on their porch. The creek banks were soiled with floodmarks, the water was not yet clear and all things were greyed by the flood; but the sun shone. They joyously hurried to the house.

Mr. Thornton gave them the key saying, "Excuse me for not a-goin' in with you. I'm very busy now with the farm. If you want anythin', come to me."

They unlocked the door. The floor was muddy. The chairs, tables, benches, windowsills and all downward surfaces were hung with beards of grey-white mould up to nine inches long. "The Spanish moss has migrated from Florida." The stove was rusted. It smelled like a cellar or cave. The cellar of the stone house was full to the opening, the steps ran down under water, a swimming pool. Thornton's secret; they laughed. They cleaned, aired and sunned everything, keeping one of the chairs to show visitors; but no visitors came yet and in a few days of sun the chair was clean. The birds sang, the woodchuck family reappeared in the vegetable patch; the grapes ripened on the outhouse. The skunks and weasels had gone, there were fewer mice; the wrens had deserted their last brood dead in the nest. After a couple of weeks everything was nearly as before; the insects had returned though they no longer thickened the air; the twanging insect in the house twanged as before. Yet it was a pity to look at the ravaged creekside from which all the delicate plants had gone. The great ravens were still there, one sitting on a naked branch and one picking in the sun on the track.

They looked through the house, peered from the windows of the little locked room. "Oh, why not buy it? It doesn't always rain." The Dilleys' land was only a hand's breadth of riverbank, a woodchuck's backyard. The surrounding hills and combing trees were blameless as before; the sunlight golden through the damp invisible vapours was like a woman's yellow mane thrown over everything; under, her damp warm meadowy skin.

"Poky was singing loudly again today. She sings in that corner of the kitchen that is under the little room. Why don't you come and look at her things, poor woman?" Sam always refused. He had seen nothing but the Indian dress and turned away from that. "I don't want to see it, don't let me see those things." They now always called it Poky's Place.

"She tries to get rid of everyone; it is still her place."

"Don't say those things."

"Why?"

"It's dangerous."

Bill Jermyn with Clare, and Joyce Jermyn with Sam, were walking along a tree-tufted edge. On one side a crumbling hillside, on the other, private unfenced woods protected by high trees linked and walled with poison ivy and poison oak.

"What do you think of the haunting by knives and axes? It isn't real," said Clare, "but it's astonishing."

Bill Jermyn was a blue-black brunette, with a melancholy nutcracker face, handsome sunk eyes and a strong-set body blanketed in hair; this hair showed through the opening of his blue shirt and on his arms. Clare looked at this hair, glanced away, thinking, Bats fly into women's hair because they don't get the echoes back. I don't get the thoughts back from hairy men. But Clare and Jermyn were close friends. They were interested in things like this.

"I say it's a low hollow where all the water and all the vapours concentrate; not only that, it's protected; things grow faster, breed thicker and then the trees and plants take the air. At night you have no oxygen at all with all those old trees bending over you taking the air from you. It's like sleeping in an old fourposter with curtains and canopy and carpet. And though you're surrounded, it's lonely. You're overlooked. That imaginary man in the attic—you're overlooked by the dark bushy hairy hill. It's lonely here, lonely and timeless, or it has jungle time, millennial time only, dangerous to man."

"Oh, no. It's millennial time we managed very well with," said Clare, laughing; "and I am not afraid."

"Are you afraid of knives?"

"I never was."

"There is something there—the vapours perhaps? This something which also appeared to you as a strong force pushing you downstairs, brought out the idea of axe-murders in Poky; and in you, a fear of knives."

"I wonder you didn't hear the mice in the night," said Clare.

"I wonder myself," said Joyce, a black-eyed impatient beauty, young, rounded. She had a rich, drawling, accusing voice. "Bill's scared of mice; they're nasty symbols to him, sex symbols, horror symbols. He got out of a property deal that way, found there were mice there and got a letter from his psychoanalyst."

When they got home, Jermyn climbed one of the trees and stayed there for forty minutes, his blue shirt visible through the leaves, an attractive blue-black four-cornered bird.

When he came down he said, "What I'd like to do is buy the place away from Thornton; he's after it for that sow daughter of his." He left them for a walk and called on Mrs. Sobieski. He was a young man with a melancholy ingratiating manner. He found out what she thought the Dilleys' place was worth and whether she would sell a bit of her field above the house. He arrived back, smoking his short-stem pipe, with the loping walk of handsome legs and when he got to where they were sitting on the porch, he slung his legs over the balustrade and said he thought he would buy it and rent it or loan it.

"Another thing is the electric light. One thing I noticed about your story was that the electric light being on all night was the storm-signal for Poky's crime down here; and it was the storm-signal for the Davies—Laban went away and the light was on all night; a lighted cabin in all these dark thickets. As in the musicians of Bremen."

And, fixing the pipe again in his mouth, he looked towards the bridge and barn, his fine tragic chinchopper face musing.

In a few moments he took the pipe out again to add, "You know Professor Abe Carter has collected funds for a writers' refuge? He's looking for a place. I can make something out of this idea. I'll get Carter to contribute some of the money he's collected, buy Dilley's place, call it Dilley's Place, summer camp for writers, say there's a ghost—you have first option. Give me a few days and I might do something with Dilley's place. Besides, I don't want old man Thornton on his hill to get it; just cussedness; because he's been playing for it. There's something to this place. Easy to work out a dam."

"Get a couple of beavers," said Clare.

"Whoever built this place? In this lap of the hills, a catchment place, a gorge? Naturally anyone who put in a deep cellar was delirious. And insane he who built it in the first place. And then, after winters and summers, he goes and builds a wing in masonry."

"He thought the cellar would take all the water," said Clare.

"Who was the architect, who the engineer? Well, here it is and beautiful as a russet apple. Where's your outhouse? It's that, smothered in grapes? I'll join you with the whole thing worked out." So saying, the handsome young man hopped off the railing, after a while came out again with the farmers' encyclopaedia and crossed the yard. They had gone for a walk to see the birds at their stations along the track, especially the buff-and-blue humming birds. When they returned, Bill Jermyn was just returning full of grace from the grape harbour, book in hand. "By the way, what is that strumming or singing that I hear coming from the grapes?"

"That is the ghost."

"It is?"

"Oh, I'm certain."

"That's very curious," said Jermyn, strolling around, climbing, sounding and poking. "Is it a loose wire, an Aeolian harp? Could be an old vine somewhere, some nails."

"The sound has been getting louder for months."

"It isn't flies in a spider's web?"

"Yes, brass flies in a brass web, I always said that," said Clare. There was a wind that night. The next morning Joyce said, "What were you people doing running up and downstairs all night? I was awake. We did our best to get a baby last night; and we overdid it, I couldn't sleep, though he did."

"It was the mice."

"The mice? That?"

"Yes. They do that every night. And fall down the walls."

Joyce looked serious and presently she and Bill Jermyn went for a walk, up and down the track, quite visible from the windows but separated by a palisade of trees, wheeling lights, the impassable barricade of *Rhus radicans*, the creek and its voice. When she came back Joyce said, "There are snakes in the water; water-snakes. Oh, I know I shall get pregnant here; the place is alive," she shuddered, "alive...and then I'll get out of here."

The next night she stumbled up the steep dark wooden stairs with a jug of water and a glass. "I may want an aspirin in the night and I wouldn't go down there at night."

She brought up her water and something to eat. "Nothing would make me go on those stairs in the dark hours. I might tread on a mouse. I hate it here. Why is it artists like to live in primitive conditions, with a john a hundred yards away, so that you can step on a snake going to it; or some bull get you or man rape you; remote from life among the farming clods, little boys with sticks driving cows, in a mice-eaten weasel-bitten shack with disgusting little vines that work themselves round your finger while you're reading a book on the back step. Would such hard luck have come to Poky in the city if her parents had had the sense to stay there? All country cottages are mistakes, follies."

At another time she said restlessly, "The trouble with me is Jermyn's not my type. I've got to find my type. I've been too long about it. Now I suppose I'm going to have a baby by him. I didn't have the sense to get out first. Jermyn's a good type for a father and he'll always be able to support the child and me. But as soon as I have it I'm getting out. What I ought to be looking for is a wolf. There are no wolves here. There's nothing here for me."

The next afternoon was warm and close. Lightning the colour of fireflies flickered; the south flared, thunder rolled in the distance, rolling iron barrels. Suddenly it roared overhead; and from the sky, violent rain. A grey long-haired animal leapt the creek, and howling, whining in fear, rushed to the porch and crawled under it, where it lay trembling.

"There couldn't be a wolf round here!" cried Joyce. "I saw a wolf!" "It's an alsatian dog!" "It's a wolf," snapped Joyce. "What a place! It's the backwoods. It's a timber wolf." "Well, you asked for a wolf and it seems that here you get what you want." "A wolf?" "Yes, you asked for a wolf. In Poky's day a wolf was a wolf." "Don't make a joke of it," cried Joyce: "it's too horrible. I'm not staying here tonight."

When the storm had passed they tried to lure the dog from the porch with a piece of meat. He lay close to the earth, in the warm damp narrow space, trembling and whining. "You do have mighty cracks of thunder here," said Jermyn. "It's like the Catskills." Joyce declared she was going back that afternoon. "I wouldn't spend another night here: by the morning you may be invaded by bears and moose. This is just a piece of the great northern world that has got loose. And I know Poky hears every word we say." "You always claim that you're not superstitious," said Bill Jermyn. "I am not. These are facts. I can believe what I see. I said wolf and a wolf came," grumbled Joyce.

When dusk came, but before they put on the light, they looked from the kitchen windows and there, almost invisible in the grass emptying of light, ran a pale animal. First he ran crouching, then he began to lope; he sped across the bridge, up the track towards the blackberries. "It's a lost dog: no one round here has an alsatian," said Clare. "It's a spectre," said Joyce. She got up early in the morning, packed and came down. "Bill is taking me away. You finish out your summer here if you can. Rather you than me. But I bet you won't finish out the summer here."

"Oh, Poky has done her worst. Now she has made us welcome."

"If you trust her you're mad."

They went. The full dropping summer days passed and trees hung out the golden bough. The Parsons had decided to go to town for the winter and return the next spring. Bill Jermyn, meanwhile, making a sketch of his own plan, was sending down two brothers named Imber to stay, look around, see what could be done to make the cottage watertight, to extend it, make it habitable for a small community. As the villages in this part of the Delaware country declined in workers, and farmers, like the ten sons of Farmer Thornton, went farther out to the plains because of big-scale farming methods, the derelict farms and follies were becoming the homes of workers in the arts. Jermyn was shaping up his idea of planting small semi-socialist, self-dependent artistic communities.

The brothers, Frederick and Walter Imber, high-school teachers, aged thirty-four and thirty-two, were indistinguishable at a distance, of great breadth and density, large limbed, moving heavily, vain of their strength. They were good-natured men, timid about their neighbours, about infringements. They did their own housework, and spent the day outside idly, but with an innocent pretence of hard work, while they agreed with each other in long discussions of political theory. They were vegetarians, abstainers and, untrained as engineers or architects or cooks or farmers, they attempted to supply their needs and their friends' needs with their own hands. They made plans for a dam and a waterwall to proceed from the dam and protect the house. But, they said, this water-wall would have to be well based in the earth, rocks at the creek's right angle would have to be blasted, the whole creek would have to be dug deeper, thus ruining the charm of its rocky shells and saucers dipping down and the first heavy rain turning the trickle into a torrent would probably flood the road. The whole thing needed planning, not to mention permission from Mr. Dilley, and the Township.

The Imbers decided to go ahead with it at once. They began to dig a new channel for the creek through the old berry patch. The trench filled with water and they were pleased. At once they had another idea. "Broaden and deepen the creek bed all the way along: you'll lose some three hundred square feet of land, but the rest will never be flooded and the track will be safe from flooding." They began on this immense project, with picks and shovels, and at once faced the tangle of elderberry, poison ivy and poison oak and other weeds whose strong woven roots held the soil together. "The creek will be the natural barrier, though we don't want a barrier. The water will keep the Strassers' chickens and stray cattle and dogs away. So we'll get rid of all this spinach," said Fred Imber, sweeping a hand over the vines and bending and thrusting the other hand into the deep tangled green.

"Be careful: you're in poison ivy!" said Clare. At this both the brothers burst out laughing. Walter came running up and Frederick said, "Surely an intelligent woman like you doesn't believe that superstition! It's created by the imagination: it's psychosomatic. You fear it, so you get a rash, or whatever you want to get."

"Well, the country people and the farmers believe it," said Clare: "and I believe it, I've had it." "Yes, they've talked it into you. Surely you know there's no one more ignorant than yokels and farmers. I've heard country people say the mushrooms all disappeared because they were pulled up by the roots." Frederick laughed. "I'll show you," he said. He threw himself down into the poison ivy and rolled about in it. "You'll see, I won't get a spot." He took handfuls of the bright ivy-shaped leaves and rubbed them over his face and neck, laughing, bathed his hands and arms in it, opened his shirt and rolled his barrel chest in the leaves, face and palms down, embracing the ground. "See, see!" he cried; "I feel nothing. You'll find out it's pure superstition. I don't believe in it, so I won't suffer from it." He turned over laughing and lay back among the plants. All around the poisonous plants moved softly, shone about him. "I'm going to sleep in it,

160

let me have forty winks," he said smiling. "To sleep, perchance to dream!"

"Good excuse, isn't it?" said Walter. Clare looked, "Don't lie there!" Frederick reached out, plucked branches of the vine and twined them around his neck and face, and put a twig in his mouth. "Now under the vine, in the arms of the vine I sleep," he said.

Sam Parsons could not stir him. An hour or so later, his brother, who had kept on with the trench, brought him in to the house, uneasy and somewhat ill. His skin everywhere was marked with a crowded red rash, trails of pinpoint spots marking the places of sprays and lengths of vine that he had worn.

"Don't send for the quack," he said; "I've heard he's an old alcoholic; all he ever knew was washed out long ago; and besides this is a psychosomatic rash, not a real one. What can he do? Let me sit inside for a while till the sun goes down; then the rash will go away; it was brought on by the sun. If you have some water, a fruit drink." He drank and began to walk up and down, through the house, standing in the three porches to get the cool air, keeping out of the sun. "At sunset it will go. I am just dyed by the sun. I'm flushed, I have a sensitive nervous skin," he said.

At night, they sent for the doctor; and that night too, the light was on many hours in the glen, till the ambulance came for the sick man. He died a few days later. His brother went back to the city distraught and deeply puzzled.

One day in September, they posted a letter to Mr. Dilley asking his price for the place. "We may as well have a refuge somewhere."

That evening she was at the leaky pump pumping water into the kitchen sink when she trod on something that felt like a mouse or bird. She moved hastily, slipped in a pool of water and fell, breaking her arm.

"Look at my funny arm," she called out to Sam Parsons who was in the stone house. He did not reply. She got up and walked to the door of the stone house. "Sam, I'm afraid you'll have to go for the doctor."

Sam set out. It was a dark starry night, slightly windy, the full treetops moving. Animals moved, the owls screeched. Sam with the lantern, an uncertain firefly on the track, stumbled and wove his way from the patch to the bridge, from the bridge past lower fields to the hilly track and so to Thornton's. Thornton took him to town and from town he came back with the doctor. All this took two hours. Meanwhile Clare with her arm suspended from the neck in a scarf, walked around the house putting on all the lights: the many bright windows of the cottage shone out like a lighthouse to all sides of the glen; and she sat and drank a bottle of wine. Presently, the doctor came. "And tomorrow you must go into town for an X-ray," he said. He was drunk, but he operated quickly, smartly. The patient was drunk too, and the whole thing passed off very well.

In the morning they sent for a taxi and went to the station with their luggage. Mr. Thornton came early in the morning, a bright warm morning, for the keys. "You can have them any time; I'll keep them up at home," he said cheerfully.

"Thank you. I don't think we'll be back this year," said Sam Parsons.

On the track at the bridge, they turned and looked; the cottage, copper-rose, brick-red, nested close in the green, spellbound, smiling. "Oh, what an enchanting place. We must come back next summer," said Clare. "Look, that is where poor Fred Imber dug his trench." The trench was still there, with a little water in it. "It looks horrible," said Parsons. "Let's get out of here. We are not coming back next summer."

"Look at it now! Oh, how lovely."

"Let the little brass guitar sing to someone else next summer."

"Oh, how superstitious you are, after all."

"Yes, I am."

Every summer the cottage enticed some new transient. The Thorntons, mother and daughter, laughed at the strange people; and talked about what they would do with the cottage when it became Maureen's, when she married. "I don't know, I don't know, I'll see," said Thornton. "Remember that poor girl is still alive. We won't touch it yet."

Girl from the Beach

NEW YORK: LATE FORTIES

George Paul came to see the Deans, man and wife, soon after dinner. Tall, ample, muscular, blue eyes in a red boyish face, thick bronze hair in a brush, he was fifty years old, but walking like a young man from the exercises he did to keep fit; and energetic, a restless worker. He looked tired and anxious.

"No, no food, no drink. I am on a diet my Paris friend Bercovici gives me. Coffee, tea and wine keep me awake. I take them if I must sit up all night to finish an article, but they give me a headache. I always have headaches," he murmured, looking towards Laura.

He sat down in an armchair, clutching the arms and looking about as if ready to jump up; he did jump up and walked about.

"I told Martin," he said to Laura, excusing himself. "I explained that it was a long story and if you hadn't the time, I wouldn't come at all. But I'm in trouble—and it's one of those times when it's better to tell someone. I'm in love, madly in love—with this girl Renee, and I'm miserable, wretched; I don't see a solution. She promised to marry me, but I'm afraid I can't hold her. It's this woman she's living with; an invalid with the clutch of an invalid and an ugly woman. When an ugly woman gets hold of something, she sticks to it. You begin by pitying her; you're lost.

Every defect, every flaw and every weakness has its cunning. You know that?" he said violently. "We say the handsome use their looks. The ugly use their looks; and the sick use their sickness; and old age uses its age. Don't pity anyone. I wake up every night at two or three o'clock. I think, I'll do some work. I jump up, drink some milk and start to work. I never lie there and torture myself. I work. If there's a solution, it will come to me while I'm working. But that's enough! I must get back to normal. My friend Bercovici gave me some pills. He understands me. I take one of these pills; I feel better. I think, That's it. It was nonsense; I'm out of it. I start my work. An hour later, my face feels wet, it's like rain. The stars are out, it's fine weather, the moon is up. It's so bright that I can work by moonlight. The rain is tears. I'm crying for her without thinking of her at all. I can't say to her, My mind's breaking up—I'm wasting months: one word from you and I'd be well. I can't ask for sympathy. Besides, I think she guesses; she says she suffers too. I can't beg! I can't do it to her.

"I woke up suddenly last night, after about two hours' sleep. The sheet's torn right down the middle. I mended it myself, but it keeps ripping. I tossed about pulling up the sheet, but I couldn't make it come up; and I said to myself, *There's such a fighting in my heart.* It came to me, out of my trouble. But isn't that from *Hamlet*? Yes, but it came to me, in the silence. I live in silence; but with me there's no real silence. Either I'm working out one of my stories, or I'm talking to her. I tell her everything. I explain everything to her. Everything she says start up an idea in me, a complete idea; it spreads out on both sides, like a landscape. That's the effect she has on me. And in silence, I explain all this to her. I talk to her in silence. I love her so deeply: in silence.

"No, it can't go on," he said, pulling out a handkerchief and wiping his eyes. "My eyes water. It's an injection I had against tetanus. I go to places—there are dogs." He put away the handkerchief. "I fought it for months. One day I said to myself, it's love and I've loved her since the first time I saw her. I stopped short and thought about it. There's a time when you do that. You stand at a signpost: Danger. After this, no going back.

"Sonne, Mond und Sterne lachen,
Und ich lache mit—und sterbe."

George turned around, stood in front of the couple and smiled, "I was happy! I was happy. You know I'm irritable—I don't like ugly old men and women. I hate old age. When I was a child, not four, my grandfather and grandmother came to see me. I was a favourite child. They sat near me, bent over in dark clothes, and they smelled of old clothes, old bodies, old hair, old snuff. They had red eyes, hands with brown spots, hairy nostrils. They tried to sing old songs to amuse me. My grandfather even had a fiddle with a thin squeak and he would caper; while my grandmother had a mannish laugh and wore starched white lace round her thick neck. They invited me to dinner and tied round my neck a stiff damask napkin that smelled of the cupboards and old oranges stuck with cloves they kept there; and their house too smelled of mould. I used to run out of the house and halloo, pretending to be a lively boy; and I ran in at the last moment to kiss their dry cheeks. When they died, I was relieved. I was not cruel. I was a kind boy. Well—last year I was kind to old men and women who annoyed me, even to an aggressive waitress in a café I go to. I can't stand her: I'm always rude to her. But last year I was nice to her, I was so happy. I didn't ask anything of Renee at first. I was in love and I was thinking of all I could do to help her. And I thought, I have never been in love before, never with the sweet feeling of forgiveness and trying to understand everything."

He walked up and down. "And now! What I have been through! What I have suspected her of! And it's I who suffer. She has her own troubles. Too many to think of me. Then I spend days forgiving her for what she never did, for the insults and mean things I invented in my trouble. I shall go mad; I believe I shall go mad. I go on inventing things about her— why she stays away from me, why she hesitates. And the situation is simple. I know what it is. I told you it was a long story. Do you mind? I can go."

"No, no."

The couple, a short dark man and a middle-sized fair woman were about George Paul's age; and they had met years before.

George Paul took a deep breath, then said, "What is it, I wonder? A deep breath is like drinking the lake, it gives you happiness. I was so happy last year, like a boy—but as a boy," he said angrily, "I was not happy. Now I have had a year of torment. My head thumps, the nerves in my brain are on fire; I can feel where they run and see them, thin red-hot wires. I know where they go, I can see the pattern, I can see their fiery tracks! I sleep an hour and wake up to feel them burning all round my brain. Perhaps I'm on the verge of brain-fever? I have been so bad for six months, up half the night, working in the daytime; and she doesn't get in touch with me or write to me, she puts me off. She says, I'll see you in two weeks. I jump and I shout, Two weeks! I'm angry and stamp off. Next time I see her, she says, I'll see you in two weeks, and watches me, to see what I will do. I smile, Yes, all right. I go back home and smile. I fooled her. I didn't stamp and shout. I am quite happy and calm. Then I begin to suffer. I suffer horribly. It goes on and on, week after week, month after month. I can't afford it. I had *grippe*. I got well. I had *grippe* again. It took me longer to get well and I am weak. Look at me," he said, turning to them. "I look strong? I'm weak. My work's slipping. I have too much to do and everyone wants work or money from me."

"But why does she torture you?" asked Laura.

"She doesn't know she's torturing me. She's only a girl. She's being tortured too. She sent me a letter—that's why I came—I have it, I brought it. I suppose the woman has been at her. See what she says."

He gave Laura the letter and took a few steps away and back, ruffling his hair with one hand.

It was a small sheet of fine-grained paper on which the words were written in an imposing girl's script.

Dear George, The woman who married you would be a miserable wife. You have been married before. You never made a woman happy. Where's the hope? I'm sorry.

I'm not happy now, but what have you to offer me?
I couldn't bear any more wandering. That's over for
me. I have a home and a job. It's over.

Renee.

"Those are not her words," said George. "And now I have to go
through the whole thing again, argue with her, argue her out of
her fears, tear her away from that vulture. Again and again. I don't
mind. At least I see her, talk to her and win her. But as soon as
I go away, she turns from me. I'm exhausted. It's her goodness.
She's sorry for that invalid. I never could endure invalids. They live
on others. They're not ashamed of anything; they beg, lie, cheat,
fake; and everyone is taken in. Because," he shouted, "because we
have an instinct, look after the weak, an instinct which betrays us
to them. She is being betrayed into a life of degrading servitude,
a bond-woman. She'll regret it. She'll end in suicide. She never
had anything. Her mother was selfish. Renee says she led a selfish
life and now she wants to be of use, and she doesn't mind if
it's degrading servitude. It's abominable. I can't stand a domestic
drudge. Renee wants to do everything for the woman. She cleans
up after her. I saw a spoiled carpet—Renee tried to wash it. I ran
out of the house. She says to me, I can't live for myself, as my
mother and I did before. If I could have a child, children, she says,
she'd be happy. If she could have children without marrying, she'd
just bring them up, she says; and she might be happy. *If I could
forget myself, entirely, have no future for myself.* That is what
has been talked into her. I won't have children. It's the big illusion
of every woman. As soon as she has a child she lives only for it;
the husband doesn't count. I said, If you have children, you won't
love me as much, you won't love me at all. She said, Oh, what
a terrible life, what a terrible empty life. If she loves me why does
she want children? If she can live for this warped invalid, why
not for me? It's these formulas women learn; obey your parents,
a woman can love only one man, a woman must have children.
I won't have it, I told her. The night is for work or love or talk, not
for squealing brats. And I am sure no charming refined girl like

169

her—how could she want disorder and wet laundry everywhere? Marriage is different, marriage is passion; it's between a man and a woman. If a woman wants children, she doesn't love the man."

"There's truth in that," said Martin Dean.

"She loves me, she said so," said George.

He stood in front of them again, searching their faces. "I must tell you everything; it has come to the point where I must or go mad. I've waited months and months, seven months, a cruel tease, a tease," he said vehemently, "and she doesn't mean it, I know, although I accuse her to myself. What am I to do? What can I do? She promises and promises and then they get her—it is like someone calling out from a wood; a trapped girl. She calls, she comes half out, she is called back again. And she is in the wood, this mythical wood, with that woman. I need you, the woman says. Her name's Ray. I have nothing, Ray says; all my life I have been a burden. I had infantile paralysis and I wish my parents had let me die. You are all I ever had. It disgusts Renee, but it calls her back."

"Is the woman perverse?"

"Yes, but Renee doesn't know it. She doesn't know. She has a pure good heart. I wouldn't mention it to her. There's enough wrong in the world. I won't corrupt her."

"There's a danger."

"That's why I can't leave," he said walking up and down. "I have to go to Paris, Vienna, other places. I meant to take her with me. She gave me a date; and now see what she writes!"

He talked about her. Her father was in business in the Middle West. He married a rich woman, himself made money. He was injured in his sex in the war and could procreate but not satisfy a woman. He had a son before the war and a daughter afterwards; this was Renee. The mother, named Lilian, soon told the father she needed men and she meant to leave him. The father agreed to a separation; and Lilian travelled all over Europe, and put the girl in good European schools, where she learned languages, music, drawing and architecture.

Lilian, the mother, went to all the fashionable places, spending money and doing as she liked, living with different men. The son stayed at home near his father, lived near his father, married.

"Renee is pretty, she has appeal, too; and she is like her mother, so that the mother never looked at her without saying, You're exactly like me, you'll go like me. But Renee is honest and she is chic, sensitive. She walks in a fetching way and she has sweet manners. But she became morbidly fanciful and made up her mind, when she was fourteen, never to marry. The sexual relation shocked her. It seemed to her that legal marriage gave men and women a terrible indecent power over each other; they were like master and slave, brute and trainer; it brutalized them towards each other and towards other people. The mother would show Renee a picture of her father that she had cut out of the home-town newspaper; she would point to his almost hairless head, scream with laughter, make offensive jokes.

"Renee lived with her mother most of the time and men were about. Her mother told her all her experiences: You're like me, you'll be like me, you may as well know. And her mother, at this time, was getting letters from the father's woman friend. This woman, Gail, often wrote to Renee's mother. She said, Sex is not everything; I had a man before and I know what physical love is, but I love your husband for what he is, his character, his courage, his wonderful mind. The wife wrote back terrible letters, coarse, dirty letters, the letters of a spiteful old harlot. Renee read all the letters.

"At last Lilian went home, went down south and found a place that suited her; and then the quarrel between mother and daughter became too bitter and Renee left to earn her living in New York. She met a man, became pregnant, would not marry him, and would not let him pay for the abortion. It took all she had, five hundred dollars. Abortionists were on the run then. There was a police crusade against them. They had gone mostly to New Jersey. But she found one up-town. She was well again, working, when one evening there was a knock at the door and there were two huskies, plain-clothes men, who told her to come along as a material witness, an abortionist was being charged. She went, but she would not speak. They tried every form of verbal coercion, everything that would frighten and shock a girl; and at last they told her they would make her speak. They put on a master record of her own voice on the telephone making an appointment with the go-between; and they showed her a photograph of herself coming out of the office, being helped by a woman. It was hopeless. They told her, if she would give the details, they would destroy the records, and give the abortionist a break; they only wanted to frighten him. She gave the evidence; the man was charged and died by suicide. One of her friends telephoned her and said to her, You spoke and you are the cause of his death.

"Her experiences made her lose faith in people. If she saw a policeman at a distance, she'd go round by another street. Her heart thumped when the doorbell rang. It began in Europe, when she and her mother were living in cheap hotels, when her mother was running through her money. There was a police raid once in a hotel in the Rue Delambre. The mother knew, though Renee did not, that it was a *maison de passe*, a hotel under suspicion. The first floor was let out to streetwalkers; the rest of the hotel was rented to students and tourists. The police came in about five in the morning and at first doubted that they were mother and daughter. Renee could not understand it; she never understood it. It was then that she told her mother they must return home.

"After the suicide Renee moved to another address; and not to be alone, she looked for a companion, a woman. The friend I mentioned, who telephoned her and told her she was guilty of the doctor's death, brought her a woman who was an invalid, a middle-aged woman who wanted to get away from her parents, with whom she was living. This was Ray. She was pathetic, limping, thin and worn, with a childish smile and a low voice, almost deaf.

"I met Renee through the police. They are co-operative with me. I was doing some research on a case, when I saw Renee's records. They had not been destroyed. I went to her, explained everything to her frankly, told her I was a free-lance journalist, working on stories of missing girls. She will listen to anyone; she's intelligent and charming. But she found it hard to understand that I was not connected with the police. I said, I'm a crime-writer.

They help me and I help them. If I find any of these lost girls, I'll tell them, for example. I sometimes happen on things. I once saved a girl's life by telling the police about an advertisement that kept appearing every few months: an old man advertising for a young housekeeper. He had buried young women in a corner of his field.

"Renee was very lonely. Her housemate was deaf and odd and tiresome, though pleasant enough. Renee's mother died and no one condoled with her, because they thought, Good riddance. But Ray said, I'm so sorry dear; it's a bad thing to lose a mother. You're very lonely now. This commonplace remark touched Renee. She said, Ray is the only person who understands that I do not hate my mother.

"I fell in love when I first saw Renee. I was soon in love, madly in love, with all the obsession of real love. I asked her to marry me as soon as I was divorced from Barby. She said she would. The lame woman made trouble; but at last, two weeks ago, when the final decree came through, Renee promised me that she would get out of it. Ray made scenes and went home to her parents. She stayed away three or four days, then sent a message that she was very ill with stomach upset, that she was vomiting hour after hour some greenish stuff and had no strength to move. Probably Ray had taken something. Renee did not see what she could do. She stayed in her room, going to work and seeing me in the evenings. We fixed everything up. Then the lame woman came back to prevent her leaving, for she had guessed. Of course, she looked ill, tragic; and then, every day, there were scenes. Renee was afraid of her. Renee wrote to her brother to come and help her; and now the sister-in-law is there, and this letter she wrote must be the advice Ray has given."

He sat down, tired and serious. "What am I to do? I have to go away; and now there are two of them in this mythical wood, holding her back."

Martin said, "I don't want to use the voice of common-sense, George, but that girl is trouble. I knew a girl like that. She couldn't help it, and your girl can't help it."

George said, "I know, but I love her. I really love her. There are times when I just want to stand by, to save her any more torture;

but that's impossible. She must be got away, and I can't stay here as long as another month."

He pondered, looking down. "I loved a few girls and I married them. I would never spoil a girl. In the work I do, you see too much trouble, too much horror. I see girls' bodies in terrible conditions. I hear stories that it would be hard for people to believe. It's impossible to write the whole truth. The stories I write for the magazines, the very worst—they're not the worst. The police have the worst on file; and I have seen them."

Martin said, "But you loved other girls, George, didn't you? The others."

George walked about the room. "You love each girl differently, to suit her nature. That is how you can love many women; each is different and the love is different. You see her reality, her difference—her charm. I loved those girls. I still do, in a way, even those—those little harpies," he said, his face changing. "And this started in the same way. I thought, There is a girl I like. And it was all unexpected. I was looking for a girl. And Renee seemed sweet; and she had been ill-treated and deceived. But this is stronger than any of the others. It is so strong! And this is why I have loved so many women; so that I can know now that this is real love.

"What will I do if it breaks up?" he asked, in a despairing voice. "I could go on; but what is the use? I couldn't take it. I've never despaired. I'm not the type. So I'd rather die. I don't want to go out of my mind. I'd rather die. And there she is! She could get me out of this with just one act—stepping out of that house. And I can't hang around waiting. I ought to take a plane next week."

"What will you do, do you think, George?"

"What am I to do, Laura? I'm worn out. Waiting and arguing and suppressing my feelings, waiting out of consideration and pride; and working through the terrible tension; and telling no one. And my work to do and the wives, all the wives, waiting their alimony."

"How many wives is it, George?"

"Three," he sang out; "three in this country. When I was a boy they introduced me to a rich girl. She was pretty and the daughter of a gold-and-silversmith. Everyone wanted her, but she liked me. I married her and they wanted me to give up teaching at the university and be a country gentleman. I had a horse. I went riding every day. I galloped, I was so angry, furious. I had gloves on and they had a river. I caught crabs in my gloves and roasted them, not to go home to lunch. My father-in-law wore white trousers and a straw hat and jingled the money in his pockets. I wanted to travel; I got my passport. With this passport you travel far and wide, my boy, he said, jingling the money in his pocket." George noisily jingled the money in his pocket, fiercely, with a Philistine laugh. "This is your passport. Make this and you need no more. My father-in-law went to business late; and as soon as he got there he telephoned home, What is there for lunch? If they changed the menu, they telephoned him back. My wife was charming. She played the piano well, she painted portraits. I couldn't stand it. I explained to her: You are charming, but I don't want to be married. I left. I have a son twenty-four years old," he said with some pride. "And I have one somewhere in France, fifteen years old—if he is alive. I have two sons. I don't know where they are. My wife divorced me. The second time I was not married." This embarrassed him. "I came here before the war and I was fascinated by the American girl, so free, so frank, like a boy, delicious and earning her own living, saying what she liked: her independence was charming. The old ones are conventional, stupid. I married an old one first, that was Alice, she was twenty-five. She behaved best. She got married again and never bothered me. Then that little angel-face, that campus-queen, that little brat who knew nothing, Sully: her name was Sullivan. Sully knew nothing! Whenever I said the most ordinary thing, remarks you can find in Ricardo or Adam Smith, she thought it was Communist. She denounced me as a Red, when it became the fashion, because of her stupid ignorance and because she fell for my agent," he said, suddenly rolling his *r*'s. "And then Barby. I am only just divorced from Barby. You see, I can marry Renee. She can have me when she wants me."

"I wish I could help," said Martin, somewhat drily, "but I can't."

"Women think I can take anything," complained George; "I look so healthy, no one believes I'm in trouble. I keep wondering if I'm very ill but the doctor says I'm well. The women pile up their troubles and unload them on to me. And Barby! Barby thinks I'm just there to be robbed, a big golden plough-ox to be kept at work. The sort of ox that soon earns a farm for the farmer and his wife; but he must be kept at work. There are two wives living off me now and I'm so strong it doesn't matter. Serve me right, the women think. He wanted all those wives, the men think. But that isn't it. I didn't. I wanted to get married. I fell in love with each; and each one," he said, getting red and shouting, "did not love me; or only as children love. Marriage was an outing. Papa would buy the candy and the ride on the loop-the-loops. I can pay. Don't worry about my health. And look too," he said bending his large bronze-red head, "I have open scratches on my scalp, behind my ear and another somewhere and they won't heal. They came in Lausanne. I thought it was the lack of iodine in the lake water. I wrote to my friend Bercovici who sent me an infallible ointment which worked for everyone else, not for me. I tried sulpha drugs and penicillin; everything is bad for me. I'm a drug-rejector. At first they work; then they don't. I don't do all the work I should. I'm exhausted. And I look like a prize-fighter. What do you think, Laura?" he said on a gentle, touching note.

"You don't eat enough."

Presently he sat down and ate something, though he worried about his diet through the meal. After eating he became calmer and began to discuss some economic questions in which he and Martin were interested. He paused and said to Laura, "You don't use that other room, do you? I see there's a bed in it."

"No. You mean, get Renee here?"

Martin said, looking unwilling, "How do you know the lame friend won't come after her?"

"Yes," said George, "it is too much to ask. I must solve it myself. She would come at once if I would have children. Children are for older women to nurse and wash. She has lovely hands. She doesn't know life. I told her she's ignorant. She's just a wax doll

176

made by a hundred hands. Do you want to start out and make another wax doll? I said. Young women, girls want children because they haven't forgotten their dolls. The old women talk it into them: they're cunning and spiteful. Wait till you have the troubles I had. Barby was the same. I wouldn't let her. It would have turned her into a drudge, a char, a babysitter. I will not live in the house with a char. I can't have that; I must work. I can't even stop for regular meals or regular sleep."

He thrust his hands through his hair and began pulling his curls. "They immediately subordinate your life to the needs of a feeble little idiot, who can't walk or talk or think or listen or love, and can scarcely eat." He shrugged. "That is the worst of these young girls: they do such crazy things, they're ignorant of life; and I have no time to argue with them. I get married; and then I must work."

The telephone rang. It was Barbara, George's third American wife. "Is George there?" she demanded.

"Yes."

"What's he doing there?"

"Talking to Martin."

"Who else is there?"

"No one."

"I know what he's doing, he's telling you about me, inventing lies, hundreds of crazy lies, he's complaining about me."

"No, he isn't, Barby."

"Tell him to come to the phone."

George had an angry conversation with Barby, then turned: "Barby says she's coming over with a crowd."

"You'd better go, George. I've had such a day—I don't know what there is about the Ides of March. People came all day and I had to go out. Let me talk to her."

Laura, who feared scenes, asked Barby not to come. "George is going out for a coffee with Martin."

Barby became very suspicious. She heckled Laura for a moment, and then said, "I'm here with a gang and I'm bringing them over with me. I'm not letting George stay there and tell lies about me. We'll make him come out of there. He's not going to sit with his head on your shoulder making up lies about me. We're all coming over."

"I can't have you, Barby; I'm tired and George is going now. I've got no room for a gang."

Barby insisted. "They're all my friends and they'll see what he's doing." She turned and spoke to the friends; and the noise of tipsy hilarious men was heard. "He won't get away with it; neither will you."

"I don't want you, Barby; now, don't come."

"I'm coming and we'll rough up the place if you don't let George go."

Laura telephoned the hall porter saying that a crowd was coming, intending to make trouble. "Don't open the doors for them."

"No," said John the porter. Before a visitor could reach their corridor, the hall porter had to operate two switches, opening two sets of doors.

"You're going abroad," said George, looking at the large trunk, half-full, which Laura had been packing. "I've got to go abroad, not only for my work but to get away from Barby. She's the worst of all. I'll do better over there; I'll get in first with the big crime stories that break over there. I must get a fast car like the one Barby and I had in Washington. We scooped everybody. I know four or five languages, I can take good photographs, and I know some of the police. I don't depend on sleepy ten-dollar hacks like other journalists; I do it myself. I've posted my story by ten in the morning."

He paused, pulled anxiously at his hair. "That crooked little tramp Barby is after me to divide up everything: that means give her everything because she needs it. My second wife Sully is going round telling all the agents and editors that I'm a Red. I said to her, Don't you want me to make money? She's dedicated! What a beautiful girl she was! One long fair curl hanging over her shoulder, braided trousers and a little white mess jacket and a soft peach face. Barby is collaborating with her in secret; though Barby is not such a fool. It's to annoy me," he shouted. He sprang up. "My God, in this country some schoolgirl only has to say so, some peach-faced all-American child. I worked for the government in the war, I did real service. That makes me for her an undercover agent. Why am I a Red? I speak Russian for one thing. It's easy for a Bulgarian to speak Russian. I did translations of documents for the information service; some of them were secret. I went with the US army to the concentration camps and spoke to the Russian prisoners. And now she says I'm a Red. That makes it very difficult for me. I must go abroad anyway. You never saw such a girl," he said with regret; "a lovely soda-shop date-queen, cute and earnest and womanly, who knows nothing, no-thing! If you say the welfare state is a good thing, it keeps the people quiet, she doesn't hear the second part; and you are a Red. My God! She has it in for me. Alice was good to me. But these others, these little tramps, they divorce me and they are out to get me. Why? Why is that? They owe it to themselves. If I get away too easily, they're not standing up for the rights of American women; I must be punished. And I am good to them. I give them all my money. I have to work day and night—my mother has money in Switzerland; it's there but I can't get it. I have got to go there and see a man. And I must go to Sofia. I've been there, I had no trouble. That makes me a Red, too."

"Well what is all this about being a Red?"

"It's poppycock, malarkey," he said furiously. "They're making themselves important; it's vengeance. Sully and Barb are doing it for the money and the excitement, and the vengeance. They're rivals but they're combining to ruin me! American girls are bloodthirsty. Their honour is in sucking a man dry; then they throw out the corpse. Why, I have known women here who destroy a man's happiness and faith in himself, ruin his career, divorce him, turn his children against him, blacken his name to all his friends, suck him dry, and then marry him again to show they own him."

He stood with his head, his back and shoulders straight. He murmured, "Of course, they are beautiful, all beautiful harpies; but only beautiful to work their game. And Barby, who is a spiteful, lying, vengeful little thief—she has just taken my typewriter and my rugs and my typewriting chair. All the sweet young girls in the American high-school plays are cute little cheats and liars, getting round everyone! They're taught it. It's in their mothers' milk. Barby is delicious," he cried out in rage, "delightful! Winning! But only to torture and curse you. I loathe her. And if she finds out about Renee she will rush right over there and tell Renee disgusting lies and turn her against me. She is on the trail now: she knows there is something. She is a little devil, a little gold-headed fiend."

He turned to Martin and said forcibly, "In Europe I won't be pestered and nagged by this swarm of little-girl gadflies. I have nowhere here to live. I have this apartment in University Place, up four stairs, a walk-up but a good roomy apartment at the top, where I have worked for three years; and now Barby is there. I won't stay there with her. I told her, We're divorced; you have no right to stay here. She said, I want a place to stay; I am doing business in New York. I said, Go away. She said, I'll sleep on the divan, I don't want to sleep with you. And the next evening, she came in late, she turned up with a Reverend she is running round with and they slept there in my bed, while I was still finishing my work; and I had to get out. I walked the streets and I had more work to do. She is there now—" He waved his arms, his eyes started and he flushed. "I ought to call the police. She is stealing everything, taking all my photographs—"

"Your photographs!"

"You know the room I had, under lock and key, the double room downstairs, dug in the ground, with a darkroom. It was full of crime photographs from my cases. I brought them here and she is stealing them. They're dynamite and not for the public and they're valuable. Some of them are police photographs. I haven't insured them and I can't call the police."

"Why not?"

"I'm not supposed to have them. They slipped them to me—or to Barby, out there, not here. We were working together. We were married and she wouldn't let me say we were married. There was a police officer crazy about her and she worked on him. They hated me. I had to pass as her bodyguard. That was reasonable, with the places she had to go to and the hours she worked. The little wicked thief claims they are all hers; and she always snuggles up to anyone; she gets them on her side. And the police would confiscate them anyway. If not, she wants me to pay her for them; and she wants everything, prints, serialization, second and third rights—she will ruin me. And she says she needs money for her business, that is why she is doing it; but I know she wants it for her uncle who is in hiding from the police, because he is involved in some deal about fake art masterpieces. She is always keeping some lame duck."

The telephone rang; and George said, "Don't answer it; it's Barby."

Barby's sharp voice said, "Laura, is George still there? I'm coming over. I'm not having him tell lies about me. Is Martin there, or are you alone? Are you alone with George? I'm coming over. I've got a big bunch of friends here, we're at Elgar Mancando's and I'm bringing them all over. They were all in Washington when George was running around there with the blondes and they want to see I get justice."

"I have nothing here, Barby, no whisky, no food, nothing. George and Martin are just going out."

"They're not going out! We're coming over!"

Laura once more telephoned to the doorman to keep them out. "Yes," he said.

George Paul was sitting with a stubborn confused face. His face cleared, became gentler. He said plaintively, "I was walking along the beach in California; and I was furious. I had a furious quarrel with Sully and I told her I was leaving her. She was working for my agent, then she fell for him and stole my story and said it was his. She looked like milk and honey. And as soon as she falls for him she goes into court and swears, swears on the Bible in which she believes, as cool as a cucumber, that she was with him when he wrote it and helped him. It was a quiet day, a weekday, hardly anyone on the beach. I saw a big sports car rolling along the beach, blue. It stopped and a little girl got out of it with a long dog. At first I thought it was a boy. She wore a little loose-fitting denim suit and had short yellow hair. And she began to run towards me, exercising the dog, which had long hair like feathers and a bow back, and loped along lamely. It could hardly run—a wolfhound. I stopped and looked and could not take my eyes off this beautiful little boy-girl. When she came near me, I saw she was crying. She was running, crying, and the dog was loping along very weakly behind, trembling and dropping on its haunches, and getting up again.

"I said to her, Isn't your dog too sick to run? She ran past me blubbering and as I turned after her, she pushed me away with her arm and ran on. I sat down. Presently she came walking back, helping the dog and when she came up to me, she dropped down in the sand, made a smooth patch in the sand and began drawing the dog which was lying on its side, panting; and she told me about it. You know the stars and starlets want pets to be photographed with, and usually dogs. They don't know what to do with them; it's only for the newspapers. Then if they flop or they move or go away, back to their gas-station or hometown or up to the top, they leave the dog behind, sometimes in the backyard. There was a scandal, a grisly tale. They said there was a wolf about that ate things at night. They followed it and it jumped over a backyard fence. It was one of these dogs, an alsatian that had been left behind. Sometimes they give it to a pet shop to board.

"Barby was living with Elgar Mancando, in his little house in one of the glens, and sleeping with him, although he was engaged to Miriam Green and waiting for his divorce to marry Miriam; and he had one or two other girls then. That is why she was crying. She wanted to marry him. He is still unmarried and she believes in him still. Barby was miserable and wanted a pet, a monkey, and she heard of this place where you could get abandoned pets cheap. She went there; a little storefront, a dark store. The man said he had a monkey in the backyard. They went through a narrow dark passage, with tiers of animal cages on both sides; and as they went through, one of the piles of cages fell over and she saw in the bottom cage where it had been lying, a starved dog. It was a large dog curled round to fit in the cage; and it just lay there. Don't you feed the animals? she asked the man. Then the man told her how the dogs and other pets were left there by the stars. Sometimes they paid a few weeks ahead, sometimes, only one week and said they were coming back; but he knew he would never get any more. If someone wants them I sell them cheap, he said.

"Barby couldn't bear to see the dog, so she bought it instead of the monkey, though the man said it was dying. She brought it home to Mancando's in her car; and she took it out every day to exercise it; or she gave it to the writer Billy Exmouth. She and Mancando were keeping Billy Exmouth then: he was living with anyone. No one believed in him but Barby. He had a manuscript written in sewer-language which he sold and which made him rich. Barby still believes in him. Barby gave Exmouth food and he took the dog out every day for exercise, and no one could say then which was the more miserable.

"Barby told me all this and took me back to her car. She was cooking Mancando all the exotic dishes he liked, but she did not believe he would marry her. So she had made up her mind to marry Billy Exmouth, to get out of it; though she had read the manuscript, all smut and excrement. I mean it," he shouted; "that is what it was. I prevented her. She married me."

He said seriously, "You see, even at that age, sixteen, she was earning big money doing sensation stories. California's full of them. An undertaker left a shed full of unburied corpses and went out to California on the money. A retired man knocked off his wife's head somewhere in New Mexico on the way out, because he calculated there wasn't enough money for both. There was a man who could live without air and who burrowed holes under the buildings in a business block in Los Angeles, and lived on the food and the cash registers. There was another man who fished ties with a fishing-rod through the mail boxes in men's stores, and sold them. There are plenty of stories; and there's a market for them. You must have something extra, get there first, have a fast car, be a good photographer, have good shock photographs; and you must be friendly with the police, who may tip you off.

"Barby had all that, but she needed a good photographer, so she took me in. I was a teacher in Sofia, but a good amateur photographer; I won prizes. I was a newcomer here, so I developed

183

my sideline. I thought I could work in the studios; I had special cameras, but they don't want art photography. So I went out on my own. She let me use her car. But she stipulated that our marriage must be secret. First, she said her parents would not like me; then she admitted that she had admirers in the police. I noticed that. She was dainty and daredevil; and some of them were wild about her. So I had to sit there at the wheel, like a heel, while they pawed her and eyed her. The police did not like me at all, even incognito, as her partner; but going where she went, at all hours, they knew she needed a strong-arm man. It made me furious. They'd stop us anywhere to give her some information and look at me with contempt. I wasn't always at the wheel. She drove that big car like a racing-driver. So I sat there. In the end they got used to me; I even got on with them. That was how we got the big stories; the tip-off and racing with the fast car, and the photographs. The police gave us some photographs too; most you couldn't use and they weren't the sort to show young girls, but they took a pleasure and a pride in their rare specimens and they thought of Barby as one of them. They respected Barby more and more for her work and for liking them. I had this chamber of horrors; no one was allowed to enter. You remember I wouldn't let you in? I had to promise that no one would ever see them. When I came to New York I burned some, gave some back and brought the others. Barby came with me, but she couldn't work in with the New York police; and she wanted to write. So now when she's desperate, lending money to the Reverend and trying to keep up with Mancando, who's wasting an inheritance his aunt left him, she wants the photographs and the typewriter for her stories. And I suspect her," he said indignantly. "There are cranks who pay anything for that sort of photograph."

At this moment the doorman spoke on the house-phone and said a lot of people were coming up. "Don't, don't, John; I asked you not to." But before Laura had finished speaking, there was a loud noise of voices and the grinding of feet in the stone corridor. "They have got in," said Laura, frightened.

Martin gave a timid grin; George sat flushing.

The bell rang. Laura opened the door. A wedge-shaped group

184

of men stood there, with a small fair girl in front, head lowered, fists doubled. Of the men, Laura knew only Mancando, a tall, pale personable man-about-town.

"You can't come in," said Laura. "I have no room and no food and I'm packing."

Barby, head lowered, started forward and led the men into the room. There was a small square entry in which stood the kitchen unit and the other kitchen stuff. Barby and the men choked their way through this, all pushing together, Laura retreating before them; and they flowed through the archway into the room beyond where, without greeting anyone, the men began laughing, passing remarks, fingering things, lounging against tables and walls, and surveying the Italian-style courtyard from the windows.

"How long have you been here telling lies about me, Pie-otter?" squealed Barby, running forward and facing George, who had got up and was standing by the table, half turned from the room, his handsome rosy face composed now.

"I have not been talking about you, Barby, and telling no lies. What did you come for? I am going out with Martin. Why did you bring these people here?" he continued, with more heat. He looked across at Elgar Mancando, who had seated himself by Laura. His large soft hands lay loosely on his thighs, drawing attention to them; and the hand nearer Laura began to move towards her. Mancando's face began to lower towards her, with obsequious insulting flattery. Laura got up and handed round glasses of California red wine, from a gallon jar. "No Scotch?" said one of the men. "Go out and get some." Taking a ten-dollar bill from his billfold he handed it to her. Laura laughed and pushed it back. The man was puzzled. The others looked on in incurious silence, as if waiting for a scene to begin.

Barby seated herself in a knot of men on a low cane stool woven with reeds, which she removed from under a looking-glass in the inner hall.

She said, "Pie-otter is going round town telling lies about me. He says I am stealing his photographs. Those photographs belong to me; I had to kiss cops to get them. That typewriter is an old one he doesn't need and I do need. When we divorced he did not share as he was told to. He was told to divide up even the coffee. Pie-otter would never have got the big stories at all if he hadn't had me helping him. I was right in business when he moved in on me. I had the connections, I had the car. I took Pie-otter because I fell for him, I fell for his big baby-blue eyes and a big baby-blue tie he had on one day. And he thought he was a bigshot, but he was a big blue-eyed goof baby, weren't you, goof baby? And Pie-otter let me down and ran around with Miriam Green when Elgar threw her out, because she had big baby tears in her eyes: he can't resist it. You know you did. And you did, too, Elgar; you threw her out with tears in her eyes. And I believed Pie-otter was my man. You were rotten to me, Pie-otter."

"Don't call me that," exclaimed George Paul.

"Isn't that your name? Your name's Pie-otter Pay-vell. His mother called him Pie-otter."

"Barby," shouted George, in a husband's voice, "you know it's Pyotr and you can say it as well as I can. Stop it now."

"Pyotr," she said, rather faintly, bending over and looking up at him; then she sat up straight, laughed. "Pie-otter. Pie-otter and Pay-vell Fornyehkatorovich," and she burst out into a rattling laugh, and the men laughed. She cried out, "Get after him, get after Pie-otter. He let me down and stole my work; and get after them, they're sitting there all evening swallowing his lies; and get after her, she's holding his hand and listening to his lies. Laura, you were at my house in the Glen and all the time I suppose you were listening to his lies about me; and all the time he was rolling his big baby-blue eyes at Miriam Green and slee-eeping with her, and anyone who would love him. He is always looking for someone to love him."

"Stop telling lies," shouted George; "stop being a cat and a bad girl, Barby. Go away and take the men with you. I am talking to my friend Martin."

"Yes, a very sudden visitation, quite an incursion," said Martin, chuckling and looking around at the sneering curious faces. Barby was now sitting on the priest's lap. "A very sudden visitation—he-he—an incursion yes—ha-ha—but I see you are getting some red ink, anyway," and he repeated, gleefully, "some California red ink, anyway."

"Martin Dean," said Mancando, standing by the bookcase and smiling at Laura, "the only man I know who carries his own echo with him; it's so good, such a treat, he encores himself, he sings the song twice over, in case you might have missed the first fine careless rapture."

The others laughed or sat dully; but Martin, who could not comprehend ill-nature and did not know what was meant, nor that this was against himself, looked around merrily to catch the drift, to join in, with a smile, half-whispered, "first fine careless rapture, first fine careless rapture," rubbed his hands, and laughed with joy. He sensed that there was a difficult situation; he did not know what it was, but he tried to get it over by laughing. He said, "Go on, boys, have a good time; drink the red ink, come on, Laura, sit down, join the brigade, the boys want you to be along." He rolled the fun and good will out of his mouth; he was tickled by what he said; he kept laughing, a long golden laugh, from the south.

"How can you be so rude?" said Laura to Mancando. "Do you go to other people's houses to insult them?"

Mancando was surprised. Barby answered from the priest's lap, "Yes, we do. We go around town insulting everybody who listens to Pie-otter's lies. And I know he has been telling you a big sob story about some girl, some girl in trouble my age he's fallen for. Big Brother Pie-otter has to make the world right for her by falling in love with her and marrying her."

The party had broken up a little. The men were insulting Martin who, talking fast, did not hear their gibes, and yet had a strange expression, like a dawn muddled by clouds. He could not believe it, but he heard it. They were telling him to get his teeth straightened, to have them cut down, not to sharpen them on his tonsils, that he must strain his soup through them. He had big creamy teeth and a wide mouth. Mancando, a liberal-minded polished literary man who thought literary people had the right to do anything, led the insults; the others, without his talent, tried and failed.

The one they called the Reverend, a Rumanian priest, gay, tall and elegant, in a long robe, rose from his seat as the baiting became ragged, picked up Barby, put her on her feet. He said to Laura, "Have you some *ikra*? What a pity. I should have brought some for your company. Let us cook something." Laura and the priest went to the kitchenette, where they looked through the cupboards. "Come out to Chicago and stay in our convent," said the priest, politely, "and we will cook for you both. We will drink Rumanian wine and every thing will amuse you. We have gardens, a swimming pool. The convent is a very gay place. We are gayer than those here." And very slightly his dark face smiled and with his eyes he indicated the ill-tempered group.

In the sitting room behind them shouting had begun. Elgar was shouting insults at a strange man, a dark hairy small man bending forward and looking keenly at his insulter; and another man, a tall strong out-of-town dandy, was taking the last of the wine and returning to the first insults. "You open your mouth so wide I can see the back of your tonsils, you got a tooth as long as your tongue," he shouted merrily. Barby was mauling George, calling him Pie-otter, while Martin, who had at last admitted the insults, had turned away to George, and, while laughing at Barby, was talking in his clear baritone. He was talking, laughing, turning up his big eyes, opening his wide white-toothed jaws, lifting his tongue and open throat to meet the light, to meet the audience as he thought of them, tossing words, ideas, jokes sideways towards the people, waiting for them to join in in a good-natured way. His face blazed with excitement. He was continuing with George Paul a conversation they had begun a while before; and in his excitement and with George's purposeful attention, he became noisier.

He was saying, "Wall Street has no wall, Broad Street no broads, there are no Germans in Nassau Street, Broadway itself at the point of Manhattan is narrow, there are no pines on Pine Street, no Cedars on Cedar, no liberty except the right to take out insurance on Liberty, few maidens on Maiden Lane and Hanover Square no memories of the house that once empested America. India House is a place for guzzling brokers, but no cinnamon from the orient, no sweet williams in William Street, Coentjes Slip has no more conies and only the well-groomed broker's typist who never slips. Whitman chanted spires but these are buried in walls of cash and even the substitute for cash, the heavenly spirit of cash and the immense cash-register bastion once the breath of hatred to every balladist of the prairies is today..."

A silence had fallen. Some were baffled, some bored, all felt flat, as Martin, apparently without taking breath, yielded to his genius.

The Rumanian priest reappeared, darkly smiling. "Barby, come over to our place and I'll make you *ikra*."

"That's good, that's better than etchings," said one of the men.

"Where's the Scotch?" said another in a brutal tone. He had been drinking out of his own bottle, now empty. He got up and lumbered over to Martin. "Where's the Scotch, mister? Where have you hidden it?"

"I haven't any Scotch, my friend," said Martin genially.

"Everyone has Scotch," insisted the man; "where the hell is it?"

"None here; we don't drink it," cried Martin cheerfully.

"What the hell kind of a dump, let's get out of here," said the man, and he led the others towards the door.

"Martin, let me talk to you about the seven year's crisis in Switzerland, 1929 to 1936," said George Paul seriously. "And what about the deposits there now? I should like to write an article too about the deposits in the USA, enemy alien deposits in other names, which will never be returned. I am told there were fortunes in Germany and other refugee money put in Switzerland and a lot of them are sitting tight. I'm not sure I'm not in that boat myself. I shall have to go there. And I've heard something. There's something blowing up—a big scandal about the Paderewski estate. I must go."

Instantly Martin said, "That crisis shook Switzerland. She had considerable investments in America. Her banks were involved in German industries—"

"For crying out loud, let's get out of here," said the rough visitor pushing the others.

"Come over to my place," the priest was saying; "I share with three other fathers—"

"Come on," said Barby, catching Elgar's coat-sleeve and pulling him along the corridor. The men milled around her. Urging and arguing she plunged down the steep stone stairs, running ahead of them, out first, impatient.

Back in the room the two friends were still discussing Switzerland. They did not appear to notice that all was now still. Laura began packing again.

Presently the two men went out to get coffee up the street. Not long after, someone knocked and Laura opened the door to admit a dark, tall man made taller by a dark, tall hat. It was their old friend, Alfred Hill.

"Do you know," she said to him, "it came to me who you look like, Alf; you look like Abe Lincoln."

"Before or after the shot?" he said, standing and looking at her. Under his arm he had a steel-strapping machine. "Is the trunk ready?"

"Yes." She helped him to move it while he put the steel strapping around it. She had rye whisky, which he liked. They had some. He drank standing up, and moved uneasily about. He stood in one of the other doors, looking at her, then said, "I'm in love with a married woman who has two children. She'd go off with me. But where should I go? I'd take the children. But do you think I could make a start in South America?"

Laura knew who the woman was. She said, "How do I know, Alf?"

"You're going; I feel I ought to go. How am I going to see you again?"

"Come to see me."

"To Europe? To see you?"

"Yes." She laughed a little. "Why not?"

He stood over her, looking down with an alert but confused expression.

"I'll be over to take you down to the boat," he said.

"All right."

190

She sat down. That day, people had been to see the furniture, strangers had spent hours talking about their affairs, Martin's cousin had come to say her husband was going to kill her. Laura had telephoned the hospitals, the police. An old friend, a studio executive, a pretty little woman whom Alfred Hill had once admired, a woman who had "given names," had come in, on her way to Los Angeles, to find out how she was now thought of in New York. Laura told Alf all this. He laughed in his humane way and gave a big sigh. They kissed and he went, shouldering the machine.

One afternoon in March, Linda Hill returned to the hotel in the Rue Monsieur-le-Prince, about half past two. She had been out to lunch with an American couple who knew her father, Alfred Hill, had met him in New York at the Deans' parties. She was disappointed. They had not seen her parents before sailing; they had brought her no message.

She said good-bye to them joylessly. They knew nothing about her; she had explained nothing to them. What was there to explain? Her parents would have understood her without many words. But she felt miserable; in a moment of raw ugly light, she saw that she was isolated. She had been up all night and was tired. Things they had said floated in her mind. What did they mean? And there had been laughter from them at her.

We thought you'd show us the Louvre.

Oh, I've never been there.

You've been in Paris a year and never been to the Louvre?

What will you eat?

I don't know. *Rognons*, what is that?

Kidneys. But you don't know French?

Oh, I always eat hamburgers if I can. There are places you can get them.

They kept laughing. She was near-sighted, but rarely wore glasses. She could not see the menu, for one thing. It was early, but Americans had started coming to Paris; some came to see her. But she lived only for her letters at the American Express, for the money they sent her; hoping that her parents would come.

Crossing the Rue Monsieur-le-Prince she was almost run over. She continued through the traffic without glancing to left or right. "Who would care? No one cares." The hotel-keeper's wife had seen her through the window. She scolded her, "*Décidément, mademoiselle*—" She gave her a letter and watched her as she opened it. Linda gave a cry of joy. "Good news?"

"It's from friends of my parents. The Deans. They've come to Paris from Switzerland and they're living quite close. At St. Germain-en-Laye. It must be near here."

"It's in the suburbs, half an hour by train from St. Lazare."

"Where is St. Lazare?"

The woman paused, then said, "I'll direct you, when you go."

"Oh, I am happy," said Linda. "I'll go there right away. No, the letter says Sunday. Oh, but I could go now. They live there. I could wait if they're out." She resumed her grave poise. "Well, I will go there for lunch on Sunday and I may stay a few days."

"Oh, have they invited you?"

"No, but they want me. They're my father's real friends. I know they like me." She smiled an open childish smile. "They have known me since I was eight years old. They always liked me."

She went out on Sunday. She missed a train or two but wasn't very late. She knew they would be waiting at the station and that they might not know her. In the train she had been thinking about the times they had met; her parents' homes at Island Beach, at Fort Tryon Park, the simple friendly life. She stopped at the top of the platform stairs to cough and looking back saw the Sunday excursionists pouring over the top of the stairs. She was close to them and looked into each face, protected by her dark sun-glasses. How many of the French had blue and blue-grey eyes: there was a man like her father—tall, dark with small blue eyes. "I never knew before that the French had blue eyes." She turned, put on her best

193

air, tall, slender, dark crop, black glasses, taking graceful large steps, an air of long-suffering celebrity. She knew she looked much older this way. They did not recognize her. She took off her glasses. "Hello, Laura, Martin; I knew you at once."

"You look like your father!" She was impassive. She had put on too much eye-shadow in which her long dark blue eyes wandered. She wore a voluminous black skirt, a red cummerbund, a white blouse, short sleeved, with falls of lace over the elbows, and peculiar Italian shoes, high-heeled with pointed toes which curled up slightly.

They stood outside the station, with a tremendous building on the left hand.

"What's that?"

"That's the chateâu."

"I didn't know it was so close to the station."

"Yes, it's like a fortress in a backyard from this angle," said Laura.

"The trees are coming out in the park, but Paris is visible," said Martin enthusiastically. A thin smile appeared on Linda's dark lips. Martin and Paris! A well-known love affair. They walked around, Martin exclaiming over everything, pointing to things and relating the history of the place. "Yes." But she did not care at all, didn't look at the people, the park, the cliff, the Seine or the castle. "The cradle of Louis Quatorze." Because of her supposed studies at the Sorbonne they threw in a lot of French, French history too. "Are you interested, Linda?"

"Yes."

"But you've been here before, know it all."

"No."

"You're tired."

Over the stone-paved streets, they took her to an old-fashioned café across the square, a very good one, Martin said; and while waiting they laughed, characterized one of the waiters, built up a story about him. She did not listen, just glanced about her, glad to be neutral.

She drank one vermouth then asked for water and drank a lot

of it. On the roof of the great Jacobite church, roof-menders were walking about tranquilly on the slopes, without ropes or ladders. "Perhaps they teach skiing in winter," said Laura: "that's what roof-menders do in Switzerland." Linda liked them to talk as if they knew everything, but she paid no attention; impassive and neutral, she rested from herself. Above, the clouds were bowling fast; blue and white, a sky in full motion, with heavy rain in the distance, and thick high rafters of raincloud, also moving fast. Laura said, "It was blue early, then a white vapour, then blue and then these rafts of rain-cloud: trying weather. How was Paris?" Their married song, the way they always thought and talked, floated past her; she was dreaming. Laura repeated, "How was Paris?"

"I don't know. Cool, I think. Are these cobbles everywhere in France?"

This started the song, their train of thought off again. Then: "Have you letters from home?"

"Yes, whenever I go to the American Express."

"What do they say politically?" inquired Martin. "What is the meaning of this silence? From the time of the Rosenbergs onward, letters to me from the USA say nothing political. Aren't they interested? Are they afraid? Have they no idea how to describe it? Has it knocked them cold? In spite of all the years of McCarthyism I know they were never prepared for anything. They were babies compared with Europeans. They never believed it could happen there. What do your parents say?"

She walked alongside them for a while, musing, then, "They don't mention it."

"And the thousands who lost their jobs, or never got any and those who were denounced and driven out—what do they do? How do they live? Do their friends stand by them, or are they afraid?"

"I never heard of them," she said thoughtfully. "I don't know what they do. I suppose it's hard for them."

"We were anxious for you with the demonstrations here, knowing how you think, how you feel."

"I was away then."

They went on walking towards the forest, over the cobbled streets, past the market-place, past long walls surrounding extensive gardens. Martin said, "They have a market here twice a week, the best food in France."

"Is there good food in France?" She looked about the square.

"There is a store down there where you can get one hundred and four different cheeses," said Martin.

"It was because of your talking about French food when I was a little girl, and all they had there, that I came," she said, looking at them intently. "Then they told me not to eat the food, and not to drink the milk."

"Do you eat in the students' canteen?"

She let the question drop, looking downward. Then she said, "I'm not at the Sorbonne. My parents think I am. I was at the *cours de perfectionnement*. I had to be there at eight and sometimes I stayed up all night working and then doing the work for the *course*. I couldn't keep it up. I missed too much."

"I thought your French was perfect. Your accent is so good."

For the first time she smiled slightly. "Yes, my accent is very good. No one knows I'm not French till I really start talking. Then, I don't know the names of anything. It's my ear. I have a very good ear, but no vocabulary."

"What do you do at night, then?" asked Laura.

"I'm auditioning for the Vieux-Colombier night club. I'm going to. I have a job, but I've only had two tries so far. It's the La Pergola night club in the Boulevard St. Germain. I was living in a hotel near there. I was paying nine thousand francs a month. They said they could get more. Now I have a sort of large divan room. I can make tea on an alcohol stove, but no cooking they say. I do some, but I'm afraid to take bread up because they'll see I'm eating there. And I don't trust French milk or water. Some of the boys steal seltzer siphons from the cafés when they can. I can't do that. My parents told me the milk was dangerous. But," she said, looking in at a large creamery, "it looks very good. I wonder if I could have some? I'm so thirsty. And I've been having the canned milk my parents send me from New York. I live on it. They send me boxes of things, they sent me a dozen cans of hamburgers, because they think—" she paused, then continued, "they think I'm broke."

"Then you want to stay on," said Martin eagerly, while they were getting the milk.

"If I go back I suppose I'll have to get married. They want me to. But I don't want to marry just because there's nothing else to do. When there's nothing else to do I'll marry, I suppose. But I don't want to, for that reason."

As they walked, Martin was commenting on the things they passed. She broke in with, "They say here I'm an essential American, no philosophy. Then they think I'm strange here. In New York I was just a normal girl, my parents' girl. They say over here that in America we have got our values confused. I thought when I came to France—" A pause. She said, "Everyone always talked about France, a place to go and where everyone understood about life. I never thought there would be any problems living here."

She looked intently at them again. "You talked so much about France. I was ten then. That time you were at our place at Island Beach." A pause.

Martin said eagerly, "Oh, you were a little girl in a thousand. We always talked about Linda. I remember you rescuing all the alley cats, thin little clawing things that didn't claw you. You held them against your thin little chest and you were like one of them yourself."

She said slowly, "And Laura, you had some red velvet slippers, the rest was gold and there were golden bells on them, real bells that rang; and you said they came from Paris."

"Oh, yes. That was a mystery. I lost them that day."

"I know. I stole them."

A pause. Then: "And what happened to them?"

She shook her head vaguely. Then she said, "I was going to get married just before I came over. They fixed it all up. Mother planned the reception at the Plaza, we bought things, father furnished the apartment."

The Deans laughed; then they saw she did not think it was funny. "Mother and I got tired running about buying everything at Bonwit's and Saks and—other places."

The Deans held their breath. She continued, "Mother just raided the bank account. And Dad got mad at us. He spent a lot on the furniture. It was all ready. Then a week before, I couldn't do it. Not to get married for that reason. I just couldn't sleep with the man. He was all right. My father liked him and Mother liked him. Dad said I let him down," she said resentfully. "I was in disgrace. I was angry. He was angry. He went off to Canada on business. Mother went with Aunt Mary to Buenos Aires to get back Uncle Ted, I was left there in the office."

"Uncle Ted ran away again?"

"Yes. They went to Buenos Aires and found him. You can always find a baker. Dad had to pay for that trip too and for bringing Uncle Ted back. He lost his hair over that. I thought they were all doing anything they liked and leaving me there in the office. So I took the money out of the cash drawer and the bank account and I sold my coat and I came over."

Since they said nothing, she explained gently, "But Mother was right. They had to get Uncle Ted back."

"Why?" said Martin. "Your Aunt Mary—" he paused.

"He has to stand by his family," she explained nicely. "A man must."

Laura expostulated. "But you know Aunt Mary herself ran away—I know you know."

She said innocently, "But a woman is different, isn't she? My mother explained it to me. A woman is always right because that is nature; she is the mother and a man has to stand by her. What a woman does is never wrong, because she has to survive. She has to live her own life because she is there to give life. If she has a strong feeling about something it's instinct, and with women instinct is always right. It is a protection."

They were silent.

They had come to the verge of the great forest. It was still fine and very mild in the forest, in which could be seen at a distance faint clouds of leaves just settling on the trees; patches and tatters of colour, people's clothes, bluebells, little children. There were villas with tea-gardens.

"Will you have tea, Linda?"

"I like tea. They send me tea-bags and I make it in my room."

"Will you have some now?"

"No, not now," she said in her reserved manner.

"You oughtn't to live at St. Germain-des-Prés," said Martin. "It's the golden mile; they see the golden Yankees coming."

"Hm—they're very nice to me—they almost—treat me like a daughter; as if they—thought—I had to be watched over. He's very strict with me, doesn't let in people who come. A boy came and he told him I'd gone out. The boy waited for me and I was upstairs all the time."

She laughed slightly: was it in a troubled way? "But I'm looking for another hotel not so dear and I did think of getting out of the American quarter, getting one near the Champs Elysées. I haven't been up there except by taxi. I'm working in a night club there! Le Faisan d'Or. I sing there."

"What do they pay you?"

"Oh, I've only sung there two nights. They promised me a thousand francs a night, but I don't know if I'll get it. You see," she continued with a clear laugh, "I can't drink. It's lucky. I was just sitting in the night club when the waiter told me to go to the bar. A man wanted to drink with me. When I went over and he asked me what I would have, I said a roast beef sandwich and some milk. So they sent to the kitchen for it. I think he was surprised though. And I'm hungry. That's how I have my supper. Perhaps they don't like it. The sandwiches are good."

"Lin, are you short of money?" asked Martin.

"Oh, I have plenty of money," she said indifferently. "The night club pays me. I get two or three nights there and at other places, the Vieux-Colombier. I'm auditioning for the Rose Rouge. And I have money from home. I sold my fur coat. A boy friend of mine brought his mother and sister and my sheepskin was hanging on the peg. The sister said, I wish I had one like that. I said, You can have it: thirty-five thousand francs. Without thinking. He said, Okay, and I got the thirty-five thousand francs. I have about seventeen thousand francs left. Not enough to go home."

"Do you want to go home?" She was silent.

They walked around a while before dinner. With a long balanced step she walked through the splendid setting, looking nowhere but ahead, in her indifferent beauty and fastidious youth.

"We were worrying about you, in the strikes," said Laura.

"No, I wasn't there." After a pause she explained, "My mother wrote to me to keep out of it. She said, Be a vegetable." Linda gave a low laugh.

"Be a vegetable—in Paris!" cried Martin.

Linda laughed. "Yes, I know; but Mother is right."

"What does your father say?" inquired Martin.

After a pause, she answered quietly, "My mother left all that behind her after Peekskill. She walked in the procession and she saw people on both sides talking at them, looking at them like enemies; and some of them were beaten afterwards. They laid for them just like dogs. Here comes another, let's get him. They were badly beaten. They waited for them in the dark," she said in her strange light thoughtfulness. She laughed in her way, troubling and troubled. "Then they wanted to get to the children's hall and some wanted to get to the cars; but they waited for them there, too. There was a banner welcoming Paul Robeson. Oh," she said laughing mildly, "they stirred up the whole town against them. They thought they were traitors, enemies and they were out to get them."

"The papers said they were in a lynch mood."

A pause. Then: "Mother said she'd been mistaken all along. Mother thought communism was a popular movement, that they were a sort of national movement. At the Beach everyone was a Communist. You said hello to anyone, because he'd be one of us. But then Mother saw how they were hated, that they didn't correspond to any national aspiration or any popular feeling, and she left. She said what was the purpose of belonging to something that wasn't a part of the American people."

"Didn't she understand the election returns?" asked Martin sharply.

Linda said, "Mother saw that it didn't mean what she thought

200

it meant. It wasn't American. They were trying to impose foreign ideas. It didn't spring from the people. Everything must spring from the people, she explained."

"Didn't your mother ever realize she was in a minority?" said Laura thoughtfully.

"Out at the Beach, everyone was with us: we were in and out of each other's houses all our lives. It was a community."

"Yes," said Laura, "it was a happy life. You understood each other."

Linda did not reply.

"And your father—Alfred?" said Martin impatiently.

"My father?"

"I know him. He hasn't given up his beliefs. He's an old fighter."

"Oh, Dad is doing business. He has offices in Montreal and in Mexico City. He has one in New York. I was working there."

"When you took the money from the cash drawer and left?" said Martin angrily.

Laura pulled his sleeve. Linda laughed. "Yes. I could take anything I wanted. We all shared always."

Outside a restaurant in the forest stood the cars of rich customers.

"Are those American cars?" she said.

"Some are. The German High Command lived here, and now the Americans are here. You can see why some of the French call them the Occupant."

"Who?" She did not understand.

Laura said, "The forest is in bad condition, you see. The Germans didn't look after it. The trees need care."

"I didn't know you had to look after trees."

Like a living frieze, riders in coloured coats, on various horses, passed along the rides among the bushes.

"Let's go riding," said Linda.

"Do you ride?"

"No; but it's nice. I could come out here and learn."

"I can't ride," said Laura.

Coming home, they passed one of the numerous riding stables in town. It had stiles around a paved yard strewn with fresh straw. The gates were open and fowls were pecking in a heap of dung at the gate. In the air of this cobbled street hung the piquant odour of fresh horse urine. Down the street rode two schoolgirls, one in breeches, one in slacks, on brown mares.

"Yes, I should like to do that. I'll come and live here and we'll do that."

"Linda, I can't do it."

Linda laughed. "Just get up and go. Horses like me. Animals like me."

Martin began to talk about Island Beach where they had known her first. "Your mother used to talk to the neighbour while they were both cooking. The houses were so close, you could step from one backstep to another, never touch the ground. The door-steps were like running-boards. It was sand underneath. The houses were like beached boats."

Linda reflected with a smile.

"I remember," said Laura, "that everyone loved Alfred. Even the bad boys, the handbag snatchers and razor-boys. They used to gather near your father's store and wait about for him. When he came out they argued with him. They wanted him to run for Congress. They said they'd work for him for nothing, go around slashing, get out the vote."

Linda suddenly had a delightful smile and said, "Did they? I never knew that."

Martin said, "Alfred was always the popular boy. I would have made speeches for him myself."

Linda said, "Mother always said that with the people he knew, our background, he ought to have got on. Mother said he wasn't doing himself justice. And she said at a certain time, after a woman has worked hard and brought up her family, she wants to relax, she expects certain comforts. She said a man who always knew fine people, artists and leading revolutionaries and writers and Congressmen, ought to be making more money, move to a better district. It's the right thing. You get a start among your own people and then you move on."

"By your own people, you mean the poor people, do you?" asked Laura.

"The poor people?" She was surprised. "Were they poor?"

Laura laughed. "You mean the gangsters who wanted to get out the vote for your father weren't poor?"

"They had plenty of money to spend. There were places they used to rob every week; and other places paid them protection money. A few went for labour goons when things were bad, but they didn't like it. It was dangerous. They never touched—the Doc, they called my father. They never hurt anyone they knew. They were all right."

"And so they weren't poor," persisted Laura.

"But there aren't any poor in America. Look at those cars we saw. They're all American cars. Look at all the money we send over. We have to help everyone."

"Why do you think?" said Laura.

She reflected and then said slowly and naively, "I don't know. Europeans are poor, I suppose."

"Why did you come over here, Lin?" Martin asked.

She did not seem to hear, musing. Then she said, very lively, "The Doc has taken up sculpture and he's good at it. Some gal of his got him into it; she said he had good hands and she was right."

She continued, "He used one of the candlesticks on the mantel-piece for an armature for a figure. He did me. He learned casting at the school. He attends classes and he has had private instruction. You know he has beautiful hands. I have a photograph of his hands dripping with clay. He was casting. The instructor stopped the class and took a photograph of the Doc as he turned to listen. The Doc did the first casting at home in the kitchen and he called out, Lin, come and look. I didn't come and he was bringing it to show me when he dropped it. He burst into tears."

They were all three silent.

Linda suddenly said, "Mother's dropped all her nonsense now. She's very good and she runs the business along with him: she gets along with everyone. Everyone likes her."

"I heard your mother was ill."

Linda became very chatty. "Oh, it's a thing, an operation. It's in the family both sides. All the families have tumours, both sides."

"It wasn't serious?"

"Oh, yes, it was serious. She had everything taken out, but it's a fad, all the gals do it. They say, Oh, I'm having everything taken out next week. No one minds. I thought of it too. I nearly did. They wanted me to do it and I thought, Save trouble. And I did—"

"You did!"

She did not reply.

She said more quietly after a pause, "The Doc was always saying he was going to quit. I thought he would quit. He did quit a few times. So Mother thought she would have this operation. And he did come back. He's too hard on Mother. She's right."

She continued earnestly, "But I am grateful to my parents. They gave us a good background. We had a real home."

After dinner Martin said that he was tired and had soon to go to bed. "I have been ill. I fell downstairs. The Germans took their stair-carpets. They were in a hurry but not too much of a hurry for that. The Colonel hasn't the money for a new carpet, so they polish the stairs to a fare-thee-well."

"I don't really want to go," said Linda nicely. "What I will do is to come out here and find a room and live near you. You have another room here. Perhaps I could stay on that sofa until tomorrow and then look for a room, a small room near the forest. There are a lot of children living round here. It must be healthy. And we could go riding."

"If you don't go now," said Martin, "you'll miss the train after nine."

"I want to stay," she said affectionately.

"No, go home tonight and see us soon. Martin is so tired."

"Will you look after him?" she said to Laura. "If he is tired when he comes to Paris for business, he can go up to my room to rest. I'll tell the man he's a friend of my parents, and he can stay."

She said in a lowered voice, "The reason I came to France was I was working for the Doc in the New York office and while he was away in Canada and Mother in South America, I came on a little drawer in the desk with letters from Laura; and in one of them you spoke about a letter the Doc had written to you, Laura. He said he was up a tree about a gal; and you said, Get a stand-in. And in another of them, the last one, you spoke about the Doc coming to Europe, as if it were all settled and you expected him in the summer. Last summer." She threw this out, not accusing, but with disillusionment.

"Yes," said Laura.

"I knew nothing about it. I was so upset I didn't speak to anyone at home for a few days after they came back. The Doc asked me what was the matter. Do you want me to do this or that? Oh, go out and do whatever you want to do, I said, leave me alone. You don't care about what I want. But they insisted; and I said nothing. But at last the Doc came down to the office with me in the subway and said, Now come on, what's the matter, Lin? I said, Were you thinking of going to France? He had to admit that he had been thinking of it; and that he had even mentioned to you that he might go in May. And Mother too? He said he had been so angry with Mother about some escapade that he had not told her, but she was going, too. And not me? I said. I thought you were getting married, Lin, he said. So I saw they were just going to marry me and then start living again, start off without me. I felt bad. I wouldn't tell him how I felt and I didn't speak to them. I made up my mind to go myself, get there before them and I would meet them here. And when the Doc went away again, that's what I did. Mother was away somewhere. I guess she was cheating on the Doc again. I rang up and got a passage. I sold my coat and got things on our credit accounts and took money out of the office and I sailed. When I got here I wrote to them."

She was, at that moment, a gentle and lovable girl, beautiful with all her sallow skin, bad complexion; and in a manner trustful and simple. Martin was irritated by this story but she did not know it. Laura took her to the station and, waiting on the platform, Linda said, "I'll come out in a few days and look for a room. Perhaps over the restaurant you showed me. You said the food is very good there. And the Doc will like this place, those walls and those streets and the forest. We will all go out together. He used to take me out every weekend to some place. We used to stay overnight sometimes. We can do it here too. We'll all go together," she repeated joyfully. "It will be very good."

"Will you have money to stay?" asked Laura.

"I have plenty of money," she answered carelessly. "I have sold my coat for twenty-seven thousand francs and I have other money."

She went away; but they did not hear from her. When Martin went to Paris a month later he called at her hotel but he found she had moved. The hotel-keeper's wife had a talk with him. "Are you her father's friend?"

"I am her father's best friend."

"Are her parents coming for her?"

"I don't know."

"She says they are."

"Yes, I know she thinks so; but they're business people."

"Some women came for her," she said significantly.

"Some women? American friends?"

"I don't think so."

She looked at him, nodded. He nodded and smiled but he did not know what she meant.

"The women came and took her."

"And you have no address?"

"I thought you would have. She talked about you."

She had no more to say. When he was going she said, "If her parents come for her, I know she will go back home. This life is not for her. She doesn't understand it."

Martin was not strong enough to make further inquiries that day. He went home and told everything to Laura, saying, "But I can't be worried by these crazy American bohemian kids. What does it add up to but an army of remittance men? They're not earning their living; they're not students; they're not studying the language or country. They're bloodsuckers living off their parents and talking about youth and revolt."

***

They unexpectedly had a call from George Paul. He was working on a feature story of the German occupation and had to come out to St. Germain-en-Laye where the German High Command had been quartered and where there had been built into a cliff a huge secret headquarters, fully provisioned, staffed, armed. It could still be seen. Everyone in St. Germain knew about it. Indeed they were full of information, since they had all served the German occupant in some manner. Some were friendly to the present occupiers, the Americans; some, like a certain café-owner whose café had been reconstructed with German money, did not try to conceal their bitterness at the good days gone, and the tongues of these were sharp against the Americans, and their late allies.

George was expected for lunch but did not get there till four in the afternoon. When the gate-bell jangled, the dog barked violently and Manette, the young maid in long hair, long apron and slippers, ran out to let him in. With her, young and beautiful, but a servant, he was rude and imperious, and imperious to Colonel de Charleville, owner of the villa. Colonel de Charleville, always described as a fine man of soldierly bearing, came around in gardening clothes to greet him. George turned his back on this man and spoke to the Deans who had run down from their upstairs flat.

"That's the Colonel," said they.

"The kind of colonel who let in the Germans," said George.

"You're late, George."

"The train didn't want to get here, French inefficiency, they have no schedules, no programme, the railroad men don't work, they have no organization; or else they took me for a German, like everyone else and led me astray, on purpose, in their crafty *bonhomme* style. Since the Germans left, they have no one to give orders to them and they're running round in circles. The Americans, of course, can't do it. They have no idea of social order.

"Even in the train they were looking at me. A man said aloud, If he's speaking French, he's a German. Fine logic. That's what the Germans told them. We are the only ones who speak your beautiful language correctly: the English, the Americans, the rest, all illiterates.

The girl said, He's Danish. I was choking but I spoke up, I'm no German, no Alsatian, no Dane; I'm an American. I didn't know where to get breakfast," he said tramping upstairs. "There's a coffee shop in the Rue St. Honoré where I had breakfast before the war and it's still there. It's run by an Englishman, good tea and the coffee is strong, a food and good for the digestion. The best coffee in Paris. The train was at 10:00 on the indicator."

While Laura was preparing food he told them a long, extraordinary story of his difficulties in getting there. "I nearly went back to Paris. But I had to get this story. Laura, you look wonderful. And is this the villa the Germans lived in and stole from?"

He followed Laura into the kitchen asking urgently about his health, what he should eat. The bread was very bad; he could hardly get any milk.

"Where's Madeline, your American girl, who was typing for you?"

"She's left me: she went back to her husband who's got a job in UNESCO. I've got to do everything for myself. I don't mind the housework; I don't need a woman for that. I type everything: but it's the copying out. I have no time. I have to keep digging up new features, and I have to get the material and copy it. This project now is taking days. There ought to be someone there typing it out."

His wants, his clothes were simple. He wore sports clothes, nylon shirts and shorts that he could wash himself.

"Your eyes look tired!"

"It's nothing," he said hastily. "The blood rushes to my head and stays there; and I feel the heat."

"Martin will take you round the town and you come back and eat a big steak and we'll see. You can get a room at the hotel in the market square. We went there for you."

"If you think so," he grumbled dubiously. "No, no, I've got to get back to Paris. I've an obligation to someone—someone I don't trust. I must ask your advice too. That's another thing that's troubling me. It's a young girl."

When they returned and were having coffee, he sat in the chair, his rosy face in the daylight and he complained, "I nearly brought her along to leave her with you where she'd be safe. I'm sorry I didn't. Barby's in town and is making a nuisance of herself. I don't want her to find out where my apartment is. She's always breaking into my lodgings. It's not that I'm afraid she'll insult the girl. It's that I'm afraid the girl will run away." He said, in his nervousness, gi*rrr*l and *rrr*un. He leaned towards them, trustfully. "She looks fifteen, a small girl with a new haircut and bright lipstick, like a schoolchild who made herself up in the cloakroom before she ran out the school-gate. She has eyes that make you uneasy, that look straight at you with a smile and then seem to peel off, and there's another eye underneath, sizing you up, a human eye that you see for a second and then the bright enamel eye is back. Expressions flick across her face as if she were trying to find one that will suit. I don't know if it's other phases of her personality, or if she is too young to have a personality. She had a room in a little hotel and ate all her meals there just as if she were at home. Then at the end of three days they gave her the bill because she had nothing but a handbag and was coming back with packets from stores. She paid them a little and promised the rest. After that, she spent a week wandering about the streets and gardens. I saw her a couple of days ago standing outside a little hotel near the Lion de Belfort, talking to the proprietor, who was saying, No, no, no, miss."

George's face showed an older grain, more flesh: he looked paternal. He said energetically, irritated, "The child flickers like water. Evidently she feels she is irresistible, a temptress. She was following a middle-aged man about the garden outside the Luxemburg, near my rooms. She was telling him some story. He made a joke and left her. She spotted me sitting near her on a seat and came straight over to me. She came right up and said, You see, my cheques are late in coming. I changed my address and I expect the hotel is holding them up because I did not pay in full. And I expect my fiancé, but he is not allowed to cross the frontier; he is having trouble. He will come. And I wonder if you know the owner of a night club. I know that's the way they earn money. I can sing and dance.

"I got her a little room in a hotel near me and I had a talk to the hotel manager. Her name was Lili Charabas, she came from Lausanne and she was eighteen, she wrote in the hotel book. Yesterday, the hotel manager and I searched her room. There was never anything left in her room and she wouldn't tell about her parents or home. But yesterday we found a little diary with notes in it, like: *Had a chocolate sundae. Danced with a nice boy at the Buffalo. Went to the movies. Had my hair washed.* Eventually we found a telephone number on a slip of paper. I knew it was a Swiss telephone number. We spoke to the girl's uncle at Morges, near Lausanne. He said, It's her third escapade. She has just turned fifteen and wants to live with men. That's what she says. She got hold of a man at home; but she turned cold, dropped him and looked for another. She promises to meet them all privately, but she never meets anyone, never keeps appointments and hangs back from kisses. She won't even let me take her elbow," he said peevishly. "She used to sneak telephone calls at home and go to a certain hotel to telephone, always telephoning men, especially married men. I believe she thinks it's safe to do so. Then she took to roaming the country, taking trains and buses. I can't let her roam about Paris; and the uncle won't send for her. Her family is finished with her. What sort of a man is that?"

He was standing at the window, looking down into the garden.

"That's Colonel de Charleville, *un beau gendarme*, as they say. As a young fellow he was a Spahi officer who, because of his connections, married a Marquise, calls himself Marquis. He's nice with the women; and he had a Frenchman's finger in cotton wool in a box. The Germans gave it to him and told him the Russians cut it off for the ring. He believes it. The German officers took over his villa, built themselves a deep dugout in his garden and allowed him and the Marquise to use it. He thinks they were very correct. When the Germans were on the run, they stopped long enough to take his household linen, tableware, pictures and carpets. But, says he, they were very correct."

"I was in Passy," said George furiously, "I know them. The Americans were parading. All the sloths and slugs, the termites of Passy were out in the street. *Comme c'est bien! Tellement corrects—impeccables!* They think me German, do they? I turned to them and said, Do you find every army of occupation impeccable? I'm an American— I'm ashamed of you."

He took a few steps about the room. "God, look at his pictures! Such pictures haven't been seen since Napoleon the Little. Perhaps she's run away, wandered off. Laura, could you come back with me and get her? I can't sleep with all these problems. I've got her there and I'm the sole person in the world responsible for her," he exclaimed irascibly. "What's the matter with that painting? On the wall there? You see, it's poorly lighted. When I am near the window I see the Duc de Guise—"

"Yes, it's the Duc de Guise. The Colonel is very loyal."

"Yes, yes, but when I am here, near the divan, I can see a screaming pétroleuse with a liberty bonnet, underneath. I can see her perfectly. Like France," he exclaimed. He stood in the window against the light looking towards the forest. "What's going on in that château over there? There are dozens of people and they are loading things in the yard."

"They waterproof raincoats over there. You can see the colours."

"Yes, I see the boxes now. What is that house at the corner?"

"It's a house that's shut in the daytime and open at night."

"Where does this street go to?"

"To the country. They come past early in the morning, three times a week. The food is good here, better than Paris."

"I hate Paris, the food is so bad," he said, worried. His face had many aspects. His eyes at this moment appeared cavernous, dark-circled. Pouches of flesh were forming along the stout jawbone. "There's Barby and this girl from Morges—Lili—and that typist I must find and I have to get a fast car. I've ordered a Mercedes-Benz and it hasn't come yet—and I have to go to Rome to see Easter Pascuale…"

"The American gangster?"

"Yes, I met him in Rome once already. He doesn't meet people; but I met him. And he isn't what they say. He told me everything. He's not engaged in drugs and prostitution. He had a big organization in the USA and part of it got involved with drugs

211

and prostitution without his knowledge. He fired the goons who were in it; then they ganged up against him and someone informed. He gave it all up. He said I could have the whole story if I'd write the truth. He consented to give me three interviews to write the truth for the American press. I can sell it for six thousand dollars; and I can get my car then, I hate these little Renaults. I gave a deposit for a Jaguar, that's a British car; know the tester; and I couldn't bear to have a German car. But the Germans are an efficient people and no strikes. They only want to work. The French only want to strike and drink red wine. As soon as you strike a red wine country, even Alsace, you find they won't work. And you can tell them from the road"—he continued, his voice rising—"from the car. They're red. They look red, red faces, red hands—the wine's in them, they're full of it. Just wineskins. I jabbed my tiepin in one day and it came out of him red, redder than nature, wine-red. If you stick a knife into one it would pour out of him like a knife in a goatskin. It runs out of their fingers," he cried shaking his broad hairy hand in the air, fingers spread. "What are all those dogs? What is that big brute who jumped at me and put his muzzle in my face like a black wolf?"

"That's Fanfan the housedog and those are his brothers and sisters. They're Greenlands."

"She's a very pretty girl," he said discontentedly, looking down at the servant, "but sluttish. I don't like that long hair in a horsetail and she has a slippery smile. What am I to do, Martin? Laura? I'm in trouble. I had to keep my apartment in New York. I can't pay hotel rates when I'm there. And now Barby has taken it over; she is there, she is doing business there with—her—gigolos," he said furiously. "Then she followed me over!"

His thick flaming hair folded itself into shells. The grey in it was hidden. His skin was rosy, his neck broader on thickening shoulders. He had loosened his tie and his broad stout chest and strong arms stuck out of the shirt. Though sixty he was still summer, strong, hot summer. "I won't keep it on any more," he said, "though it is so cheap. I've paid but I'll give notice. And now she wants me to help her here. She's making a big mistake. We're divorced. I wrote to her, I'm not your man. I need certain conditions for my work, quiet, peace. I used to eat at a *pension* round the corner. It's for Swiss students, it's run by a German Swiss. The Germans are the same everywhere. They eat swill. They eat in platters, troughs I call them, piled to the top with sour cabbage and one sour sausage on top! At the end of the meal all the troughs are empty but mine; and those hills of sour grass and those lakes of sour sauce are inside; and inside them is buried the sour sausage. And because I speak German everyone sidles up to me and starts propaganda. It's frightful. It's torment. I don't know what to do. But I must eat."

He said in a gentle sad voice, turning to Laura, "What am I to do, Laura? Advise me!"

"Tell them you're Viennese."

"No."

"You were brought up in Vienna."

"I am not Viennese," he said, squeaking with rage. "I never saw the Viennese golden heart. All over central Europe the traces of the German brute. I am an American! In the war I fought for the USA and it was a pleasure, because it was against the Germans. Oh, you fought them, but you don't know them as I do. Why did not you throttle every one of them? There is not one good one."

"That is race prejudice, pure, absurd race prejudice," said Martin.

"The Germans are no race, but a mess," said George. "What am I to do with this girl? I have to get my work done. I can't put her on the train for Lausanne. I can't hand her over to the police. I can't be in Switzerland for several months. I have a book lined up, about refugees. I hate them but I will get money for it. I interview refugees, from Eastern Germany or Russia, I listen to their ridiculous stories, and then I write a good book, *I was an Eastern Refugee* or some such thing. I'll get five thousand dollars for it; more perhaps, eight thousand. I have to sell outright because I need the money; and it could be a movie."

"Perhaps the girl Lili will be gone when you go back and you can forget her."

213

"I can't forget her. Besides she will be there. I asked Bunny Branch to look after her."

"Is that the Mrs. Bunny Branch I met in New York?"

Still irritated but laughing he said, "She bummed her way to London as soon as the war was over, went over in a freighter that was empty because it went to New York full of Scotch. Bunny Branch was sick of New York. She's not one of the multimillionaire Branches. She married one; he left her and they don't give her anything; and she won't sue. I'm not a highwayman, she says. She had to leave London because she got into the clutches of a society drug fiend, a doctor—a Yugoslav," he said with fury.

The Deans began to laugh. George became serious.

"Oh, he is safe; he just married a title. He went around poisoning everyone, getting people down with synthetics and getting women in his clut-ches, picking and choosing and at last he got one that suited him. He made plenty of money. He gave anyone drugs that came to him. When he first took Mrs. Branch for a patient, he thought she was one of the rich Branches; but he dropped her; and so she was able to escape. But she said, In London I was only a shuddering crying rag, freezing and hungry and unable to eat. She came to Paris without anything and came to me, and said, Georrrge, I am going to shack down with you; she had nowhere to go. I've only a little room for my bed, a bathroom and a sitting-room where my files and photographs are and there is a sofa there. I must work out on the landing, for she is there now. So there," he finished, dejected, "she is and I can't turn her out. She doesn't know how to do anything. I look after her. I bring her her breakfast. Poor thing. I have got her to eat now. But I want a secretary who will do my typing. And I must make love to her. She expects it. But she is fifty! She did some typing for me and she is a good typist. But I don't like her to do it. And I have no room for myself."

"George, you have a woman ranch."

"I do not," he said indignantly, getting up and going to the window again. "I do not ask them to come and live with me. I don't love them. I need money. I have to work. I have these frightful headaches and stomach-aches. What do you think it is?"

"You must wear glasses. And eat properly."

"But I am too hot-headed! I must avoid alcohol and sugar and red meat. I must eat lightly."

Laura said, "A hot-headed man feels worse when he is hungry. When he eats, the blood goes from his head to his stomach."

"Do you think so?" said George hopefully.

"And lead a quieter life," said Martin with annoyance. "Women don't shack down with me. I don't find lunatic adolescents in the park. You must marry an older woman, George, and stick to her."

He stuck out his chin and an ugly look crossed his face. "Older women are good for aunts and mothers." Then, afraid he had offended, he said, "But I had a very good housekeeper in Paris last year, an older woman who said she loved to look after me. You must eat more; yes, she told me that."

He moved about restlessly, "You see this is all a waste of time. A publisher in New York will give me this big lump sum for the confession book. I have a good title and I call myself Pavlovich; it has a good simple Slavic sound, humble, not too reliable. It is supposed to be the experiences of a man escaped from the East. It is a work of fiction but they will say it is true. It will be good," he exclaimed. "Refugees are like pianists and dancers, they must all have Slavic names. It will be good, just the mixture of fiction and non-fiction that sells nowadays. But unfortunately, I must sell it outright and not have my name on it. I sold a story to a newspaper, and got a lump sum for letting the editor put his name on it. I can't wait for royalties and pyramiding rights. And perhaps it will be a bestseller, serial rights, TV."

"Do you really think the Russian horror story still goes?"

"German," he said, "German. He went with the Russian army to Berlin, my Pavlovich. I don't mind anyway what I do to the Germans, even East Germans. Where was Buchenwald? Right next to Weimar, the home of culture. That's the picture of German life. Don't try to make me think it over," he exclaimed, gesturing towards Martin. "I need money for my Mercedes, I will get stories faster if I drive up in a Mercedes. And there are my wive-z, my ex-wive-z. And I suppose I must take back this silly little goose from Morges."

"She is sure to get into trouble; why bother?" said Martin.

"But there are so many terrible tragedies with young girls," said George. "I am afraid for her. I know too much."

"Is that why you marry the young girls?" asked Laura.

He straightened, looked shocked. "I would not harm a young girl. Besides, they want to marry me," he said. "They are glad to marry me. They love me—besides—you cannot trust them. You must make up their minds for them. If you don't marry them they would run off tomorrow or the next day. I must have peace for my work."

"But you don't have it, George; you have nothing but misery, disappointment and anxiety."

"Because they are little idiots, little ignorant gold-diggers," he exclaimed. "When I first went to the USA and saw the glorious free little creatures, I nearly fell for every girl I saw. Then I married an old one, Alice, who was no good for me; and then Sully, she was twenty-two but she was like an old woman waging war against me all the time, always showing me up, misunderstanding everything and then—" He took steps about the room. "And I must get to Sofia to see my mother about the two houses there that are mine. Look at my eyes, Laura! They are red. Every time I lie down for a nap that happens. I get up with a headache. But I can't lead a quieter life. Anyone in my profession who gets rooted becomes a hack. He rewrites stories others have uncovered, his price goes down, he is nothing and has nothing."

"You love the excitement; you're a knight errant," said Laura.

"Don't analyze me, don't criticize me—I'm built this way, this is the only way I can live. Any other way would be the way down for me. I'm looking for someone. I got out of it with Barby and I must find someone."

"What about Renee?" asked Martin.

"Renee?" he said, abstractedly, looking at the picture of the Due de Guise.

"I never asked you, what happened to Renee, the girl in New York? Just before we sailed."

"She left me: she said she didn't want me," he exclaimed with sulky anger. "The women got her. I don't know where she is."

"You couldn't have saved her," said Laura.

George Paul looked at her seriously, the full cheek and neck, the side of his head, with the mingled bronze and silver hair, all his solidity showing his age in its full splendour, in the light. "I could have saved her; but it is too late—it's all over now. That's finished."

Presently they all three set out for the station, a long walk across the town.

They had not gone far when a young couple on a motorbike hailed them and drew up. It was Linda Hill with a young man she called Arthur. "We've just come back from Strasburg and I thought I'd come and see you." She was delighted to see them.

"In New York in the war I used to slip out to go dancing and skating. I met this pompom from Strasburg and he told me to call him when I came to France. Arthur is studying medicine here, and when I mentioned Strasburg, he said he wanted to see it too; so we went there. But I didn't know where the pompom lived. I thought Strasburg was just one street with wooden houses along it. It's a big town, with a lot of streets. We rode up and down for a while but I didn't see anyone I knew. Arthur was surprised I hadn't got the address. I thought I'd just have to ride up and down and he'd wave to me. Perhaps I've forgotten what he looks like." She laughed, and Arthur smiled.

They said they were going to the station. She said she wanted to show Arthur the forest; and then he'd drop her at their place for tea. "Arthur has to go back to Paris." They rode off.

"Who is that beautiful girl?" said George.

"I hope she hasn't come to settle on us again," said Martin.

They commented upon her and her ways. "I'll come back with you and take her back to Paris," said George at once.

Martin was indignant. She had been to Italy, to Strasburg now; she was flying about, a madcap, and knew nothing. "To me ignorance and irresponsibility are not endearing. Her parents are working their heads off to pay for all this."

"All the youngsters think they have to spend a year or two in the waste-land," said Laura.

George wanted to know all about her and they told him; her childhood, her youth, her family. Said Martin, "She is not going to shack down with us."

"I have never seen such a beautiful girl," said George.

When they got back, Linda was already there in the garden waiting for them, playing with Fanfan the puppy. She had dismissed Arthur. "I told him I was going to find a room here and stay."

They went upstairs. She said another pompom she knew lived in Bordeaux and she had promised to go to see him; but Arthur said it could not be done this time.

"I had no idea the towns were so far," she said laughing.

"Do you expect to go there?" said Martin tartly.

"Oh I guess I'll go down there and have a look," she said gaily. "Arthur can't, but someone will take me."

"I'll take you," said George.

She looked at him for the first time. Her face became grave and elongated; she held her head back and eyed him carefully. A faint smile appeared and she said, "Thank you; all right. Some day we could go."

"You can come back to Paris with me this evening, if you like," said George.

"Oh, I'm staying here," she said confidently.

"No, Lin, you can't stay here," said Martin.

Linda went into the other room, to inspect the sofa there.

Martin spoke about her father. "Linda worships him," he said.

"Why does she worship him?"

"Alfred Hill is a fine man. He's good to her. The mother, Daisy, is a flighty screwball."

"And Alfred takes Linda out every weekend," said Laura: "they go dancing; they go to roadhouses and places he knows from prohibition days."

"I'll take her out; she can forget her—father," said George.

Laura said, "She adores him. He's a big fighting man. He hails from IWW days. They were great men."

George looked at her. Laura began to laugh. "And he enter-tains her with stories, the wildest rigmaroles; and it all happened to him. I'm sure it did, too." Martin began to laugh. "I wish Alfred were here now. He's the only man I miss from the USA."

He became serious, "I wish that girl would go home. She's a worry to me. She has no more sense of direction than a packet of firecrackers, firing off in all directions. She's doing no good here."

"You needn't worry about her; I'll look after her," said George.

"She probably hasn't even a place to sleep tonight," said Laura, looking at Linda, who was coming in for an answer.

"I have a hotel room. They kept it for me," said Linda; and she gave the address, a number in the Rue Monsieur-le-Prince.

They had a brief meal. George sat beside the girl, kept looking at her.

The Deans were very cheerful. They were glad to let George take her in charge. Linda became more languid as train time drew near. Her replies told nothing; or else she let a grave pause answer for her. She hung back, but she got ready to go at last. At the last moment, she said she had nowhere to go in Paris; they had let her room. She could easily sleep here on the sofa. Her luggage was downstairs in the hotel office. The hotel was crowded. George took both her hands, looked down at them, thin, pale muscular hands.

"I'll see to all that. You must not worry about anything. I know the damned French—if you don't pay ahead, if you don't leave a deposit—no credit; you're out. Linda! I have a place to take you to. A friend of mine—"

The two men went downstairs, George explaining about a friend of his, Clare Cane, who ran a hostel for American girls.

"Clare did not know whether to marry me or set up this hostel. There are so many American girls who come to Paris and get lost. They won't go home again and they have nothing here. She wanted me to go into it with her. I didn't. I give her money for it when I can. In the end she decided she didn't want to get married. She's quite old, thirty; but she is a splendid woman—I respect her. I would have married her."

219

The two women stood at the stair-head listening. Linda turned quickly to Laura and said, "Don't let me go with him. Keep me! I don't want to go with him."

"I can't help it, Linda!"

Linda turned, her face showed great agitation. "Please keep me!"

"Martin won't let me. He's been ill. He's been up here a month. There's no sun in these rooms; and the Colonel never asked us to go into the garden. Martin slipped on the stairs and the Colonel is afraid of a lawsuit. Martin is not himself."

Linda stood looking at her. Laura said, "George is a very good man; we know him. He's honest."

But Linda lowered her eyes. "What can I do?" she said in a low voice.

The men had begun to call. "You're free, Linda."

Linda muttered. "The trouble is I do what people want me to; I can't say no. I never do what I want to do. I wish I could stay here."

Laura started towards the stairs and Linda followed. They said good-bye. The new couple turned the corner of the street. It was evening. The silent house was now alive, lighted up within behind the shutters, like a stage house; as if soon the shutters would burst open on an upper balcony and a girl would come out to sing.

Martin said, "What a blessing that George Paul was here and took charge of her. I couldn't have stood another hour of that tramp."

"She isn't a tramp. Don't they all come to Europe with a guitar?"

"To me she's a tramp wasting her father's money. She's a thief who stole his money."

"We must help her for Alfred. He loves her."

"Yes."

"I'll write to him to get her back. She was afraid to go with George."

"Afraid!"

"Yes. We don't know everything, do we? We don't know what she has been through."

"I don't want to know."

In the train Linda talked to George about her father. "I told the boy to bring me out to St. Germain-en-Laye to stay with friends of my father, until my father came. Arthur was going to bring my luggage in the morning. I thought they'd keep me."

"Is your father coming?"

"My parents will come for me."

"Can they make the trip this year?"

"I know they will come for me. We could go to Czechoslovakia. I know a boy in an agency."

"Is that why you came over?"

She was thoughtful for a while. She said, "I found two grey hairs this morning. I will have to go home, I suppose. I can't sing, you know." She opened her purse and took out a creased letter. "My mother wrote to me. She wants me to be happy." She began to read, "Don't worry about anything; leave the worry to us; we're here for that. We can always send you the rent. Don't worry about politics. Be a vegetable. Everyone is turning into a vegetable. Leave it alone. Have a girl's life. Remember everyone's proud of you. You gave us a big surprise, but we adjusted to that; and we're on your side. We're here for that." She gave him the letter, her eyes shining. "I read it so many times, I know it by heart," she said with a quiet laugh. He read it and gave it back. She folded it away. "And my father writes to me too. He never writes to anybody." After a moment she said in a low voice, "He wrote to Laura; and she wrote to him. I didn't know that. I found the letters. He never said a word."

"We'll work it all out, darling," said George. "If you want me, I'll write to your parents. They can write to me if they want to. I'll find out if they intend to come over."

She sat looking downward for a moment; then she put her arms around him and kissed him. "Oh," said she, "you are so good to me."

He took her into a popular café-tabac on her way home and while they were standing at the zinc, having coffee, she pointed to a young man standing with his back to her. "You see that boy? The one standing by the PMU. It's nobody. But he used to like me, now he detests me. He said he loved me. But not now. I don't want to be with him or see him. They get tired of me. It's something I do. If I knew what was wrong I'd change. I even ask them. They say, *Tu triches avec la vie*; one said, *T'es gentille, mais sans âme, tu tuerais sans souffrir.* It always means I don't understand something. There's an age between seventeen and twenty-one when you feel old: you seem to have lost your way. Philosophy can't help you: that's for old people who know their way. I don't understand philosophy. I don't know what it's about. It doesn't help with the life you lead. And that's why a lot of girls get married. And that's why I came over."

After a pause, she added, "They say I'm an essential American; I have no plan for living; and they say that's why we depend on getting more gadgets. But I don't like gadgets. In New York I was all right. Everyone liked me. Laura and Martin always talked about France; and I thought when I got here—" She sounded resentful, but she said no more.

"You're not lost, Linda. I'll take care of you and you'll be all right. There's nothing wrong with you, baby. The French will always prove to you you're wrong. They talk this claptrap in cafés just to pass the time till it's time for the apéritif, when they'll meet a man, another phoney like themselves, for some shoestring business. They have no philosophy! The Germans had philosophy and that is why they were organized and could overrun them. Forget them." He paused and continued, "Leave it all to me. We'll go to the hotel and get your luggage and find a hotel near me. Then I can look after you. I'm very busy; I want you near me."

She confessed that she had a room in a students' hotel near the Boulevard St. Germain. "They're nice to me."

"Let me come and see the kind of place they've given you. Say I'm your father's friend."

"Are you?" she said eagerly. "I didn't know that. Oh, I'm glad, I didn't know. I'm glad. I want to see my parents. I've been here over a year, waiting. I wish they would come. Will you really write to them? They love me, you see."

"I love you, too," said George.

"Do you love me?" she said earnestly. He kissed her. She withdrew and looked around. When he came to the door of the hotel, she said quickly, "Don't come up. It's not convenient. They'd think it funny. I have someone there."

He stared at her.

"It's a boy," she explained. "An American boy. If I don't have him, he'll sleep in a doorway, or walk about sleeping on his feet. Or he'll go to an all-night café. There's one down the street. I've often been there. We're all friends. But it's bad for him. They have coffee or wine and smoke drugged cigarettes or just plain cigarettes and they sing and talk a bit and they sleep on the tables and seats. The proprietor lets them, if they buy some little thing. There are plenty of boys there I know." After a moment's thought she said, "They're my best friends. They would let me sleep in their rooms if I had nowhere. But they haven't all got rooms. This boy's been sleeping with me for nearly two months." Seeing George's shock, she explained, "He's a homosexual. He has a sleeping bag and sleeps on the floor beside my bed. He gets up early in the morning and rolls up his bag and puts it in the closet and we arrange it to look as if he's slept in my bed. The proprietor thinks he's my boy friend. Otherwise, he would think something was wrong and might turn the boy out. The reason I went to Strasburg was I thought my parents might be coming and they would find the boy there. I told him to find another place, and I asked the proprietor to let him stay until he found something. And when I got back I found him there still. He hasn't anything— nothing," she said, a reflected despair in her face. "He nearly starved while I was away. I don't know what to do. I wanted to break it up. I can't let you go up. He would be scared. He's so—miserable. He's so thin. I think he'll die."

When he went there in the morning Linda was out for a walk. She returned just then. He was startled. She was in a close-fitting black dress which showed her beautiful figure, broad thin shoulders, a long triangle to a small waist around which she wore two Great Dane dog collars in a belt. "My God!" muttered George to himself. Trembling, almost weeping with joy, he kissed her respectfully and said what he had come to say. He wanted her to give up the room here and move near him. He was getting rid of the two women who camped with him: she was to come there in a few days. He took her out to lunch and went on with his plans. He had written to her father, told him he would marry her as soon as he could.

"I want you, that is all I want in my future life," he told her. "I don't want to settle down and furnish, I don't want children. We can go around together. You can learn to drive and, if you like, you can type my work; but I'll get a typist. I don't care about cooking and housework. That's not for young girls."

But he thought, he went on, that she should return to the *cours de perfectionnement* and go from there to the Sorbonne and get a degree, so that she could teach. He was older than she, one never knew what would happen; he would probably never have any money; she must be prepared. He would pay for everything; though, if her parents wanted to help, they could.

"But I can pay, don't worry them. And now I am worried, darling, because I have to go away and leave you for at least three days, to Rome. Then I have to go to Spain, there's a story there; and to Gibraltar, which is a free port, and to Algeciras. I have to investigate a story about pirate ships on the Mediterranean smuggling these drugs. Some say Easter Pascuale is in it, some say the Communists. We'll find you a room this afternoon and you'll wait for me, like a good girl. I'll be back as soon as I can."

By the end of lunch he had decided to pack off Mrs. Branch, with Lili to Switzerland in his Renault. Linda could stay in his flat and see that Barby did not move in.

They went back to her hotel. She went upstairs and came down. "You can come up," she said, "Mervyn's gone out."

They went up two stairs. Her room opened out of a crooked passage, a blank wall on the other side. It was evident that two buildings had been put together, long ago. Her room looked on the street. Behind it was a small bathroom, with a window on a lightwell. A double bed took up much space; and Linda's bags and trunks stood about in disorder. One, with the lid up, showed a lot of ski pants and sweaters. "Have you been skiing?"

"Oh no, but I thought I might and bought those. I'm going to pack my souvenirs in those soft things."

They sat down on the bed facing the wall. There hung a large photograph of an art class on folding chairs. One middle-aged man with long face and long hands had turned to face the camera, clay dripping from his hands.

"That's my father, that's the Doc."

"You have his eyes and hands, though your eyes are larger, and your hands are smaller. Why do you call him the Doc?"

"He wanted to be a doctor but he had to quit. He had no money.

"You say you work all night?" she said.

"I often do."

"That's good then, because I'm having tryouts in night clubs, and I could not get back early. I'd have to have a key. I'm up all night anyway. I go to that little café I told you about where the boys are."

"You say you can't sing, Lin."

She smiled simply. "Oh, you don't have to have a good voice. If you have good songs. They don't like good voices here. I sing Union songs and campfire songs to young French people. I call them American folksongs. But there's no build-up, no explanation, because I don't know the French words. I give a little talk, but in English. I just have to give it to them cold and it's hard to put over. They try me once or twice and then they don't want me because they don't understand."

"Couldn't you work it out with friends, tell them what it's about?"

"Oh, they'd find out they're radical songs and the proprietor mightn't like that."

"They're radical here."

"Oh, I don't want to get known as someone singing American radical songs over here. I don't want to get a record. I might want a clearance some day. I have friends in Heidelberg. They had to get clearances. Even in New York you have to have a clearance. That's why I started working for Dad."

"Couldn't you get a clearance?"

225

"Oh, you know—at the Beach," she began to laugh affectionately, "there wasn't anyone who could get a clearance. You would have to give names to get a clearance. And the Deans always said the French thought the same here. I thought it would be like the Beach." After a pause, she laughed and said, "Well, I'm in trouble with the police anyway. I was going to tell the Deans. That's why I went out with that boy; partly. I thought I'd stay there. It's another *département*. But anyhow everywhere I go people seem to know about me."

"What do you mean, they know about you?"

She did not answer for a while, then she said, "At the Commissariat, the police said, *Les américains sont terribles*. I couldn't understand it. I kept thinking about it."

"Were you at the Commissariat? For your papers?"

"I had to show my papers. They're okay. I really went out to see the Deans to ask their advice because I'm in trouble. At this hotel I'm in now, the proprietor got difficult at one moment and called the police."

"Why?"

"I did tell the Deans, but I didn't make them understand— well, I left out something and all they said was, Go to the Embassy. But I didn't feel like it. I was waiting for my parents to come and they could have taken my luggage with them and we could all have gone home. I told the Deans the proprietor was angry because I was drinking milk in my room at midday with two boys; Mervyn was one of them. But he allows visitors in reason. That wasn't the whole story. I was showing the boys my souvenirs when he came in. And the police came in my absence and found a good many souvenirs."

George was puzzled. "What souvenirs, honey?"

"Oh, creamers [cream-jugs], silver forks and spoons from cafés and hotel towels. If I go into a bathroom in a hotel and they're not nice to me or the place is dirty or anything like that, I take a towel or a napkin or fork from the table. It's to make them pay. Because they ought to be nice to us; they owe us everything, don't they?"

"My God," said George.

"Oh, I've been doing it since I got here. I told the Deans the first time I was out there. I just said a teaspoon. They told me not to, but everyone does it. Every American boy I know does it; not only boys, middle-aged people too, those Middle-Westerners too. They think it's a joke. They say, Oh, it's all in the bill. They take them home for souvenirs. I've collected dozens of them. Of course, they have the names of the hotels on them," she said, with a reflective laugh. "You couldn't hide where you got them; but that's what you show when you get home, the names. Or I just go into a different café or hotel to get a different name. I don't think about it. It's just a craze."

"And so he called the police and they found them here?"

After a pause, she continued, "It's a craze not only with the whacky young Americans but with everybody. I don't know what they think, but I work it out this way; it's coming to them for saving Europe. The Germans took more; the Deans said so."

"It's just plain thieving," said George angrily. "I don't care who does it."

"Is that what you think?" she asked in surprise. "Oh, it isn't that. I don't think so. Perhaps it is." She laughed. "It doesn't matter what it is, does it? They do it. Well, once the police had been here I stayed here; and besides I couldn't move very easily. And that was the night I told Mervyn he could stay here."

"What night?"

"The night the police called and found the creamers and had me in the station. They kept me a few hours at the station and they told me I had a file. And they called on me at the hotel here the next day. I would have moved, but I had all this luggage. I suppose they would have caught up with me."

"It won't do, Linda," said George, running his hands through his hair. "They catch up with you—you talk to everyone, you trust everyone. What do you think they do with all those papers you fill in?" Seeing a certain expression on her face, he said, "I hope you haven't filled in aliases; that would be much worse."

"Oh, they were quite nice to me," she said, not answering, "at the Commissariat. I pulled it off all right. I think. I told them I had to see a doctor or a psychiatrist, because I was a kleptomaniac."

George laughed.

"But they wouldn't let me. So I told them I didn't really steal them, that the boy friends I have and I don't know all their names, just Bill and Irving and Françoise, they steal them and give them to me to keep or to sell."

"What?" shouted George, "You said that? That makes you a receiver of stolen goods."

"I never thought of that," she said with enjoyment. "They have a lot on me, haven't they? But I don't think they believed all I said."

George became very serious. "Look, darling, once they put down to joyous youth; twice, you're in trouble; so no more youthful high spirits of that sort, please. Besides, they hate us; they're just waiting to hand us carbolic acid."

"But why?" she persisted, with droll insolence. "The French have always been our friends; because of Lafayette; we're sister republics."

George did not answer. After a moment Linda said, "This is the skirt I always wear to cafés." She picked up off the bed a very full skirt which she held up against herself, a dark plaid. "It's not in style," he said. Pleased, she pointed to the folds, "I had it made specially. I have a thin waist and it hangs very full. It's lined. It has long pockets that hang right down all round. It just swings. Oh, the pockets are inside!"

He got up impatiently. "It's for the souvenirs," she said mischievously.

"Eh?"

"I can wear this skirt full of souvenirs and no one would guess. I want to take it home to show my parents. They will laugh."

He looked at the skirt, looked hard at her, "I don't think they'll laugh. Only moral rapscallions would laugh."

"Oh, perhaps—they are moral rapscallions. Mother and I always laugh."

He was angry and went to close the trunk, tossing the skirt on top. She said, "Oh, don't. Is the door locked?"

He looked up. She said in a low tone. "You see, I couldn't move because of all the other things. Come in here."

She took him into the bathroom and pointed to four posters on the wall behind the bath-heater. "Behind those four posters is a big hole where the wall is broken; and the police never thought to look there. They looked everywhere; and even the proprietor doesn't know. I have all my best souvenirs there. I stole all of them myself in this skirt. The police only found a few, three or four. The rest are here; and we must pack them. We can paste the posters back. It won't matter after."

"Some day, Linda darling, when workmen tear down this rats' nest, they'll find them. We are not taking them."

"Then I must stay here. I won't leave them. I want to take them home. What did I do it for? We will have such a laugh when I unpack all that. Otherwise why have I been over here so long? There's nothing; only the things I brought over. And I lost a lot of those."

"You will never get them through the customs! Don't be such a child," he stormed. Then he began to pity her. "Come along with me; child, baby. We're moving now."

Sadly, full of reserve, she went down and asked the proprietor to help them with the luggage.

"*Et monsieur?*" asked the proprietor, meaning her roommate, Mervyn.

"Oh, it doesn't matter about him," she said to George. "Let's go if we have to. I don't want to have to explain to him," and she said to the proprietor, "Tell monsieur that I've gone; he must go somewhere else."

"I'll do that," said the proprietor.

Some of the luggage had to be left to be called for. At the last moment, she kissed the proprietor, a middle-aged, sallow man, thanked him for his kindness, "for looking after me like a father," and she said rather sadly to him, "There's no need to look in my luggage, there is nothing there; it is all gone." The proprietor, saying nothing, stood and watched her go, with a strange expression, sour and longing.

In the taxi she was crying. "I hate to leave them, I wanted to take them home. My mother loves silver things. She never had any. A boy friend gave her a creamer and she is always putting it on the table. The Doc doesn't like her to do it. If we had a lot he wouldn't mind. Oh, I'm making this up, I guess."

He was touched. He took her hands and kissed them.

"I've nothing to show for all the trouble I had," she said.

"You will have something to show, you poor baby, you little child. You'll marry me and grow up. I'll look after you. You don't know where to look. That's all it is."

"I could have done something, I suppose," she said. "It was all because of a pair of slippers, Laura's slippers, she brought to Island Beach one time when I was nine." She laughed and then became silent.

He felt the darkness in her and leaned towards her. He took off her smoked glasses and watched her pale face in the whirling streetlamps. "What is it, baby?"

She spoke up sombrely, "I'm a thief. I stole those slippers. And they never said anything; just, They're gone. And they brought retribution. Those slippers were always bringing retribution. A friend of hers died, I think. I'm not sure. A boy, I think."

He found her a room in the little hotel near him where Lili had first stayed, and asked her to come over to his rooms for breakfast, to meet Mrs. Branch and Lili before they left.

They spent part of the next day making arrangements. George did his mailing, had a nap, then went out again. He came back very much excited.

Mrs. Branch, a middle-aged woman in black, sitting with her swollen feet on the sofa, had a broad face with dark eyes and a beautiful smile. Against the wall, talking to her, was a fair small girl.

George said to them, "I wish I had the Mercedes now. You have to take the Renault; so I must fly from Orly in an hour or so. Something has happened. I've got to get down to Alpes-Maritimes this evening. It's a triple murder, an assassination, probably political; and the assassins have murdered a little girl, too. I'll be away a week. It's terrific, the biggest thing in years."

Packing his bag, changing, he gave them a few details about the Hammond triple murder.

"Rumours are thick already. I must cable New York, call a taxi."

He told them about Linda, and arranged for them to leave for Switzerland the next morning. Mrs. Branch said she could find another bed; she had friends, not too glad to see her, but they wouldn't let her sleep under the bridges.

"And you know me, George, I don't care if I do sleep under bridges."

But George said the best thing was for her to take the Renault, after that to Rome, where he had arranged to sell it to two girls he knew, girls who were working there.

"You can use part of the money to come back to Paris," he said to Mrs. Branch.

George left that night and the two women left for Switzerland the next morning. Linda, with her key, came in the same day.

Linda was left alone in her new home and at first did nothing. She trailed along the near-by boulevards, went into the Luxemburg, came home and cooked something. She was glad that she had lost contact with her Latin Quarter friends. She wrote to her mother in New York giving her new address and saying, "I am working for a journalist, doing his typing. When I have the money, I am going to the Sorbonne."

That evening George was back again. He had milk and a sandwich and sat straight down to his article; and when it was finished he went out and posted it. Then he returned and explained it to her. "They'll pay me for that but they won't get any more. This case is too hot to handle. They can get the news from AP; I'm not going to end up a headless body in the bushes on a byroad."

She listened to his brief remarks without comment, believing him. She had heard cruel stories always. They went out to dinner and when they came back, he began to make love to her. She withdrew. "I'm not a tease," she explained; "but I can't yet, George.

I do it with a boy if he wants it, if he expects it. I'd rather than make a fuss. But you're not a boy, you're different, you're older; and it makes a difference."

"You don't mind love-making with a youngster who doesn't give a damn, but not with a man who loves you?"

"I don't know why. I don't want to get involved, I expect." She laughed a bit. "It's the slippers, perhaps." She became very sober and put on her smoked glasses.

"What slippers?" He looked down: he was wearing cream sandals with blue socks.

"Not those. It was the Deans. They stayed with us, one night, out at Island Beach. My parents had put up a folding cot for them; it swayed and creaked. I was next door. In our house all the doors and windows were always open in summer. I was only nine and heard all sorts of things I didn't understand but I was frightened and I stayed awake. I didn't sleep all night. Perhaps towards morning. It was hot then. Laura was wearing those slippers in the morning; you could hear the bells ringing in the other rooms. The Doc was crazy about those slippers. They all went to the beach and I stole the slippers and hid them in a drawer under clothes. When the Deans went, I showed the slippers to a man, the father of one of my friends, who was always nice to me. I told him to come and see them. He came into the house, everyone was down at the beach and he raped me!"

"Linda!"

"I didn't know I couldn't have a baby. I waited for two or three years, expecting to have a baby. I was so frightened I would begin to swell like the women, and my mother would scold me. It wasn't till three years later that I knew I couldn't at that age."

He was silent.

"No one knows. I never told anyone but you. The man never spoke to me after that. He used to cross over the street if he saw me. I thought he liked me. He didn't. They didn't know what was wrong with me. They thought I was a crazy, nervous kid."

"Oh, how terrible," muttered George.

"I couldn't tell anyone. My father would have gone after the man. And I liked the man. I thought he liked me."

232

"What age was he?"

"About my father's age."

"My God," said George, getting up and walking about the room. "I'll look after you, Linda. I'll do anything you like."

"We're not married and I'm so afraid of affairs," she said, taking off her glasses and looking straight at him with her clever dark-blue eyes. "There must be something else. I look like a failure, don't I? But there must be something. If I only knew what to do—I'd like to go in with someone, work along with someone. I don't like money. It's just dead. I don't spend it for weeks and then I spend all I have to get rid of it. Like those ski things. I didn't want them, it was a joke; I went to the tourist agency to get those ski posters to put over the hole where the creamers are—" She paused and evidently thought about the creamers. "I just bought clothes like the poster-girl. I never thought of a skiing holiday," she said wearily. "I guess I'm a sort of black sheep. People like me, and then they—" She began to laugh. "I don't know what it is. It means nothing to me here. It must be me. Everyone likes it here. But if I go home I don't know what to do. How do you find out what to do? I don't believe in things, that's the trouble. They all say there's something wrong with me. They fixed up a marriage for me. I couldn't sleep with him. I thought of having my womb taken out, then I'd have no troubles. I wouldn't have to like men and no one would want to marry me."

"A beautiful girl like you! You're going to forget all that. You'll be all right, baby. This is just a black spot."

He made some food for them. Neither of them ate much; they drank milk. He began to tell her all his plans, the money he would make, what he owed his wives, the money needed still for the Mercedes, the money he expected from the sale of the Renault; what he did with his cheques. It grew late and she did not seem to be listening. "What are you thinking about, baby?"

"I'm sorry I did not bring the souvenirs."

He made her promise not to go back for them when he was away.

He continued, "The lawyers, the doctors want money. Sully wants one thousand dollars to have her teeth fixed. And Barby wants money. I have to go to Germany to get my car, it's the best way. And then I must go to England. I am so worried, so overworked, so short of money. I'm afraid of a nervous breakdown. And it's only the thought that you are here, that you're going to marry me and that you'll be here waiting for me while I'm away that will keep me going. I have always kept my head clear. My work has always cured me. But there is so much to do. I am disappointed about this Hammond affair. I could have made thousands out of it. But everyone is going to pull his punches. A triple assassination, international implications; and you'll see, it'll fizzle out. So, dear, I have got to get to London and to Rome to earn our bread. And I only hope they don't find a skeleton under a tree in the Forest of Fontainebleau tomorrow morning. I'd have to do it and, even if it's a missing young English girl, it's only good for one article and in a second-rate magazine at that."

He went on talking, telling her his troubles. She rested her head on the back of the sofa and folded her hands in her lap.

Suddenly, she laughed. "Oh, I'm sorry, George. It is the time of night Mother often comes home. It used to be from meetings. She was a very good women's organizer. Now it's from work, some night job she has. Sometimes she stays there all night, when she's doing two shifts. It was like that in the war too. She couldn't get back. She has fine hands: she was doing some job only women can do. I never get to sleep. I'm sleepy, ready to go to bed; then Mother comes in, and we begin to giggle; then I'm not sleepy and we stay up half the night. That's when the Doc has to flop downtown. He used to flop with the Deans."

George asked questions and, after a few more words, went back to his typewriter, placed on a little pine table in the entry under a naked electric bulb.

"I've got a few hours," he said; "I can get on with a refugee chapter."

After a long time, he looked and saw her looking very tired. "Poor girl! I'll make some tea."

"George, take me with you to England. Don't let me stay here. I'd like to see England."

"No, love. I must travel around and I have not time."

"I might go and see the Deans."

"All right."

"I'm tired," she said, "because I went to various tourist agencies this afternoon, and I ended up at Cedok to ask about rates to Czechoslovakia. I've written to my parents to come over and we'll go there and then I could go home with them. But I think they spent all their money on their new business. I guess they have none and I'm on my own."

"But you're going to marry me. I have to get proofs of my previous divorces, that is all."

"It would be nice to have a place to stay, not move from hotel to hotel; and I'd like to work with you, George. But I don't think I'm right for you. I don't believe in marriage or having children or anything. I'm too old."

"How old are you?" he said sharply.

"Oh, twenty-two; but I've been around. I don't think it would last five years. So why would I get into all that trouble for nothing? Perhaps I'd better go home."

George said, in a weary tone, "We'll talk it over in the morning. I have to get my car, and then I can take you with me. Did you ever drive a car?"

"My father was going to give me a car." She paused, reflected, and added, "No, he didn't say that. It was someone else."

"I'll take you with me when I get the Mercedes. I'll teach you to drive. Barby was a wonderful driver. I'll take you everywhere. You'll really see Europe, not from a motorbike."

In the morning he left early, excited and joyful about the German car. He gave her money, addresses, the key to the garage. "Lock the door at night. Don't let anyone in. I know Barby is in Paris or just going to fly in. When I get back I'll finish the refugee book. That will solve my problem. You go out and look at wedding-dresses. And stay here, baby, stay here, won't you?"

He kissed her with tears in his eyes. "You can read all my letters. And I may telephone you to find out what my lousy agent is doing. I'm furious with her and I wrote her a blistering letter."

Two days later he was back with the Mercedes, shouting about what the French had done at the frontier; it had taken hours. The wine was running out of their fingers, noses and eyes; some had admired it, others insulted the German car. He had to leave at once for England. He drove her around a bit, then gave her the keys, took his little bag and flat typewriter and went back to the airport.

He wrote, telegraphed and telephoned her; there was no reply. He returned at the end of ten days, found no one; and the grocer next door said no one had been in for several days; he had not seen mademoiselle. George sat down to his work. His first dispatch took him all day. Then he took the Metro to the Sorbonne quarter. He searched all the morning and found no trace of Linda. He returned home, ate some bread and began on another article. Days passed. It was one of the most miserable weeks of his existence. He started at noises, there were tears in his eyes, his stomach pained him. But he went on working and mailing what he had written. He stuck so close to his work that he had not yet used the big fast car which meant so much to him. When he had time, he found that he had not the garage or car keys. Linda had taken them with her, probably. Some of her luggage was missing. He sat down; he did not know what to do.

One afternoon she came up the stairs looking very travel-worn. She was carrying two bags.

"Linda! Where have you been?"

"In Spain," she said and sat down. "I had a good time."

"I thought you didn't approve of people who went to Spain."

She did not answer. She seemed exhausted. He got her some food and put her bags in his own room. "You must go in now and sleep. But give me the keys. Have you got the keys?"

"I just got back," she said. "It was tiring and I had no food. I just had some pills."

"Pills?"

"The boys gave me. I met some boys at the American Express when I went for my mail. They were American boys who had been here a long time. We got to talking. They said they were going to Spain; and you said something about Spain, Algeciras, the pirate ships. So I told them and they thought it was interesting. We had all got some money from our parents, so we bought a *kilometrico*, that's a mileage-ticket. You can travel all over the railroads up to a certain mileage. We bought a lot of mileage. They gave me the *kilometrico* for us three, to keep safe. One of the boys didn't like me at all. If I accidentally touched his knee or elbow, he'd pull away and make a face. And when we got to Tangier, he quarrelled with me; and I left them and went with another boy to the Casbah. I didn't know it was the Casbah or what it was. It was all right. But I don't like the people."

"What would your parents say to that, going to the Casbah?"

"Oh, I don't write them everything. It takes too long; and they don't know. But they're on my side."

"Linda, you take too many chances."

She seemed surprised. "Why? I was with a boy I knew. Everyone's very nice."

"How long have you known this boy?"

"Oh," she said dreamily, "I met him. He was a nice boy. I got back to Algeciras, I think that's it, with the two boys and I still had their *kilometrico*; and there I lost them. There was no restaurant car, so they went for some bread and missed the train. So I used up the *kilometrico* myself. I went to Barcelona and Madrid. I fell asleep in the train. I was hungry and thirsty and no one had anything, so I went to sleep. While I was asleep someone took out of my valises all my valuables, some South American jewellery my father brought me and my clothes and a leather belt with turquoises in it and a lot of things. I don't think it was the passengers."

"It could have been the customs officers, or the train police," said George indignantly. "Every tramp gets into government service, then they starve, then they steal. They have to steal to eat."

"Well, it could be. The people are very nice. But there's something funny about me," she said laughing. She had recovered her spirits since the meal. "If they come into the carriage, they just look at me and say, Show your passport; or, Open your bags. They pick on me always and no one else. They all thought I could speak Spanish because with my five words of Spanish I have a good accent. Spain is terribly poor." She mused. "In Barcelona I tried to locate a hotel, asking cops and other people and I couldn't understand anything they said. But two Spanish men found me a hotel and took me out for a drive in a horse-carriage the next day. We were driving for hours; and I didn't know where we were. They showed me everything; only I didn't understand. They paid for my dinner and took me home and the next day I found they had also paid my hotel bill."

"Did they go up to your room?" asked George sternly.

"No, it was on the level. They didn't even ask." She laughed boyishly. "And of course, there was an *agente* in the hotel lobby when I came down. Then I found out I was followed; they knew all about me. I didn't like that. So I came back. I had no money left."

"What became of the boys? You had their *kilometrico*."

"I don't know what they did. I don't know if they got back. The Embassy can send them home." She said dolefully, "I thought my parents would come while I was away. I must go for my letters. We can go over tomorrow in the Mercedes."

"Yes, I'll take you."

She became sombre. "My parents broke up my home. They were fixing a business in Canada and Mexico and they were planning to go to Europe and never told me. My father said I was old enough to be on my own."

"Linda! Have you got the keys—the keys I gave you, the car keys—"

"Oh, yes. Where can they be?" She searched and thought. "I didn't take them with me. I'm sure of that."

George flew into a frenzy: they searched his quarters. He became morose and near to tears. "Baby, you must learn, you must grow up! My darling, that is to earn my living. I need a fast car. To get there first, do my type of work, I need the Mercedes."

She was contrite, searched everywhere. "I know I'll find it, George."

George cooked bacon and eggs, they drank caffeineless coffee, and, quite worn out, they went to bed, Linda for the first time sharing George's narrow cot. It was not long before she was on the floor beside the cot, wrapped in a blanket and a coat. "You are not comfortable: come back, come back," he said.

"No, no, leave me alone. I like sleeping on the floor, it keeps my back straight, I feel calm." He looked over to her.

"What a long girl with long feet!"

She laughed, "Yes, my feet stick out."

George did not sleep for a long time. Hours later he awoke in the cold and heard sounds. He thought Linda was laughing to herself, and he waited a while; then he realized that she was crying quietly. He said nothing for some time thinking it would cease and he need take no notice; but presently he reached down and touched her shoulder.

"What is the matter? Are you cold? Come back here."

She got up and got into the cot, and wept on his breast. "Why, my darling? You miss your parents? Your friends?"

She turned over and said in a youthful voice, trustingly, "Why must it be? Is that all? Isn't there anything else? It was all right, when I was a child, and when I was growing up—it always seemed there was something. Now, now—" She began to sob and could hardly speak. "There isn't anything—there's nothing!" He let her cry for a while, then turned his back, muttering, "I have to get some sleep, I must get up early, I'm sorry, darling. I must sleep." And he did soon sleep.

But in the morning he awoke very early, about five and began thinking about the lost keys. He got up at once, and made breakfast for them both and began to search. As he searched he became more anxious and began to think of the money spent on the car, and of his present assignments which he could not work at because of his worry. At breakfast he began to plead with Linda, "Think, honey, stand in the middle of the room, there, and try to think where you put them. I must have the car. I am behind with Sully's alimony, I should have sent it to her, but I spent it on the car because I need the car. My agent is sitting on my cheques and if anything urgent comes up, like the Hammond affair, I must have it. I need to make ten thousand dollars right away to get out of my muddle. I won't live in a muddle. I've always been hard-working, decent, temperate,

239

I've never spent money on myself—only on women, on my wives—and I can't stand this muddle. If this goes on, I shall have to sell the Mercedes, but the girls in Rome are selling my Renault. I should have to buy a new one—I'll never put up again with the wretched little French tin can. Of course I make it go! I'm a good driver. I've driven a Renault all over Europe and to the borders of Asia! Wait till the mail comes, you'll see there'll be something in it. I may have to go straight off to Nancy or Berne or Nice and I must have a good car. It's not for swank. I need it. No, stand up there, my darling, or—how do you think best?—lie down there—and concentrate."

Linda did as he asked but could not remember. "Oh, you are so scatter-brained! American girls are terrible!" She lay there and fell asleep. He covered her up and paced about. When she awoke he had thought of other dangers, miseries. He harassed her. "You will see, this is a bad omen. I must write and explain the whole thing and try to get duplicate keys. I shall have to break in the garage door and pay for it." He stopped short, stood and stared at her. "Linda, my girl! Have you sold the car?" She was astonished.

"No. I never thought of it."

"Barby would—that would be the first thing," he lamented. "You are sure the car is there? I must go round at once." He left her and while he was away, she got ready, took her overnight bag and handbag, took the Metro and crossed Paris to the American Express. There was a letter for her with fifty dollars from her parents. She went back to the Latin Quarter and tried to get back her old room, which had the posters in the bathroom. It was taken, so she moved into a tiny room in the attic in the same hotel, the hotel-keeper promising her that room as soon as it was empty. He was fond of her. She could see he desired her and expected a return. She smiled at him with understanding each time she passed, but she was wondering whether she could not go away somewhere to avoid this entanglement, and she went around the quarter to the places that knew her, looking for someone. She did not mind that they greeted her strangely, jocularly, coldly. She always smiled eagerly and began to chat as with old friends. She was sad if they had forgotten her—too many customers, a new waiter— and began at once to make new friends, to be sure they would think of her.

George called at the hotel, judging she might have returned to her souvenirs, hidden in the wall, but the hotel-keeper told him that he not seen mademoiselle for nearly two months.

"She owes me rent. I was really mad to trust an American girl."

George answered him angrily and left; but, coming back, gave him his address and giving him some money, begged him to give him any news of Linda.

"She's my fiancée: we are going to be married."

"I understand," said the man with a peculiar smile. George did not know what it meant and was short with the man, having a poor opinion of hotel-keepers, knowing that most of them were informers, had to be, had a police function.

When George was some way off the man called him, "Monsieur!"

"Yes?"

"I saw her in Furstemberg Square with these women."

"What women?"

The man did not reply, but gave George a hard persistent look.

"What do you mean?" said George.

"If you spend some time around the quarter, no doubt you will see them," said the man shrugging his shoulders. "They are well-known ladies." And the man burst out into a bitter jeering laugh.

"You must tell her to come to see me. She has my keys," cried George; "it's no joke. I can't open the garage; I can't drive my car. I'm in a terrible state and my work is being held up; I'm weeks behind. It's two months already, that I've been like this. Two months ago, she went off and took all my keys. I saw her for one day, and she went off again."

"Ah, yes, one can't do anything with these mad children," said the man, indifferently. "They're barbarians, terribly savage, in a state of nature. There's no education over there; and the parents—the parents are worse than the children. Monsieur—"

"I must go. Tell her, tell her to bring the keys."

"I will do that. Monsieur is not French?"

"I'm an American," said George, furious at the insinuation.

"An American? But I should have said—"

"Good-bye!" cried George, striding off.

"He's a German for sure," said the man to himself, turning; "it's the accent. And then no American can speak French. Well—the little one, the girl—yes—" He sat down at the window and watched the street. At any moment she might go past with the four beautiful perverse women who had taken her up.

George looked for her day and night, whenever he could. He knew Linda well by this time. One day, he sat down to eat in a little cheap restaurant in the Rue du Dragon. He was tired out. He sat on the bench at a table for two. The restaurant, catering chiefly to poor American students, served meals in single dishes cheap and served fast, so that they could get in three or four sittings during the lunch-hour. Americans liked it that way, and so did George. He was too impatient to sit for hours over a meal unless he had an interesting companion, like Martin Dean, someone who could give him information. He ate escalope viennoise, something he never had at home, ate it fast, drank some water and was looking for the waitress to pay, when someone came up to the little table.

"I'm just going," he said looking up. It was Linda. "Oh, my God! Linda!"

"May I sit down?" she said, as if fatigued.

"Sit down! Eat something. You look used up."

She sat down, took the menu from the waitress. "Do you want to pay, monsieur?"

"No, no, mademoiselle is going to have lunch. What will you eat, Linda?"

Linda put down the menu. "I don't know the names of French food. What is good?" she said with lassitude to the waitress.

The waitress mentioned a few dishes that were still to be had. "Yes, that," she said, stopping the waitress; "that—or if it's off, anything."

"Do you like *bœuf à la mode*?"

"*Bœuf* is beef, I need some meat."

242

"Where have you been, my dearest? I have been looking for you for two months."

She was looking around the restaurant with interest. She turned her thin pale face to him and took off her glasses. He looked into her eyes with pain. The eyes were sunken and sick; they were like half-dried raisins; and in them was hopeless misery. She was thinking of suicide.

George kept talking lightly and kindly while he pondered. "Where are you living, Lin?"

"Nowhere. I have just come out of hospital," she said indifferently.

"What were you in hospital for?"

"I had boils. I was covered in boils. I suppose it was the food."

"Why didn't you let me know?"

"People came to see me. I didn't want them to. I looked bad." She ate the beef when it was brought. "It is very good," she said to him.

"What hospital was it?"

"I don't know. They took me there. They looked after me."

"Who took you?"

"Some women. They were good to me."

Sitting straight, he looked at her anxiously, but did not probe. She ordered some dessert, looked at him and her eyes were now fuller; but old, tired. "I thought I was going to die and if I had told my father he would have come straight over and I couldn't do that."

"Because he's busy?"

"I couldn't let him see me like that." She lowered her eyes and bent down to her handbag. She brought out his keys and handed them to him. "I found them. I had rolled them in a stocking and put them in one of the pockets of my skirt. They dropped right down to the bottom and I didn't feel them till I put my skirt on today. Then I was so—" She laughed for the first time. "I had so little strength I felt the weight! And I took them out. I was going to bring them to you." After a silence she said, "I went to the American Express and I got some letters from home. There's a hundred dollars they sent me and they tell me to come home.

243

My father is angry with me. Mother says to come home, even if I haven't got my degree. They sent someone to look for me last month, a tourist, and he couldn't find me and he went to the Sorbonne and couldn't find me there. So I had better go home. But they won't send me the ticket. They'll only send it to the Deans. They don't trust me. They think I'll sell the ticket." And again she looked around vaguely, mournfully, looking at the floor. She was saying something he didn't catch. She looked sideways up at him, "They don't love me; they don't care about me." She was silent and he could not get her to speak again. She simply shook her head.

"Lin, let's go home."

She got up, put on her glasses and strolled out after him. She was wearing the long tartan skirt with the deep pockets. When she got out she said, "I never used to take anything from that restaurant, because they have such bad forks and knives; but I took one this time, because they give us such bad things; they treat Americans like Algerians."

He took it from her. "I'll give it back." He took her to a café, gave her coffee and brandy and explained to her that she stole because she felt miserable and homeless, of no account. She would come home with him; he'd buy her her ticket to New York and she would go there to wait for him. She lived in New York and he had had an address there for years. They could marry there. "You go to your parents, tell them you're engaged. I will come as soon as I've finished this assignment. I must go back in any case because of my citizenship."

She agreed to this, and they returned to his lodgings.

"You must stay there, Lin, till I make all the arrangements; you need rest and reassurance. It'll be on the up and up. We'll be married soon. I won't bother you."

"I can work for you," she said quickly. "I'll do your typing. I'm a good typist, but no foreign languages. I don't like them."

She was no sooner there than she sat down at the typewriter and began typing out the last chapter of his refugee book.

The next day he left her at it, when he went out for a lunch appointment with Martin Dean who had come into Paris for his doctor. She said she did not want to see him. "Better not. He'll ask me things. He'll write to my parents. They're my father's friends, not mine. Besides"—she looked at him plainly—"there are a lot of people I don't want to see any more. I'm tired of it." She hesitated, but added, "You see, in the hospital I thought I'd die and I wouldn't see my parents or anyone again. I didn't care for the women either, though they were kind to me. I don't love anyone," she said, looking at him and shaking her head slightly. "I know that now. That is what is wrong with me. I don't want to see all those people I never loved. It makes me miserable. I suppose I had better get married."

"You mean, I am your new life: all the rest is gone?"

She did not answer.

The next day, he met Martin Dean. They went to a restaurant halfway along the block. It was cheap and the food poor, but Martin praised the cheapness and the food, admired the students who were working as waiters; and George took no notice of what he was eating. They had neither wine nor bread. "It costs practically nothing to eat in Paris," said Martin happily.

"But when I was a child they said pig's liver and pig's brain sent you mad; what do you think? A superstition?" said George. They had both tried the pig's kidneys.

"That was before hygienic sties," said Martin.

"But there was a man in New York, one summer, who claimed trichinosis was superstition and ate raw pig's liver and went mad and died," said George, in a worried tone.

"It was raw. Our kidneys were cooked to a fare-thee-well," laughed Martin.

They walked back towards George's quarters. "You worry about your health because you live alone," said Martin. "All bachelors worry about their health."

"I am going to marry Linda, your friend's daughter," said George. "She is a good age, twenty-two and quiet; and she wants to forget all the past. She wants to live for me. She has nothing else. I never thought of that before. One night, the other night, I stopped typing. I leaned back and thought, I am going to be happy. It never happened before. I loved them, I married them, but I never looked ahead and thought of being happy. It is not my age," he said hastily, "it is the girl. Wait while I drop in my airmail. Airmail ruins me. I was up till three, I hardly slept."

They walked on; and went up and down a few steps in the garden alley which leads to the Luxemburg Gardens. The whole country was still talking about the Hammond affair; and Martin asked whether George thought there was any connection between it and other murders of foreigners in lonely places that summer—on a seabeach, in a forest, on a road in the Pyrenees. "I don't know," said George; "but I kept out of it. I didn't want to end up a trunk murder; and there was that in it. Too many foreign services. I have to dig out the bones, name names or I have no following; and I couldn't do that. I could have made thousands. I hate all this; I hate murder; but it is my business."

"You once taught history in a university," said Martin, with slight reproach.

"I often wanted to go back, but where? Too much time has passed. I'm out of it; and this other business I can do. And I make more."

"But you spend more in this bohemian life."

"I can't settle down, I can't lead what they call a normal life. It would be the end of me," cried George. "Linda does not want a home, she does not want children. She will live anywhere. I must never settle down. Never! It's fatal. People who settle down get old. I'm ageless this way. What is to stop me?" Suddenly he said eagerly, "I have my keys: come and see my Mercedes. I'll run you out to St. Germain; we can take Linda along, and see Laura."

They turned and walked up the avenue again. Out of an apartment on the third floor of a white-faced building on one side came stirring music, a quartet led by a strident violin. After a few steps George stopped. "What's that? I know that. It gets to you. It hurts you. It has a dreadful message."

"It's Schubert's 'Death and the Maiden'."

"My God! Death and the Maiden! This little girl was eleven years old and they murdered her too. What sort of men were they? It's a Feme type of murder. I made up my mind to get them; and no sooner had I got down there, then I knew. It was known. I could not get them. Too big for me. And it presses down on me. She cries to me."

"Yes, there was a clue," said Martin, with interest.

"Don't talk about it!" George said.

"The maiden always dies and it is sad for us," said Martin in a jolly tone to distract George.

"What do you mean?" he cried.

Martin said, "A woman can't be, until a girl dies; I don't mean it indecently. I mean the sprites that girls are, so different from us, all their fancies, their illusions, their flower world, the dreams they live in."

"Women!" said George stormily. "No, there is not a dead girl in them. They are just clay. When the girl dies there is nothing. Just an army of aunts and mothers, midwives and charwomen."

"And yet, George, you have many true friends among women; Clare Cane, Mrs. Branch, you're like a brother to Laura. I wouldn't put up with women shacking down with me, or trouble about that sprite from Lausanne. I'm not nearly the knight errant you are and yet I love real women—I see nothing in girls. They're undeveloped as souls."

"I never think about these things," said George energetically. "It doesn't help. I have no time to think. I must write my stories without sentiment, and how I see them. I see girls without sentiment, but I see how beautiful they are. I cannot marry a woman who is a dead girl. I must marry a living beautiful wonderful girl. I am going to marry Linda. She will never know what she wants. I am going to make her know."

"Well, it's a relief to us, George."

George exhibited the car, and ran Martin to the station in it. Then he went back to his lodgings to take Linda out for a spin. He left the car outside and started up the stairs. He stopped. There were voices in his rooms; and one of them was Barby's. He ran upstairs.

There was Barby standing in the middle of the room, in a smart New York dress, her yellow hair piled and lacquered, holding forth. Linda was in a corner of the sofa, entranced. Against the window stood a graceful dark man about thirty-four. He was looking out of the window and at the same time holding a hand tenderly. The hand, of white ivory, with a smooth finish, like young flesh, was cut off at the wrist, but with such art that it seemed living and delightful.

Barby was saying, "This man lives in the cemetery, in the lodge-gate and he adores me; he told me there are dozens of real art masterpieces he can get for me. I pay him two or three thousand francs or even four or five hundred. I take them to New York and I can sell them for ten thousand, fifteen thousand, twenty thousand—any price. I don't go to the big galleries, I go to a little gallery on Sixth or Seventh Avenue or somewhere in Newark. I just tell someone, I pay someone commission and I can make all my expenses and big money. Then I'll set up a big gallery on Fifth Avenue—"

The man at the window stopped and kissed the ivory hand. He saw George.

"Barby!" said George, "what are you doing there?"

"Oh, she has some wonderful paintings," said Linda.

"Georgie, baby," said Barby, turning and rushing to him. "We have just got off the plane from Vienna. I went straight to Asnières because I got this tip. If you want to go in with me, baby, you can. This is my husband, George Paul, Dimitri; George, this is Prince Dimitri, my partner. Georgie darling, come into the bedroom. I want to talk to you."

"Talk here," said George.

"I can't, baby darling, I must tell you something. Do come. There, I must give my blue-eyed baby a kiss." She reached up and kissed him on the mouth and pulling at his hand began to drag him into the small room on the landing towards George's tiny bedroom.

"Get away, Barby, I'm not going with you."

Barby stopped and looked downstairs. "Pie-otter!" she cried, "is that yours? You got the Mercedes!"

"Oh, my God," said George.

She rushed to the Prince and took his arm, "Dimitri, darling, come and see George's Mercedes!" The Prince stepped along with her, with a faint agreeable smile, leaving the hand on the table, where it shone in the afternoon light. They admired the car and Barby called out to George for the keys.

"Pie-otter! I must try her. Let me take Dimitri round the block."

"What block?" said George sourly. "You mean round Paris."

"If you don't trust me, baby, you can drive us yourself. But I'd like to feel her myself."

"No," said George, "you are not driving and I am not driving. Come upstairs and tell me what you want. Because you must get out of here, Barby: I am busy."

Barby said that she had thought he was out of town and that she and Prince Dmitri could stay at his place overnight. "Who is that beautiful long girl? Are you going to marry her? Does she live here? Then we will have to go to a hotel. It is only till tomorrow, George. I am taking the plane to New York. But I need money."

"Nothing doing," said George. "I just sent you five hundred dollars. Where is that?"

"It is just that, George. It is not enough now. I need funds. I have this wonderful business, a tipoff I had. You know everybody in the States is buying art masterpieces from Europe, Utrillos, van Goghs, Cézannes, and all those, and giving them to the local art gallery. It comes off their income tax. They don't mind what they pay, it comes off the income tax. And they don't get in experts; they don't mind. They want to pay high prices and get a brass plate up in the museum or school. Well, I heard of this man in the cemetery—"

"What man? What cemetery?" George was interjecting.

"Baby darling, listen. You know your baby can unearth anything. I had a tipoff and I went along and this man—I can't tell you where he is or who, baby, of course—has dozens of art masterpieces that he'll sell me for a few dollars any time I come along. He can't tell me exactly where he found them but it's in a mausoleum, a derelict vault in the cemetery grounds. They're stacked there. So I bought a few, some Utrillos and van Goghs; and I'm leaving them here with you, baby, unless I can take them with me tomorrow. I want to take them on the plane with me, so I can make a quick sale. I know someone in New York is waiting for me. And I'll get the money, I'll get fifty thousand or more dollars as soon as I land. I'll fly straight back, baby, and pay you back."

"You won't pay me back, because I'm not lending you any money," shouted George. "And who is this man? What has he to do with it, this Prince?"

"Prince Dimitri is my partner. Now do come uptairs, Georgie, I must talk to you about something; about business. I want to show you the paintings."

George returned with them upstairs and went inside with her, Barby shutting the two intervening doors.

Prince Dimitri sauntered in, took the hand from the table and brought it over to Linda. He sat beside her, at a little distance. He spoke a graceful English, with a pretty foreign accent, not Teutonic, not Slavic. "My wife is a beautiful girl," he said with a smile to Linda; "and this is a copy of her hand. I have to travel so much for my business, and I cannot have her with me. She loves her home and her parents. We live on a little estate; it is not a park, only a garden and some acres of grass and trees—and she loves it. She loves me too and I love her. You see, because I cannot take her with me, I asked a friend of mine, who is an artist, to make me a copy of her right hand. I take it everywhere with me." He held the hand with respectful tenderness, looking at it. "Would you like to take it?" he asked, giving the hand a slight movement towards her. Linda took it and turned it over.

"It is beautiful," she said, "like a real hand."

"When I go to sleep at night, I put this hand on the pillow beside me and if I wake up I kiss it," he said with sincere tenderness. Linda, touched, looked at the hand and gave it back to him. The Prince held the hand in his lap and began to murmur to her, asking her about herself, her parents. "I see you love your parents just as my wife does."

Linda began to tell him about New York. "I'm going back soon," she said with joy. Tears came into her eyes. "I shall be so glad to see them. I've been away nearly two years. All the time I expected them to come. Now I am going home in a month."

"And you are going to marry Mr. Paul?" She did not answer. Two voices exploded behind the closed doors. The Prince got up and went over to the window, placing the hand on the table and resuming his original pose.

They heard George crossing the room in a temper, a door opened, after a moment George shouted, "Take them out, I won't have them! Take them away at once!" and once more his steps. He opened the door and appeared red-faced. Barby ran after him.

"Just till tomorrow, Georgie baby, and I will take them to the airport. If you won't lend me the Mercedes, you can lend me the Renault, you could give me the Renault if you were nice," she said, pouting. "You don't need two cars, and I need one. I can't do business, going in the subway. The Prince can drive me and I'll do the business. So will you give me your Renault, baby? You owe me something. You did not share your estate with me fifty-fifty as you were told to do."

"The Renault is sold," said George, "you won't get anything out of it. It's in Rome. You just keep your hands off me, Barby. We're divorced. I owe you nothing. I've paid you your alimony."

"I don't want alimony, I want you to go into business with me, be partners," she said pouting, and hanging around him. "George, darling, go into the bedroom and get my handbag, I left it there."

"I'll get it and you must go," said George. "Take your rubbishy paintings and get out."

"They are not rubbish, they are van Goghs and Utrillos and Rouaults."

"They are van Fakes, every last one," shouted George. He went into the bedroom and was away a few minutes. At last he returned. "You spilled everything all over the bedcover," he said stormily, "I had to pick it all up."

"I didn't spill it, Georgie, you must have done it," she said taking the bag and rummaging in it. "Georgie, you have taken two thousand francs."

"Don't be ridiculous," he shouted. "Don't pull anything."

"George, when I came I had five thousand francs and I left my handbag on your bed and you spilled the things out and looked

251

for money because you have a Mercedes and you are going to get married, but you have no money, you are broke and you found two thousand francs and you thought, I will take it back because I have to pay her alimony."

"Don't tell such terrible lies, Barby," he shouted; "you know you didn't have another two thousand francs."

"Yes, I did, George," she pouted; "and this is the second money I have lost today. I had a lot of dollars in my bra. Some were in my bag; they took those and I thought I would put five hundred dollars safely into my bra and pin it and so I did. But somehow it slipped out and someone picked it up—the customs officers or the hostess on the plane, I expect. Perhaps I dropped it in the ladies' room. So I am without a cent, I am broke, and you will have to help me out. The Prince has friends, perhaps; but I have not. You are my friend, my husband, and you owe it to me. You are always behind with the alimony. But I don't want alimony. I came to you to make a proposition. I paid for the pictures, you give me the money for the freight and I will fly back as quick as I can and pay you back and we'll make a business arrangement. But the Prince must be in it too."

"Barby, you're a little liar and thief and cheat," he shouted, outraged, "if you had any money, you stole it yourself. Now get out. And take those van Fakes. I'm not having the police here." She persisted that they were genuine masterpieces; but George said, "I saw them, I saw them. A cat could see they're fakes."

"No matter what they are, baby, though they're genuine. I can sell them in New York and California and Texas; I have contacts," she said, amiably.

In the end, Barby refused to remove the canvasses unless George drove her and the Prince to a small hotel. She whipped into the car first, took the wheel and could not be dislodged; she drove them away. George was away a long time. He came back about eight o'clock at night very tired.

"I am so tired, I don't sleep, I don't dare take sleeping pills because they are bad for me, I'm a drug-rejector," he said to Linda; "and Barby has finished me. She knows how to drive me mad.

I ought to go to South America, take you with me, we could both go now. When Barby is around and knows I have a car or money or even a roof over my head, she will try to take it all from me. I am used to her hangers-on, all good-for-nothings she picks up. They never give any trouble. It is Barby! It is Barby!"

"But she must be good in business," said Linda. "Do you think she will make money? Perhaps we could help her. I'd like to go into business. I think I could do that, sell pictures."

"We are never going to touch those crazy van Fakes," said George firmly. "I know what cemetery she got them in. I think I know the man. But this Prince is in it; and Barby is completely without morals."

"But how do you know they are fakes?"

"I know," said George. "Do you think they have van Gogh and Cézanne and Rouault lying around Paris in heaps? The place is skinned. There can only be fakes left. I know all about it from a friend. Besides," he cried testily, "Barby would never touch a genuine article. It wouldn't appeal to her. She only likes the phoney; because the market for the real is known, whereas the market for the fake is anything you can get. She loves that."

Linda desisted; but often during the afternoon she lay back, her eyes wandered and she began to smile.

This evening they celebrated the engagement; they laughed, but Linda became pensive. This was her third engagement. They all wanted her to marry. It had just occurred to her that if she married George, she would not have a home in New York, an apartment and furniture; she would be his secretary in Paris or Vienna, sometimes flying to New York. Or would her parents come to visit her? She did not think about George's remark, "I don't want any children, honey; I want you to love me." This passed in one ear and out the other. She lived from day to day: and she liked to see how things worked themselves out.

The next day, George was meeting refugees in Montparnasse. He despised them; "mendicant riffraff" he called them. He did not take the car, so that they would not try to pump money out of him. Linda was typing some of the refugee manuscript when

Barby, alone, ran up the stairs, called out cheerily, threw her arms around her, kissed her and called her darling. Linda, delighted by the sharp, smart, irritable New York voice, hugged and kissed her; they moved around the rooms, talking and laughing. Barby had brought a bottle of wine and some steaks.

"I'll cook you an American meal; I know you must be home-sick for it."

"Oh, I am."

Barby asked questions about George and Linda answered. "Are you going to marry him? You don't seem to me his sort of girl."

"I don't know," said Linda, with friendly frankness; "he says so and the Deans seem to want it. I think everybody wants to get rid of the problem. I'm a problem."

"George is the biggest problem you'll ever run into," said Barby, decidedly. "Listen to me, honey. I'll tell you about George. I don't want you to make a big mistake. I did. I was only sixteen. Georgie-Porgie likes girls young. I'm twenty-four now. He'll marry you and in two or three years, he'll get a middle-aged typist, he likes them, and he'll fall flat on his nose for some other American kid. He's got a complex. But you haven't, have you? I mean, when you get married you have to be sure the other one has a sort of complementary complex. Then there's a balance. But have you got a complex?"

"I suppose I must have," said Linda; "I don't seem to get anywhere, no one likes me and I don't know what I want."

"That's nothing, you're a kid of twenty-two. Go home and marry a straight American and you'll have the same values. George's a European. He hates Americans. Only Baby Blue-eyes doesn't know it. He keeps marrying them to make them into his own little girl."

She cantered along, rushed along, honeying and laughing and Linda felt that she had not been so cheerful since she came abroad. "I suppose I'm a real American and I can't change," she said. "George wants me to go home and he'll come and join me in a couple of months."

"Don't do it, honey," urged Barby. She went on talking fast, "You go home and see your parents and see what it is you really want. Over here you're lost, you feel frustrated, you're disoriented. You'll be okay at home."

"Yes," said Linda eagerly.

Presently she asked her about the Prince. "I liked him."

"I think I'll marry him," said Barby.

"But what about his wife?"

"What wife?" said Barby in the sharpest tone.

"He carries this beautiful hand with him that he had yesterday, to think of his wife. He says he puts it on the pillow at night."

"Dimitri is a damned liar, he'll spin any yarn," cried Barby indignantly. "He bought that hand yesterday and he spent nearly all my money on it. He's crazy about curios and antiques. I was so—fur*r*rious—" She paused. "I was so mad at him, he promised me he'd sell it this afternoon; and he's gone to sell it."

Linda reflected. "Well, all he did was talk about his wife."

Barby pouted, asked many questions; presently, she had the story. "He's such a liar," she said anxiously; "I've only known him three months and most of the time, I've been flying around Europe on George's money, looking for art masterpieces. I knew there were stacks of them somewhere. I was tipped off. I finally, this week—" She paused. "And there's a lot in Rome, I know that. Americans are buying them there. It's a pity George left his typewriter in Rome; and the Renault—I could have taken it down there myself and done business." She began thinking. "Are you sure they've sold the Renault?"

"Yes. They've got the money there for George. He's waiting for someone to bring it up."

"I'll go and get it," said Barby jumping up. "Barby, let's give Georgie a great big surprise. Let's do something for that cute little Pie-otter." She became silent again; and then began wheedling and persuading. Linda had never seen Rome. Why not go there and then set sail from Genoa or fly from Rome to New York? Let them both go to Rome and get the money for George; and Linda could leave right away.

"See your parents, make up your mind. See how you feel about Baby Honey when you're in New York. Pie-otter is just an alien in New York. He isn't a real American. He thinks he speaks without an accent," she said, bursting into girlish laughter. "He's so naive. He's funny in New York." She walked about thinking, "You see, Lin, I can't take the paintings over till I get some money. I have to let Dimitri have what he gets for the ivory hand. I don't have to, but he'd starve or run off with some pick-up—he can't spend a day without a woman. And he's such a liar—he's got his head stuffed with film stories. He makes it up as he goes along. I want to keep him around in case I need him. He has a very good eye; he has natural taste. I never lose a man if I can help it, because you need contacts. The freight is enormous by air and the customs—at the customs I'll say they're copies, just to get them through; and I'll say they're for my family."

She had by now a complete plan in her head. "Do you know where George's keys are? That's such a swell car and I'm crazy about fast cars. I could get to Rome, if he'd only lend her to me. He knows I'm safe. But he'll be arguing about his darling baby Mercedes for weeks. I've got to get to Rome. I know someone there, a contact, who will give me money. He's crazy to be my partner. Come with me, baby; will you come?"

It did not take long to persuade Linda. She hesitated at Barby's suggestion that they should run off, take George's car, leave him high and dry. "For a couple of days only, baby. We'll come right back with the money from the Renault and then he can lend me that for the plane fare and the freight." She talked on rapidly, intently. Linda liked to be led by an astute and busy New Yorker, and allowed it all to go forward; Linda knew all George's affairs, had the addresses. Within an hour, Barby had set off with Linda in the Mercedes, with Linda's few remaining bags in the back. In eleven hours they were in Switzerland. They stayed the night with some friends of George, who ran a little hotel Swiss-Touring in Montreux, where they put the rooms down to George's account; and by seven in the morning, they were off again, promising to stay at the hotel on the way back, in two days. Barby spoke a fair

French and her papers were in order. She was still described as George's wife on her passport; but her true passport was that she knew men and understood officials. Barby had not wanted to leave word for George; but Linda had privately left a typed notice in the typewriter: *Dear George, Barby is going to get some money and we will soon be back, Love, Linda.*

It was not till Prince Dimitri turned up at George's lodgings that George had an inkling of the trouble. "My partner has gone to Rome," and the Prince, placidly. "She wants to buy a few more canvasses down there, and then she will be back. But perhaps she will fly from Rome airport to New York; and then come back here. Or she may sell the paintings in Rome to Americans she knows there. Perhaps you know?"

George said, "What is it? Where is she? Where is Linda? Where are my keys? I can't find them. If I find out that that wicked little thief has taken them—" He suddenly turned scarlet. "Oh, my God! I know. She has taken the car." He telephoned the garage: it was so. He began to rave, rushing up and down the apartment, almost out of his mind. "Oh, what a wicked scheming little devil! She will sell it. I know her. I'll never see it again."

It was some time before he began to think more about Linda. Had she gone with Barby? He threw himself down on the sofa and sank back. "I know Linda went with her. Linda says yes to everyone. She adored Barby. She is so naive, so ignorant, she thought Barby was a business woman."

At some time in this tirade, the Prince left. Many miserable hours George tramped about. He telephoned the Deans at St. Germain, on the off chance; but no, no, he knew where she had gone. At this moment she was speeding through Italy, with Barby, streaking along the road under the cypresses, roaring through the towns, enjoying the sensation, being admired by the speed-crazy Italians, tearing into Rome; remarkable, wicked Barby. "My curse, oh, my God, a vengeful, greedy, lying capricious dangerous woman, with no brains at all, nothing but crazy whims, which she calls business. And the world's so crazy, and America is so crazy, that they think she's wonderful. And what stories has she told Linda?

That's nothing. I can get Linda back—but my car! I will never get the Mercedes back."

He telephoned his friends in Rome, the two American girls, Madeline and Louise, who had his Renault for him and who were living in the little room he kept in Rome, for interviewing Easter Pascuale and other work. There was no reply: "The ladies are out." "Tell them to call me back." But he had little hope. "These Italians, all these insouciant Latins, unreliable, with no idea of efficiency; they won't do anything."

He kept telephoning but had no reply till very late at night. Then Madeline spoke to him and said they had already given the money for the Renault as well as the typewriter to his young wife, Barby. Barby was returning to France at once.

"And Linda—did you see Linda—an American girl, dark, beautiful—wasn't she with her?"

"No. Barby was alone. She came down alone. She is brave, isn't she?"

"Oh, for heaven's sake, you all admire that highwayman," he shouted. "She is robbing me. I'll never see the money or the car again. And where is the girl? What has she done with Linda?"

He did not sleep all night, raving and crying. At last he took the train out, to see his friends in St. Germain; but there was no help there. They could only look at him in fear, the poor worn man, with pouched face, hair showing grey and his red-rimmed eyes. They knew nothing of Linda. "We'll write to her parents: that's all we can do." He returned, shrugging, waving his arms, talking to himself. Presently he got a telephone call from the girls in Rome. They were full of enthusiasm for Barby and full of anecdotes. Barby had come over the Alps with a girl friend; and they had nearly been killed. Tearing down a slope in bad light, they had almost run into a wagon loaded with newly felled trees, roughly trimmed, and with the tops over the end of the wagon. By good luck, the ground dipped and they had passed under the projecting spikes, but skidded; and there had been some trouble. Barby had made the trip to Rome. The other girl went to hospital, but was soon out; and now Barby had arranged for her to fly to New York. She had gone, Barby generously helping with the fare. Barby could not make the trip back in the slightly damaged car, so she had sold it; but she had enough to take her canvasses to New York. She would meet George in New York.

George was made more miserable by this news, that Barby had stripped him and Linda had left him without a word. He felt the top of his head lifting slowly upward and the wind blowing in; and at other times, he felt the fiery network that he thought was brain fever. He was unable to work. He visited several of his friends, including the doctor who always looked after him and told all his troubles. One of them put him to bed and looked after him for a few days. But when he returned to his lodgings there was rent, the agent who had cabled for his work; and there were one or two agonizing business problems to think about. Sully had written to say that she needed money for her psychoanalyst and that she had already tried to commit suicide. No word at all from Linda.

"I will simply have to go to New York," said George. Gradually he righted his affairs, did some writing which seemed good enough to him, but which the agent did not like. After some weeks he had a note from Linda. She was working in her father's office and liked it. "I am glad I am back in New York. When are you coming over?" It took him four months before he could take a plane over. He saw his agent and handed her the completed refugee book, as well as the plan of another book he had roughed out on the plane. He then went to the office address given him by Linda, the Alfhill Manufacturing Company. There he met, not Linda, but her mother, a gay sheep-faced woman, about forty who put her arm around his waist and laughed upward. He introduced himself as a friend of the Deans. After cheerfully flirting with him, she gave in to his irritation and told him where Linda was. She was at a Madison Avenue address decorating her new home. She was just about to marry someone she had known as a child, a boy from the Beach who was going on to get his master's degree. Alfred Hill would be supporting them both for the time being. "He is a warm, lovely boy, though a bit defensive," she said; "but he is right for Lin: she can mother him; and he needs the build-up we are giving him. I told Alf we'll have to sweat it out a bit, till he settles down. We're here for that."

George went to the place, rang and Linda opened the door. "Come in, George," she said sweetly. "Mother telephoned me you were coming. I am so glad to see you before I get married and explain. I decided when I came back and met this boy again. This is the best way. I was just wasting my time, wasn't I?" She listened to his protests quietly, but without answer: she was calm and content. She showed him the curtains, furniture, the wall-to-wall carpeting. "Dad had to sell some shares to get this, but we felt Nick needed the build-up. So did I." She put on her coat to go out with him. "This is the best way for me, George. My mother thinks I'm right. You must go in the folkways, she says. There was nothing for me—" She paused, turned to him. "Do you know, George," she said with a laugh, "I can hardly remember what I did in Paris, I don't remember what it was like. I know it's there," she touched her forehead, "but it's fading, like a dream. It was a waking dream, wasn't it? I don't want to think about it any more. I think Americans need their country more than other people. It's in them."

George was going to take her in the subway: she hailed a taxi. "I never go in the subway now," she said with a laugh. "I never think of it."

George went and sat in Washington Square. He felt calm, as one does when something exceptional has happened. A man beside him spoke. George looked. He was an elderly man, with creased neck, tanned skin, coarse grey hair, cut short, alert blue eyes in slits. An old man, sitting on a park bench, thought George.

"People of our age," said the man to George, "don't want to be pushed around." George pretended to listen to the absurd old man: he thought everyone as old as himself. The old man told him something about his son and daughter-in-law: "The basement was flooded and they were in Karachi." George said good-bye, got up and walked off. How can he see that I am his age? thought George to himself; I look so young. I am not interested in flooded basements.

He went back to the apartment in New York for which he paid rent and he found Barby there with some friends. She welcomed him excitedly. "You were going to be evicted, George—I paid the rent and we were just celebrating. Come and have a drink."

"If I don't have something, I'll drop dead. It's a wonder I'm not dead already," said George, taking what was offered him, a glass of Scotch whisky. He never drank whisky. Barby kept egging him on to tell his experiences; and while he was looking elsewhere, flushed, talking wildly, she slyly, grinning at the others, poured Scotch into his glass, filling it again and again. George remained himself, but suddenly lay down on the floor and became unconscious. The party went on. Presently, leaving him there, they went out to eat. Barby spent the night at another apartment; though, not forgetting her prize, she went home early in the morning. George was still on the floor and feverish. He caught cold, was ill and took a long time to recover. When he did recover he did not for a long time speak of leaving Barby or going back to Paris. She got him back to work. Presently he went away, left her; and for years no one heard of him. He was seen in Paris, Sofia, Vienna, in Buenos Aires: then there was no news of him at all. Some said he was very disturbed, he thought various foreign services were after him, that he was a hunted man; others said he had quite recovered, had taken hold of himself and married a quiet young woman.

Just before her wedding, Linda's father said to her. "You cabled me for money from Rome. What were you doing in Rome?"

"Oh, I was doing some work for that journalist I told you about. He went away and I had no money; so I thought I'd come home."

"I had a letter from some fella in Paris. He came here and saw your mother. What was he to you?"

"Oh, he was a father to me."

"Wasn't he going to marry you?"

"I don't think he cared for me. He was always doing what he wanted to. So I thought I'd come home."

Text Classics

textclassics.com.au